BURNING QUESTION

Sagorn looked ill, haggard and livid. "I can hide—"

"No!" Rap grabbed the old man by his bony shoulders. "That won't work! The dragon will blow fire in at you. Tell me your word! Tell me now, or we're all going to die."

The dragon hurtled forward, seething down the slope. Thornbushes vanished in flashes of white flame as it went by.

Sagorn wailed. "I can't. It hurts!"

Rap shook him like a feather bolster. "It'll hurt a lot more in two seconds! Tell me!"

The dragon was on the flat and coming faster than anything Rap had ever seen. Bigger and bigger. Jewel eyes blazing . . .

The old man choked, staggered, then slumped over Rap's shoulder, suddenly a dead weight.

Perilous
Seas

Perilous Seas

Dave Duncan

This book is a work of fiction. Names, characters, places and incidents
are products of the author's imagination or are used fictitiously. Any
resemblance to actual events or locals or persons, living or dead, is
entirely coincidental.

© Copyright 1991 by D.J. Duncan
First e-reads publication 1999
www.e-reads.com
ISBN 0-7592-3948-7

Other works by Dave Duncan

also available in e-reads editions

Dedicated to
George Melnyk,
Ron Robertson, &
Shirlee Smith Matheson,
who showed through their work at AFLA
that a government agency could actually be
efficient, effective, friendly, helpful . . .
and too good to last.

The voice I hear this passing night was heard
In ancient days, by emperor and clown:
Perhaps the self-same song that found a path
Through the sad heart of Ruth, when sick for home,
She stood in tears amid the alien corn;
    The same that oft-times hath
Charmed magic casements, opening on the foam
Of perilous seas, in faery lands forlorn.

                        KEATS, *Ode to a Nightingale*

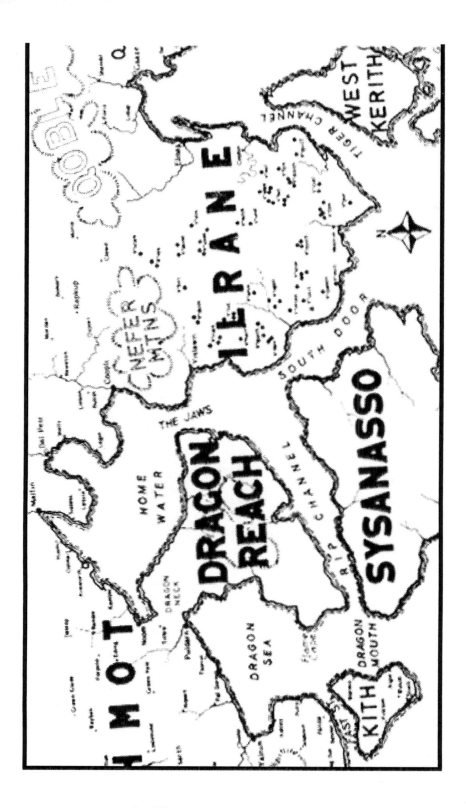

Table of Contents

Perilous
Seas

1

Favor the deceit

1

I n all the Impire, there was no more prosperous province than the island of
Kith. Ever since its conquest in the expansive days of the Xth Dynasty, it
had been the imps' main bastion in the Summer Seas.
    It had rich mines, fertile farmland, and a substantial shipping industry.
Once in a while a typhoon would do some damage, or dragons might lay
waste along the northeast shore, but neither had troubled the western coast
in centuries, and there the city of Finrain was the largest and richest on the
island, as well as the greatest port.

Ports needed sailors. The best sailors were jotnar. Imps had good reason to
be jumpy when there were jotnar around, and they firmly encouraged the
sailors who manned Finrain's shipping to make their homes at Durthing, a couple of hours to the south—close enough to be handy but distant enough that
their violent impulses could do no damage to Finrain itself, nor its citizens.

Durthing was home also to a few trolls, most of them descendants of slaves
imported from the Mosweeps, because the aboriginal population had pretty
much died out after the Impire came. There were also some mixed bloods,
and of course gnomes to handle the sanitary arrangements. There were even

a few imps, but any imp who chose to live in a jotunnish settlement must have very good reasons, of the sort that were better not discussed.

Lately, a young sailor of mixed faun-jotunn ancestry had taken up residence. Although he had been a thrall purchased at enormous expense by Gathmor, the new master of *Stormdancer*, he had subsequently been given his freedom. Within limits. His shipmates did not exactly take turns at keeping an eye on him, but . . . Well, he was a good kid and never lacked for company. He had shown no interest in departing, anyway, but he was much too valuable to be allowed the opportunity. Moreover, there was only one land road out of Durthing, and it ran by a post of the Imperial army. Imps were notoriously nosy.

Its fondest resident could not have called Durthing a town, and barely even a village, for its huts and hovels were scattered at random around the sides of a shallow, bowl-shaped hollow. The only break in the bowl's symmetry was a notch where the sea had broken through, back before the oldest Gods. With clear, calm water and smooth sand for beaching, the near-circular bay was one of the finest harbors in all of Pandemia. Three little streams watered the slopes, the sea teemed with fish, and the climate was perfect. Usually a dozen ships lay anchored there, or pulled up on the beach, and most often two or three more were under construction.

There was no formal land law in Durthing, for there was no formal law at all. The sea was a demanding mistress and whenever she stole a lover from his family, his home was soon abandoned to weeds and swallowed up by scrubby woodland.

A woman bereft must find herself another protector at once, and her children likely died soon anyway. Even among jotnar, few men would actually kill a child in cold blood, but even fewer would care overmuch for brats spawned by a predecessor. The work was done by neglect and indifference, or in mindless drunken rages. A widow who did not find another guardian was soon driven out by the other women and vanished into the nightmare slums of Finrain.

But in every evil there was some good, as the priests said, and housing was thus no problem for a newcomer. He might pick a pleasant spot not too far from one of the streams and build the home of his dreams, or he could just move into one of the empties. The selection was wide: impish wooden shacks, or low, dark sod hovels of the Nordland type favored by jotnar, or the rambling piles of masonry constructed by trolls. There were also some abandoned gnome burrows, but even the rats shunned those.

The faun had selected an ancient log cabin off by itself, and labored to make it shipshape while he settled down to life as a sailor. After every voyage he added more improvements. The months slipped by imperceptibly in that silken halcyon climate, and spring had become summer already.

2

2

Far to the east, under a harsher sun, the caravan road from the great port of Ullacarn ran eastward through the foothills of the Progistes before swinging north to branch and divide and become a stein of paths into the Central Desert. Squeezed between sand and mountains, the single way was known to the merchants as the Gauntlet. Their guards called it the Slaughterhouse. In some places the road was so constricted that drivers heading seaward could shout insults or greetings to those bound for the interior, while the bells on their respective camels rang in rondelet together. Many trader trains came through there, but not as many as tried, for banditry was the main source of employment in the district. The names of the passes told the tale: Bone Pass, Bodkin's Eye, One Out, Bloody Spring, High Death, Low Death, Buzzard's Gizzard, and Eight Men Dead.

Additional guards could be hired at either end of the Gauntlet, but they might not be of authentic royal blood. The genuine lionslayers distrusted them utterly, and with good reason.

After many weeks of trekking across the wastes of Zark, the caravan led by the venerable Sheik Elkarath had come at last to the Gauntlet. A few dangerous days ahead lay the fair city of Ullacarn, representing rest, profit, and well-earned comfort. The camels that had borne necessities to the humble folk of the interior—shovels and mattocks of tough dwarvish steel, cunning elvish dyestuffs, strong linen thread—were laden now with produce that the rest of Pandemia would greet as luxuries: wool of mountain goats and bright rugs woven from it, uncut emeralds, and durable garments of leather or camel hair, crafted by humble, hungry folk, whose only resource was unlimited time.

Many times in a long life, the sheik had traversed the Gauntlet. He had met violence there on occasion, yet he had never suffered loss of man or substance. If pressed to explain his remarkable good fortune, he would merely smile cryptically into his snowy beard and speak of vigilance and devotion to the precepts of holy writ. This time, he was confident, his passage would be similarly untroubled. This time his party was no larger nor richer than it had been in the past.

Portly and dignified, Sheik Elkarath rode high on his camel, serenely surveying the sun-blasted rocky landscape from under his snowbank brows as he led his long train down to the Oasis of Tall Cranes. Here he was in the very center of the Gauntlet, the most dangerous stretch of all. The barren crags around him concealed a dozen dark ravines that only the locals knew, any one of which might hold a band of armed brigands lying in wait. The jagged peaks of the Progistes pressed close along the northwestern skyline.

3

The tiny settlement in the valley below comprised a few dozen adobe houses, a welcome pond of clear water, and a hundred or so gangly palm trees. It owned no mines and grew no crops of any substance. Yet the people of Tall Cranes were well fed and prosperous. Their paddocks held many fine camels. Among other peoples, all djinns had a reputation for perfidy, but within Zark itself, the inhabitants of Tall Cranes were notorious.

From long experience, Sheik Elkarath anticipated a productive evening of trading. Always he brought gold to Tall Cranes, because the elders would accept nothing less for the jewels and crafts and livestock they offered. To inquire into the source of their wealth would have been grossly discourteous and insanely rash.

Behind the sheik, tall in the saddle, rode his chief guard. By the ancient tradition of the camel roads, he was referred to always as First Lionslayer. In his case the anonymity was especially valuable, because that spectacular young man was Sultan Azak of Arakkaran, literally worth a king's ransom. Much farther back in the caravan, the young woman professing to be his wife was Queen Inosolan of Krasnegar. She, however, would be worth nothing to the average kidnapper, except brief carnal satisfaction. To the wardens, the four occult guardians of the world, she was apparently worth considerably more.

But Sheik Elkarath would not be speaking of magic, or politics, during his visit to the Oasis of Tall Cranes.

3

Ogi called out, "Shipmate ahoy!" as he drew near to the faun's cabin. The sun had only just set and he was quite visible as he came through the low shrubs and spindly trees, but life in a jotunn settlement like Durthing made caution second nature to a man—startle a jotunn and he might kill first and apologize later. Some would not apologize even then.

The hammering ceased, and a moment later Rap's face appeared in the window, a homely face below a mop of brown hair like a tangle of dry ferns. He wiped his forehead with a bare arm.

"Got some carp," Ogi yelled, holding them up. "And wine!"

"Wine? What's the occasion?"

"Just thought a working man might like a break."

The faun smiled his usual diffident little smile. "Great!" he shouted, and disappeared.

Ogi headed over to the fire pit and was pleased to discover a few live embers remaining. He added some twigs and blew up a flame. Then he settled on a boulder and made certain that the wine had survived the journey unharmed.

4

A gray bird flew in to perch on a twig and eye him with deep suspicion. There were rocks enough to seat at least a dozen more people, so whoever had built it must have had a large family . . . no, the shack was small, so he'd just enjoyed throwing big parties. It was a pleasant spot, though, set in a little dell and sheltered from the tropic sun by a couple of half-decent trees— in Durthing any worthwhile timber soon vanished into cooking fires—but too far from a spring to be a prime location; more private than most.

In a few minutes Rap came wandering out, pulling on a shirt. He was still comically modest about clothing, considering the complete absence of privacy in a sailor's working life, but a good lad, steady beyond his years. In appearance he was pretty much straight faun, except for his hair and his size, and he had a faun's disinclination to conform to social pressures. Like being cleanshaven, for instance. He was the only man on *Stormdancer* not trying to grow a floorbrush mustache like Gathmor's. He was also the only man in Durthing who wore long pants all the time. Ogi often wondered whether that was just another of his odd ideas about propriety, or if he was touchy about his faun legs.

There were a lot of things about him that puzzled Ogi.

Already the fire was crackling nicely. Ogi began peeling onions. Rap settled on the next boulder, wiping his forehead again.

"Working too hard! Meant to go for a swim." He hefted the wine jar and tilted his head for a long, hard swig—which was a pleasant surprise to the imp. Maybe getting him drunk tonight wouldn't be the swine of a job they'd expected.

Rap lowered the flask with a gasp. "I'll go later."

"Hey, swimming in the dark . . . All right, smarty, you needn't smirk like that!" Ogi did not usually cluck like a mother hen, but young Rap was a newcomer to swimming. "So it's not dangerous for you—but don't go too soon after you've eaten, okay?" In any case, certain parties had plans for this sailor's evening, and swimming was not among them. He'd get to those later. "How's the builder doing?"

"Come and see?" Rap asked shyly. He jumped up and led the way over to the little hovel he now called home. It was a lot more homelike than it had been two months before, and he proudly displayed his latest achievement, a shutter for the window. It would keep rain out, if not wind. He had no furniture yet except a hammock and a chair, although Ogi had often offered to lend him some money to get settled in. At suitable interest rates, of course.

As always, Ogi wondered why a faun-jotunn hybrid had chosen an impish shack. In their homeland of Sysanasso, fauns lived in flimsy huts of wicker and thatch, and yet Rap had selected an ancient log cabin, built by some long-lost imp in this lonely dell. He had seemed surprised that his choice

5

would surprise anyone, muttering something about his hometown being impish even if he wasn't. To have picked somewhere less isolated would have
seemed more friendly.

He had fixed the roof and made the place quite astonishingly clean. Ogi
viewed, admired, and complimented. Then they headed back to the fire pit
and the wine.

Ogi proposed a few toasts, and got some more of the wine into the kid
that way. Then he pulled out the day's catch and set to work cleaning them.

"Arrivals?" Rap muttered, peering over his head, apparently at the
stringy trees.

"One of them's likely *Petrel*. She's due. Don't know the other."

Ships arriving were always of interest, but the juvenile forest around Rap's
cabin blocked a clear view of the harbor. He, of course, could see through
anything, but either the ships were still out of his range or he just didn't care
much. He sat down again and stared at the flickering flames in silence.

The swift tropical dark was settling in all around, and the birdcalls were
fading away. Bright smoke and sparks and crackling fire . . . oversexed crickets racketing already . . . It was a pleasant night.

As Ogi cut off the fish heads, he tossed them over his shoulder for dogs
or gnomes to find. Likewise, when he slit the bellies, he scraped out the guts
on the dirt behind him. Quite likely there would be a gnome child or two
hovering nearby already, drawn by the fire.

"Something wrong?" Ogi asked.

Rap had been staring fixedly at the flames. He smiled faintly and
shrugged. "Nothing you can help with."

"Please yourself. But if you want to talk it out to a friend, I'm available. And
despite what you may have been told ever since you were weaned, some imps
can keep secrets."

That brought the little smile again, briefly, and Ogi realized that the wide
faun mouth almost never smiled more than that.

"It's just that I'm not finding it easy settling down here."

Yes, that was very odd.

"Durthing's not perfect," Ogi said loyally, "but there's nowhere much better. You've gotten yourself a pretty fair house there for just the cost of a few
days' work, and there's a very wide selection of girls. I know of lots who'd be
willing to help you fill it with babies."

Rap shuddered.

"You get used to the little pests," Ogi said complacently. Uala had two now
and another on the way already. Perhaps twins, the way she was bulging. "At
times they're quite lovable. Don't quote me."

Rap went back to staring at flames.

6

There was a mystery even about the way the kid had gotten to Faerie in the first place, and it probably involved magic. Ogi was enough of a sailor to dislike talking about that. Still, it was curious.

"A girl, was it? " he asked softly. "Or a dream?"

"A girl," Rap told the fire, "but not the way you mean."

"Son, I've tried every way there is," Ogi said nostalgically.

Rap wrinkled his wide faun nose. "A promise, then."

"What sort of promise?"

Rap shot him a brief, cryptic glance. "A crazy one." He took another swallow from the wine jar and wiped his mouth with the back of his hand. "I don't really want to be a sailor. There's the nub."

He wasn't going to be very popular if Gathmor heard him talking like that. Or any jotunn, for that matter.

"Then you're fooling all of us, buddy. There was talk you might be made coxswain's mate when Larg got promoted."

Rap snorted disbelievingly and went back to leaning elbows on knees. He'd rowed to Faerie and back three times now. Men grew fast at his age, and he had a rower's shoulders already. He was going to need those tonight—for a moment Ogi felt a gloating touch of avarice. Lovely gold! Then he wet a finger and flipped a drop of spit at the griddle. It hissed and danced satisfactorily. He threw on the onions and began buttering the fish with his dagger.

"Gathmor said he paid forty-six imperials for me and the goblin," Rap murmured. "If I save all I can, how long would it take me to pay it off?"

"With interest, about thirty-nine hundred years."

"Oh—that soon, you think?"

"Be realistic, Rap! If you were Gathmor, would you let you go? Your farsight's beyond any price to him. He loves his ship, he's responsible for his crew—he isn't going to let you go."

The faun sighed and fell silent.

His farsight talent made him unique, of course, and yet it was a freakish thing. *Stormdancer* had not needed it since his first voyage. His subsequent trips had been hard work, with too much rowing and not enough sailing, but completely uneventful.

And the lad had more to him than just an occult knack. He had the makings of a very fine sailor. He was competent and trustworthy. He never complained or picked fights. He did whatever he was told to do as if he were grateful for the opportunity. Even without his farsight, he was not a man Gathmor would readily let slip away. Almost all the unattached girls in Durthing were giving serious thought to the big faun, too,

"They say," Ogi remarked, "that happiness is pretending you always wanted what you're getting."

Rap chuckled, but he kept his gaze on the flames.

Ogi began to feel worried. If the kid was out of sorts, then tonight's operation might turn into a disaster. Before he could explore that possibility, Rap spoke.

"You're an imp. Why d'you live among these maniacs?"

Ogi twitched nervously. "I suggest you don't say that word too loud, friend. And you shouldn't ask questions like that here."

"Oh! Sorry! Didn't think."

"It's all right with me. I'll just tell you to mind your own business—"

"But a jotunn would knock my head off," Rap finished. "That's what I meant."

"And you don't need to ask anyway. The only possible reason a nonjotunn would live here is that it's pleasanter than the imperor's jails. Come on, lad— it's a great life! Space and freedom! Women? You don't get women in jail unless you're real rich. Enjoy it!"

None of which was true in Ogi's case. He had never fallen afoul of the law, and he lived in Durthing simply because he loved the sea and loved being a sailor. Trouble was, the only possible explanation for that was much harder to talk about than a criminal past would have been. He knew his grandfather had died when jotunn raiders razed Kolvane; his father had been a posthumous baby. Although the family would never discuss the matter, and although Ogi himself was impishly short and broad and swarthy, he was quite certain that he must be one-quarter jotunn. To say so would greatly boost his standing in Durthing and among *Stormdancer's* crew, but it would increase his risks, too, and the kidding would never end. Ogi was not enough of a jotunn to find such matters funny.

"But they are maniacs," Rap muttered. "Kani's still after me to go pick a fight with someone. Why, for the Good's sake? I've shown I'll defend myself!"

Ogi began flipping fish over with the point of his dagger. He hadn't meant to raise the matter yet, and the kid wasn't close to drunk. "Well, there's a difference, Rap."

"What sort of difference?"

He passed the wine. "Here—you're not drinking your share! Yes, you've had a couple of fights. But they don't really count."

Rap put the jar down on the ground beside him and fixed a cold gaze on his companion. "Don't count? Why not?"

The carp were done. Feeling his mouth watering already, Ogi began scooping them onto the platters with his dagger. At least he need not look his friend in the eye while doing so. He hoped they would still be friends tomorrow.

"You know the standings round here, Rap. Lowest are the nonjotunn, like me. Especially me, 'cause jotnar rank imps just barely above gnomes. Then the part jotunn, like you. Fauns are quite well thought of, actually—probably because they're so pigheaded that they never know when they're beaten—and

8

you're almost jotunn size, so you rate just below pure jotunn." He waited, but got no comment. He worked more on the fish. "And then they have their own levels. Tops are the Nordland-born, like Brual—"

"And Kani's a third-generation southerner and hates himself for it. So? So what are you getting at?"

"Well, I know a couple of guys decided to try you out. You did very well, too, but Dirp is a third-generation exile, like Kani, and old Hagmad is a second, and neither is much thought of as a fighter. Besides, they were just playing."

"It didn't feel like play," Rap growled. "It bloody hurt!"

Ogi had scraped the griddle clean. He had no option but to hand Rap his platter and meet his eye.

"Tell me the worst," Rap said sourly. "I've lost my appetite already."

Ogi sighed. "You want them off your back? Well, then, you've got to have a punch party with a full-blooded, Nordland-born jotunn. One of the good ones."

"Oh, great! I used to think Gathmor was bad—"

"I'm not finished. You've got to pick the quarrel, not him. Your fight, see? And you've got to make him mad. Really mad! We can't settle for just a playful testing to see what's in the uppity faun mongrel. You bait him till he's one man-eating, homicidal, kill-crazy jotunn, who really wants to smash you. Then—no mercy! You beat him to a jelly."

"You lost me right at the end there."

"I'm serious, Rap. Eat up. More important—drink up! you're new. They give new boys time, but you've got your rower's arms now. You're looking sort of ready, so you're going to be measured soon. Today? Tomorrow? Best to pick your own match, right? The important thing is to try for the highest standing you can possibly hope to hold on to. In the end that'll mean a lot less pain and blood than if they're all using you for practice on the way up."

Rap laid the platter aside and crossed his arms. "What's your part in this?"

This was where Ogi could give the kid some good news. He spoke with his mouth full. 'Important! I found out who Verg and that crazy Kani had picked out for you: Turbrok! Or even Radrik! Gods! They'd have gotten you maimed or killed."

Rap put his elbows on his knees and scowled sideways at his companion. "And you won't?"

"Hope not. This fish is delicious. Try it—you need the strength. No, I took over, and you can trust me. Sure, I've been setting you up, Rap, I admit, but I know what I'm doing."

Well, he was three-fourths sure he did.

"Setting me up?"

9

"Who suggested you take the charming Wulli to the dance?"

Rap straightened, taut and furious. "You told me she wasn't anyone's girl! So did she!"

"Yes, well, she would. They do, here. But what I said was right, so far as I know. No engagements or understandings. How far have you got with her, by the way?"

"Mind your own Evil-begotten business!"

"Awright! But the previous dance she went to with Grindrog. He's been at sea, so he hasn't squired any ladies since."

Rap groaned. He had turned pale, understandably; in fact his face held a sort of greenish tinge in the fire's dancing glow. "So he'll assume I'm muscling in?"

"Well, you are, in the way things are done here. Grindrog never dropped her, you see. His choice, never hers. And of course, she's pure jotunn, and you're not. Mongrels aren't allowed near—"

"Bastard! But I should've thought of that, at least. God of Liars! You did set me up, you sneaky bunch of bastards! And I really don't like her much. She's all 'Yes, Rap,' 'No, Rap,' without an original thought in her head."

Wulli was a mouth-wateringly sweet kid, about sixteen, with the sort of face and body that the sailors called a shipping hazard—breathtaking, in fact. No male jotunn would worry at all about her mental processes, pro or con.

"Maybe Grindrog doesn't like her either. But that's irrelevant."

"*Petrel?* He's bosun on *Petrel?*"

"Right. Don't let your meal get cold—"

"About twenty-four, twenty-five? Twice my size, with a cast in one eye and his nose pushed over to the right? That one?"

"That's him."

"And *Petrel* just berthed. I suppose there's no chance that he might not find out?"

"None whatsoever," Ogi said complacently. "Kani's making sure he gets the news right away, as soon as she beaches, while all his crewmates are still around to sympathize."

Rap picked up his platter absentmindedly and began to eat, staring into the fire again. "I've saved up about half an imperial, Ogi. It's on the rafter over the hammock. You and Kani are my best friends, and I'd like you to share that. My boots are worth—"

"Oh, shut up! Do you think I'd do that to you?"

Rap glanced seaward. "Someone's coming now. He'll be here in a minute. Yes, it's Kani, running. Coming to tell you that the trap's set? So out with it— what's the ploy?" He seemed to be taking this better than he had done a moment before.

"The ploy is Grindrog. He's rated ninth or tenth in Durthing."

"You can have one boot, and Kani the other."

"Shut up! Listen—Grindrog hasn't fought in over a year now! He challenged Rathkrun himself. Rathkrun put him to sleep for a week."

Rap gulped, as if swallowing fish bones.

"But," Ogi said triumphantly, "he hasn't picked a fight since! Now I happened to notice him baiting a hook, last time he was in port. He held it right up here, on his left. Real close. And he's right-handed!"

Rap chewed in thoughtful silence.

"Rathkrun kicked his head about quite a bit! Rap, I don't think he can see worth a cod's ankles! I've been watching him. He trips over things. He slobbers when he talks. And if you get him mad enough tonight, he'll be fighting in the dark."

"That's cheating!"

Absurd! If the kid thought like that then he wasn't old enough to be allowed out alone, certainly not in a jotunn community—and yet Ogi had half expected that objection.

"That's partly why we snared you. You've got to go down there and drive him so wild that he'll try to fight a seer in the dark. If he loses his jotunn temper, then you've got him."

"Or the other way," Rap said calmly, chewing, gazing levelly at Ogi—who was beginning to find that steady stare unnerving.

"You've got your shoulders now. Rap. You can deliver."

"It isn't going to work. Not for long. Everyone knows I have farsight, so if I win I'll get a daylight challenge real soon, and you're trying to rank a mule above hundreds of purebred jotnar . . . But I suppose the main thing is to live through tonight, isn't it?"

He had some good points there, but tomorrow could look after itself. "Right. Just get him so mad he can't wait to get at you."

"If I said that Wulli told me he couldn't get it up for her, not even once . . . that would do it, wouldn't it?"

Ogi's forehead broke out in sweat at the thought of what that accusation would do to a drunken jotunn. "Just about. You may have her father to worry about tomorrow, but he's pretty old."

Rap threw his platter aside and wiped his mouth, as if he had reached a decision. Ogi held out the wine jug, but he shook his head.

"I'd rather be sober."

"Oh, you're weird! Sober, for Gods' sake? Fight sober? Jotnar think that's unmanly. That's worse cheating than using far-sight!"

In silence, Rap stood up and stretched. Apparently he'd accepted his destiny. Ogi had expected a much longer argument, and he began to wonder if this was a trick and the faun was planning to disappear into the woods. He certainly did not look like a tyro preparing to fight one of the top killers in Durthing.

11

Sounds of smashing shrubbery heralded the approach of Kani.

"You're taking this very well," Ogi said uneasily.

Rap smiled, humorlessly. "It'll be a pleasure."

"Oh?" Ogi was dumbfounded.

The kid stepped closer, eyes glinting in the firelight. "What Wulli told me about Grindrog was something different. I'd have been tempted anyway, if I'd thought I had any chance at all. Now you say I have, and you've trapped me, so I have no choice. Fine! Friend Grindrog deserves to have his head kicked a few more times. And other things."

Ogi opened his mouth and then closed it again.

"But we've got time to kill, haven't we?" Rap said gently. "I'd like to borrow some heavier boots from someone, and we must let Grindrog do his drinking and meditate on his troubles . . . *mustn't we?*"

Suddenly, somehow, the faun had hold of Ogi's shirt and was twisting it, hauling him right up off his seat and higher, up on tiptoe. And smiling. The first big smile all night. Not a cheerful smile, all teeth and much too close to Ogi's nose.

"How much?" Rap demanded. "How much are you going to make if the faun mule beats the blind champion? Or is the blindness just a worm to hook me?"

"No, Rap. I really think he's almost blind. And I was just about to talk about your share of my . . . our winnings . . . and—"

"And I may have time for a practice bout or two first!"

Rap, of course, was half jotunn. It just didn't show, usually.

It showed now.

Ogi should have thought of that sooner.

The fist at his throat was choking him. His knees began to quiver. He could *smell* that jotunnish anger. Imps fought best when they had numbers on their side, and he was no great bruiser. He'd brawled a little when he first arrived, because he'd had to, and he was hefty enough, but usually he just groveled. Few jotnar in Durthing would even bother to jostle an imp.

"You and Kani and who else in this?"

Hefty or not, now Ogi had been lifted right into the air. The faun was holding him up one-handed, holding him close enough to stare right into those big faun eyes, and they were full of jotunn madness. He should certainly have thought of this possibility.

"You and Kani and who else?"

"Verg," Ogi said with some difficulty.

"I'll start with you, then—practice the jelly thing."

Ogi muttered a silent prayer to every God in the lists.

Kani burst into the circle of firelight, so breathless he could hardly speak. Obviously he had more on his mind than the proposed Rap-Grindrog con-

12

test, for he did not seem to notice the confrontation in progress. He gasped, pointed back over his shoulder, gasped again.

He said, "Orca!"

"What?" Rap released Ogi, who dropped and staggered backward. By the time he had recovered his balance, Rap was gone in the darkness, the sounds of his progress through the shrubbery already growing fainter.

"Rap! Wait! that's, that's suicide!" The noises cont nued to move away. "Rap, we have no weapons!" But obviously shouting was not going to stop the faun.

Orca?

Far, far more frightened now than he had been by the thought of a beating from Rap, Ogi took off after him, leaving the winded Kani to follow as best he could.

If he dared.

4

At the Oasis of Tall Cranes, Inos achieved the impossible.

It started when Azak smiled to her as he strode by.

A smile from Azak was a fearsome sight. It displaced large quantities of copper-red hair. Since leaving Arakkaran he had let his beard grow in full, and it was a very full beard indeed. With his hook nose and scarlet djinn eyes, with his great height and unshakable arrogance, Azak was not a person easily overlooked.

For a moment Inos stood and watched him go, heading for the camel paddock, stalking along in his voluminous desert robes, one ruddy hand resting on the hilt of his scimitar. She sighed. Azak ak'Azakar was a problem. His proposals of marriage were becoming more frequent and more insistent every day, as the long journey neared its end. His logic was impeccable and his arguments unanswerable. Only sorcery could ever put her on the throne of her ancestors, the throne of Krasnegar. Only the wardens were permitted to use sorcery for political ends, and the Four would be much more likely to approve her petition if she had a competent husband at her side. Especially if he was a strong and proven ruler already. Like Azak.

A match foretold by the Gods.

The only flaw in this plan was that she did not feel ready to accept Azak as a husband, despite his obvious qualifications on all counts; despite the command of a God. She could not imagine him surviving the boredom of a Krasnegarian winter; and if the wardens refused to uphold her claim, she would then be faced with the alternative of being sultana of Arakkaran. That would not be the same thing at all.

As he vanished into the roaring melee of unloading camels, Inos returned to her immediate task, which was helping Kade erect the tent. Kade was waiting patiently, regarding her niece with faded old blue eyes—and a glimpse of those eyes could sometimes startle even Inos now, so accustomed was she to seeing only djinns around her.

"First Lionslayer seems remarkably relaxed," Kade said.

"Oh, I'm sure it takes more than a few brigands to frighten Azak . . . Now, which way is the wind blowing?"

But as the two of them set to work with practiced skill, Kade's comment began to bubble in Inos's mind like yeast in a beer vat. For weeks the women of the caravan had talked uneasily of the dangers of the Gauntlet. Here at the infamous Oasis of Tall Cranes, they were right in the middle of it, and most of them were visibly jumpy. The lionslayers' wives muttered discreetly about their husbands' ill temper, for the lionslayers were red-eyed in more ways than one, standing watch all night and riding camel all day.

But Azak had been smiling?

Well, why not? No matter how the rest of the party had fretted, Azak had remained quite untroubled by the promised perils. Chuckling into his red bush of a beard, he had pointed out that Sheik Elkarath had traversed the Gauntlet many times unscathed. And of course Inos had known what he was hinting—that the old sheik could never be endangered by mere mundane bandits.

That must be what Kade was thinking at the moment, also.

It just wasn't something that could be said out loud, though. Kade had been unusually brash, or strong-willed, to say even as much as she had.

Inos glanced around at the gaunt, rubbly hills and the sharp peaks of the Progistes, dark against the setting sun like gigantic legionaries. There were no cranes in sight, tall or short, but then there had been no dragons at the Oasis of Three Dragons, either. The world had changed since place names were invented.

She scowled at the white cottages, the pampered trees, and even at the welcome little lake. Some long-forgotten sorcerer had dammed an intermittent stream to make this settlement possible. If the stories were true, he had thereby created a long-lived aristocracy of highwaymen and caused the deaths of untold innocent travelers.

But not Elkarath.

She stared thoughtfully at her aunt, now busily hammering in a tent peg. Kade did not normally discuss the sheik, even in such oblique hints. Nor did Azak, or Inos herself. But she could recall a couple of times on the journey when the conversation had come close to the subject of magic—and both times had been late in the day, as now.

Her eyes went again to the forbidding barrier of mountains. Beyond them lay Thume, the Accursed Place. No one ever went there.

Did they?

And so . . .

The temptation was irresistible. What did she have to lose?

She drew a deep breath, ignoring the sudden thumping of her heart while cautiously glancing around to confirm that there was no one within earshot. In these trailing Zarkian costumes with their floppy hoods a woman never knew who might be creeping up on her, but the nearest tent on the right was already standing and obviously empty, its sides folded up to let the evening breeze sift through. The one on the left was being erected by a jabbering band of youngsters, the daughters of Sixth Lionslayer.

"A favor, Aunt?"

Kade looked up and nodded, her jotunnish blue eyes puzzled, and the rest of her invisible below yashmak and draperies.

"Tonight take your cue from me? No arguments?"

The blue eyes widened, then quickly narrowed in a frown. "You aren't planning something *impulsive*, are you, dear?"

"Impulsive? Me? Of course not! But, please. Aunt? Trust me?"

"I always do, dear," Kade said suspiciously.

Nevertheless, Inos knew she would cooperate. "Well, if you can spare me for a moment . . . I need a quick word with Jarthia.' She turned and trudged off between the trees.

She thought she almost approved of Tall Cranes despite the sinister reputation of its inhabitants. Yet not long ago an isolated hamlet like this would have seemed squalid and pathetic to her. How fast one's standards could change! Probably the Ullacarn place would feel like a grand city when she reached it, after so many lonely little desert settlements, most much smaller and more poverty-stricken than this. She did not yearn for grand cities. She would cheerfully have turned down a visit to Hub itself in place of a quiet afternoon in Krasnegar—dull, scruffy old Krasnegar!

Cheerfully she returned the greetings of familiar fellow travelers as she passed their tents, women and children with whom she had shared the ordeals of the Central Desert: thirst and killer heat and the terrors of a sandstorm. She should have brought a water jug as an excuse for this excursion. Kade was much better at carrying water on her head than she was. Patience had never been her strong suit.

Then she reached the tent of Fourth Lionslayer. Fourth would be engaged elsewhere, helping Azak oversee the unloading. His wife, Jarthia, was about the same age as Inos and admittedly striking, in a voluptuous djinnish way, with hair of deep chestnut and eyes as red as any Inos had ever seen. Shortly after the caravan had left Arakkaran, Jarthia had given birth to a large and healthy son. Now that her belly had flattened again and her breasts were still large with milk, her figure was even more lush than usual. None of that was visible at the moment, of course, or ever would be visible to any man except Fourth himself. He was elderly and utterly enslaved by his beautiful son-bearing wife, whose predecessors had produced only a double handful of daughters. All these factors found their place in Inos's devious inspiration.

Kneeling on the rugs spread before her tent, Jarthia was lighting the brazier. Just another anonymously shrouded female, she looked up in wonder at the visitor, for this was the time of day when the women must rush to prepare the day's meal for their hungry, hot, and hot-tempered menfolk.

"Mistress Harthak?" Jarthia murmured respectfully, and inscrutably. That was Inos's current name, Azak's choice. It was certainly better than the name he had bestowed upon Kade, which had unfortunate implications—at times the young sultan's ferocious mien concealed a wicked sense of humor.

Mistress Harthak had not thought to prepare what she wanted to say. She mumbled some sort of greeting, then decided to sit down. She settled stiffly on the rug.

Jarthia's surprise increased to became distrust. She muttered the customary welcome from, "My husband's house is honored," to the final offer of water.

Inos declined the water. "I was wondering," she began, remembering to harden the Hubban accent she had cultivated so painstakingly at Kinvale, "whether you were planning to visit the bathhouse this evening."

Jarthia sat back and studied her visitor with unblinking red eyes. "The lionslayer insists. He is a very demanding husband."

Inos doubted that. "Oh, that's good . . . but not quite what I meant. Actually, I was more concerned about *thali* . . . if you had thought of playing *thali* this evening?"

Thali was a popular women's game. Inos had played it at Kinvale a few times.

Jarthia was the caravan's lady champion. Her hot gaze flashed briefly over the buildings on the far side of the pond and then returned to Inos. "Possibly." The women of Tall Cranes would certainly have more valuables to lose than those of more honest settlements.

"Oh, good. My aunt and I might like to join in, for a change."

"Mistress Phattas and yourself are always welcome." Jarthia's voice was becoming quite sinister with suspicion.

"Yes. Well . . . what I had in mind . . . actually . . ."

Inos really ought to have planned how best to say this. "What I had in mind actually was . . . was gambling, and . . . er, *cheating?*"

Favor the deceit:
   When I consider life, 'tis all a cheat;
   Yet, fool'd with hope, men favour the deceit;
      Trust on, and think tomorrow will repay:
   Tomorrow's falser than the former day.
                                        Dryden, *Aureng-Zebe*

2

Piety nor wit

1

A way from tile fire there was moonlight, and even a few stars. There were many other fires twinkling around Durthing, their smoke drifting up vaguely in the moonlight. Moonlight was gleaming also on some very brawny clouds banked up in the west, but if there was wind, it did not penetrate the little valley.

And there was no sound! That was the eeriest thing of all. Ogi could hear nothing but the irregular slither of his own boots on the slope and his own panting. If Kani had not been imagining things, then every throat in the set-tlement should be in full chorus, every cook pot clamoring the alarm.

He had thought briefly of going for Uala and the kids, but either he didn't think he could move them out fast enough, or else his damnable impish curiosity had gotten the better of him. He was following Rap to the moot-stow.

If there was going to be a massacre, it would start there.

The moot-stow was where the men met to talk and drink and fight. If the Rap-Grindrog match occurred, it would be held at the moot-stow. Homing Durthing vessels always docked first in Finrain to unload cargo or passengers, and they always loaded beer. So the night after a ship returned was always rowdy. The crew itself would be in a mood for blood after weeks at sea. So would everyone else when the beer ran out. The moot-stow was an open square of packed clay by the shore with a raised bank around three sides; on that grew the only large trees left in the valley, giving shade and rain cover, serving when necessary as grandstands.

On nights when no ship had docked, there was music and dancing there, with lanterns hung in the trees. When there was beer, then a bonfire blazed in the middle; so a man could see what he was doing. Those nights the women stayed home. *Sea Eagle* and *Petrel* had both beached that day.

Soon Ogi saw the flicker of the bonfire and the shapes of men standing on the nearer bank under the trees. He sensed other men running in from other directions. But still he heard no sound.

There was no law in Durthing—except maybe one. If it had ever been passed by the Senate and the People's Assembly in Hub, or signed by some long-dead imperor, then no copy of the original survived. The jotnar would not have accepted a written law anyway, but there was an unwritten law, and the Imperial army had standing orders.

The only jotunn settlements tolerated within the Impire were *unarmed* jotunn settlements. The lictor at Finrain kept spies in Durthing, and any attempt to collect weapons would have brought the entire XXIIIrd Legion marching in, five thousand strong. The jotnar pretended not to know that. They themselves outlawed weapons, they said, so that quarrels would be settled by more manly means—with fists and boots. And teeth. Or rocks and tree branches. Daggers were permissible sometimes, but swords were for cowards.

And every law had its exceptions. The senior jotunn in Durthing was Brual, unofficial mayor. He was aging now, but he was Nordland-born, and he kept the disorder within some limits with the aid of his five sons, of whom Gathmor was the youngest. Ogi was fairly sure that Brual must have a few swords tucked away somewhere.

Never enough! Not if Kani had truly seen what he had claimed. Not if that second boat had borne an orca emblem on its sail.

An orca was a killer whale, but it meant more than that in Nordland. It meant a thane's ship—raiders.

Gasping and sweating, Ogi came reeling up the bank and recklessly pushed his way through the line of blond, bare-chested sailors standing in ghostly silence, watching what was happening in the moot-stow.

The wide space was almost empty, except for the fire and Brual himself, flanked by the only two of his sons who were in port at the moment, Rathkrun and Gathmor. Brual had an ax and his sons bore swords. Their shadows stretched long on the ground behind them.

Three strangers were striding up from the sea—jotnar, of course, recognizable by their pale skin. They wore metal helmets and leather breeches and boots. They seemed to be unarmed.

But far behind them, an unfamiliar longship glimmered in the darkness on the placid waters of the bay, and men were wading ashore and lining up along the beach. Seeing no glint of weapons, Ogi decided that they also were unarmed. They must be, because their round shields still hung along the low side of that sinister boat. They wore helmets, though.

One group of waders was carrying a hogshead, and another had already been set on the sand. The ship had anchored, not beached; that was ominous. Yet the barrels suggested gifts, and might be a hopeful sign.

The entire male population of Durthing was there. It seemed to be holding its breath.

The three strangers stopped at a safe distance, and the night silence grew deeper and heavier, as if even the sea and the crickets had stopped to listen. Fear drifted though the trees like an invisible fog.

"What ship?" That was Brual, loud and harsh.

The stranger in the middle stepped forward one pace from his companions. He was tall and young and muscular. He was clean-shaven, while they were heavily bearded.

"*Blood Wave*. And I am her master, Salthan, son of Ridkrol."

"What is your business, Captain?" Brual's voice was strong, but curiously flat.

"Who asks?" Salthan was quieter, and he seemed completely at ease, although he was much closer to the ax and the swords man he was to his own crew.

"I am Brual, son of Gathrun. These are my sons."

Salthan put his fists on his hips and the gesture blazed with arrogance. "We came in peace, Brual, son of Gathrun, but your manner is beginning to irk me. We brought some beer to share with you, to exchange, perhaps, for some traditional jotunnish hospitality?"

Silence fell again. Nobody moved. Perhaps Brual was thinking. Perhaps he was already admitting disaster.

Then a man broke out of the crowd around the edges and ran a few steps forward and stopped, ill lit by the blaze of the bonfire. Almost alone in the whole crowd, he was dark-haired.

"He lies!" the newcomer shouted. "His name is not Salthan! He is Kalkor, the thane of Gark."

The entire male population of Durthing seemed to draw breath in the same instant. Ogi heard a low moan, and realized that it came from himself.

When the faun picked a quarrel, he picked a good one.

The stranger let the tension grow until Ogi wanted to scream. Then he said the inevitable: "Who calls me a liar?"

It was Gathmor who answered, without taming his head to look.

"He is a thrall. If you would answer the charge, then answer it to me, who owns him."

"That's not true!" Rap yelled shrilly. "You freed me!" And he went stalking forward defiantly until he stood at Gathmor's side.

Kalkor—for Ogi had no doubts at all that the faun had spoken the truth, however he knew it, and this was the most notorious raider on the four oceans—Kalkor seemed more amused than ever.

"Is this a three-way dispute, then? Both of you call me a liar, but he also calls you one, Son-of-Brual? Do we settle it in some sort of order, or in one big free-for-all?"

"You answer it to me." Gathmor had not taken his eyes off Kalkor. He was ignoring the crazy faun beside him, but Rap leaned close to his ear, as if whispering something important.

Ogi tore his attention from the main action and looked seaward. About fifty of the half-naked giants had come ashore now and were standing, watching. Firelight gleamed on their beards and flashed from their helmets. They were shifting, though, gradually edging in around the two hogsheads, and Ogi was suddenly frantic to know what really was in those barrels. Rap would know, and that must have been what he had just whispered to Gathmor, but Gathmor might already have guessed what Ogi was starting to fear.

He thought of Uala and the children and realized that he had never been more terrified in his life. Women and children could not run fast enough.

"I will take the thrall and consider the debt paid," Kalkor said. Even at that distance, Ogi somehow sensed the arrogant smile on the killer's face.

Trust me?

"What brings you to Durthing, Thane?" Gathmor demanded. His father seemed to be leaving it to him.

Kalkor cocked his head. "You repeat the challenge? I come for many reasons. My business is varied. I am mostly anxious to see how the summer sailors fare."

A low noise like a groan swept through the watching crowd. The jotnar of Nordland despised those who dwelt in the gentle southern lands. Their jotunn blood would bring them no better treatment from a Nordland raider than an imp could expect, or a faun, or anybody. The bloodlust might even burn hotter against them, fanned by contempt.

Ogi started praying—for a squadron of the Imperial navy, or a couple of cohorts from the XXIIIrd Legion.

"You have seen. Now go in peace." Gathmor's voice held none of the bottled anger that Ogi had heard many times in the past just before some errant sailor was beaten bloody. Something was keeping it in check. Gathmor had a wife and children, also.

"But I came for that faun. And I will also enlist a pilot who knows the Nogids, as my course lies westward."

Again the watchers seemed to breathe in unison, and this time the sound was certainly a sigh. The thane was offering terms.

"He won't dare sail tonight," whispered a voice near to Ogi's shoulder. He glanced around and recognized one of *Petrel's* crew.

"Why not?" asked another whisper.

"There's a mother-and-father of a blow brewing out there, or I'm no sailor."

Ogi wiped his ribs where the sweat ran; now he recognized the urgent, muggy feel in the air. He should have noticed sooner. But if Kalkor dared not leave, then equally he could linger without worry that there might be Imperial ships out hunting for any reported orca.

Brual reached out a hand to stay his son, and Gathmor struck it away.

"I know the Nogids as well as any man."

A very long silence this time—Kalkor certainly had a sense of drama. Then he gestured toward his ship.

Gathmor rammed his sword into the ground and released it. He said something to the faun beside him and the two of them began to walk. Brual and Rathkrun stood where they were.

A strange whimper rose from the watchers, a most unjotunnish sound. They were ashamed. Their leaders had given up without a fight. *And they were afraid!* Hundreds of jotnar, every one of them a terror, men who would kill in a blind mad rage, or hurl themselves at fighters twice their size, men who would brave the worst the sea could throw at them without hesitation—they were all chilled to stony terror by that arrogant young thane. In the face of certain death they were no better than imps, Ogi thought bitterly. But they knew what raiders did to men, to children, to women, and they had no weapons. Kalkor did.

Gathmor and Rap reached the waiting raiders, and the line opened to let them through. They waded out into the water, heading for *Blood Wave*. Kalkor said nothing, and did not move. Nor did anyone. The whole island might have been frozen, except for the two men wading out into the warm waters of the bay. Then they reached the ship, caught handholds, and simultaneously swung themselves up and over the side.

Faintly over the water came the sound of two hard blows, and a grunt.

Kalkor bowed ironically and turned. He and his two companions began to walk seaward.

It had always been inevitable.

Brual and Rathkrun leaped forward simultaneously, raising their weapons. The barrels were hurled over, spilling axes that flashed in the light of the moon. Kalkor and his two henchmen swung around to meet the attack. Brual

22

struck one, but Kalkor himself somehow stepped around Rathkrun's thrust, felled him with a punch too fast for the eye to follow, and flattened Brual with a kick. Then the raiders had their weapons in hand, and they charged.

The jotnar of Durthing fled screaming.

By morning, the settlement was only a memory.

2

Thume, the Accursed Place . . . The War of the Five Warlocks . . .

History had never been one of Inos's interests. Throughout her childhood she had rejected history with a passion second only to the fanatic fervor with which she had spurned mathematics. Her long-suffering tutor, Master Poraganu, had learned to temper their mutual excursions into history to a tolerable minimum.

But even Inos had heard of the Accursed Place. It had a romantic name.

As Elkarath's caravan had drawn near the foothills of the Progiste Range, she had heard more of it. Azak had spoken of Thume a few times, as they ate their evening meal outside the tent. To him it was a place of annoying mystery, an untidy tangle in the military logic of Pandemia—a hazard when Zark wished to invade the Impire, an unreliable defense when the Impire attacked Zark. The local women in their bathhouses and bazaars had spoken of Thume with hushed voices and stretched eyes, muttering tales of ancestors who had wandered too far into the mountains and been Seen No More. To them it was a place of dread.

Ulien' quith had been warlock of the south, and a sorcerer of renown, cut from the cloth of such legendary masters as Thraine, and Ojilotho. Ulien', it was said, had sought to become supreme, to overthrow the Protocol and dominate the Council of Four. He had been balked, repudiated, and cast out. He had fled to Thume; the other wardens had appointed another South, and had pursued him to wreak vengeance. The resulting War of the Five Warlocks had continued for thirty years.

To be exact, there had then been three warlocks and two witches, and the war should rightwise have been called the War of the Five Wardens—a point Inos had made forcibly to Master Poraganu—but Five Warlocks was how it was known.

Even before that disaster, Thume had always been a cockpit. Trapped between imps and djinns, between the gnomes of Guwash and the merfolk of the Keriths, it had been doomed to eternal struggle. Its two long coasts had doubtless brought double trouble from jotnar raiders also. The native race, the pixies, had been looted, raped, massacred, and enslaved without respite since before the coming of the Gods.

23

The War of the Five Warlocks had been merely the final catastrophe. Fire and earthquake, storm and monsters, bronze-clad armies and rampaging hordes—all had struck at Thume, or at one another. Death and destruction had swept back and forth with no clear victory for anyone. Not being bound by the Protocol, Ulien' quith and his unknown allies had resisted even the legions, dragons, and jotunn raiders that were normally immune to the ravages of sorcery. He had destroyed them, or turned them on their nominal masters and their allies. For thirty years. At the end of that time, seemingly, everyone just stopped fighting and went home.

Not the least of the irritations of history in Inos's view was that it so often failed to end its stories tidily.

No one ever went back, said the legends. There was nobody there now, nothing left to fight over. Solitary travelers returned reporting an empty land, forest and game in abundance.

Or else they did not return.

Intruding armies either passed through unmolested or mysteriously disappeared. Attempts to colonize the empty land never prospered, the settlers fleeing in inexplicable terror or just vanishing without trace.

No one had seen a pixie in almost a thousand years.

3

Princess Kadolan of Krasnegar was *concerned.*

With her comfortable girth wrapped in a couple of towels, she sat on a rather lumpy cushion in a very hot and overcrowded bathhouse and listened politely to the troubles of a Bloody Phlegm on one side and a Hardened Liver on the other.

She was not especially worried that this remote mountain hamlet was reputedly the worst nest of cutthroats in all Zark. Whatever evil might be planned, it was not going to occur in the village women's bathhouse, and almost certainly not until after the caravan's departure the next day.

She was not even troubled at the moment over the mysterious Sheik Elkarath, who might or might not be a servant of the sorceress Rasha. Either way, his lifelong immunity to the dangers of the Gauntlet merely confirmed her previous suspicions that he was a sorcerer. The second danger canceled out the first.

No, Kade was apprehensive about Inosolan, who was clearly plotting something. Inos was always more of a leaper than a looker. Kadolan had learned to be prepared for the worst when her niece was in this mood, and the worst in this situation might be very bad. Inos resented restraint of any kind, and she was probably scheming some way to make the first danger cancel out the second.

Every evening, after serving their menfolk's meal, the womenfolk of Zark
headed for their local bathhouse. There they shed their all-enveloping robes
and veils and lounged around in comfort upon cushions set on ancient floors
of tile or clay. They talked of their children, their health, their husbands, and
their husbands' problems. Often they played *tbali*. In some places the women's
bathhouse was little better than a shack over a mud pit, but the larger, better
houses were well equipped for socializing and recreation.

The men, of course, would similarly gather at their own establishment,
and talk of serious matters: trade and politics, health and poverty . . . horses,
dogs, camels, and women. Visitors were always welcome. In the sparsely settled Interior, the caravans were prized as much for news and gossip as for their
trade goods. The drab lives of the inhabitants held few excitements.

The bathhouse at the Oasis of Tall Cranes was as spacious and comfortable as any, but the population was large, and at least a hundred women and
girls were crowded around in the dimness. The massive walls had kept out the
worst of the day's heat, but they took a long time to cool, and the windows
were so heavily shuttered that the room had become headachingly stuffy.
Lamps smoked and sputtered, insects buzzed, and voices droned. Babies snuf-
fled and whimpered in a dark corner.

Bloody Phlegm was again explaining the difficulty she had in sleeping at
all now, growing hoarse as she tried to drown out details of Hardened Liver's
grandmother's guaranteed physic. Kadolan nodded and smiled, or frowned as
required, and meanwhile she tried to keep an eye on Inosolan.

Inosolan sat in a group of younger wives in a relatively bright corner,
under a patch of lamplight. She was still combing out her hair, a stream of
moonlight in the gloom. The upper half of her face had darkened in the
desert glare, a trait inherited from her jotunn ancestors; without her veil she
looked as if she were wearing a mask.

Of course there had been the usual questions earlier, provoked by her
green eyes, Kadolan's blue eyes, and their pale skins. Tonight Inosolan had
stayed with the simplest explanation—jotunn blood in the family, too far
back for details. The local ladies had sighed understandingly. Some nights
Inosolan went into lurid particulars involving longships, or she might invent
elvish ancestors instead. After an especially hard day, she was capable of
including both elves and rape, in highly unlikely combinations.

The Tall Cranes bathhouse was acceptable. The women, Kade noticed, were
better dressed than most. There was no ostentatious flaunting of jewelry, but
the negligees and even towels were of fine stuff. Of course the oasis lay only
three days or so from a great city, and should not be compared with some hamlet in the middle of the desert. On the other hand, there was no local industry
to account for the prosperity, as Azak had wryly pointed out only that evening.

25

Thoughts of the sultan made Kadolan realize that she had not heard him mentioned in the bathhouse. He was a noticeable man and lionslayers were romantic figures. Almost invariably on other evenings, some of the younger women had directed wistful queries about him to his supposed wife. The women of Tall Cranes had not. That discretion might have pleased Inosolan, but it was an ominous break with routine.

But so far Inosolan herself had done nothing out of the ordinary. There had been no further mention of the mysterious favor she had requested earlier. Bedtime was approaching. The younger women were already dressing, preparing to leave when impatient husbands would arrive and lead them home to perform their final duties of the day.

Hardened Liver was occupied now in supervising a pedicure being administered by one of her granddaughters. Bloody Phlegm had drifted off to sleep in the middle of her complaints about insomnia. Kade struggled to her feet; she donned her sandals and wrapped herself in her chaddar. Then she wandered across to join the younger group.

Inosolan glanced up and smiled rather tightly.

As Kade sat down, she was startled by the first thunderous bang on the door. Inosolan yawned.

One of the girls went to open the peephole flap, and then turned to call out names. The women indicated either hurried away at once, or jumped up and started pulling on their robes. They were all locals. The visitors began preparing themselves also, for if the village men were coming to take their wives home, then the merchants, camel drivers, and guards would be arriving shortly. Kade herself suppressed an enormous yawn as she saw Inosolan turn to catch the expectant eye of Jarthia, Fourth's young wife. So here it came, whatever it was.

Jarthia emptied a bag of *thali* tokens onto the floor. "Anyone care for a quick game before bedtime?"

Some of the villagers paused in their dressing, tempted.

"I should love a throw or two," Inosolan trilled. Kade stiffened in astonishment, having warned her niece months ago that Jarthia used marked tiles.

"Me, too," Kade said loyally. "But I forgot to—"

"I can lend you some, dear," Inosolan said, and produced a clinking bag, which for a moment bewildered Kade totally. Then she recalled Inosolan taking Azak aside after the evening meal. What possible reason could Inosolan have given for needing money in a place like this? But Azak likely would not have argued. He was infatuated by Inosolan. Dangerously infatuated. By the sound of it, that bag contained a small fortune.

In moments play had started. The game was childishly easy, the only skill required being a good memory, to recall tokens' values while they were turned facedown. Jarthia's set was very old, scratched and stained by long use, and much craft.

Kade stifled another yawn. The hour was late, and she was very tired. Desert air seemed to have that effect on her. Plus o'd age, of course.

She yawned again.

At first she managed to hold her own in the game, struggling to note and remember the illicit markings on the tiles. But the light was dim, her eyes were not what they had been, and oh, but she was sleepy! She had never enjoyed gambling, an entirely stupid pastime. Soon she was losing disastrously. Inosolan was doing even worse.

So was Jarthia—and the more she lost, the higher she raised the stakes.

Fuzzily Kade tried to work out the plot, for obviously there must be a plot. Azak's gold was disappearing at a scandalous rate. Of course the village women could not stop the game while they were ahead and doing so well— that was mere good manners. Soon the girl posted by the door was calling more names, and the players were excusing themselves to go and whisper urgently to their husbands outside, and then return to the circle. Kade and Inosolan yawned and fought their weariness, and watched the small fortune grow steadily smaller.

"Mistress Jarthia?"

Jarthia rose and went to the door. Predictably, Fourth would refuse nothing to his delectable, son-bearing young wife. After a brief muttering, Jarthia hurried back to rejoin the play.

Kade yawned again, then snapped awake . . . So that was it!

"Mistress Hathark?"

Inosolan shot a guilty glance at her aunt from under sleep-soaked eyelids, then heaved herself to her feet. She was visibly dragging as she went to the door. But certainly Azak would cooperate also, because he had duties to perform while the encampment bedded down, with no marital joys to look forward to.

In a moment Inosolan came stumbling back, yawning. "He says we may stay while Jarthia does," she told Kade seriously, "and Fourth will escort us."

The game continued; the stakes increased. Kade squirmed as she saw how much this escapade was costing. What on earth was Inosolan hoping to accomplish? As the room emptied it seemed to grow larger, and eerie echoes developed in the shadowed corners. Soon only half a dozen players remained, the three locals all twittering excitedly over their astonishing good fortune. Inosolan passed her aunt more "loans." Kade yawned shamelessly, and struggled to stay awake, and fought against logical inner voices that told her not to be silly, she was too old for this and she certainly ought to insist on going off to bed, and they had a long way to go the next day . . .

But another, very tiny, inner voice was whispering that she surely wasn't as old as that, and the hour was far from late by Kinvale standards, and Inosolan must surely have something serious in mind if she was throwing away money like this.

Somehow Kade battled on, against brain-numbing exhaustion, losing ridiculously and watching Inosolan doing little better. The dim room swayed; her head lolled; her eyes blurred. She did not see a signal pass, but there must have been one, for Jarthia suddenly went on the offensive. The money began to move inexorably in her direction, and the chuckling and joking of the locals became rarer, then stopped altogether, as their gains dwindled.

Soon it would be over, Kade thought with relief. Soon Jarthia would have all the coins in the room, and then the gamblers must call it a night.

And suddenly the pressure eased . . . returned . . . faded altogether. The world came back into terrifying focus.

Kade glanced up in horror and saw triumph blaze up on Inosolan's face.

4

Hospitality was a duty to the God of Travelers. Violence within Tall Cranes itself was extremely unlikely—Azak had said so at supper. He had then ruined the reassurance by pointing out how few men were present in the village. The rest, he had suggested cheerfully, might well be preparing an ambush for the morrow, at some respectable distance.

Nevertheless, Fourth Lionslayer escorted the ladies back to the encampment grounds. It was a distance of a few hundred paces only, and the worst dangers it offered were barking curs, but the way wound along between the tiny settlement's squat stone cottages, and therefore was not a journey women should make without a man to guard them. There was also the matter of passwords when the duty lionslayer challenged—passwords were men's business. This attitude riled Inos to frenzy, but Kade rather enjoyed being treated as a fragile halfwit, having cultivated the role for years at Kinvale.

The air was cool already, because of the altitude; the desert sky was a fiery tessellation of stars so low that they seemed to peer over people's shoulders. A few clouds sailed in dark majesty on that sparkling sea.

Fourth delivered his charges to their tent and went off with his arm tight around his beloved Jarthia, who had already told him about her night's winnings, understating them by four-fifths.

Inos made no move to enter the tent. She leaned back against a palm tree and folded her arms and said, "Ha!" in a gloating manner.

Kade no longer felt sleepy at all. She felt very apprehensive.

And rather foolish.

"Can I have an explanation now, dear?" she asked, annoyed that she could not keep her annoyance out of her voice. There was enough wind to muffle quiet conversation, and the rest of the encampment seemed to be asleep.

"I'll try," Inosolan said grimly. "But it's not easy to talk about—is it?"

No, it wasn't. But Kadolan had thought it often enough. Sheik Elkarath had gained Azak's trust, and Azak normally trusted nobody. Sheik Elkarath had persuaded Inosolan to embark on the mad flight from Arakkaran into the desert—and although she was often impulsive, that had been an absurd venture even for her. And finally, Sheik Elkarath had apparently succeeded in eluding any pursuit by Rasha. Who but a sorcerer could outwit another?

So Elkarath must have occult power. Either he had stolen Inosolan away from the sultana to play the same sort of political game she had been playing, or he was her minion, her votary, and Rasha had used him to hide the merchandise in the desert until her bargaining with the wardens could be completed

Of course the sheik might be a votary of someone else—one of the wardens, probably, and most likely Olybino, warlock of the east. But in that case, why had Inosolan been allowed to continue her journey unmolested? If she had political value, it was as queen of Krasnegar, not as a pretend wife to a pretend lionslayer in the middle of a desert. Weeks had gone by while the caravan traversed the desert.

All of which was ominously difficult to put into words.

"I think I know what you mean, dear."

Inos chuckled. "He must have seen where we were, but *thali* would seem innocent enough, and it's not something you can just walk out on as soon as you start feeling sleepy. Then he dozed off himself—he's had a hard day, and he's old."

"I worked out that much! What I mean is what do you hope to gain?"

"Surely it is obvious? Every night for months you and I have dropped off to sleep like chimney pots falling off a roof."

"Camel riding is very tiring."

"Some days we had not been riding." Inosolan paused, and for a few moments there was only the rustle of the palm fronds in the wind, tents flopping sleepily, and distant dog yowls from the houses. "Remember when Azak burned you?"

"Of course. It still isn't quite healed." Azak's hand had touched Kadolan's in the night and charred her skin, but she had not wakened. She had not known of it until morning. She made sure now that his blanket was never placed so close.

"Well?" Inosolan demanded. "That was not normal sleep!" For a moment she glanced up at the dancing palms, her face a pale blur in the starlight. She drew several deep breaths, as if enjoying an unexpected liberty. Crickets chirped,

29

and camels bellowed in the paddock. Their bells jangled in a sound as familiar to Kadolan now as the boom of surf below the castle windows in Krasnegar.

"Yes, it's getting easier to talk," Inosolan said. "Remember the door at the top of Inisso's tower—how hard it was to approach? Aversion, Doctor Sagorn called it. What are you thinking now?"

Kadolan glanced around at the darkness. "That I should like to sit down in a comfortable armchair." She was evading the question, of course, but certainly not telling a lie. She was too old for camels. She could hardly recall what a not-sore back felt like.

"Hogswill!" Sounding as if she were forcing the words, Inos said, "Well, I'll tell you what I'm thinking. Which is that we have been duped. Elkarath is in league with Rasha, and always has been. Gods, talking about it still makes my head hurt! It was just too easy, Aunt! She can spirit people from Krasnegar to Arakkaran, across the whole width of Pandemia, and we merely hop on camels and ride off into the desert? She meant us to escape. She set it up!"

Kadolan sighed. "It's possible, I suppose."

"It's obvious!"

"What about the wraith you saw, the ghost?"

"Ah. Rap is dead. We know that. But I still think that was a sending. From Rasha—or someone."

She meant that Elkarath might have been responsible himself, of course. He had never met the young faun, but perhaps a sorcerer could conjure up pictures of the dead from other people's memories. Who knew what a sorcerer could do?

"It told you to run away!"

"And we did the exact opposite—we stayed! We all agreed a wraith of evil could give only evil counsel. Of course that was what we thought! It was what we were meant to think, a double bluff. Obvious, really. So why have we never said so?"

Kadolan sighed again, and shivered. She had wondered such things many, many times, and never been able to bring herself to put them into words. She had been unable even to worry about them. She had prayed quite often to the God of Humility, though.

"*Magic!*" Inos snapped out the forbidden word triumphantly. "By day. He makes us afraid or ashamed to talk about it by day. And at night he puts a sleep spell on us; you and me. Talking gets easier at night, though—have you noticed? Maybe he gets tired, or he puts on the spell in the morning and it fades. Now it seems to be wearing off!"

"Well, now you've given us a chance to talk about it," Kadolan said. "I suggest you don't mention it to Azak."

"Why not?" said Azak.

"Oook!" Kade jumped like a rabbit, clasping her hands to her mouth. Despite his size, the sultan could move like floating gossamer, and she wondered how long he had been standing mere behind her—dark and big and menacing, with eyes that glinted in the starlight.

"Why not tell Azak?" he growled.

She sought to calm her fluttering heart. Even by daylight, Azak flustered her. "Maybe . . . maybe we have been sleeping very soundly, but that hasn't happened to you."

"True. No other reasons?"

"Er . . . no." Just that Azak hated Rasha so much that he might not react rationally to the news that she had outsmarted him.

"Mmph?" Azak transferred his attention to Inosolan, who was still leaning against the tree. "I congratulate you! You outwitted him. I did not think it was possible."

"He's only a man."

"You knew?" Kadolan exclaimed.

"Certainly. As Inos says, it is obvious—in the night. It is obvious by day also, but so absurd that I cannot bring myself to discuss it. I have known for months."

Inos and Kade said, "Oh!" together.

He was right—it had been months. Kadolan had lost count of weeks, but two or even three months . . . In the distance, camel bells clanked faintly. The night was rapidly becoming colder. She wished she had her camel-hair shawl with her, but she wasn't going to go and get it and m ss whatever madcap talk was coming next.

The big man was looking at her. "It was an accident, I assure you."

"What was?"

"When I burned your hand. I had tried to awaken both of you without success, several times, and given up trying. I had even considered loading you both on camels like baggage and fleeing away across the desert, but I dared not risk it. I worried that you might never awaken. The burn was an accident."

Maybe! But even if he had not been testing to see if he could waken her, he might have been testing to see if Rasha's curse still prevented him from touching a woman.

Azak stepped closer to Inosolan, who did not move.

"You have outwitted him. What do you propose, my dove?"

Kade's heart had quieted down somewhat; now it lurched nervously. Behind her, the tent flapped in the wind and the ropes hummed.

"We tried to leave once," Inos said bitterly. "And failed. Let's leave now!"

Kadolan's knees bent with very little direction from her, and she sat down on the rug rather heavily, not thinking of scorpions until she had done so. Oh, for a comfortable armchair!

31

"Here?" Azak exclaimed, from somewhere high above, near the stars.

"Yes, here! Don't you see?" Inosolan spoke quickly, as if trying to convince herself as much as him, or perhaps not giving herself time to change her mind. "That's why he . . . why we aren't so sleepy tonight! He didn't bother! He decided we wouldn't dare try to run away from him here in the Gauntlet!"

It would certainly be an insane act, her aunt decided.

Azak's voice came deeper and slower. "There is another possibility. Sorcerers can detect power being used. The sheik showed us his ring—he might have invented that story, I suppose—but he did tell us that it had revealed sorcerers at work in Ullacarn. Mages, I think he said. It is more logical that there would be full sorcerers there, an Imperial outpost. May it not be that . . . that a sorcerer . . . would prefer not to use his abilities so close to Ullacarn? You are right, you know. This is easier to talk about."

Kadolan resisted a temptation to quote an impish proverb about fine words salting no cutlets. As long as they only talked! But Azak was infatuated. Inos's slightest wish was a royal edict to him.

"Then that's another reason!" Inos agreed excitedly. "That means we have a much better chance of getting away! And what can he do when he wakes up and finds us gone? If he comes after us himself, he leaves everyone else at the mercy of the brigands!"

Most of the traders and drivers were the sheik's relatives.

"He might send the lionslayers," Azak growled. "A trail that fresh would be no trouble to a lionslayer."

Inosolan said, "Oh!" in a disappointed voice. "Then it is hopeless?" A challenge from her would spur him to any madness, and she was woman enough to know that. Vixen!

He chuckled. "No."

"Ah! You can deal with them?"

"Gold and promises. If they head off along the Ullacarn road, and we go north—"

"North?" Even Inosolan sounded shocked.

He could not be serious!

But he was. "Northwest. Did you not notice the ruins we passed this afternoon? A large city, very old. Cities near mountains usually mean passes. Once there must have been a pass. The roadway may be gone, but the pass itself must still exist."

"And the bandits?"

"If they are anywhere, they will be waiting on the Ullacarn road."

"I suppose. North? Dare we?"

"I dare. Do you?"

Challenge worked both ways, evidently. Even before her niece's agreement, Kadolan knew it was coming. She heaved herself to her feet, ignoring her complaining old joints as she mustered her arguments. All her instincts were against this folly.

"Inos!" she said. "Your Majesty! Even if we are right, and his Greatness is a . . . has been deceiving us . . . at least we have his protection at the moment. This is notorious bandit country, Sire; you told us so yourself, and—"

"They will certainly not be looking for victims heading in that direction." Azak's voice was a deep certainty in the darkness. Then he added thoughtfully, "I wonder how many of the legends are spread around for just that purpose—to keep the caravans from seeking ways around the Slaughterhouse?"

Kade tried another tack. "But travelers in Thume vanish and are never seen again!"

"Not necessarily. I have heard minstrels talk of it. Third Lionslayer's father crossed Thume, so he says."

"But what good will it do? Surely the fastest way to Hub—"

"The fastest way to Hub is a ship from Ullacarn," Inos agreed, sounding excited. Her logic was often shaky; it became notably precarious when she was excited. "But if we are still in Rasha's clutches, then she will make sure we never get near a ship in Ullacarn. She will certainly never let us appeal to the Four, Aunt. She has been meddling in politics—abducting me from my kingdom, interfering in Azak's rule in Arakkaran. The wardens will squash her, and she knows it! We can travel to Hub through Thume, can't we?"

"If we are not molested," Azak agreed. "A month's ride, perhaps, to Qoble. We can be there before winter closes the passes."

Another month on a camel! Or was he thinking of horses? Kadolan wanted an armchair, a stationary, down-filled armchair. And there was no guarantee that the wardens would be of any assistance, anyway. This was all just a dream of idealistic youth. These two youngsters could not believe that the world could be a place of injustice, which it certainly was, much of the time. The Four might well spurn their pleas without a thought, or decree some solution even worse than the present situation, murky though that seemed.

"A month?" Kadolan protested, knowing that all her protests were vain, but determined to try. "By then Nordland and the Impire will have come to some agreement about Krasnegar, and—with all due respect, Sire—the emerald sash of Arakkaran may well be gracing some other ruler. The wardens will dismiss your petitions as historical curiosities!"

"Perchance!" Azak said equitably. "Then I shall merely ask that they remove my curse, so that I may marry your niece. That matters more to me than all the kingdoms in Pandemia."

There was a pause, when Inosolan should have agreed, and said nothing.

Kadolan reached for another arrow, and there were only two left in her quiver. One of those she must not use, so she tried the other. "But to anger a sorcerer?"

"Personally I should like to disembowel him with a gardening fork!" said Inos. "Horrid old fat fool, messing around with my mind! I am not going to hang around here so that Rasha and Warlock Olybino can marry me off to a goblin. Can you get us out of here, First Lionslayer?"

"Your wish is my command, my love."

"Are you coming, Aunt?"

Kadolan sighed. "Yes, dear. If you insist," she said, and she left the other argument unspoken. For weeks that giant young djinn had been wooing Inosolan as best he could, but for a Zarkian male to be seen spending time in the company of a woman, and especially his supposed wife, was to risk seeming unmanly. Thus Azak's courting had been seriously handicapped. Now he would have Inosolan all to himself, from dawn to dusk, uninterrupted. True, he would still be hampered by his inability to touch her—what a blessing that curse was!—but she would have his undiluted attention.

Inos had been handling him very well. She had neither spurned nor encouraged. She had been tactful and kind, promising nothing, committing to nothing. The poise she had learned so well at Kinvale had stood her in good stead so far. But she was very young; she was homeless and friendless, and in great need of support. Alone with Azak for an entire month or longer, could even Inos continue to resist his logic, his persistence, his undeniable charm?

Kadolan was not a gambling person, but she knew a long shot when she saw one.

5

Day dawned through a strangely undesertlike fog. It might have been a cloud, for by then the travelers were already high into the hills.

Departure from Tall Cranes had been a very educational procedure. Inos had listened in fascination as Azak reduced both hamlet and caravan to utter confusion. Although the visual detail had been obscured by darkness, she had been able to make out enough from the sounds alone.

The famous Code of the Lionslayers had proved to be much less reliable than the proverbs about not trusting djinns. Gold and promises had worked their usual wonders. Although she did not hear the actual words of treachery, Inos could guess that exiled princes would readily succumb to offers of future royal status in the court of Arakkaran—even though they had no reason to expect Azak's pledges to be any more reliable than their own oaths. However he did it, Azak prevailed and Elkarath was betrayed

If the villagers had guards of their own posted, then the lionslayers dealt with them—Inos preferred not to know—but probably the foxes had not expected danger from the chickens. Most of the men were absent, anyway.

The camels had been freed of their hobbles and bells, and driven from their paddocks. By dawn they might be anywhere. The rest of the livestock—mules, cattle, horses, even poultry—had also been chased out into the night. Some had tried to follow the fugitives for a while, but had eventually given up. The lionslayers had loaded their familes and taken off south, to Ullacarn. When the old sheik awoke, he was going to have much to keep him occupied—marooned and defenseless amid a very hostile population. No one was going to be starting a pursuit for quite some time.

Mules would be better than camels in the mountains, Azak had said, so it was from the back of a mule that Inos greeted the dawn. A mule was not a smooth ride, but the tough little beasts had climbed and climbed and climbed without protest. Already Tall Cranes was a long way back and a long way down.

The night wind had gone, or else it was confined to the valley and the mule train was now above it. A pearly glow filled the air, and she could smell dampness for the first time in weeks. Delicious! The mules' small hooves clopped on a smooth stone surface.

"A road?" Inos said.

Azak and his mule loomed large and dark at her side, just foggy enough to hint that they were not quite corporeal. His red-bearded smile was visible now, but she had been hearing it for some time in his voice.

"The road to the city, certainly. We have been following it for an hour. It comes and goes. See?" The paving vanished below a bank of sand.

Inos twisted around and confirmed that Kade was in view now also, although misty. She waved and received a wave in reply. Wonderful old Kade! Inos herself sat the lead mule of a string of four, with her aunt bringing up the rear. Azak had kept his mount free, and rode ahead or alongside, as the terrain dictated. Even mules did not argue with Azak ak' Azakar.

Escape! Freedom!

Boulders and a few scraggy bushes appeared out of the fog, paid their respects, and withdrew to the rear like a procession of courtiers. The light was growing brighter, the fog drifting. A few minutes later the pavement was back again. After a furlong or so, the mules reached a gully where it had been washed away, but Azak found it again on the far side

He was very pleased with himself. He had reason to be. The current confusion in the Oasis of Tall Cranes did not bear thinking about—meaning that
it was very enjoyable to think about. Revenge!

Weary as she was, not having slept all night, Inos could still convince herself that she was thinking more clearly than she had done in weeks. She said
so. "I feel as if my mind has been wrapped in a blanket! Sleazy, deceitful old
man! Everything feels sharper and clearer."

"Then you agree to many me?"

She parried with a jest, and won a laugh. Azak seemed to be feeling the
same sense of relief she did. He was flippant and high-spirited. He was totally unrecognizable as the saturnine sultan who had ruled a palaceful of ferocious princes by brute terror. He was in love.

She had seen the same transformation happen at Kinvale, although never
on quite such a scale. A man in love reverted to boyhood. He rediscovered fun
and frolic, and cheerfully played the fool in ways he would never otherwise
have considered. She had seen a normally lordly tribune leap into a fish pond
to recover a lady's hat. Temporary mating plumage, the girls had called it
among themselves. It suited Azak. It made him seem much more credible as a
husband in Krasnegar. But how long would it last after the courtship was over?

And he was very persistent. Even at dawn, on a mule, after a sleepless night,
heading into unknown dangers, possibly being pursued by an angry sorcerer,
Azak was busily wooing. He badgered, and he deflected every objection. "Tell
me!" he said. "Describe these customs that you find so unacceptable."

"Murder, for one thing. I know you poisoned your grandfather . . . how
about Hakaraz and his snakebite? Did the snake have help?"

"Certainly. Asps do not infest royal apartments from choice, and there
were six of them. The one in his boot got him."

Inos shivered. "How many brothers have you killed?"

"Eighteen. Do you want to know about uncles and cousins?"

She shook her head, not wishing to look at him. The mules were back on
the made road again, and the surrounding slopes were coated in rank brown
grass, wet with dew. The air was cold yet.

"Do you wish to hear my reasons?"

"No. I'm sure you had reasons. And I know that it is the custom of the
country, so they couldn't complain that they—"

"Complaints were some of the reasons." He was mocking, and yet serious,
too. "But I shall have no relatives around in Krasnegar to vent my barbarous
impulses on. It just isn't as much fun with commoners, somehow."

"Oh, Azak! I know you don't do it for fun, but . . . Oh, Azak! Look!"

The fog swirled as if bowing farewell, and withdrew like a drapery.
Sunlight blazed hot and bright. Inos stared up in amazement at a rugged

mountain that filled the sky, seeming to overhang her, and yet the craggy hills directly ahead were sizable in their own right. Then even more dramatic, the crumbled yellow landscape seemed to waken like a sleeping dragon and transform itself before her eyes into the ruined city that was their immediate goal. Cliff became wall, peak tower, gorge gateway.

And Kade cried out.

Azak wheeled his mule even before Inos had hauled hers to a stop. She dropped the reins and scrambled off its back, suddenly aware of stiffness and stabbing aches. And she was not a quarter of Kade's age! How could she have been so thoughtless as to drag the old lady up here without any decent respite? Keeping her up all night . . .

By the time she had limped back to the fourth mule and her aunt, Azak was dismounting a short way farther back, and Kade was full of apologies. She had dropped her breviary, was all.

Well, if she could attempt to read and ride a mule at the same time, she was in not too bad a shape.

"We must take a break, though," Inos said.

Azak nodded agreement as he returned with the missing book, leading his mule. Although his mule was larger than any of the others, in the light of day he seemed absurdly huge alongside it, like a man walking a dog.

The sky was blue, the sun hot, and sunward the land tumbled away in scrawny ridges to the hazy immensity of the desert. Inos had a sudden heady sensation of being a bird. The view was breathtaking. She was amazed at the height they reached already, at the vastness of the world spread out before her.

Somewhere down there in that jumble of rock was the Oasis of Tall Cranes, full of enraged brigands and a very angry sorcerer. Doubtless the local men knew of this road and would follow as soon as they had recovered their livestock, but so far the sorcerer had not reacted. He had not called the fugitives back to him. He might have lost them, or they might be beyond his range already.

But a rest, and hot tea, and food . . .

"Which God?" Azak murmured politely, thumbing through Kade's breviary. "Travelers?"

"Humility," said Kade.

Without hesitation, he expertly flipped the pages and found the place, but as he handed back the book, he raised one copper-red eyebrow. "And why should you choose to invoke Them, ma'am?"

Normally Kade deferred to Azak as thoroughly as any Zarkian woman would. This time she met his mocking gaze with a royal confidence of her own. On muleback, she was almost at his eye level, which no doubt helped, and perhaps she no longer wished to play the Mistress Phattas role, for there

37

was no deference in her ice-blue eyes as she replied. "Because I am convinced
we have made a terrible error, your Majesty."

He flushed. "I trust that you are mistaken!"

"I hope I am. I pray that I may live to apologize."

Azak's red eyes flashed anger, and he turned away, yanking his mule's reins.

6

Someone slapped Rap's face to get his attention. He was still bound,
crammed in on top of some angular sacks and under a bench. He could not
feel his feet at all, and his hands were only more anonymous lumps twisted
underneath him. Day and night were a blur, as if he had been lying there for
weeks, unwanted baggage on *Blood Wave*. Even in the taiga, he had never felt
so cold. His head throbbed from the effects of the blow that had felled him
as he boarded, although he had detected the ambush in time to dodge and
avoid some of the impact. Gathmor had not been so lucky, and he remained
an inanimate bundle jammed in beside Rap.

The storm roared unabated. Kalkor had set sail into the middle of it, with
brazen insanity, and *Blood Wave* had been whirling around like a feather ever
since—standing on her bow or her stern or her beam ends, never still. She
groaned and creaked under the battering, but an orca ship was as near to indestructible as a jotunn raider himself. Even in the dark. Rap had been able to
see the waves, and from his low vantage they had been green mountains,
taller than the mast. They were still coming.

"Water!" he croaked. The only water he had tasted had been the rain on
his face mingled with the salt spray that drenched him and everything else
aboard every few minutes.

Then he recognized the hairy giant kneeling over him.

"What's it worth. Stupid?" His sibilant growl was familiar, too. That voice
came with the nightmares.

"Water!"

Darad thumped a fist on Rap's right eye. Cold and numb as he was, the
pain was unexpectedly overwhelming. For a moment it blocked out the whole
world, crushing, deadening, nauseating. Lights blazed around in his head.

When his mind cleared a little, the jotunn was grinning his wolf grin, the big
canines emphasized by the missing front teeth, top and bottom. "Andor told you
he'd find a way to get you off that stupid little tub. Well, we did, didn't we? *I* did!"

"Friend of yours, is he?" Rap croaked. "Kalkor an old friend?"

Darad nodded, leering. He was ugly as a troll, and almost as big. With any
other of the sequential five it was possible to argue, but Darad was too witless
to be distracted.

38

"And he was willing to do me a favor!"

"How'd you meet up with him?"

"Luck, Stupid. Just luck. My word makes me lucky, see? Yours doesn't! You're mine now, faun. A gift from Kalkor! You're going to tell me your word."

"I don't know—" The other eye was thumped now, harder.

Oh, Gods! That was worse.

"Thinal thinks you do. That's good enough for me." Darad raised a thick finger and stroked his goblin tattoos. "You'll talk."

Rap had recognized Darad among the raiders. That was the main reason he had rushed forward like a maniac to denounce Kalkor—he had known then why the jotnar had come to Durthing. But some of his madness had been the remains of his own killer anger. Without that he might just have run away, and he would have escaped, unless he had lingered to help the women and children. He had been within seconds of beating Ogi; now he was getting what he deserved for losing his temper.

And for being so stupid! He had known that Darad would always be a danger—Darad and Andor and the rest of the five—but he had thought he could shelter in Durthing, guarded by a few hundred jotnar. Had he used the wits he was born with, he'd have guessed that Darad might enlist some jotnar of his own. So Rap had brought down the full horrors of a Nordland thane on the settlement, and for that evil he deserved more punishment than even the Gods could decree.

Whining was not going to help, and telling his word would mean instant drowning. He wasn't ready for that yet, not quite.

So he gave Darad a very obscene instruction he had learned from Gathmor. The resulting punches knocked him out for a while, and that was an improvement.

Piety nor wit:
>   The moving Finger writes; and, having writ,
>   Moves on: nor all your Piety nor Wit
>   Shall lure it back to cancel half a Line,
>   Nor all your Tears wash out a Word of it.
>   Fitzgerald, *Rubaiyat of Omer Khayyam* (§71,1879)

3

Where are you roaming?

1

"**N**od if you're awake," said a whisper in his ear.
Only pain was convincing Rap that he was even alive, but
he nodded slightly.

"Can you get free?" Gathmor really didn't need to whisper
when the storm still howled in the rigging and every rope and spar and strake
on *Blood Wave* was screaming in the torment of the monstrous waves. In any
case, the raiders had apparently forgotten their captives altogether.

Rap shook his head. Seawater blew in his face.

"How long've we been here?"

"About two days, by the stubble on your chin."

Gathmor was deathly pale, his hair matted with old blood. The crazy look
in his eye might have worried Rap had there been anything left in the world
that could worry Rap.

"Did they fight?"

Rap nodded. He'd heard snippets of the bragging; he'd seen the bloodstained axes being cleaned and resharpened. He'd even recognized some
items among the pitiful handfuls of loot that had been thrown aboard and
now lay scattered around in the bilge: brooches and trinkets.

Gathmor let out a long sigh and closed his eyes He'd doted on his three sons, and he'd shown his wife as much affection in public as a jotunn ever did. His beloved *Stormdancer* would be a heap of ashes or the beach by now.

"I think they're leaving us here to die," Rap croaked.

The sailor shook his head. "Just softening us up."

Rap fell silent, frightened he might start to sob. He was so weak! Courage or stubbornness were easier to fake when a man had his strength, but days and nights in bonds, thirst, hunger, cold, pain—he could feel them sapping his will. A man had far more trouble being strong in spirit when his body had been so badly damaged. And uncertainty helped, too. Call that fear.

Farsight made the ordeal worse. Every roll to port and his ribs were ground against a lumpy sack—but those lumps were stoneware flagons of wine. He could even read the labels. Rolls to starboard brought a heavy keg thumping against his knee—and he knew it contained salt beef. Most of the baggage on *Blood Wave* was loot: gold and jewels and finery, stuffed in bags and jammed into odd corners, much of it broken or ruined already; but within his reach, were he not bound, there was food and drink aplenty.

He could also watch every mouthful as the raiders feasted and drank. They ate well. Even at the height of the storm, when he expected *Blood Wave* to founder at any minute, the mariners went calmly about their business and pleasure. To display fear or even reasonable doubts would be unjotunnish and probably a capital offense on this ship.

If softening him up was what Kalkor intended, then Rap thought he would make a very fine feather mattress already.

Dark and cold . . . Splash after splash after splash of salt water . . . Rain, sometimes, which helped.

Being rolled to and fro on a rock pile until half his bones felt raw.

Thirst, monstrous torments of thirst.

A boot in the ribs if he called out.

You volunteered for this voyage, Pea-brain! Did you expect the luxury cabin?

Hunger. Cold. Thirst.

Fouling his own clothes.

Thirst. Cold. Cramps like hot coals.

Gathmor, whispering: "Why'd you interfere? If you knew it was Kalkor, why not just get the Evil out of there?"

"I knew he'd come to Durthing to find me."

"And you thought he might be satisfied? Spare the town?"

"Maybe."

"Feeling guilty for bringing bad luck?"

"Maybe. And you? Your reason?"

41

"The same."

Thirst. Splash. Roll. Cold. Dark . . .

A punch or two whenever Darad went by. Testing for softness.

Gathmor again: "So Kalkor has a seer now. You'll be his eyes?"

"No!"

Truly, Master Rap? Suppose he made you an offer right now, Master Rap? Pilot for an orca—easy work for a seer. Just guide the death and rape up the river by night, Master Rap. Outflank the guards. Locate the hidden treasures: gold below the bricks, virgins in the attic. Good pay—all the booty you can carry, all the women you can catch. Will you accept that offer, or stay where you are, Master Rap?

Take all the time you need to think about it.

Kill yourself, Master Rap? You're not man enough. Do it later, when you feel better?

Cold. Thirst. Delirium starting. Inos on a horse. Darad and Inos. Andor. Bright Water the mad witch.

They're eating again. Drinking again.

Splash after splash . . .

Blood Wave was a lower, longer, sleeker vessel than *Stormdancer* and yet she was still only an open boat, for there were no unnecessary luxuries like cabins on an orca longship. One small triangle of deck at the stern supported the helmsmen—the steering oar needed two men or more in this weather, and if the wind ever caught *Blood Wave* broadside she would be on her beam ends instantly. Below that tiny deck was the only relatively sheltered spot on board. There Thane Kalkor hung his hammock. He had a chair there, also, a throne, and when awake he sat in bored glory, rarely speaking to anyone, waiting for better killing weather.

The sailors bailed, prepared food, tended weapons, but mostly they just lounged about, being idle. The storm would take them somewhere and they had no say in where; rowing was impossible in weather like this. There might be rocks dead ahead, but jotnar would never admit to fear.

Despite the howling wind and thrashing rain, few wore more clothing than leather breeches. Their beards and hair flew wild in the breeze, or clung in soaked tangles of silver or gold or even copper. There was a manic, ruthless quality in their appearance, an animal ferocity that would have persuaded Rap to believe their reputation even without the evidence of the cargo. Their conversations were ravings of nightmare. He would accept any story told of such men. They competed in cruelty and sought to outdo each other in atrocities. To them compassion would be worse than cowardice. Brutality was their creed and their ambition.

He had no doubt that they had killed everyone they had managed to catch in Durthing—women, children, even the harmless little gnomes, for he had overheard jokes about the problem of cleaning gnome off an ax.

And it worked! Kalkor had lost only one man in Durthing, the one Brual had taken, yet there had been more than enough able fighters in the settlement to put up a resistance. They could have driven the raiders off with rocks, or at least have made them pay for their sport; but instead they had crumpled before the orca reputation and thus themselves become part of the legend. Atrocity fed on itself.

But who was Rap to judge? Only Kalkor's arrival had stopped him from beating Ogi to a pulp—squat Ogi, who had probably truly believed he was doing a friend a favor by setting up a match for him, while at the same time enriching himself by backing a dark horse. Typical imp! Rap had not lost control of his temper since he was thirteen, the time he broke Gith's jaw, but the madness was still there underneath. He had been going to maim Ogi, and only chance had stopped him. Kalkor felt that way more often, perhaps, but Rap was of the same jotunn blood.

He was in the same boat.

And now maybe one of the crew.

2

Strong hands dragged Rap out of his cramped corner and untied his bonds. He was so numb that he could not clasp the beaker he was offered, so it was held to his lips by a fleece-bearded blond giant who looked no older than himself, and who so much resembled Rap's old friend Kratharkran that at first he thought he was hallucinating. But Kratharkran must be safely home in Krasnegar, earning an honest living; this young jotunn was a killer, and his attitude to the foul and stinking captive was one of understandable dislike.

Fortunately there was still no shortage of fresh air, although the storm was waning. The sky had brightened, and Rap could have seen with his eyes almost as well now as he could without them, except that both his eyes were swollen mostly shut, thanks to Darad's little chats. The waves had not subsided, though, and might not do so for days. Fresh air and rain, and cold. He was almost too weak to shiver.

"Thane wants you," said the young colossus, with the same unexpectedly high-pitched voice as Kratharkran. "Can you walk?"

Rap shook his head, and even that was an effort. The water had added nausea to his pains; he should have drunk more slowly. Apparently he was not going to be fed yet, but he didn't care overmuch at the moment.

The sailor rose, took hold of Rap's feet, and headed aft, dragging him along the narrow central gangway between the rowers' benches. Unfortunately the oars were stored there when not in use, and the narrow walk space remaining was wide enough for a boot, but not a man's shoulders. He bounced on blades and counterweights. The first half of the journey was downhill, the second half up, as *Blood Wave* continued her trek over the gray-green ranges of the Summer Seas. Arriving at the stern, the gangling raider dropped Rap's feet, hauled him up by the shoulders, and adjusted him so he was half kneeling, half sitting on the planks.

"Thanks, Vurjuk," Kalkor said. "Be sure and wash your hands now."

"Aye, sir!" The young raider grinned and stalked away, swaying in easy balance as the ship tilted its bow to the sky again.

Rap could not even control his whirling, reeling mind, let alone his despicably useless body. He slumped on the planks before the thane's bare feet like a dog, or a heap of refuse. He wanted to stand up like a man, and his contemptible muscles refused to obey his commands. They would do nothing but shiver. His hands were starting to throb painfully.

Lording above him on his throne, Kalkor reached out one horny foot and nudged Rap's head up, so he could study the ruins.

"Darad?"

"Aye, sir."

"It's enough to spoil a man's lunch." Kalkor pushed the offending face down again, still using his foot.

The thane's private kennel was crammed with sacks and bales, which Rap had long since inspected and judged to contain the choicest loot. The overhead deck was too low for a man of any of the large races to stand upright; indeed it had not even been high enough for Thane Kalkor's chair.

Once that chair must have belonged to a king, or perhaps a bishop. It was big and intricately carved, inset with jewels and enamels and filigree of gold. It was padded in fine scarlet velvet. But the tall back had been shortened with an ax to fit under the low headroom, and now half the jewels were gone and the velvet was stained and rotted by salt water. Even the legs were splintered where the chair had been spiked to the deck to stop it sliding around.

Now the throne belonged to a half-naked jotunn pirate, who was lounging back in it and regarding with wry amusement the wretched near-corpse that had just been dumped at his feet. He was exactly as Rap had seen him in the magic casement: big and young, powerful in every way imaginable. His hair was the color of white gold, hanging heavily like plate; his eyebrows were white seagulls' wings of irony on his bronzed face, a face of hard, angular beauty and diabolic cruelty. Unlike the rest of the men aboard, he wore no tattoos.

44

His eyes were the most intensely blue eyes Rap had ever met. They burned like fragments of sky, full of cold and deadly fire. They smiled with the joy of madness. Lesser jotnar, like Gathmor, might rouse themselves to killer frenzy. Kalkor would never lose it.

And this notorious killer Kalkor, Thane of dark, was a distant relative of Queen Inosolan and supposedly holder of a word of power handed down from their remote common ancestor, the sorcerer Inisso.

"You are Rap."

"Aye, sir." It hurt to speak. It might hurt much more not to.

"I have some questions," Kalkor said. He was shouting, as *Blood Wave* balanced momentarily on a high green crest, and the wind shrieked in the rigging, hurling a stinging salt spray with the rain. Even his covered nook did not keep him dry. "You will answer them truthfully." *Blood Wave* pitched her bow down and began the long slide into the next valley.

Rap nodded and almost fell over backward. He managed another "Aye, sir." It was quieter in the troughs, so he needn't shout.

Then a sudden shadow, and he looked up with farsight. The troll-like Darad loomed over him, scowling monstrously. He was stooping to see in under the helmsman's deck, steadying himself against the edge with one giant furry paw. The hair on his shoulders stirred in the wind like ripe barley.

Kalkor's attention left Rap and fixed itself on the newcomer with no change in its disdain.

"You promised he would be mine!" Darad bellowed.

"Did I?" Kalkor waited for a moment, and then repeated, "Did I?" in a slightly more pointed tone.

"Yes! You said he would be mine. You gave him to me! A gift to me!"

"I don't remember. Are you sure?"

Kalkor had not raised his voice any more than necessary to let it be heard over the wind, and his calm, steady smile did not vary by a twinkle, except when rain or spray blew in his face. Darad likely had little more intelligence than a starving dog and no compunctions at all about anyone else's life or death. Yet apparently his own fate still mattered to him, for he flinched before Kalkor's unspoken threat.

"Well . . . I thought so, sir. Must've misunderstood you."

"You do that quite often, Wolf. Don't you?"

Incredibly, the ogre cringed even further. "No, sir I mean, aye, sir . . . I mean I'll not do it anymore, sir."

"I certainly wouldn't advise it."

Darad hesitated, lips moving, and then growled, 'But you remember this, Thane: He's a liar! He'll lie to you."

45

"I don't think so."

The giant hesitated, puzzled, knowing he had been dismissed and yet unwilling to go away and leave Rap babbling of sorcerers and Sagorn and Thinal and Andor and Jalon. Had he really expected Kalkor to kidnap Rap for him from a jotunn settlement, and then never want to know *why?*

"He's mad, too. Imagines things."

"Darad," Kalkor said in the same conversational tone as before,' "it is my custom to present gifts to my guests when they depart. Would you care to choose something now? Something heavy?"

The monster took a moment to work that out, and then his eyes turned toward the ranks of green hills marching at the ship.

"North for Pandemia," Kalkor said, "but I can't give you any clearer directions, because I don't know."

Darad turned and rushed off downhill, along the gangway.

The blue fires came back to look at Rap. The quiet smile almost seemed to want to share amusement; but that would be a dangerous assumption to make.

"I see I have more questions to ask than I thought I had. His stupidity is disgusting. Now . . . Have you ever seen one of these?"

The thane reached behind him and produced a gruesome artifact that Rap had not noticed tucked in there. The handle was a wooden cylinder, short and polished, possibly even smoothed by long use. Attached to one end were many fine chains, each about as long as a man's arm. They looked as if they might have been dipped in black mud, and dark pellets still clung to the tiny links.

Rap could only shake his head. His voice had failed him. He licked salt from his lips.

"This one's of dwarvish make, I think, but the imps use them in their jails. They use them on their troops, too. Now I find that absurd! If a man doesn't measure up, kill him and find another—why mess around? Yes, this is an impish punishment. Jotnar don't use such barbarities." The gull-wing eyebrows rose inquiringly.

"No, sir."

Kalkor beamed. "Wrong!—*Aye, sir!* Sometimes wanton cruelty is useful. One has a reputation to maintain, after all. It's messy, though, and best done ashore. Find a suitable tree, tie the subject up by his wrists . . . The men take turns. The one who kills him wins. I have yet to see a man survive more than twenty-two lashes, but he was a quite elderly bishop who didn't want to part with a minor treasure he had hidden away, so you might do better. Five strokes would ruin a man for life, I think—applied with enthusiasm, the chains will cut to the bone, you do understand?"

"Aye, sir."

"So, faun, I am going to ask some questions, and you are going to answer. I am very good at detecting lies, and every lie earns you one stroke with the cat-o'-nine-tails. Behave yourself and I won't hurt you. I may kill you, but it will be quick. Now, are we clear on the rules?"

"Aye, sir. Sir . . . may I have a drink of water?"

"No. First question: Who is king of Krasnegar?"

"There isn't one. Holindarn is dead."

Kalkor nodded, as if pleased—as if Rap was confirming Darad's news. Kalkor had not known, so obviously Foronod's letter had never reached him.

Had the factor guessed what he was inviting into Krasnegar? Or had he seen Kalkor as inevitable and just wanted to get on his good side as soon as possible? All Kalkor's sides were bad. Rap's feet were starting to throb worse than his hands.

"Second question: Describe Inosolan."

Rap took a deep breath and weighed the agony of being flayed against the probability that nothing he could possibly say could ever make any difference . . . but his mouth had started speaking already. Cowardice had a thousand disguises and if it called itself exhaustion and weakness and exposure and *don't-matter-anyway*, cowardice it was still. Nevertheless, he was not man enough to stop himself talking.

"Somewhere between an imp and a jotunn in height. Mangold . . . darker gold than . . . well, that man sewing the boot? About that shade. Green eyes. Slim. She rides and—"

"I'm only interested in her body. Is she beautiful?"

"Aye, sir."

"Face me while you're speaking. Show me how big her breasts are. Mm. I like them bigger. Is she a virgin?"

"I don't know!" Rap almost managed a shout.

Kalkor chuckled softly, the sharp sapphire fires never leaving Rap's face. "You have occult farsight, don't you?"

"Me, sir? No, sir."

"That's one, Rap! I warned you! One stroke. Can you control it, turn it on and off at will?"

"Sometimes," Rap muttered. Darad had the brains of a herring. He had talked far too much for his own purposes. Like Gathmor, Kalkor would never willingly part with a seer.

"It's not easy, is it? So you're discreet? Do you love her?"

"Inos? Love her? Me? I was . . . No, of course not!"

"That's two."

47

"Two what?" Rap snarled. The pain of those chains could never be worse than the pain now pounding in his hands as the blood came back. And his feet . . . Oh, Gods! . . . his feet . . .

"Two lies, two strokes." Kalkor waved the whip gently, letting the chains swing like a pendulum, jingling.

In his sudden, utter shock, Rap forgot the torment in his hands and feet. "No! I was a stableb—" *Oh, Gods!* Love Inos?

Kalkor shook his head wonderingly. "You didn't know? You hadn't realized! How sweet! My heart bleeds, my gorge rises. Rap, I'll take back that 'two'! I haven't felt so moved since the praetor of Clastral offered me his daughters. But let's be quite clear on this. You lust after Inosolan?"

Rap nodded, too shattered to speak. How had he dared? So that was why he had this crazy dream of finding his way to her side—to be a lover, not just a servant? She had kissed him once, and then let turn return the favor. They had held hands. Puppy love! Hopeless love. It was unthinkable—she was a queen and he was a churl. He had been deceiving himself all this time. Gods, Gods!

And that was why he had been so disturbed when he had seen a man coming out of her tent in the looking glass vision. *He had been jealous!* Fool! Fool! Fool!

And Kalkor was watching him with amused contempt as if he could read all this appalling revelation unwinding in Rap's mind.

"More than you lust after any other woman?"

"Aye, sir." By the Powers, it was true!

"Well, that is a recommendation, but I don't know how reliable a faun's taste would be. Where is she now?"

"I don't know."

The bright-blue eyes seemed to grow even brighter as Kalkor frowned, regarding Rap carefully. He waited while the ship topped another spume-swept crest, then he probed with care: "Roughly?"

"Probably in Zark, sir. A sorceress abducted her, and she was a djinn."

The thane was surprised. "Truly? I really thought the Wolf had gotten his head banged once too often! How did you know my name?"

"Saw you . . . in the . . . magic casement." Rap had to force the words out. The pain was knotting him now and getting worse. His arms and legs would have been a torment by themselves, but he was barely noticing them over what his extremities were doing to him.

"Do you know where in Zark she is?"

"Arakkaran, sir."

"That's two now, Rap! The truth?"

Struggling to concentrate, barely managing to speak instead of just scream. Rap said, "The sorceress said she came from Arakkaran."

"But you don't think Inosolan is in Arakkaran. Why not?"

Shocked, and hurting too much to plan any convincing lies, Rap blurted out a confused account of his meeting with Bright Water and Zinixo, and how the wardens had all been trying to steal Inos away from the sorceress and one another. He expected the thane to throw him overboard for spinning such a yarn—and it would have been a blissful release—but Kalkor, amazingly, seemed to believe him.

The questions thudded home like arrows, Rap croaked out answers in a blur. Describe Milflor harbor . . . how many men in the Krasnegarian army . . . He shaved the truth as much as he could manage, until Kalkor shook his head gently and said, "We're up to five, Rap. I thought I'd warn you. We're looking at real damage now, I'm afraid. Next question . . ."

His instinct for truth and falsehood seemed to be infallible, although Rap's face was so battered that it must be very hard to read, and often the wind whipped the words from his lips. The penalty count was up to "Nine!" before Rap abandoned any further efforts to deceive. Thereafter he just let his tongue babble. He didn't care anymore. The pain in his hands and feet was driving him mad. If he had the strength, he'd climb over the ship's side and drown himself.

He must have fainted, because afterward he remembered speaking while lying flat, his bruised cheek against the cold wet planks. Later he sensed two enormous dirty feet right in front of his nose. From them young Vurjuk sprouted like a spare mast.

". . . clean him up," Kalkor was saying. "Can you trawl him on a rope without killing him?"

"Can try, sir."

"Well, make it brief and find him some clothes afterward, because I would prefer that he live awhile yet."

"A flogging match?" Vurjuk's voice rang with boyish eagerness.

Thane Kalkor did not answer impertinent questions; the look in his eye was enough to make the kid bleat, "Aye, sir!" and jump to obey orders.

Stripped, trawled, dried, clothed, watered, and fed, Rap discovered to his surprise that he was still alive, although he wished he wasn't. He was still incapable of walking, but he crawled aft to where Gathmor lay, and gave him a drink. Then he dragged over a battle-ax, which was the only sharp thing within reasonable distance, and found even that hard to hold in hands so grotesquely swollen. The jotnar must have noticed what he was doing but they did not interfere. By the time the last of Gathmor's bonds parted, Rap was so weary that he was capable of nothing more. He fell asleep where he was, in much the same place he had been before.

49

3

Rap was kicked awake and told to report to the thane.

Reeling and stumbling, he hurried aft, confused by the ship's new motion. Falling was inevitable in his state, but he managed he make all his impacts on inanimate things—oars, benches, tubs. To land on a sleeping jotunn might cost him half his teeth.

The sun was just rising into a blue and promising sky. The wind was strong, but no longer dangerous, and *Blood Wave* was singing northward over the last remnants of the storm swell. Even the creak of wood and rope had taken on a more cheerful note. Perhaps today he might get dry for the first time since Durthing? Then he reached the stern and sank to his knees before the throne, where Kalkor was just making himself comfortable.

For a few minutes Rap was ignored as the man rummaged in a leather bag, looking for something. All over the boat, men were stirring, rising, stretching, scratching, cursing.

"Roll that up." The thane's gesture indicated his hammock, so Rap rose and attended to the hammock. He could not straighten under the low headroom, but in his condition he had very little desire to. He was as shaky and weak as a sick kitten, staggering with every pitch and roll.

He tucked hammock and blanket on top of the mountain of loot, but before he could kneel—or just fall—down again, Kalkor held out a hand to him. Rap stared at its burden in dumb incomprehension, and then looked into the jotunn's arrogant blue contempt.

"You lose a finger for every nick."

It was without question a razor. Still gaping, Rap took it, opened it, and found the finest steel blade he had ever seen, obviously dwarvish. He tried the edge; before he felt anything, his thumb was oozing fine specks of blood.

"Idiot!" Kalkor said. "Well, you know the rules. Get busy."

Rap's hands were still stiff and swollen, and if they had not been shaking before, then they certainly were now. He moved near to the chair and tried to steady his head against the overhead beams—had he been a fraction taller he could have rested his shoulders against them instead. He was stooped over Kalkor, and much too close for comfort or even for easy work. The thane was offering his face . . . and neck.

Why shouldn't Rap just cut his throat?

Kalkor's sky-blue eyes gleamed. He knew what Rap was thinking, and he smiled up at him as fondly as a lover. When he spoke his voice was very soft, "Don't even be tempted."

To dry-shave a man on a leaping, heaving boat in a state of shivering weakness when the slightest knick would bring mutilation—for Kalkor's threats would never be idle—that was a totally impossible task. The very prospect brought sweat leaping out all over Rap's body. It was utterly, completely, insanely impossible! As well ask him to fly to Zark.

"I'll give you about five more seconds," Kalkor said.

Rap took him by the nose and lifted. The jotunn stretched his upper lip and Rap stroked it with the razor. He did not forfeit a finger with that one. He wiped the blade on his sleeve and prepared to try again. Kalkor had missed shaving for several days; his golden stubble was long and tough, his skin dry and surprisingly soft. Rap's own face was streaming, as was all of him. He could not have been wetter had he just emerged from the sea.

Why shouldn't he just slit Kalkor's throat? The man was an egregious monster, a killing, raping, looting horror without peer. Even this whole shaving charade was a form of torture. The crew would be watching and laughing— and admiring their leader's courage. Rap's opportunity to make the world a safer place for human beings was one that any half-decent man should be glad to sacrifice his life for. Trouble was, he might not reach the rail in time to gain an easy death, and if the rest of the jotnar caught him, what unspeakable torments would they inflict on him?

Kalkor was watching with a sleepy sort of disdain. He looked completely relaxed, lounging on his throne, being shaved by his new thrall, but he wasn't relaxed to Rap's farsight. His eyes were half closed, and yet alert, and while his hands hung slack and loose, the muscles in his shoulders were knotted hard as steel. Thane Kalkor was not quite the uncaring suicidal hero he was trying to portray.

Rap realized he had stopped breathing, and paused to resume. He wiped his forehead, although the sweat wasn't running into his eyes, which were still puffed and blurred. He had been working with them closed.

Kalkor was still watching.

"Strop?" Rap croaked.

"In the bag."

Rap fished out the belt and began sharpening. When he was ready to shave again, Kalkor tilted his head back, baring his throat.

"Tell me about Darad and this curse of his."

Rap pulled skin taut with fingertips, slit off whiskers with a deft stroke. A slash would be so easy, the world so much better! He could not remember what he had told Kalkor about Darad the day before. "There are five of him." He must watch the crests—*Blood Wave* had a nasty habit of twitching her tail when she went over the tops, as the wind caught her hull; if he lost his balance he would lose a finger for certain. "Only one of them can exist at a time. They were a gang of wild kids. About a hundred years ago . . ."

So easy to kill. Was he not man enough? He felt no real guilt about Yggingi, and this jotunn was a thousand times worse man the imp had been. Make the try and get it over! He pushed Kalkor's chin to a better angle. He was steadying his own head against a beam and getting splinters in his scalp. This would be easier if he could stand upright. Without the acuity of farsight it would be impossible.

"Each of the five has a talent . . ." Now the razor seemed to be tugging more, and it wasn't for lack of sharpening. Kalkor was starting to sweat too. He was still striving to seem relaxed and limp in his chair, and yet he was growing tauter and tauter. A fine sheen of damp showed on his forehead and chest. Was this ordeal going on longer than he had anticipated? Likely he had expected Rap to nick him on the first or second stroke . . . all right so far; half done now. Probably Kalkor had planned to end the game when he got to ten nicks. A seer with no hands would be easier to keep prisoner. But if he wanted to mutilate Rap like that, he would do so anyway, regardless of how many times Rap cut him.

Talk was easier while stropping than while shaving. "Darad doesn't need to call for help very often, so he's aged. He stays too long. Thinal, on the other hand, is still just a kid." Rap gripped Kalkor's ear and pulled a little harder than necessary.

Not a game—it was a trap. Nicks were not what the jotunn expected, but an attack. Rap moving to cut his throat. Strop some more. "Jalon's the minstrel, the artist . . ." He was talking without thinking, but he didn't mind revealing the gang's great secret. He owed nothing to any of them. The only thing he left out was the word of power. Kalkor already had a word of his own, and might be tempted to become an adept. He might very well extract Rap's word, also, and three words made a mage. Kalkor as a mage was a brain-curdling thought.

His talent was fighting, so Andor had said. Could a mere occult genius fend off a razor attack even if it was launched from such close quarters? Perhaps. Probably. So Kalkor was not nearly as vulnerable as he looked. If Rap tried to avenge Durthing, then Kalkor could still block him.

And the man was really sweating now. It made the shaving harder, but Rap could afford to take his time. He was beginning to think he could win this game, unless Kalkor deliberately cheated by moving, and so far he had played fair. So Rap was stropping after almost every stroke, dragging it out.

"Sagorn is the wise man—"

"Never mind him. Tell me again what you saw in the casement."

"Which time? You, or the dragon, or the goblin?"

"All of them. Start with Inosolan's prophecy."

"You, wearing a fur and nothing else." Rap was enjoying pushing the thane's head into odd angles. "An old man giving you an ax . . ."

52

But any ordeal must end eventually. Rap had no sooner closed the razor and replaced it in the bag with the strop than his knees folded of their own accord. He slumped down, with one leg twisted under him; he doubled over and shivered convulsively, as if he had a fever. He retched, but his stomach was empty and nothing happened. It was over. Over! He shivered and shivered.

After a moment, a dirty toe poked under his chin and nudged his head up. There was a very strange glint in those deadly blue eyes.

"Tell me again of the place where we were supposed to fight this interesting duel, you and me?"

Rap licked his lips and managed to steady his quivering jaw enough to use it for speaking. "I told you, sir—it wasn't clear at all. Short grass; scythed or grazed. Mist and rain. A ring of people all around. That was all. Nothing in the distance, no landmarks."

"The Place of Ravens on Nintor," Kalkor said, staring intently, "has a circle of great stones around it. The spectators must stay back from those. Stay outside. There are no predators or scavengers on Nintor, except the ravens, and the bones of the losers are left where they fall. Did you see any bones, or the monoliths?"

"No, sir."

"Mmm." Kalkor rubbed his fresh-shaven chin and seemed to ponder. "Reckonings are almost always done at the Place of Ravens, but they need not be. They can be held anywhere, if certain conditions are met."

Rap almost gagged again. He could think of nothing to say, so he didn't try. Sagorn had interpreted the vision as showing Rap being Inos's champion; but he might equally well be Kalkor's plaything. The shaving episode had just demonstrated that the jotunn's sense of humor was as warped as his morals, and if he found the idea of a ritual battle with Rap an amusing prospect, then he could stage it at the next landfall, wherever that might be.

"And when you tried for a vision from the casement?"

"I never did, sir. I approached it twice, and each time it . . . well, it sort of blazed. Very bright. All shining. Eerie!"

Kalkor nodded. Then, slowly, his smile widened—and yet his eyes seemed to narrow. He stepped off his chair and moved out from under the helmsman's deck. "Up!"

Rap rose also and cautiously straightened. He was shorter and slighter than the jotunn. He felt very frail beside that potent killing machine.

Kalkor looked him up and down twice, perhaps making the same comparison and feeling reassured by it. Then he folded his arms and shook his head mockingly. "Just be glad I'm a gambler, sailor."

"Sir?"

Rap staggered on a roll, and the thane's hand flashed out to grip his shoulder and steady him. His fingers dug in like skewers.

"There is something very odd about you, halfman. Very odd! My instincts for self-preservation tell me I should gift you a full suit of armor and send you out to push. I just tested you, you realize?"

Here came the job offer. "Sir?"

"You passed, but not in the way I expected. I would have taken odds of a thousand to one that what I demanded was humanly impossible for a mundane in your condition. But you weren't using occult power, were you?"

"No, sir. Just farsight. I can't see well at the moment."

"Farsight . . . and something else, but not magic!" Kalkor chuckled, and it was a sound to freeze bones. "I had decided to kill you if you did pass." He sighed. "But, as I said, I'm a gambler. Just a sentimental softie, I am. I will accept that you are not an adept in spite of the test."

He raised a quizzical eyebrow, and Rap said, "Thank you, sir."

"Indeed. You may be a mage or even a sorcerer, of course, but then I am helpless—and you certainly don't look like either at the moment. Faun, I am going to be very surprised if we do not fulfill that absurd prophecy one day, you and I. That intrigues me! I have raised twelve heads in the Place of Ravens. I should like very much to raise yours, also."

"I will bet on you, sir, not me."

Sudden anger blazed in the inhumanly blue eyes. "Do not joke about sacred matters! I am no imp to wager squalid, worthless things like money! A Reckoning is a solemn ritual, an offering of courage and a sacrifice of life. Few things less than life itself are worth gambling." For a moment Rap thought Kalkor was going to flash into jotunn madness, but then the eerie smile returned. "Two strong men battling to the death, entering the circle knowing that one of them will never leave? There is the ultimate gamble, the finest game of all. I hope that one day I do leave my bones for the ravens of Nintor—it is the noblest death for a thane. And I ask only one favor from the Gods, Master Rap."

Rap saw that he was supposed to question. "What's that, sir?"

"That my slayer be worthy, a man of courage. Tell Darad I want him."

4

It was a real pleasure to pass the message to Darad and see apprehension spread over the nightmare face. There were not many pleasures on *Blood Wave*. Gathmor was conscious, but too weak even to sit up. Rap found water for both of them and eventually begged some food, also. Then he set to work on the problems of cleaning up his fellow prisoner and finding fresh clothes for him. The jotnar did not interfere, but they were surly and uncooperative.

And yet even a captive could have moments less miserable than others. Boat and contents steamed in the hot tropic sun. The sea shone like silver, flashing bands of glory across the minatory obscenity of the orca crudely painted on the sail. White birds followed, rocking on the arcs of their wings. Given blue sky and a fine breeze, a half jotunn could not be totally unhappy on a sprightly vessel like Blood Wave on a fine day.

Rap had noted Darad cowering at the thane's feet and then forgotten him. The next development was Kalkor himself striding past, stopping to drag one of the sacks of loot out from under a bench near the bow. Rap knew what was coming before it emerged, and he swung his farsight aft again. Cowering under the poop deck was the flaxen-haired minstrel, Jalon, struggling to adjust Darad's oversize breeches to his slender form. Small and unassertive, Jalon was a most unlikely jotunn, as he himself had pointed out to Rap once when they shared a picnic lunch in the hills, long ago. His skin was pallid, sickly compared to all the bronzed sailors, and certainly there was no more terrified minstrel on the Summer Seas.

What the crew thought of the magical transformation was impossible to tell. Blue-eyed glances flashed under golden brows questioning and commenting in surly silence. Kalkor had not deigned to explain, and not a man aboard would dare show fear.

The thane headed aft again, carrying a bejeweled ivory harp. In a few minutes Jalon had done the best he could to tune the battered, impractical instrument and was sitting on the helmsman's deck, with his legs dangling.

And then—pure miracle! Somehow he wrung a flawless, angelic thread of music from the harp and on it wove tapestries of the finest singing in all Pandemia. A couple of sea chanties, then a ballad, and more and more, and either every one was perfectly fitted to the timing set by the ship's motion, or else Blood Wave herself now danced to the minstrel's beat.

Glory! It soared, it floated in the warm sky like a flight of rainbows. It lifted the heart or wrung it as he chose. Murderous brutes those jotnar certainly were, but at times Rap could see tears in their eyes, while he himself was tormented by thoughts of Inos and could not help but weep. Then Jalon would switch to some rousing warrior song. Rap's heart would pound, his spirit surge, and he was ready to storm Zark single-handed. At those times the jotnar were roaring, waving battle-axes and eager to waste the entire Impire.

"God of Madness!" Gathmor whispered during a brief pause. "Who is he and where did he come from and how does he do that?" But then the mystery came again, and everyone hushed to listen. Kalkor kept Jalon at it for hours, while *Blood Wave* rushed over the ever-rolling waves in search of land.

As each song ended, harsh jotunn voices called out the names of others, and there were very few that Jalon did not know or could not sing; his repertoire was enormous. But even he had his limits, and eventually his voice began to falter. To say that Kalkor took pity on him would have been an absurdity, but at last he acknowledged human frailty and sent the minstrel off with Vurjuk to eat and drink and rest. The other jotnar began to talk fiercely among themselves, discussing what they had just heard.

Gathmor was asleep. Rap was hungry, but the sailors were eating and he felt it wiser to wait awhile than dare to interrupt. Instead he gave some more thought to his own troubles and prospects.

To start with, where exactly was the ship? The storm could have moved it an immense distance; he had no experience to guess how far. Direction he always knew fairly well, a talent that seemed to be part of his farsight, and in any case he could always read the helmsman's binnacle. After his first two or three days aboard, though, his attention had been distracted by weakness and pain and he had stopped caring. The wind had first carried *Blood Wave* southward, then northeast, but she had not piled up against the coasts of either Kith or Sysanasso. One or other likely by ahead, then, for the helmsman was holding the most northerly course he could manage in a southwesterly, and although she, too, bore only a single square sail, this was a much more weatherly vessel than the top-heavy *Stormdancer.*

And if *Blood Wave* had not gone westward, then Gathmor was in terrible danger, because he was no longer needed as a pilot for the Nogids. Kalkor could find another of those anytime.

All Pandemia lay somewhere to the north. If *Blood Wave* passed west of Sysanasso, she would enter the Dragon Sea, rife with commerce and good pickings for a merciless raider. Alternatively, east of the big island lay Ilrane and elves or Kerith and merfolk, areas Rap had never studied. Farther east still was Zark, although one storm could not possibly move a ship that far.

Which brought his thoughts back again to Inos.

How ironic that a callous killer and rapist like Kalkor should have seen what Rap himself had never before realized. He was in love with his queen! How blind could a man be?

Or how crazy? A stableboy falling in love with a princess—the very idea had been stupid beyond dreams, too stupid even to contemplate. It still was.

And so what? She still deserved his loyalty as a subject. That loyalty should be even stronger if he loved her.

She did not return his love. How could she? A very lowly factor's clerk . . . not even that now, only a vagabond with a knack for horses and a smattering of sailoring skills. On that mad night when her father died, Inos had been cour-teous and kindly to her childhood friend, as she would always be. She had thanked him for his help. She had not flinched before his occult abilities, because she was a sophisticated, educated lady, not one of the ignorant, super-stitious rustics of Krasnegar. Like him.

And if by some miracle he could ever find her, she would certainly by then be married into some noble family. The wardens might just possibly have installed her on the throne of her fathers, with a compromise consort accept-able to both thanes and imperor . . . not, thank the Gods, Little Chicken!

Never Rap.

The man in her tent had been a swordsman, almost certainty an aristocrat. Big, handsome fellow.

So Rap must continue his search if it took a lifetime. She would welcome him into her household, perhaps make him master-of-horse, as they had joked together when they were children. She need never suspect how he felt about her. He would serve her loyally as subject and worship as lover from afar.

And if all he was feeling was an overaged juvenile infatuation, then he would grow out of it in time.

Could a juvenile infatuation hurt this much?

Now he knew why the fairy child had not told him her word of power—her name, or possibly the name of her guardian elemental, if that is what the words were. She had told Little Chicken because he had truly known his life's great desire, and because he had wanted it enough to die for it. Rap had not said that he loved Inos, only that he wanted to find her and be her loyal sub-ject. Not the whole truth! Had he known the truth, and said it, then he would be an adept now, with two words. And the fairy would have died in his arms, not the goblin's.

What if Kalkor got to Inos first?

Or changed his mind and slew Rap out of hand? He obviously took the prophecy seriously.

Or decided to torture his word out of him to become an adept?

Better not to think about that.

No, somehow Rap must escape from the thane's clutches. He'd escaped from the goblins, hadn't he? And from the imps, and from a warlock.

How obvious now was the advice that King Holindarn had given him, and even Andor—that occult powers must be kept secret at all costs. Too late! A jotunn raider would never willingly release a seer. Before landfall, Rap would find himself chained or deliberately crippled so he could neither run nor swim.

"Rap?"

The whisper startled him out of his brooding, and he jerked around to stare at a brilliantly flushed face. For a moment the redness suggested an

extreme, comical embarrassment; then he saw that it was only a very bad case
of tropic sunburn. Jalon had now found a shirt to give him some protection,
but he must be suffering. Under his pain, he was pathetically bewildered and
frightened. He still clutched the frivolously ornate harp in one hand and was
holding up his oversized breeches with the other.

Once Jalon had confessed to having elvish blood in him. Seeing him now
alongside so many pure jotnar. Rap thought he could detect a goldish tinge
to his skin, and a slant to his eyes. And of course he lacked the height and
muscle. It would be unkind to comment on that, though.

"Take a chair," Rap said sadly. "Wine? Sweetmeats?"

"Don't!" the minstrel said, crouching down. "Don't mock, Rap! Gods, man,
but you've grown!"

"I have?"

"It was only two days ago we met, you know. For me, that is."

"You share memories, don't you?" Rap thought of Thinal and Sagorn and
Darad, and all that had happened in the year since that picnic . . . more than
a year.

"Yes. But mine are the clearest to me. The others never *see* things properly!" That was the artist speaking, the painter. He took a harder look at Rap's
face and grimaced. "It wasn't me set Darad on you, Rap!"

"Oh, no!"

"Really!" Jalon's dreamy blue eyes filled with tears. "I warned you about
him, remember! Then I got lost in the forest, and I was tempted to call him,
because he knows that country, but I knew he'd head straight back to get you,
so I called Andor instead. He recognized the danger. Rap, too. Andor's not all
that bad! He managed to find his way south . . ."

"Did he meet any goblins?" Rap asked, suddenly curious.

The minstrel nodded. "A few, in ones and twos, and of course he could
charm that many. They're fairly harmless in the summer, anyway."

"Not now, they're not! Or so I've heard."

"Well, they were! But I did try to keep Darad off you. And I haven't been
back since."

"Not at all?" Rap thought he saw a shiftiness.

"Well . . . once. Just for a few minutes. I wrote a letter that Andor needed,
a letter of introduction. And he'd trapped me, because he called me in a room
where lots of people had seen him going in. They would've seen me if I tried
to leave."

Rap chuckled. The gang of five exploited one another without scruple. He
wondered how many little tricks they had like that.

Jalon glanced around nervously, then looked doubtfully at Gathmor, who
was glaring at him. "Rap, I need some help!"

"Don't we all?"

"No, immediate help! I have to compose an epic, a jotunn war song."

"Good luck."

A flicker of anger appeared in Jalon's washed blue eyes, or perhaps it was only fear. "Kalkor told me to. You know the sort of thing he wants?"

"No. Do you?"

"Oh, yes. It's to be about the battle of Durthing."

Gathmor snarled, and Rap stretched out a hand to restrain him as he struggled to sit up.

"It's not my idea!" the minstrel squealed, flinching. "But there's a convention to these battle songs. Every man has to be mentioned, so I have to talk to every man aboard and get his name. Then I have to fit him into a verse, telling of his exploits. That's not hard; I'll just lift stuff from all the old classics. But I need to know the names of their opponents, see? They have to be in there, too."

"And these brutes didn't think to ask who they were killing?" Rap asked bitterly.

Jalon nodded. "Please, Rap?"

"Why bother? Call Darad."

"I *daren't!* Kalkor says if I call any of the others he'l put his eyes out!"

His distress and his red face made Jalon seem almost farcical. The sequential gang had a man for every situation, and Darad was the man for this one, never Jalon.

"Have you five ever been trapped like this before?"

The minstrel shook his head, looking ready to weep. He was much better at singing about warfare than he was at being involved in it.

"All right!" Rap said, ignoring Gathmor's growls. "I'll list the best fighters in Durthing for you. They're dead, so it won't hurt them. But you'll owe me, Master Jalon!"

Jalon nodded vigorously. "I won't forget, Rap. And the others will remember and be grateful, too."

That seemed doubtful. Even more doubtful was the possibility that Rap would ever be able to collect on the debt.

Jalon was too fine an artist to displease any audience, and probably too great a coward to disappoint this one. By nightfall he had completed his jotunn battle song about the sack of Durthing. It was all pure fantasy, and a stupendous success. It listed every member of *Blood Wave's* crew by name and credited him with some gruesome exploit or other. Even Rap could tell that most of these tales were verses pirated from well-known ballads or epics, but that did not seem to matter at all. The jotnar cheered and roared and applauded every line.

And when at last the blood-soaked narrative drew to its close with the youngest and most junior of the raiders, who turned out to be the oversized Vurjuk, the baby giant who so much reminded Rap of his boyhood friend Katharkran. For the finale, Jalon had saved a famous feat of arms attributed to the ancient jotunn hero Stoneheart. Legend told how Stoneheart had pursued three mighty foes up a great tree and there hacked them to pieces, so that when he departed the branches were all decorated with severed limbs and organs and the grass around was drenched with blood. In Jalon's version there were six enemies, not three, and all were dismembered single-handedly in midair by young Vurjuk and his ax. The sailors screamed with joy, rolling around in their mirth, while the juvenile champion turned an excited fiery red and cheered with the rest of them, quite willing to pretend that every word of this had really happened.

The sky was dark, but the wind held, and *Blood Wave* sailed on. Long into the night Jalon had to keep repeating his masterpiece, over and over, until it seemed as if all the raiders had come to accept that things had actually happened exactly as he said. In the end they were congratulating one another, and especially complimenting the boy champion who had slaughtered six men single-handed, in a tree.

In some ways they were like children, Rap decided, oddly incomplete. It was not bloodlines that made them monsters, for he knew many decent, likable jotnar—like many of his former shipmates on *Stormdancer*, or like Kratharkran, who'd apprenticed to his uncle the farrier. Nor was it climate, for Krasnegar was every bit as cold and bleak as Nordland itself. It could only be custom. In other circumstances Vurjuk might have made a very fine blacksmith, and were Kratharkran here and a proud member of Kalkor's crew, then likely he also would be striving to be a man as they were men, to be like his hero Kalkor. But now, however ruthless he might have been before, Vurjuk had been given a reputation to live up to. He would be worse than ever, if that was possible.

Meanwhile, *Blood Wave* sailed on, into the unknown.

5

Her recent long ordeal on camels, Inos decided, had given her a very sentimental view of horses. Camels' gait was a sickening sway, and her joints grew stiff with the unnatural posture. Camels were stupid and bad-tempered and smelly.

But after three days on a mule she discovered she was looking back on both camels and horses with nostalgia. Mules *bounced.* They raised blisters in unmentionable places. They were stupid and bad-tempered and smelly. The absurd Zaridan robe she wore had never been designed for riding, while her primitive saddle had been stuffed with flints.

After three nights on the bare ground at ever-greater altitudes, she remembered the tents in the desert with much greater affection than she had expected, but a lady never complained, as her aunt had taught her, and if poor old Kade was managing to look on the bright side—and she stubbornly was—then her much younger niece must strive to do much better. Azak expected courage in royalty. So Inos smiled and smiled, and cracked jokes, and once in a while actually deceived herself, as well.

This was, after all, a great adventure. All the rest of her life she would be able to silence a whole dinnertable with the simple words, "When I was in Thume . . ."

The escape seemed to be working. Elkarath had not appeared in their path with a roar of thunder. The brigands of Tall Cranes had not come in pursuit, seeking vengeance. Perhaps they believed their own stories of uncanny horrors preying upon travelers rash enough to venture into Thume, but those horrors had not materialized, either.

The scenery was remarkable, she told herself firmly through chattering teeth.

The gloom-filled forest was redolent with arboreal mystery. Or something. Big trees, anyway. Creepy, haunted.

The ruins had been spectacular—vast tumbled towers and walls of unthinkable antiquity, hidden in forest, beetling over chasms, half buried in silt in the tree-choked valleys. What cities had these been? Who were their brave warriors and fair queens? How long since children had laughed in the deserted courts or horses had plied the empty streets? Now only the wind moved, in blank doorways and crazy staring windows, whispering forgotten names in tongues unknown.

And she was with Azak. Azak was a problem, but he was also a superb protector, and in his strange guise of lover, he had turned out to be extremely good company. Very rarely now did he send shivers of distaste down her spine as he had done sometimes in Arakkaran when he raged at the princes. He was courteous and considerate, and at times even fun. He had a quite astonishing sense of humor, although it was unpredictable, as if it were something he had suppressed in his childhood as unworthy and was now trying to rediscover. And to be wooed by a giant young sultan was certainly a powerful aid to a girl's self-esteem.

Azak as traveling companion—fine. As defender in the wilds—also fine. But Azak in Krasnegar? Azak as *husband*?

Could this really be the love the God had promised Inos? She must trust in love, They had said. She was inclined to believe now that Azak was, incredibly, truly in love with her. He certainly displayed all the symptoms. She must trust the God, then. She must not listen to the insidious tremors of doubt she felt when she tried to think of Azak ruling the prosaic merchants of Krasnegar.

She tried not to think of Krasnegar at all, especially in the gloomy dark of night. She slept badly, missing Elkarath's sleep spell, and even missing the straw pallets of caravan life. Those had seemed very uncomfortable at first, but a single blanket on bare ground was much worse. So her nights were filled with restless turnings and gloomy thoughts.

Krasnegar, more than likely, had no further need of her now. The wardens would have settled the matter somehow, and there had never been anything Inos could have done to honor the promise she had given her father. So what now, Inosolan?

Had the God been telling her she was destined to love a barbarian and live as sultana of Arakkaran?

The idea of a sultana riding out to hunt in Arakkaran was almost as difficult to grasp as the idea of Azak contentedly spearing white bears in a polar night . . . Well, she must trust in love, as the God had directed.

And trust Azak.

At times the mountain road was a paved highway, snaking through the eerily deserted valleys, its ancient blocks heaved and moved by roots and landslides. At other times there was no visible path at all, and then progress became unbearably slow.

But the third day brought the explorers to the barren crest of the pass, a gravelly desert scrolled with strange patterns of rocks and overlooked by magnificent ice-sheathed mountains. Inos thought she would remember the wind here, more than anything.

Late that third day they began descending along a made road, old and battered but still mostly passable, twisting steeply down a dark and gloomy gorge into the unknown lands of Thume.

Where are you roaming:
> O mistress mine! where are you roaming?
> O! stay and hear; your true love's coming,
>   That can sing both high and low.
> Trip no further, pretty sweeting;
> Journeys end in lovers meeting,
>   Every wise man's son doth know.
>   Shakespeare, *Twelfth Night*

4

Battles long ago

1

J alon's ordeal on *Blood Wave* lasted for three days. He sang and played
until he was hoarse and his fingers bled, and every second song had to
be the "Battle Song of Durthing." Soon Rap knew it as well as Jalon did.
He detested every note and every word, hating the callous mockery of
honest sailors cruelly murdered; he mourned their wives and children even
more. *Gods forgive me!*

The minstrel obviously wearied of it, also. He tried to vary it, but the
crew insisted on the original version. They did accept one minor
change—at about the fortieth rendition, Jalon performed the final verse in
a perfect mimicry of young Vurjuk's squeaky treble. He would never have
dared mock any of the others like that, but they all found this embellish-
ment of the climax even funnier, and thereafter it had always to be done
that way. Vurjuk glowered dangerously, and then reluctantly accepted it
and pretended to like it. Apparently mimicry was yet another facet of
Jalon's occult genius.

Several times Rap was ordered aft to answer more questions from Kalkor.
He tried to deflect danger away from Inos and Krasnegar as well as he could,
but the thane detected every deviation from strict truth, no matter how slight.

63

Steadily the toll mounted until Rap was being promised thirty-two strokes from the cat-o'-nine-tails.

He shrugged—which was hard to do convincingly while kneeling at a man's feet—and he tried to put some of his contempt into his still-puffy eyes. "That's a death sentence, then?"

Kalkor looked amused. "I never bluff, lad."

"Then why should I answer any more of your questions? You're going to kill me in about as nasty a way as you can find."

The white eyebrows rose in disbelief. "You underrate my imagination! Besides, I never said you'd have to take all thirty-two strokes at the same time. We can spread them out—one or two a day. You can make a career out of it." The blue-blue eyes glinted. "A seer deserves some consideration."

A truly brave man ought to prefer dying on the first handy tree, rather than be conscripted into a pack of jotunn raiders.

"Thirty-two and counting," Kalkor said. "Next question . . ."

On one topic only could Rap deceive the sharp-witted thane, and there he had no choice. As soon as the questions drew near to the importance of Faerie and the source of magic, Rap's tongue would run away with him and he would start lying like a vagrant horse trader. Those lies Kalkor seemingly accepted, however fantastic they seemed to the man telling them, but of course they sprang from sorcery, the forbiddance laid upon Rap by Oothiana. He could not tell that secret if he tried.

Except for those interrogations, Rap was completely ignored, and so was Gathmor. The sailor was recovering his physical strength, but his mind seemed to have snapped under the strain of captivity, or else from the loss of his ship and family. Dull-eyed and morose, he spent hours curled up, ignoring everything, not even replying to questions. The prisoners were given food and water, but only if they begged for them on their knees. Gathmor either could not or would not do such a thing, so Rap had to beg for two, begging being better than hunger. If he hoped to live beyond the next landfall, he must hope to escape, and for escape he would need his strength—so he told himself as he groveled, but the sustenance he gained thereby seemed strangely tasteless.

The wind faltered, recovered, veered southerly, then westerly, yet it never failed enough for Kalkor to order rowing; it never again became a full gale. And on the third afternoon, at about the fiftieth repetition of Jalon's battle song, the lookout spied land.

Like Andor's and unlike Rap's, Kalkor's word of power seemed to bring him luck. His ship was bearing down on an unknown lee shore in a spanking

64

wind, but his course brought him within sight of exactly what he wanted, an isolated village.

The land was green, hilly and wooded, if not as lush as Faerie or Kith. Within the stretches of forest, too, lay many stretches of open grassland and even barren rock, which Rap found puzzling. By and large, though, the country seemed fertile—why was it not more populated?

And when *Blood Wave* was close enough for sharp eyes and farsight to make out details, there was a river mouth coming up ahead, and a cluster of small cottages. None of the buildings could possibly be a barracks, and if there were boats, they must be small. So this was no Imperial outpost with a naval squadron or a garrison, and those were all that raiders need fear.

The jotnar took out their axes for more sharpening, and demanded the most spirited songs the minstrel knew; they began talking themselves up into bloodlust. Rap found the process horrible and in some perverse way fascinating. The pirates never paused to consider that a tiny fraction of the wealth their vessel carried would buy them all the food and shelter they could use—the idea of a peaceful visit never entered their minds. They bragged of how they would kill and kill, rape and rape. They challenged each other to fiendish contests in atrocity. Before long they were so aroused that they could hardly contain themselves. Their eyes rolled in their heads, and some were drooling like imbeciles. Many stripped naked as if even their usual scanty clothing might somehow restrain their actions. And yet this was the crew that had lined up in solid silent discipline along the beach at Durthing—small wonder that the raiders of Nordland were the terror of Pandemia.

Suddenly the minstrel was ordered to cease, although he had been barely audible over the manic babble anyway. Kalkor was up on the half deck beside the helmsman, roaring orders through a trumpet. Men leaped to their benches and the oars were run out. Rap and Gathmor, who had been huddling in the bow, making themselves inconspicuous amid the madness, were ordered aft. Amidships they passed Jalon as he staggered forward, ashen pale under his sunburn, sucking swollen, bleeding fingers. The sail was furled in the bunt; the coxswain began piping a stroke.

Now Rap received the job offer he had been expecting all along. Kalkor stepped to the edge of the tiny half deck and stared down at him with contempt gleaming in too-blue eyes. "Well, faun? I was told you were pilot on that floating brothel your friend ran?"

"Aye, sir."

"Then let us see how you manage a longship. Up here with you. And if you prove yourself useful, I may decide to postpone the flogging for a while. Some of it, anyway."

Seeing no viable alternative, Rap clambered up the little ladder to join the thane and his helmsman on the poop.

"And you—whatever your name is—" Kalkor said to the scowling Gathmor. "Cast an eye at that shore and tell me where we are."

Gathmor was pale and sullen, not the man Rap had known. No jotunn should have taken such a tone, especially him, but he turned obediently to study the landscape and then looked back up at Kalkor.

"I have never seen its like. It is not Kith, nor any part of Sysannaso I have ever visited."

"And not Pithmot, I think," Kalkor said, with a smirk. "So we know where we are, don't we?"

Dragon Reach? It had to be Dragon Reach! A strange warm thrill tingled Rap's skin as he realized the implications of Dragon Reach.

"Vurjuk!" shouted Kalkor.

The gangling young raider was sitting on the nearest bench, wearing nothing but a conical steel helmet and a self-conscious expression. He was unpaired and thus had not put out an oar. He sprang up. "Aye, sir?"

"Get a weapon and keep an eye on this jotunn woman. If he causes any trouble, kill him."

"*Aye, aye, sir!*" Vurjuk said in an enthusiastic squeak. He stooped to find his battle-ax under the bench. A sword or dagger would have been more appropriate at such close quarters, Rap thought, but the youth hefted the huge ax in one hand and stepped closer to Gathmor. He was a head taller and dangerous in the extreme, yet Gathmor did not even deign to look at him.

Rap, meanwhile, had been studying the approach, both with farsight and with eyes that were gradually recovering from Darad's brutality. Farsight worked better—the sun was close to the horizon, the light tricky.

Either way, the problem was obvious. Hastened along by the rush of the tide. *Blood Wave* was skirting a long spit of rock and sand, keeping step with the breaking swell that raked it in white plumes of spray. Beyond that sinister barrier beckoned a clear lagoon and a friendly yellow beach, and back of them were trees and a hamlet at the base of steep cliffs—a safe haven, with fresh water and shelter, plus unhindered opportunity to enjoy the bloody sports of raiders.

Up ahead, the narrow hook ended, plunging below the shining water in a frothy confusion of rocks. And beyond them was open channel through which surged the fearsome tide. But the rocks were what sent Rap's heart racing. Deceptive to the eye . . . Deep below the smoothly coiling surface, he saw the frenzied streaming of the kelp. He checked *Blood Wave*'s draft, and it was less than *Stormdancer*'s. But it was enough.

Now he must see what he was really made of.

He was new to the ship, so Kalkor would be wary of him, but another chance might not come again for months, and he might never find a better natural trap. Under the low sun that tidal rip was barely visible at all to mundane vision. If he could position *Blood Wave* crosswise in that, then she would whip around and oars would never control her. For several minutes she would be completely at the mercy of the current, and some of those rocky teeth were shallow enough.

Other words of power brought good fortune; perhaps his was going to come through with some at last.

Peep! said the coxswain's pipe.

"Steady as she goes, sir."

Peep!

"The gap's clear?" Kalkor demanded suspiciously.

"Aye, sir. Plenty." And that was true, except that the longship would never reach the opening Rap was looking at. Would that partial lie deceive the jotunn? Rap's heart was racing as it never had. He kept his face turned to the sea. *Peep!*

Please, Gods! Please let me rid the world of this monster!

Rap would die, too, of course. If the waves did not smash him on the rocks, then he would swim ashore and the other survivors would catch him there. But surely this so-perfect ambush had been provided by the Gods themselves?

God of Sailors, God of Mercy, God of Justice . . . As I seek to aid the Good and shun the Evil, grant me this day courage.

Peep! Peep! Oars creaked against thole pins, heaving *Blood Wave* closer and closer to that sinister, inconspicuous ripple. *Peep!*

Twenty strokes should do it.

Swiftly, swiftly to destruction.

Eighteen.

Sixteen.

"You're sure of this, are you, Master Rap?" Kalkor murmured.

"Aye, sir. Quite sure. Steady as she goes, helmsman."

Fourteen.

Twelve.

Then Kalkor raised his trumpet and roared orders—helm hard over, port watch backwater. *Blood Wave* seemed to stand on her stern as she came about, her bow swinging seaward, away from the waiting race.

The thane's rugged hand grabbed Rap by the throat, thrusting him back against the gunwale, bending him over it until his feet left the deck, flailing helplessly, and he was sure he was about to crack. Through a choking black mist he saw blue eyes blaze above him in a killer rage. "Sink my ship, would you, faun scum?"

Gathmor lifted the battle-ax from Vurjuk's unresisting hand and swung it against the back of Kalkor's knees. The thane leaped straight up, so it passed below him and thudded into the side of the ship between Rap's legs. Momentarily released from that choking grip. Rap toppled himself over the rail in a back somersault and plummeted into the sea. Vurjuk reached both hands for his prisoner and was doubled up by a punch that would have felled an oak. Gathmor vaulted over the side, following Rap.

Blood Wave surged away seaward, out of danger.

2

Swimming in the calm of Durthing Bay was no preparation for what happened when a man fell into a riptide crossing a reef. Nothing in Rap's past had ever prepared him for the experience; nothing he could do now made the slightest difference. His farsight was warning him of jagged teeth in all directions; seaweed streaming in the water like hair in a wind; sand swirling in clouds along the bottom; strange marine growths and slippery things writhing all around him. And he, stirred in some giant's silent soup pot, rolled over and over, going down and up and down again, was all the time being rushed helpless between those terribly sharp-looking rocks, coated with abrasive barnacles. Fish fled from this improbable terrestrial monster invading their realm.

Then calm! He fought his way to the surface, to the world of air and life and sound. Gasp! He was into the lagoon—dazed and shaken but unhurt . . . almost so, for he had lost some skin on his shoulders and knees. But alive!

His first thought was to head ashore and warn the villagers, but that was already impossible. He was long past the huts, being borne northward parallel to the coast, and moreover he had left the beach behind also, and there was nothing to landward except rocks and a cliff. So he concentrated on saving his strength, keeping his head up, and searching for *Blood Wave*. He found her at the limit of his range, far out from shore, northward bound like himself.

Then he could relax a little. With wind and current behind him, Kalkor would not turn back to loot a humble handful of hovels, else he would exhaust his rowers to small purpose. Rather he would search for better pickings up ahead. The immediate danger was past.

But soon Rap found himself being forced inexorably shoreward, to where the surf broke upon monstrous boulders that would love to break him also. He had never swum in real waves, honest waves, and he was appalled at how little his efforts seemed to matter. The sea moved him as it moved the weeds, and if it chose to shatter him and color the spray a momentary red, then that would be his lot.

Try as he might, he moved ever closer to the fury and madness of the breakers, the white thunderclap explosions, the myriad rocky claws stretching out to rend him. Crosscurrents spun him around in mockery, so at times he was swimming toward his destruction. At last one careless eddy slid him into the lee of an especially large boulder. He flailed water with hands and feet, resisting the drag of the water, fighting for his life. For one desperate minute he held his position, then he began to drift away. His fingers touched trailing weed. He grabbed, pulled, and slid easily to the rock, a land animal rooted again.

Once he had his breath back, he scrambled up to safety. So far so good! The tidal flow seemed to be easing already, meaning he would not be washed off his rocky perch, but the surf still lay between him and the shore, the sun had gone, and so had every stitch of his clothing. He could hope to swim the few yards to shore when the current slackened in a couple of hours, or he might have to wait for low tide and wade, but he could certainly reach the land in time, and then hope to walk back to the village. On bare feet? Oh, well—at the moment he was king of his own island.

Which was certainly better than being Kalkor's prisoner.

On the other hand, this deserted land was neither Kith nor Sysannasso nor Pithmot, and thus it must indeed be Dragon Reach, the eastern shore of the Dragon Sea. Things were certainly beginning to shape up like the first of the magic casement's prophecies. One of the three men in the vision had been Rap, one Sagorn, and the other a jotunn sailor. The first time Rap had met Gathmor, on the dock at Milflor, there had been something oddly familiar about him.

For the thousandth time Rap wondered how those three dread visions should be interpreted. Were they alternatives, with him fated to die in one of those ways? Kalkor had gone, Little Chicken was dead, the dragon was perhaps not far off. Or were they a sequence—would he survive the dragon and at some future date survive Kalkor? And in that case, where was the goblin?

What a choice!

Either the pounding of the surf or the nerve-racking strain of the last week had exhausted him. He wanted to stretch out and sleep, but the rock was not flat enough. In any case, he must not miss the tide. How far to Zark from here? He huddled himself small, shivering in the clammy sea wind and the cold touch of spray.

So he had escaped from the raiders. He wondered if his occult genius included more than just farsight and mastery over animals. Could there be such a thing as a talent for escaping from awkward situations?

Mainland! Apart from a few yards of turbulent water, he was within reach of Zark. A long walk, maybe, but possible. Inos might be in Hub, of course, or back in Krasnegar, or anywhere; but he'd told her he was coming, and that meant following her to Zark, and if he couldn't find her there, then he'd try the other places afterward. Now he could begin, and that was very satisfying.

He had failed to destroy Kalkor, but by all the Gods he had tried! Tried his damndest. He felt even more satisfied when he looked back at that effort. Maybe, just maybe, he could take a little pride in that honest failure. He must no longer think of himself as a stableboy. He was a man now. He hadn't been one long enough to really get to know himself. Oh, he was accustomed to his size; he knew how his ugly face looked, and the amusement on other people's faces when they registered it and tried to place him, and he had accepted his absurdly furry faun legs. But the stranger behind his eyes—he was still an untested quantity. Now he could begin to hope that the man in there was not one to be ashamed of. Nice try, lad, nice try! Not bad at all, faun.

So? Maybe it was time to start asserting himself. Maybe he, too, had a destiny to find.

Dragons, huh?

He was unsurprised, an hour or so later, to sense a boat coming from the south, riding the last curl of the tide. It was a cumbersome craft, hollowed from a single great log, being paddled by a burly, naked savage. Even in the dark, farsight said that his hair and mustache and stubbly beard were jotunnish silver.

"Shipmate ahoy!" Rap called.

The boat turned in his direction and a familiar voice came on the wind: "How much will you pay for supper?"

"All the money I've got."

The tidal race was slackening now, and the wind dying. Rap shouted directions, and in a few minutes the sturdy craft thumped against his rock. He grabbed hold of one side.

"Here, take the painter," said Gathmor.

"There's nothing to tie it to."

"Tie it round your neck! Tide's turning, so we'll get a free ride back. You never heard of the tides in the Dragon Sea? Stir it like soup." He was grinning in the dark.

Rap looped the rope round his leg. "The villagers let you borrow this?"

"The villagers had the sense to be long gone. They must know a raider when they see one. I helped myself, but I expect they won't mind when we explain. If they do, I'll kick their heads in."

Gathmor, apparently, was restored to his old self.

"We're in Dragon Reach?"

"Right."

"I thought no one lived here?"

Gathmor shrugged, and passed up a basket. "Help yourself—you can see better than I can. No, there are people here. It must be like living on the rim of a volcano. Escaped convicts, I expect. Shipwrecked jotnar, merfolk . . . runaway slaves, of course. They'll be a rag-bag lot, but probably quite friendly. So I've heard."

"But dragons?"

"I said. Like living on a volcano, and people do that. But remember that it's metal that attracts dragons. Gold, of course, or silver, but any metal to some extent. There wasn't as much as a nail in that hamlet that I could see. Stone axes, stone knives. If they can get by without metal, the dragons may not bother them much."

"You warned them?" Gathmor was an infinitely more powerful swimmer than Rap.

"I told you, lad—they'd already gone. But I would have done. They might have thumped me first, of course, seeing as how I'm a jotunn, but I figured if you'd survived you'd be along here somewhere. So I thought I'd come and look for you."

"Thanks." Then Rap added cautiously, "I think there's another somewhere."

"Who?"

"The minstrel, maybe." If it was Darad or Andor, Rap would be happy to let him die of starvation and exposure. Jalon or Thinal would be worth saving. Sagorn it would never be, not yet. Having laid a selection of fruits and crusts beside him on the rock, Rap passed the basket back down to the canoe.

"Did he jump, too?"

"I didn't see him, but . . ." Rap considered trying to explain, and weariness settled over him like a blanket of snow. "I think maybe he did."

Gathmor grunted, his mouth full of black bread. 'You really tried to sink the longship?"

"Yes."

"Nice try! Good man!" The jotunn chewed for a while. "Wish I'd felled the bastard with that ax, though! Never saw a man jump like that."

"He has farsight, too," Rap said sadly.

"Stow that!" Gathmor would never discuss the occult, nor let it be discussed in his presence. Sailors believed such talk was unlucky.

But obviously Kalkor had seen the battle-ax coming. When he had wanted a harp for his minstrel, he had gone straight to the correct sack among a boatful of loot. The test with the razor had been a lot less dangerous than it seemed, for he had been watching all Rap's muscles, as Rap had been watching his. He had known the dangers of the reef and understood them perfectly,

71

waiting until the last minute just to be certain of Rap's ill intent. Kalkor had never needed a seer; he was one.

"What're you going to do next?" Rap asked, nibbling at a thickskinned fruit he did not recognize. It was sickly and bitter at the same time, and the juice ran down into his stubble.

The jotunn paused in his chewing and bared his teeth. "Find an Imperial post and warn them of Kalkor. If we can get word to the navy soon enough, they might bottle him up here."

"How far?"

"Let's see . . . We passed Flame Cape two days ago—"

"We did?"

"We did. Clouds. Birds. Wave patterns. Those northerners don't know these waters. I wasn't certain it was Flame, of course, but I knew we were close to land. So two days northeast of that . . ." He pondered for a moment, screwing up his face. "We must be close to Pithmot. Dragon Neck, they call the bit next the mainland. Not far to Puldarn, but it might still take us days. The devil may be long gone by men. Not much chance of catching him, really." He fell to brooding, chewing as impassively as an ox, locking to and fro as waves flowed under him. The painter tagged stubbornly at Rap's ankle.

"Then," Gathmor said at last, "from Puldarn we head home to Durthing. The other crews'll be in now, or very soon. Expect they're organizing something."

"Hunt him down?" How could anyone ever hope to corner a single raider on the immensity of the four oceans?

"Course not. We'll go to Gark. Return the compliment—burn his steadings, carry off the young women."

Rap shuddered. He could see where the manpower would come from, and the galleys could be adapted readily enough, but . . . "Where do you get the weapons?"

"The praetor. Impire's always willing to support an outing like that."

Of course. It would never end. Moreover, Gathmor was obviously assuming that he still had the right to give Rap orders and have them obeyed. That was a matter that would have to be settled soon, but this was neither the time nor the place. It would mean a fight. "You're feeling better, anyway."

Gathmor bristled. "And what does that mean?"

"Just that I'm glad!" Rap said hastily. Yet the sailor had made a miraculous recovery from me paralysis that had seized him aboard *Blood Wave*. That withdrawal could have been genuinely due to weakness and shock, but it had more likely been faked. While a faun could cower and beg for food, another jotunn doing so might provoke a lethal contempt. His strange lethargy could very well have saved Gathmor from cold-blooded execution, but he would never admit that he had stooped to using deceit.

72

So change the subject quickly.

"I'd like to explore a little farther north before the tide turns, sir. If you don't mind."

Gathmor grunted uncooperatively.

"I thought I caught a glimpse of the minstrel jumping," Rap said with complete untruth, "but if you think it's too dangerous—"

"We can risk it. Get in, then."

The canoe was an absurdly awkward thing, constantly shipping water, but it was better than swimming or walking. Just around the next headland, Rap's farsight detected Jalon stretched out on a small patch of sand. He was unhurt, and effusively grateful for being rescued. The prophecy had passed its test and the trio was now complete.

The tide began to ebb, and soon the clumsy dugout was whirling southward, perilously overloaded. Jalon had deliberately followed the other captives over *Blood Wave's* side, which was a surprising act of courage or desperation from him. Although he had already guessed that this deserted countryside must be Dragon Reach, he did not seem to connect it with the vision in the magic casement. Any of the other four would have done so, but Jalon was notoriously impractical. When the dragon appeared, he would call Sagorn and the prophecy would be fulfilled, the hidden ending revealed.

Gathmor did not know of the prophecy, and his sole intent now was to be revenged on Kalkor. Dragons held no interest for him.

So Rap was the only one who could see what was going to happen. He had his own ambitions, and it felt like his turn to be ruthless for a change.

Ever since the night encounter with Bright Water's fire chick in the Gazebo, he had known that his mastery over animals could control dragons. Neither Sagorn nor any of his four alternates knew that, not having been there, and Rap could see how this situation might be used in the near future to extract certain information. He would have to fake enough terror to deceive Sagorn.

That might be the tricky part, for of course he would be in no real danger.

3

The little hamlet had no name. Its people were mostly old or middle age, with few young adults and even fewer children. They were a varied lot, as Gathmor had predicted: hulking trolls, tall jotnar, squat imps, and a couple of male fauns like shorter, slighter versions of Rap himself, plus people of obvious mixed blood. He was curious to farsee one of the women being hustled away by two men as the strangers arrived. They put her in the farthest shack and stayed there with her, as if guarding.

Among the adults, men far outnumbered women, and many of both bore ownership brands to prove that slavery still lingered in the outer reaches of the Impire. All seemed bitter and listless—from sickness, perhaps, or poor diet, or just excessive toil. Everyone and everywhere stank of fish.

On the edge of the firelight, the naked castaways were challenged, and came to a halt before a bristle of spears and axes, tight-clutched in male hands and backed by the glint of angry, distrustful eyes in shadowed faces.

Gathmor told his story, or the parts that mattered, and for an uneasy few minutes after that Rap was acutely aware of numbers and the utter lack of law. Only brute force reigned here in the wilds. He saw the poverty and emaciation; he smelled the resentment. Who was he to come begging at such a door?

Then a woman called out from behind the ring of men, "Bring you metal, strangers?"

"No metal!" Gathmor said. "We have nothing, as you can see."

"Be welcome then."

With no argument, but certainly without enthusiasm, the men accepted her decision and lowered their weapons. Clothes were passed forward, and the visitors brought into the group.

Thus Rap soon found himself joining a single great circle, cross-legged around the central fire. The fare thrust upon him was sparse, fish and roasted roots, but he felt guilty at accepting even that, hungry though he was. His meager portion was larger than any other in sight, and he could see the gaunt children huddling behind their elders and peering out at the newcomers with sullen awe. He thought they needed the food more man he did.

The buildings on the edge of the firelight were ramshackle hovels of driftwood and wicker; sparks and smoke drifted up into indistinct overhanging boughs, and somewhere the stream made excited chatter on its way to the sea. The night was heavy and sticky and rife with insects. In the distance, surf boomed an endless, mindless, changeless knell.

Across from Rap, Gathmor sat beside the hamlet's wise woman, an ancient half troll named Nagg. She was undoubtedly the ugliest person Rap had ever seen, a giantess of haggard skin and crooked bones, scanty of tooth and hair. Gathmor and Jalon had done a poor job of concealing their mirth at the idea of a wise troll, but Rap suspected that much cunning might lurk behind that nightmare parody of a face. On *Stormdancer* he had prized Ballast as a friend and one of the best men aboard; in Durthing he had concluded that the trolls were rarely as stupid as they often pretended. It had been Nagg alone who had chosen to admit Gathmor and his companions; the villagers had accepted her decision at once, as if her judgment could be trusted.

She nodded and clucked and drooled while Gathmor explained how he must hasten on to Puldarn to warn the Imperial navy of the raider, but in his efforts to seem friendly, he became pompous. "We shall not tell of meeting you," he said. "We shall not report this village."

Nagg screeched with merriment even as she stuffed her mouth full of fish. "Tell all you want, jotunn," she mumbled. "You've seen the marks here. Some have been here long enough." She pulled her rags aside to show her own shoulder. "Was only a child when I left the Impire. Long, long ago, sailor. Legions don't chase runaways into Dragon Reach—right?" she appealed to the others, and they hooted and laughed. "Lots more like us along the coast, too. Here and there."

Gathmor flinched as she patted his thigh.

"Gold tastes best," she said, "but bronze near as good, they say. Nothing hots up a dragon more'n a well-armored warrior. It'll waste half a country partying after." She cackled and chewed some more.

And so the talk inevitably turned to the dragons, and metal. The villagers themselves possessed no metal at all; they scraped their narrow living from the miserous land with tools of wood and stone. Knives of fractured dragon glass were sharp enough to shave with, although they soon lost their edge. To raise crops the women turned the sod with wooden plows pulled by men or other women. Men speared or netted fish, children scrounged roots and berries from the woodlands. To Rap it was the life of a brute, worse than anything any sane slaveowner would inflict on his stock, but the fisherfolk seemed to think freedom alone worth something, and themselves better off for it. He could not visualize a past bad enough to be worse than their present.

Yes, dragons came over once in a while, Nagg admitted placidly, but rarely threatened unless they sensed metal. In her life she could recall only two attacks. You could see them dance in the dawn sky almost any morning if you looked—oftentimes one or two, rarely a whole blaze of them. They would not fly over water, not usually.

"Gold is what draws them most?" Rap asked his neighbor, an elderly, crooked-tooth faun named something like Shyo S'sinap.

The old man nodded so vigorously that his scraggy neck and straggly beard flapped. "Worm'll find a gold ring at ten leagues, so's said."

Gathmor described *Blood Wave's* cargo, and his audience reacted with stark disbelief. That much gold should have fetched worms from all over Dragon Reach. The drakes did fly over water sometimes, and a shipful of gold would be ample excuse. Kalkor's luck was apparently effective even against dragons, Rap thought.

Just a couple of good handfuls might do it, Shyo opined solemnly.

Rap chuckled around the chunk of coconut he was gnawing. "You don't have any handfuls handy, though?"

75

The old man screwed up his wrinkles in a smile, letting firelight scroll shadows on his leathery brown face. "Did once. 'Bout thirty years ago, I expect." He noted Rap's doubt with satisfaction and snickered. "Used to work in the gold mines!"

Rap glanced at the faded numbers burned into the bony shoulder. Then he looked at the old faun's protruding ribs, his furry faun legs, thin as a spider's. He glanced around the dilapidated hovels at the edge of the dark. "And this is better?"

"Freedom, lad!"

"You can't eat freedom. Freedom doesn't keep you warm of a night, or heal your children's—"

"Ever seen a man worked to death as an example to his mates?" the old man asked, wheezing softly. "Ever watched your best friend die of shock after he'd been gelded?"

Rap shook his head. He'd spoken rashly.

The faun bared the skewed yellow pegs in his mouth. "Or get Nagg to tell you how it feels to be kept as breeding stock, raising mongrel quarry boys. Harkor, there . . . The bones in his back are fused. See the slope of his shoulders? That's what slave work does."

"How about the others, then? Not all of you were slaves."

"No. Srapa, there? Killed a man who raped her. He was of a *good* family. Hers wasn't, so she had to run. Real beauty, she was, when she got here." The old man sighed, shaking his head. He stopped his pointing and just stared at the fire for a moment. "Gave me a son once. Was going to look like me when . . . He died. We got thieves here, o'course. Honesty's easier when you're not hungry, for some reason. Widows. Unwanted concubines and embarrassing bastards. Mutineers? We have several mutineers. A spiteful centurion's worse than a bad slave boss, lad, 'cause he needn't worry about what you cost his master."

Rap wiped his forehead and wished he could ease back from the heat of the fire; but that would seem as if he were moving away from the smelly old man. "You've got a merwoman here, too?"

"Evil rend me! How's you know that? You planning on staying?"

"No."

Shyo scowled. "That's the only way you'll get a share."

"I didn't mean that!" Rap shouted, louder than he meant.

"Sure you didn't?" The old man looked angry and suspicious.

"All I meant was why would a merwoman be here?"

"Same reason as any of us, of course! She stays because the outside's worse. She came by chance, but she stays 'cause it's better."

"What sort of chance?" Rap's mouth asked the question before he could stop it. It was none of his business. He had never seen a mermaid before and he was naturally curious. This one wasn't young, but the way she was cavorting with her guards in the most distant shack suggested that the old stories had a lot of truth in them.

"She was shipwrecked. She and her man."

"Merman?"

"Course."

"And what—"

"Couple o' husbands knifed him the first night."

"It's true, then?"

"Course." Suddenly Shyo cackled. "Did you never hear about the legions' last try at invading the Keriths, back in Emthar's reign? Not the first time, of course, but some bright tribune dreamed up the idea that they might make it stick if they took along enough camp followers, but o'course what happened was exactly the opposite, and . . ."

Rap had heard versions of the story in Durthing, and didn't care to hear any more. It was a standard tale whenever the conversation turned to the irresistible attractions of merfolk.

Then he realized that Gathmor was again questioning old Nagg, and arguing at her answers. Growing steadily sleepier and sleepier, he struggled to follow the conversation. The castaways could walk to Puldarn easy, she said. Three days maybe; far enough to get hungry, not far enough to starve. Gathmor inquired cautiously about the sea route. Very dangerous, Nagg assured him. The tides of the Dragon Sea were notorious. Very rocky coast. No, he and his friends should walk.

Of course they were going to walk, Rap thought drowsily. The casement had said so.

Can't walk on bare feet, Gathmor insisted. Three days in the sun with no food and little water . . . and eventually Nagg promised to provide clothes.

Robes, Rap thought, yawning. Black, green, and brown.

They would be plain wear, Nagg said, just gowns of the coarse stuff the women made, but they'd keep out sun and wind and thorns.

Rap wondered if the robes, when they appeared, would trigger Jalon's memories of the casement—Jalon's memories of Sagorn's memories. He wished Gathmor could sound a little more grateful. These poor fisherfolk had no need to give the strangers as much as a smile. The jotnar would have meant little to them, for they had nothing to lose except their lives, and Rap wasn't sure he would care very much about life if he had to spend it here. *Yawn!* His mind wandered away to the merwoman and her two fortunate guards. Still at it! . . . He scolded himself for prying and forced his attention back to the negotiations.

At long last Gathmor solemnly thanked Nagg for her offer of the shoes and clothes, and promised that he and his companions would set off at first light, so as not to waste any of the cool hours. And the weather was so fine, they would sleep outdoors here.

Even the outdoors smelled bad enough, Rap thought. Those heaps of drying seaweed over there would make good bedding, the villagers said.

Right now a bank of shingle would make good bedding.

The kelp, when he was led to it, proved to be springy and less smelly than he had feared. It crackled and popped in his ears when he moved, but he was not expecting to move much. He closed his eyes and indulged in one last— long—slow—yawn. And was asleep.

Gathmor shook him awake in pitch darkness. "Sh!"

"Huh? What time is it?"

"Sh, I said! 'bout midnight."

Rap noted Jalon kneeling, half up, grumpily rubbing his eyes.

"What's wrong? Won't be dawn for hours."

"We're going to leave now," Gathmor whispered. "On the tide."

"But . . . Oh!" Down on the beach lay the village's four dugout canoes, one of which Gathmor had borrowed earlier, and then returned. "Steal . . .?" Blurred with sleep, Rap tried to imagine the amount of labor involved in making a dugout canoe with stone tools.

"Ride the tide to Puldarn," Gathmor added in a determined whisper. "We'll be there by nightfall."

Rap was not going to steal a canoe.

Rap was not going to Puldarn. Rap was going to Zark.

But to tell Gathmor that would mean a brawl, and he didn't feel like fighting a jotunn right now, in the middle of the night.

The seaweed crackled and crunched as he raised his head, although he didn't need to do that to see.

"No we won't."

Now it was Gathmor who made the "Huh?" sound.

"She's posted guards," Rap mumbled. "Six of them, on the beach. They've got spears 'nd axes." He lay back and crackled himself comfortable again. "And they're all awake," he added with sleepy satisfaction. He rolled over and went back to sleep.

Gathmor ran off a string of nautical obscenities.

He didn't think to go and see for himself.

4

The western descent was taking longer than the ascent had, which Inos considered unfair. The food was running out and the nights were cold and

78

there was nothing to see except endlessly winding walls of rock. The valley widened, it brought in tributaries, and it steadily descended; it just would not arrive anywhere.

Wolves lived in those hills and howled after sundown; Azak had reported bear tracks. He chose defensible campsites on principle, being a distrustful man.

On the fourth night of the descent he found a cave that had once been an arched gateway into a small castle, most of which had been swept away or overthrown by old floods. Mud had settled around the rest until little was now visible above me grass and bushes; but the barrel roof of the adit was there and one end was blocked by rubble. Azak insisted he could hold it single-handed against an army.

Inos and Kade huddled together through yet another frigid mountain night, wrapped up in their two blankets like a single load of laundry. Azak did not seem to sleep at all, sitting cross-legged by the fire, scowling at the darkness of the valley outside. He said afterward that he saw eyes out there once, but the howling never came really close.

Chilled and stiff, the travelers settled for a quick snack of dates and stale bread at first light, then broke camp. The valley had perversely narrowed again. Its beetling walls still clutched the nighttime chill, holding the sun at bay and filling the air with blue shadow. Even the mules seemed glad to be on their way.

The road they had followed down from the pass continued, broken here and there where it had been washed away or buried. The scale of it fascinated Azak. He had been speculating on what great king or sorcerer could have attempted such a work, for much of the roadbed was paved with huge slabs, and other parts had been chiseled out of bedrock, and six men could have ridden it abreast. It leaped chasms on rainbows of masonry as graceful as arrows' flights. In its prime it must have been a marvel. He tried to estimate how many had labored for how long to create it, and seemed awed by has answers. It must be more than a thousand years old, he pointed out, and it would obviously last as long again. Yet perhaps he and his companions were the first to travel it in centuries.

Even when buried in soil, the highway had often resisted tree roots. Then it formed a ribbon of turf snaking through the forest. Conifers had dwindled; here the valley was filled with hardwoods. The frothy white stream had become a river of stature, still flowing strangely milky water.

Nothing like a mule ride to shake out the last crumbs of sleep. "These eyes you saw," Inos said. "Were they mundane?"

Azak chuckled throatily. "I'm still here, my love."

Not demons.

They had talked the old tales to tatters. Azak believed in the demon hypothesis. Someone in that awful war had released demons, and a few still lingered, preying on hapless travelers, but not so many that they caught everyone who came through. Not much anyone could do about demons except hope to stay out of their way.

Inos did not like the idea of demons. She preferred the invisibility story, which said that Ulien'quith had rendered all pixies invisible, and their descendants lived on like that still, under their own warlock. Azak scoffed at that. If pixies were at all like other men, he said, they would have long since used their invisibility advantage to conquer the whole world.

Now Inos was beginning to fashion a theory of her own—that the missing travelers were ensnared by curses of nonarrival. This valley, for example, never seemed to be getting to anywhere. Perhaps she and Kade and Azak would ride down it forever, or until they died of old age.

She was just about to mention that cheerful possibility when the travelers rounded a bend and saw their first pixie standing in the middle of me road. The flash of Azak's sword alarmed his mule. The others reacted along with it, and for a moment there was confusion. By the time the animals were calmed, though, their riders could see that the danger had been over for ten centuries.

They rode cautiously forward to inspect the solitary figure. Weathering had pitted the grayish surface and blotched it in white and yellow lichen, but all the details and features were clearly visible still—a perfect statue of a youth running; naked because whatever garments he had been wearing had long since rotted away. Silt had washed in around him until now he was buried to the ankles, and the grass stalks waved around his knees. He could not have been much older than Inos, and the face he raised to the mountains ahead seemed to her to be filled with stern resolution, a determination to conquer no matter what the cost.

Inos reined in the lead mule and dismounted. Kade remained in the saddle, four mules back, and pulled out her breviary so she would not appear to be looking. Inos had seen much worse than mere nudity among the statuary in Rasha's bedroom. Azak had come to stand beside her and would be noting her reaction. She must demonstrate the sophisticated attitude of an Imperial lady. It was only stone, no excuse for prudery. So that's what they look like?

"A messenger," she said sadly. "Running to warn someone?"

"Or a coward running away?"

"No." Sorrow soaked into her bones like the damp of the gloomy valley. The shadows chilled her heart—a road going nowhere, traveled by no one, a boy turned into a monument to a lost cause.

"That is not the face of a coward," she said. "The eyes are strange . . . pixie eyes?"

"They're sort of elvish," Azak said, "set at an angle. But not big enough. And sort-of-elvish ears, too, but not pointed enough. He's too brawny for an elf. They're skinny. Too much chest for an imp, and not enough for a dwarf.

And that stepped-on nose looks faunish. A little bit of everything. I suppose he was a pixie."

Inos saw nothing wrong with the nose. Not every man looked good with the eagle beak of a djinn.

She moved closer, until she was between the figure and the peaks, so the unseeing eyes glared right at her. The gray stone, roughened by centuries of rain and wind, was yet eerily realistic, like a living man coated in mud.

"Turn back, pixie," she said. "They can't hear your message. They won't come to your call." She expected Azak to make fun of her, but he seemed to have caught the same dark mood.

"The Accursed Place may have worse things to show us yet."

She shook her head. "Nothing could be sadder than this. Go home, pixie, back to your loved ones. Tell them the war is over."

"They will ask who won," Azak said softly.

"Just tell them you lost."

"They will ask why."

"'Why' doesn't matter to the dead. Tell them you died in vain." For a moment there was silence. Even the wind dared not speak as it stirred the grass around the youth's calves.

Azak spoke again: "Remember what the poet says—nothing frightens like tomorrow's war, inspires like today's, or saddens like yesterday's."

She glanced up at him in surprise. "You believe that?"

He looked abashed and showed his teeth. "I care nothing for yesterday, and today we must ride. Say good-bye to your pixie, my lady. He will keep his vigil here until long after we are gone."

Once more Inos met the accusing stare of the stone eyes. Then she shivered and headed back to the mules.

But that pixie was only the first. Soon they came to two others, lying facedown. And then more, and more. The forest died away, as if ashamed to conceal such disaster, and the whole width of the valley floor was exposed, all littered with stone corpses. The road itself was completely blocked, compelling the travelers to leave it and pick their way across the turf and rocks, around and between the silent multitude.

The river, wandering to and fro over the centuries, had swept whole areas clear of the gruesome remains, piling them in shoals and burying them in sand, but it would need many centuries yet before one river could hide so great a slaughter. Creepers and ivy had tried, also, wrapping some of the figures in grotesque green fur.

Many lay flat, especially solitary runners, who would have been off balance, and the fallen had often shattered. In the more crowded areas, and

81

where the ground had been soft, most were still upright, or leaning against their neighbors. Unless broken, though, every statue in that great naked throng was as well preserved as the first: roughened in spots by erosion and splotched with lichen, but exact in every detail of hair and muscle.

Hundreds and thousands of them . . . faceup or facedown or standing in their huddles like mourners . . . all had been going the same way. As Azak had guessed, they had been fleeing from something, and now the intruders must ride their trembling mules into the warning, accusing glares of a myriad stone faces.

Most were young males, a routed army, but there were many civilians also. Inos saw women of all ages, and one whole heap of old men with their knees up, all traces of their wagon long since vanished. She saw family groups: children grasping adults' hands, men bearing toddlers on their shoulders, and one stone infant clutched to a stone nipple. She saw men stooped beneath burdens of earthly possessions that had long since disappeared, leaving only the memory of their weight. She saw helmeted soldiers brandishing rusted swords to clear a way through the mob, with plates of bronze tumbled around their feet because the leather had perished.

Some armored men lay on their backs with their legs bent, nested in the shattered bones of their horses. The weeds must hide not only stirrups and bits and buckles, but also coins and jewels, gold plate and works of art. With a bag and a shovel, Inos thought, she could gather a great fortune here in a few days—and lose her wits in the process. Those eyes . . .

She developed a shiver that she could not control. She kept glancing hopefully at Kade, wishing her aunt would insist that they all turn back and find another way over the hills or even flee back to Zark; but Kade said nothing, although her face was pale and drawn with horror. Even Azak looked nauseated. No one spoke as the little caravan wound its way through the grisly mausoleum.

Beyond the last stragglers, the valley was again deserted for a space and then ended abruptly in blue sky framed by spectacular cliffs.

Once a mighty fortress had stood proud on a high spur, guarding the mouth of the pass. Some trace of the eastern salient and tower still remained, bent and grotesquely twisted. But the main buildings and much of the spur itself had melted like butter, flowing down to engulf the little town below. All that was left was a great frozen spill of black glass and a few protruding gables and chimneys, burned red and fractured by the ancient heat, warped and half melted themselves. Here was what the pixies had been fleeing.

Inos did not say so, and neither did the others. They had lost the pavement, and the forest returned. They rode through in single file without a word or a shared glance, all bearing thoughts too somber to profane with speech.

Then daylight showed through the trunks, the land fell away, and the valley had ended. Azak reined in and the others came to a halt at his side, overlooking an open meadow, sloping gently westward. In the far distance silver flashed from a very large river, twisting lazily over the plain. Beyond that the sky and the land went on forever, merging eventually at the limits of human vision in a vague orchid haze. A warm breeze rustled leaves overhead, bringing a faint hint of the sea.

"Thume," Azak said softly. "The Accursed Place!"

"It doesn't look accursed to me," Inos retorted. "It looks peaceful. Welcoming." But anything might look welcome after that petrified army.

She glanced across at her aunt, and was astonished to see an expression of . . . worry? Concern . . . almost an expression of fear. Kade's normally plump and contented face seemed haggard and sickly. True, for an elderly lady accustomed to a life of genteel inactivity, she had endured an incredibly wearying journey—but she had survived the rigors of the desert and the hardships of the taiga without looking like that. Her scanty silver hair was tousled and tangled, floating like wisps in the breeze. Her wrinkles were scored like scars; her mouth sagged. Why should the petrified army have done this to her?

"What do you think, Aunt?"

Kade shook her head and gnawed her weathered lip. "I don't know, dear. I suppose I'm just being a superstitious old woman, but . . . but I don't like it!"

"Go back, you mean?"

Stiffly Kade glanced over her shoulder, to where the steep western escarpment loomed above the treetops. She shivered. "Oh, no! Not back!"

"Well, we don't exactly have many other choices. Big Man?"

Azak studied Kade for a moment, narrowing his eyes as he peered over the bristling red yashmak of his beard. Then he flashed his teeth at Inos. "I see no sign of people. What do you think, my precious one?"

He expected courage in royalty. Inos took another look at that serene idyllic landscape.

"I say we have no choice!" She slammed her heels into her mule's flanks, and the startled little beast seemed to leap forward with all four feet at once. Then it charged off down the slope, and the others came thumping after.

Battles long ago:
> Perhaps me plaintive numbers flow,
> For old, unhappy, far-off things,
> And battles long ago.

Wordsworth, *The Reaper*

5

Man's worth something

1

"Now I went down to Ilrane
My ladylove to see.
Most fair the maids of Ilrane,
But none more fair than she."

If you wanted a man to find poison ivy, hornets' nests, or the wickedest
thorn bushes, then Jalon was the obvious choice. If you needed a companion who would slip off a steppingstone and lose his sandal in fast
water, or let a campfire go out when he was supposed to be minding it, or
fall asleep five minutes after his watch started . . . Jalon, without hesitation.
He could also vanish inexplicably and be discovered an hour later, twenty
paces away, lost in rapturous admiration of an orchid.

Jalon, in short, was a gigantic pain in the spinal column.

But if you enjoyed unfailing good humor and cheerfulness, an unflagging
willingness to apologize, laugh at himself, and promise to do better in
future—well, he had those in abundance, although he never actually *did* manage to do better. And if you appreciated a comrade who could suddenly open
his mouth and pour forth a strain of purest melody to banish fatigue, uplift the

soul, and melt away the aches and worries of a long march . . . Even Gathmor could not stay mad at Jalon for long.

The three adventurers had seen their first dragons less than an hour after leaving the fisher village, a blaze of four or five, but very far off, mere specks weaving and circling above a distant hill. By then, too, the light had been bright enough to reveal the colors of the robes donated by the villagers—brown for Jalon, green for Gathmor, black for Rap. Even so, Jalon had not associated the casement's prophecy with the steady march of events. He was far more interested in wildflowers than in dragons. In the next few days the only signs of the worms had been a few faint smudges of smoke on the horizon, and he still had not remembered the prophecy.

Nearing the edge of a small forest around noon, the travelers had found a patch of wild melons and stayed to indulge in their first good meal in two days. Afterward, sated and drowsy in the heat, they had lingered to enjoy the shade, for ahead of them stretched open sand and black rock that made a man uncomfortable just looking.

But Gathmor was a demanding leader, who insisted on a harsh pace. "Time to go!" he announced, as Rap was starting to nod.

"Let's trade sandals," Rap suggested, seeking to gain time.

"You and me, then. Not him."

Owning no leather, the fisherfolk made their footwear from slabs of wood and loops of rope. These removed the skin from a mans toes in about ten minutes and thereafter became very irksome. They were better than being barefoot, but not by much. As every sandal was different, the travelers traded them around to distribute the discomfort evenly. Jalor had stumbled into yet another swamp an hour or so before, and the ropes were even more abrasive when wet.

The exchange extended the rest a few minutes. Then, lounging against a moss-soft trunk and perhaps thinking that it was his turn to find a delay, the minstrel launched into a song about the elven maidens of Ilrane. It began as a pleasant romantic ballad, but swiftly deteriorated into the sort of scabrous bawdiness that amused sailors. Gathmor barked with mirth as the tale unfolded, and even Rap found himself chuckling.

One more day should see the expedition safely out of Dragon Reach, if Nagg's estimate had been correct. Without Jalon, the other two would have traveled much faster, and he must know that. In his way, he was apologizing to them yet again.

He stopped suddenly, in midverse. The other two looked up.

"That ridge!" he said. "Look at it!"

Beyond the trees lay hot sand, a small desert valley encircled by gentle hills. The hills were wooded, but the forest cut off as sharply as a horse's mane and the hollow grew little but scabby tufts of thornweed.

A long, rugged buttress of twisted black rock rose like an island in the middle of the clearing, crested by a few trees rooted in cracks. Loose boulders lay scattered around it. Rap studied the scene and glanced inquiringly at Gathmor, who shrugged.

They had seen many similar places. The countryside was rugged, and although they would have preferred to skirt the coast, they had been forced inland to avoid the rocky gorges by which the many streams plunged down to the sea. Everywhere they had noticed traces of old fires, from ancient charred logs half buried in jungle to much more recent evidence: long, grim stretches of bare poles with grass and weeds just becoming established in the mud between them. As obstacles, neither of those was too serious. Much worse were the intermediate stages, where the trunks had become deadfall entangled with secondary scrub of thorns and creepers.

But some of the fiercest blazes had cauterized the soil all the way to bedrock—melting even that in some cases—and left only patches of desert that resisted the forest's attempts to return. Whole hills seemed to have been favorite targets of dragons throughout the ages, and those had been reduced to battered carcasses, ripped and melted away in streams of glass as the monsters quarried for veins of metal within the rock. The valley ahead seemed to be nothing other than that, a scar that could be thousands of years old, and might remain unchanged until the end of time.

"What am I supposed to see?" Rap asked sleepily.

"A dragon."

That brought instant alertness, but of course Jalon meant a *dead* dragon, and in a moment Rap made out what the artist's eye had detected: head, legs . . . The ridge was indeed the body of a dragon, long since turned to stone and weathered to ruins, half buried in the sand.

"Gods!" Gathmor said. "It must be older than the Impire. And I never knew the beggars grew *that* big!"

"A primal male, likely!" Jalon flushed with excitement like a child. "Isn't it gorgeous?"

"Gruesome," Rap said. His flesh crawled at the thought of that hill-size monster alive, an indestructible destroyer as big as Inisso's castle; but that was the life cycle of dragons. They started as wraiths of pure fire, like the flame he had seen burning on Bright Water's shoulder. They gained substance as they aged, and they ended as gigantic beings of pure mineral. This one had crawled here to die, and in its death agonies it had burned away the forest and the very soil beneath it.

"How old would it have been, do you suppose?" Gathmor asked, rising and stamping a few times to adjust his footwear.

"Centuries," Jalon said. "Come on! Let's go and have a closer look. Maybe its eyes are still there!"

Dragons' eyes were supposedly worth a fortune, but they also bore a reputation for bringing bad luck, and Rap certainly did not fancy the idea of rolling one all the way to Puldarn. Jalon would not have thought of that practical matter.

As the others set off toward the great petrified carcass, Rap rose and stretched to ease his aches, then picked up his stone-pointed spear. In theory he carried that to defend himself against leopards, but in practice it was useful only as a staff. He tended to agree with Jalon's theory that the easiest way to escape an attack by leopards was just to die of fright. He trudged off after the others.

As he emerged from the trees, the noon sun struck brutally. He flipped up the loose corner of his robe that served as a hood. A few steps worked the gritty sand up into his sandal ropes and he was soon limping, but so were the others. He caught up with them about halfway to the petrified dragon.

Gold?

"What?"

"What 'what'?" Jalon asked, turning a wide gaze of blue innocence on Rap. "Did you speak?"

Minstrel and sailor both shook their heads.

"Funny. I thought . . . Well, never mind."

The dragon fossil was farther away than Rap had realized, and therefore even bigger. The sand had drifted deep on one side, half burying it. The exposed flank still showed curves of muscle under the patterned hide, but many scales had fallen off and lay littered on the ground at the base of the cliff, as if a legion had thrown down its shields. Great cracks were being opened by tree roots; half the hind leg had collapsed. It all looked older than anything he had ever imagined.

In one searing flash of recognition, the scenery changed in his mind.

Gods deliver us!

This was it! Why had he not realized sooner?

"Those rocks!" Rap cried. "Jalon! Forget the dragon. We've seen this place before."

The minstrel stopped dead. His face was still burned and blistered and peeling, yet now it turned an impossibly pale color.

Gathmor was in the lead. He turned and noticed, and his fog-gray eyes narrowed dangerously. "Seen what?"

Gold?

87

Again recognition—an alien, metallic, bitter voice in Rap's mind. Of course! A thrill ran through him, mingled fear and excitement.

He scanned the sky. It was blue, cloudless, and as deep as forever. "There's a live one around somewhere." Of course.

"How the Evil do you know?"

"I can hear it . . . and Jalon knows. Don't you?"

The little minstrel was cowering like a terrified child. His teeth chattered as he nodded, and his staring blue eyes held both terror and accusation. "You knew!" His voice was shrill.

"No! *Don't call Darad!*"

"Why not? Why shouldn't I? You trapped us! You knew, and you didn't say!" Jalon half raised his spear, and Gathmor's chopped down to strike it from his hand. He did not even seem to notice. He pointed an accusing finger at Rap instead. "You knew the vision was being fulfilled!"

Gold?

The call was stronger now, echoing in Rap's head. Still he could see nothing in the empty blue sky, not even birds. His farsight detected only trees on the ground—hills were opaque to farsight, though. The dragon might be down behind any one of a dozen hillocks, and yet its voice certainly seemed to be coming closer. He did not think he could summon a dragon unless he could see it.

Bright Water's tiny fire chick had not spoken in words.

Jalon was still screaming at him.

"I knew nothing you didn't!" Rap shouted. "Dragon Reach, and the gowns? You should have seen, too."

"Fool! Fool! We could have split up! Traveled separately!"

Maybe, although Rap suspected that the magic casement's prophecy had been too inevitable for that. Besides, he'd lied to Gathmor to stop him stealing a canoe. He'd been helping the prophecy along. He felt a little guilty about that, seeing how upset Jalon was.

Before he could answer, though, Gathmor roared. "Will one of you tell me what's going on?"

Rap opened his mouth, and then the alien voice boomed in his mind again, louder than ever and filled with strange reverberations and ringing metallic echoes: GOLD? It half stunned him, so that he clutched both hands to his head, dropping his spear.

By the time his wits settled, Jalon was explaining to Gathmor how he and Rap had seen a prophecy in a magic casement. The sailor's face was pale, too, now, but with fury, not fear.

"There it is!" Rap yelled, pointing. A speck, low in the sky. Far, far away. Coming. Still beyond the range of farsight. Only one.

A sudden surge of doubt sent prickles racing over his skin.

Oh Gods! If its voice is that strong now . . .

Gathmor grabbed the front of Rap's robe in one massive fist and brandished the other. "You young bastard! You knew about this and you trapped me?"

"Let him be!" Sagorn snapped.

Gathmor whirled to find the source of the new voice, and staggered when he found himself looking up into the shrewd and angry eyes of the old scholar.

"Who the Evil are you?"

"Never mind now. Do not blame him—magic prophecies cannot readily be evaded or nullified. We must take cover. Sometimes these draconic vestiges are cavernous. Come!" The old man set off, striding across the hot sand with surprising agility.

"Yes. He's right," Rap said. And yet . . . how inevitable was the prophecy, how significant its details? It had shown the three of them at the base of the cliff where the dragon's ribs rose from the sand. If they split up now, could they still balk it?

Gold? trumpeted the fanfare voice. *Is gold?*

Rap felt as if someone had dropped a metal bucket over his head and thrown a house at it. Deafened, blinded, he sprawled to his knees. Gathmor hauled him up and began hustling him across the sand after Sagorn.

His farsight was picking it up now, coming low over the forest, the blast from its great wings stirring the trees in dancing turmoil. It did not compare in size with the mountainous fossil, it was silvery and not black, but it was still as big as *Blood Wave* or *Stormdancer.*

He tried to answer Gathmor's questions while the sailor hauled him—half carried him—toward the towering pile of black rock ahead, but that last word from the dragon had left him too dazed. This was no tiny fire chick, and its sheer intensity overwhelmed him. He had blundered hopelessly. Miscalculated. Everything was lost, and they were all going to die.

Twice more the gigantic voice rang in Rap's mind, exulting, gloating, ravening after gold . . . yet curious and querying also, as if a current of doubt ran deep below. The power of that voice was unbearable now, every blast an impact of pain that made him think his head was being crushed, that sickened him, that blanked out everything else except the awareness of failure and stupidity.

Sagorn had picked his way between the litter of giant scales and was peering into a crevice in the ropy black face of the cliff itself. He turned as Gathmor released Rap to fall on the scorching sand at his feet.

"Now will you explain—"

89

"No. These gaps are too shallow. But there may be a cavern of some considerable size within this cadaver." The old man glared down at Rap. "Fool! I suppose you thought your mastery might work on dragons?"

Rap croaked hoarsely, then forced himself to sit up. "It worked on a fire chick."

Sagorn roared in exasperation and shook both fists at the sky. "Where did you meet a fire chick?"

"In Milflor. Bright Water had one."

Gold? Two legs have gold?

The worm was close now. Its voice was a brass band inside Rap's head, and an earthquake also, and being crushed flat. His skull would fall apart.

Inos! He must think of Inos. He was doing this for her, and he sought to draw strength from her memory.

"Bright Water! You met the witch again?" Sagorn grimaced, baring his teeth like an angry skeleton. "Moron! Young idiot! You should have consulted me! You should have told Andor."

Rap began hauling himself upright, pushing himself up the rough black face of the cliff. It burned, hotter even than the sand. His head was still ringing from the dragon's last fanfare, and already the worm was much closer, sunlight flashing on silver scales as it soared swiftly over the forest. The beat of its wings was rhythmic thunder thudding against his eardrums. Huge! The next word it said was going to kill him. He cringed in expectation, waiting for the next bolt of agony like a felon hung on the whipping post, able to think of nothing but the coming lash.

"Too strong!" he muttered.

"Obviously!" Sagorn snapped. "Have you tried, though? Have you even tried to send it away?"

Rap shook his head. He was still leaning against the furnace of the rock, as he dared not trust his legs to support him. The dragon was close enough now that he could believe he was looking up at it, a silvery sky-snake, thrashing through the air on wings as wide as the courtyard of the castle in Krasnegar, its tail trailing behind it in long curves, two monstrous jeweled eyes flashing. Beneath it, trees were tumbling and shattering like matchwood in the blast.

"It wants gold," he mumbled. "It thinks we have gold."

Sagorn spun around and stalked off. "We must take cover!" he shouted over his shoulder. "I must find cover."

"Why you?" Gathmor followed, firing angry questions. "Just you? And where did you come from, anyway?"

Rap pushed himself erect and tottered after the other two. He ought to try sending a command to the dragon, he knew, but he was terrified that it might reply. That voice was worse agony than anything he had ever known. It would burn his brain to ashes.

Oh, Inos! I tried! I tried too hard.

Sagorn rounded a rock fragment as large as a cottage, which might have been a part of a fetlock. He was scanning the cliff that rose so high above, looking for an opening into that mythical cavern he hoped for. Even if he found it, it would be only a death trap.

Then a gigantic shadow flashed over them, and they all stopped.

The casement! This was the moment. Rap turned to stare across the heat-distorted sand, and for one tiny instant thought he saw a flicker of darkness there, where the observers must have been, where he must have been. If it was there, it had gone . . .

"This prophecy?" Gammor shouted. "What happens?"

"We don't know," Sagorn growled, watching the sky monster sweep around in a curve, coming in lower for another pass. "This is as far as it went."

"You mean we may die?"

"We probably shall. Unless Rap can sent it away."

It was up to him. Rap braced himself, trying to imagine he was dealing with Firedragon, the Krasnegar stallion—or a dog, maybe, like Fleabag. He tried to recall how he had influenced the fire chick. He took a deep breath. *Go away!* he commanded.

The response was even worse than he had expected—a shrill explosion of fright that struck like agony, that hurled him bodily backward to sprawl on the sand. His head came down a hands-breadth from a jagged rock, but he hardly noticed. The dragon shied like a foal, whirled around in the sky as if knotting itself, then spiraled down out of sight behind a hilltop. The forest exploded in a red-black mushroom of flame and smoke.

A moment later, a sound of thunder rolled over the clearing. The pillar of smoke roiled skyward, ever thicker, its feet bright with fire. Sharp booms suggested tree trunks exploding in the heat.

Gold?

That had been a quieter, almost timorous query, but there was tenacity in it. Rap did not think the dragon had given up. It was merely startled, and puzzled.

Sagorn loomed over Rap, staring down with grim fury. His ghostly pale face was slick with sweat, his bony nose and lantern jaw more skull-like than ever.

"Fool! You thought to frighten my word of power from me?"

Rap grunted and struggled to rise. In the back of his mind he could feel the dragon's thoughts now—low self-mutterings of gold and of two-legses by the ancestral relic. It was not even speech, just musings, and it filled his mind with metallic alien echoes so torturous that he could not think.

"You thought you could control dragons!" Sagorn snarled. "You were going to coerce me into telling you my word of power!"

Rap nodded miserably and forced himself to his knees. "I might have—but it believes we have gold."

Sagorn sneered. "The slightest hint of gold will drive a dragon crazy. Even you must know that! It puts them into a frenzy. They need metal to drive their metamorphoses, gold most of all."

"Have we gold?" Gathmor demanded suspiciously, appearing at the old man's side.

Sagorn kept his eyes on Rap. "Thinal has."

"What!" Rap shouted.

"In Finrain, he stole for Andor again; to bankroll more of his philanderings." The old man closed his eyes and seemed to crumple. "Before he went away, he put a coin in his mouth."

Rap howled. He struggled to his feet, swaying.

The fire beyond the hill was growing larger, and louder. Trees were exploding, smoke pulsing up in huge black clouds. High overhead, the column was drifting westward. The dragon was coming.

"Why?" Rap demanded. Frowning, Gathmor reached out a hand to steady him.

"He almost always does," Sagorn said sadly. "It is the only way any of us can keep anything for himself. What is inside us goes with us—so Thinal usually hides away a coin like that. When he returns, he has that much, at least. He is only a common sneak thief, remember."

"And the dragon can tell?"

"Maybe it can. Dragons are not wholly mundane. They have powers of their own. This one may be sensing Thinal's gold."

GOLD!

Rap staggered and almost fell as another twisting wave of torment tore at his mind. Could the dragon even hear his thoughts, as he seemed to be hearing its? He wished Sagorn had not told him about the gold.

"Then call Thinal! We'll throw the coin away and run!"

Fire was glowing through the forest at the crest of the hill as the dragon ascended the far slope.

Sagorn shook his head. "Useless! A taste of gold and the drake would devastate the countryside for leagues. Its frenzy would last for days while it went through another stage of metamorphosis. We should never escape."

"Then tell him the damned word!" Gathmor bellowed. Apparently he had gathered a fair idea of what was going on.

"No!" The old man glared stubbornly. "I am too old! I need it all!"

"You won't need it very long—here she comes!"

At the top of the hill, the last fringe of trees erupted in one brilliant flash, and the dragon emerged, its whole incredible length pouring out like a string. Not pausing at all, it continued down the slope, slithering at a speed that would have left a racehorse standing. With wings furled, it looked very much like a gigantic metal worm, every scale flashing color in the sunlight, and even at that distance, Rap could feel the heat from it.

In desperation he gathered all his strength and hurled a command: *Go back!*

The monster shied, spreading wings to brake and shooting out a hail of sand and rocks beneath its talons. It reared up on its hind legs, tall as a castle tower, jetting a deafening howl of white fire. Returning waves of power battered into Rap's mind with stunning force; he felt as helpless as he had in the surf and tide. Half stunned, he reeled back, and only Gathmor's steely grip stayed him from falling.

Ishist? came the thought. *Two-legs speaks? Is Ishist?* The silver form curled forward, front claws sinking into the ground. The great back was curved like a cat's as the dragon pondered, but Rap thought more of a dog encountering its first porcupine. The massive triangular head swayed from side to side on the scaly neck, regarding the problem from different angles; while all around the sand darkened as it began to melt, then the closer regions started to glow. The whole monster was hotter than a smith's furnace. Heat wraiths blurred the air around it, molten glass puddled below.

"The word?" Rap cried.

"Tell me yours!" Sagorn demanded.

Rap tried to rally what little courage he had left. He felt ill and faint and very stupid. But he wasn't going to yield his word now. Not if he died for it.

"No! Remember what Andor said when we met the goblins? The tables are turned, Sagorn. It's my talent that's needed now, not his! Not yours! Mine! But I must have more power."

This was what he had planned, the reason he had let Jalon walk into the trap; but he had thought he would be bluffing. He had thought he would be able to control the dragon and bully Sagorn into telling him the gang's word. Now it was no bluff. He could no more control this monster than he could arm-wrestle it. He greatly doubted he would do any better as an adept, either. Probably only a full sorcerer could coerce a dragon.

Sagorn looked ill also, haggard and livid. His eyes flickered toward the cliff. "There may be a cave. If I can hide from it, it may not sense Thinal in me . . ."

"No!" Rap lurched forward and grabbed the old man by his bony shoulders. "That won't work, and you know it! It will blow fire in at you. Tell me! Tell me now, or we're all going to die."

Not Ishist! the dragon concluded. *Two-legs not Ishist.*

It hurtled forward, splashing molten rock behind it. It came seething down the slope. Thornbushes vanished in flashes of white flame as it went by.

Sagorn wailed, and bent his head near to Rap's.

"Well?" Rap screamed. "Speak!"

"I can't! It hurts!"

Rap shook him like a feather bolster. "It'll hurt a lot more in two seconds!"

The old man choked, staggered, and slumped over Rap's shoulder, suddenly a dead weight. Strange noises grated in his throat, as if he were having a fit. Rap was struggling to hold him up.

"Sagorn!" Rap yelled. "Doctor! Tell me!"

The dragon was on the flat and coming faster than anything Rap had ever seen, faster than a swooping falcon. Bigger and bigger, jewel eyes blazing . . .

And then Sagorn roused himself just enough to mumble his word of power into Rap's ear.

2

Being struck by lightning might be an experience like learning a word of power. Nothing else was.

For one eternal, lifeless moment, Rap thought he had blown apart. Lights seemed to soar all around in darkness, and there was music and a great silence. Fanfares and carillons and a deep, deep stillness like the musings of mountains. Solitude and whirling stars. There was pain. There was ecstasy.

There was no time to enjoy the experience. He looked up and the dragon's monstrous head was almost on top of him, its heat was blistering his face. He smelled burning cloth from his robe. Sagorn and Gathmor had turned and were staggering away, screaming. The giant gemlike eyes shone down on all of them with a deadly inhuman intelligence, with thoughts no man could think, with alien emotions no human would ever comprehend; the vast mouth was opening to reveal rows of crystalline teeth around an internal blaze like a captive sun. Scales shone like metal, radiating heat.

GO AWAY! Rap yelled, not knowing whether he spoke the words aloud or not.

Again the dragon reared up into the sky in shock, and this time it toppled backward. Claws grappled air; it impacted with a concussion that shook the world and blasted a belch of purple fire from its mouth. Boulders came crashing down from the ridge at Rap's back: scales and armored back plates and half a rib. He ignored those. The live dragon was much more perilous than the dead one.

A barrage of mental explosions seemed to pour from it, and at that range they should have burned out Rap's brain, but he blocked them.

94

"Go home!" he commanded fiercely. "There is no gold here. Go away!" He felt a shimmering response. It was unreal and outlandish, but vaguely reminiscent of Firedragon, the Krasnegar stallion: anger, and shame, and fear, and a juvenile silliness.

No gold?

"None! No metal! GO!"

The dragon spun around in coils, like a snake, and went rushing back up the slope, somehow seeming to slink at the same time. Its wings spread, flapped. Dust whirled up in thunderclaps as the monster rose to run on its hind legs. A few more hurricane beats and it took to the air. It veered past the column of smoke still rising from the burning forest, causing it to swirl and writhe like a candle flame, sending a wall of fire roaring through the trees. The dragon dwindled rapidly into the distance.

Rap heard tiny mutterings of complaint—*no gold*—and then even those faded away.

He stank of scorched cloth and hair, but cowl and stubble had protected most of his face. His tattoos hurt, and he could see tiny blisters on them. Apparently his farsight would now work like a mirror, and he couldn't remember being able to use it like that before. He could see the backs of the hills, though, which was certainly new. The whole world had a sparkle, a sharpness, that he could not recall noticing earlier, but some of that glamour might be the afterglow of a very narrow escape. Life felt extremely good right now.

He turned around to face Gathmor, who had his arms crossed over his chest, his feet well planted, and was glaring at Rap with intent to terrify. "So you planned all this, did you, sonny?"

The man was frightened of Rap! It was written all over him.

"I didn't plan to . . ." Rap sighed. "Yes, I did! Yes, I planned it." He could hardly believe that he was still alive. And he knew two words of power. He was an adept. The world spun brightly for him now.

"You knew that we would meet a dragon. You led us into a trap. What sort of shipmate would—"

"Yes. I lied to you, Cap'n, but—" But nothing, obviously. Rap ought to be quaking and quivering as the sailor talked himself up into fighting frenzy. The rage was draining all the color out of his face, even his lips. His hair seemed to bristle. Killer jotunn! What Rap saw, though, was a man frightened by the unknown powers of the occult, a man who was also furious at the fear he had felt before the dragon, who was desperate to restore his self-respect by taking out his rage on someone—or by suffering, perhaps. Now he must take the measure of this young upstart magician and establish who was the better man. Soon his rage had mounted until he was spitting more than he was speaking.

95

"Snake!" he screamed. "Ingrate! Reptile!"

Unable to get in a word, Rap turned and walked away. It didn't work. Behind him Gathmor tore off his gown and threw it away.

Rap wheeled. "Stop that!" he shouted. "It's all a big act! It's stupid and childish."

"I'll show you stupid and childish—I'm going to break every bone in your damned faun carcass!" Gathmor stepped out of his sandals. "Worm! You haven't any bones to break!" Keeping a steady glare on Rap, he balled his fists and stalked forward. A killer jotunn, out for blood.

Rap was not impressed. "You can control that damned temper of yours when you want to," he said sadly. "You were a sweet little bunny *on Blood Wave.*" He kicked off his shoes, but he left his robe alone.

Gathmor leaped. Rap sidestepped in a swirl of sackcloth.

"I wish you'd listen a minute, Cap'n. I'm an adept now. You can't expect—"

But Gathmor did expect. Gathmor was lightning fast. Every man in Durthing had agreed that others might punch harder or meaner or absorb punishment better, but as long as he was reasonably sober there was no one faster than Gathmor of *Stormdancer.* He seemed very slow now. Perhaps it was the sand, or the hard day, but when he pivoted and swung again, Rap was not there again. Screaming, the jotunn tried a third time, and now he was ready to grab, in either direction. That left him open. This time Rap stood his ground and laid a fist into that hard hairy abdomen with all the force he could muster. It felt like hitting Inisso's castle. Apparently it felt worse to Gathmor.

For a few moments he seemed to be dead, but then he began to breathe again, very noisily, curled up small on the sand. Rap stepped back into his sandals, because his toes were being fried like sausages. He studied the sailor for a moment and decided that he was in no danger. Sucking his throbbing knuckles, he wandered over to where Andor was watching.

Of course the gang would have chosen Andor at a time like this. Looking almost elegant in Jalon's brown robe, he was relaxing in the shade of an overhang, seated on a slab of black rock that had once been part of a spinal armor plate.

He greeted Rap with a white-tooth smile and a silent mime of hand clapping. "I'm sure that felt good?"

"Not really." Rap had not wanted to humiliate Gathmor. The defeat would hurt the sailor much more than victory pleased the faun. Not a faun—an adept! Fighting now was cheating. Almost anything was going to be cheating in future.

Andor's face, for example. The polished impish good looks no longer impressed. He wasn't ugly, but his charm didn't work on Rap anymore. He looked unpleasantly effeminate, in fact.

96

"I'd have enjoyed it! You're a good man, Master Rap. Most men would get a lot of pleasure out of stuffing that jotunn in a bottle." He nodded solemnly. "I don't think you do, though. You don't enjoy humiliating other people." The automatic compliment.

Rap shrugged. He ought to be finding pleasure in his new immunity to Andor, but he didn't think he was. Behind the quizzical smile he could see anger and fear, and cold calculations in progress. Andor was frightened that Rap was going to kill him to gain the rest of the word of power. *Gods!*

And now he was being disconcerted by Rap's silent scrutiny. A spurious twinkle came into his eye. "So what happens next, great sorcerer?" Under the humor, there was something long dead in those deep dark eyes. Andor had manipulated people until he couldn't think of them as people anymore.

"I'll make a deal with you," Rap said, and watched the surge of relief and pleasure. He even saw the calculations speed up. Probably Andor was wondering if he could kill Rap to regain the share of their power that Sagorn had given away.

"Name it! I told you on the ship, Rap—I think you have a destiny, so I'd like to stick around. More than that, though, I really do want to be your friend. I always have."

If the man had *Liar* tattooed on his forehead, it couldn't be more obvious. Then Rap glanced at his own face with farsight and was disgusted to see the innocent smile on it, the boyish appeal. He tried to change that, and saw himself become an earnest, rather innocent young man facing great challenges. He couldn't help it! He was bedazzling Andor as Andor had bedazzled him in the past, and he could no more stop himself than he could turn off his farsight. He must just hope that some practice with his new powers would teach him how to be an honest man again. Meanwhile he watched Andor being impressed, and he felt sick.

"We've had one of the three prophecies, Andor. That leaves two. I think they'll turn up in time." His mind shied at the sudden memory of himself on the floor of the goblins' lodge with his bones showing. "If I can beat a dragon, I can beat Kalkor."

"Easily. Like you felled Gathmor."

"So I can put Inos on her throne. That's all I want. So here's my proposal—you help me with that, and afterward I'll help you with your problem, getting rid of your curse."

"Fine!" Andor flashed teeth and held out a smooth brown hand. "You can count on me. I can't bind the others, though. You know that. But anything you need of me, you just ask."

"You'll trust me to keep my side of the deal later?"

97

"Of course!" Andor's face said that if Rap was fool enough not to kill him now, then he was probably even stupid enough to keep a bargain after he had got what he needed. Andor would honor a promise only if it suited him to do so.

In the background, Gathmor groaned and levered himself up on one elbow. Rap wiped sweat. "There's water just over there," he said, waving at the trees. "Let's head that way."

"Your hairy friend can track us when he's finished his rest," Andor agreed, rising.

"I think Jalon next, please." Rap did not look at his companion as they walked side by side, but he saw the annoyance that did not show in the voice when Andor said, "Of course."

Then Rap's companion was Jalon.

His blue eyes filled with tears, and he limped along for a while without speaking.

"You said you owed me one," Rap said. "I agree you didn't expect it to be that big."

"My fault for not looking, as you did. I should have seen." He groaned. "And now I can't!"

There was no deceit showing on his sun-broiled face, only pain, and a sort of nausea.

"What does that mean?"

Jalon waved a hand at the woods ahead. "It's all gone dead. The life's gone out of it, the beauty. You stole my power, Rap. I feel blind and deaf! I couldn't paint a barn door now. And I don't suppose I could outsing an alleycat."

"Never met a man who could." Rap walked for a while in silence, wondering what to say, wondering also if the new sparkle he saw in everything was exactly what had gone out of Jalon's vision. There were butterflies everywhere in the forest, and millions of tiny flowers that no one but a mouse would ever notice, and bright birds by the score, motionless on twig or nest, and leaves of every shape imaginable. Even the sand beneath his feet glinted with myriad sparkles of mica flakes and crystal edges. He marveled at a variety and vitality he had never noticed before, while Jalon slouched at his side, chewing his lip and seeming ready to weep.

Then a glitter of anger . . . and a whine. "Rap? We could both be adepts."

Power was not easily relinquished, obviously. Jalon was a dreamer, the least ambitious or assertive of men, but he resented his loss. Even Jalon craved power.

"No." So did Rap. "First," he said, "Sagorn insists that sharing usually doesn't reduce a word to half. So you have lost only a small part of your power.

98

Second, you've just had a very bad shock, and those always make things look blacker . . ."

He tried to be convincing and was disgusted when he succeeded. Jalon began to smile, slowly, shyly, letting confidence be talked back into him. Eventually, and just as the two of them reached the edge of the trees, Rap persuaded him to sing a little. He ran off a couple more verses of "The Maidens of Ilrane," the song he had interrupted to draw attention to the petrified dragon. Gods! That could have been no more than half an hour ago at most, back when the world was a simple, easy sort of place.

It was fine singing, if not quite the old Jalon, and these verses were the most disgusting yet, but Rap bellowed out laughter that sounded to him as unlikely as a three-legged racehorse. Relief bloomed in the minstrel's face like a reprieve from imminent death.

"All right?" he whispered.

Rap wiped tears from his eyes. "I'm no musician, friend, but you can still sing better than any other four guys I know. I honestly can't tell any difference."

God of Liars! There could be good in lies, though, just as in everything else. Jalon was smiling again.

Rap had wanted power so he might help Inos. He had not wanted it to be like this.

The edge of the open clearing was a sand dune. Behind that, thick forest offered immediate cool shade like a divine blessing. More blessed still, the mossy trunks cuddled tight around the edges of a dark and shining pool. Rap dropped his gown, walked out of his sandals, and waded in. Jalon was close behind. They sank gratefully into warm bliss, reclining on a squishily soft matting of leaves and mud. For some minutes they just lay.

Then Jalon tried again. "Rap? You . . . you wouldn't . . . you won't share?"

If Andor had asked, the plea would have been more skilled and refusal much easier. What had Jalon ever done to deserve his portion of Rap's vengeance?

Plenty! When he'd met an innocent boy who didn't even know what a word of power was or that he even knew one, Jalon had not explained, and he had certainly not mentioned the dangers. He'd merely muttered a cryptic and useless warning about Darad. Jalon had lost any claim on Rap's friendship at their first meeting, so Rap was now entitled to . . .

Power was very easy to justify to one's conscience.

"No. My aim is to help Inos. For that I'm going to need all the power I can muster." He would not share the word his mother had told him. "But I make you the same promise I made Andor: You help me first, and then I'll help you. Maybe then, when Inos is safely on her throne . . . Maybe then I'll even tell you my own word. If it's necessary to lift your curse, I will." Promises were easy.

Jalon nodded solemnly and offered a hand on it. And there was no guile on his face, damn him!

The water was marvelously soothing on sun-battered, travel-worn bodies, and the dim peace of the forest was balm for nerves that still rang with memories of dragons. Rap could hear dragons, if he strained, but they were very distant, a fault mumbling and squabbling, no threat to anyone. They sounded rather like sleepy chickens, in fact.

Gathmor lurched in over the sand ridge, walking with a pronounced stoop. He dropped the robe he was carrying and waded into the pool.

"I'd like to talk to Sagorn, please," Rap said.

The water was up to Jalon's chin and when he shook his head, he spread circles of ripples.

"Why not?"

"He's dying—or at least very sick. He really did have some sort of seizure. And he told you the word!" Jalon shuddered. "That hurt! Gods, that hurt him! And then . . . Well, it's amazing he had the strength to call Andor." He screwed up his face at the memories of approaching death.

So Rap had killed Sagorn! Even if he was not in any true sense dead, none of the gang would ever dare call him again.

Revenge was a very sour fruit.

And what of his soul? Sagorn had not seemed especially evil, although the Gods would know more of him than Rap ever could. Sagorn had tried to steal Rap's word of power. That was an evil to cancel out a lot of good. But the man was not truly dead! How could his soul go before the Gods for weighing if he wasn't dead? Would it remain forever in some sort of limbo, holding unreleased forever the spark of residue, the balance that should go to join the Evil or the Good? The undead dark?

God of Fools!

Gathmor had been sitting hunched up. Now he lay back gingerly, wincing as if something hurt. He glanced suspiciously at the other two, alert for traces of amusement.

"Rap!" Jalon said. "You used power against a dragon!"

"I know. I'm trying not to think about it." The warlock of the south might be on Rap's trail right now. "Let me talk to Darad, please." That would be magic, but Oothiana had said the transformations were too brief to be located.

Jalon blinked, seemed about to argue, then nodded. The giant jotunn appeared in his place with a stupendous splash, sending waves surging across the pool. Gathmor, taken by surprise, tried to sit up and obviously regretted the hasty move.

Darad looked hard at Rap, then opened his mouth in a huge crocodile grin, displaying his fangs. Rap was tensed, prepared to jump up and treat him as he had treated Gathmor, but there was no need. The fighter's face was hideously battered and disfigured with tattoos, yet as easy to read as a child's, and it was filled now with great amusement.

Chuckling hoarsely, Darad offered a hand larger than Rap's foot. "Thanks, faun! You sure fixed them!"

Rap clasped hands, saw the inevitable squeeze coming, and calmly bettered it. Darad looked comically astonished at the resistance, then alarmed, and finally howled very satisfactorily, raising flocks of birds from the trees. Rap released him, suddenly ashamed. He was no better than they were, these crude, sadistic jotnar! No, he was worse because he was cheating, not using honest muscle.

Unabashed, gently massaging his damaged hand with the other one, the ogre resumed his grin. "That primpy, prissy Sagorn! You made him look pretty stupid!"

"Liked that, did you?"

"Loved it!" The wolf teeth flashed again. "Been wait ng a hundred years for him to get what's coming to him! He was a snotty, smartass kid, and he only got worse. But you watch that Andor! Don't trust him!'

"I won't." Rap studied the dim-witted warrior for a moment. "How about you? Will you take the same deal?"

Darad nodded vigorously. "You bet! You can count on me, sir! You'll get this spell off of us if anyone can—and it won't take you a hundred years, neither! I'm your man, Master Rap!"

He meant it! Even as a mundane. Rap would never have been deceived by Darad. His new occult sense of truth detected no reservations, and now he could readily see that Darad was a born follower who preferred having a superior around to tell him who to kill or maim. Once he gave his word he would be more loyal than Andor or Thinal, and infinitely more reliable than Jalon, within the narrow bounds of his abilities. Amazing!

But Rap had not yet said he would accept this new henchman, and his hesitation had provoked a very worried expression on the jotunn's grotesque features. He could have no real conscience, but he apparently had some sense of justice. "Sir?" he muttered. "I guess I did a job on your face back on the boat there. Got a bit carried away, see? If you want a few free ones to make us even . . . well, I'd understand."

So Darad would humbly stand still while Rap systematically battered his eyes? The image was enough to make the new adept explode in his first genuine laughter for days, and the resulting perplexity on Darad's face only increased his mirth.

"I think we're about quits," Rap said, catching his breath. "You sold me to the goblins. I set my dog on you. Little Chicken began the eye work, but I gave the orders. Princess Kadolan burned your back, so we'll count that in, too, right?" Then, as Darad nodded and leered his agreement, Rap had a vision of himself walking up to Inos's aunt and blacking her eyes to settle her account, and that absurdity convulsed him in more howls of mirth, while the two jotnar sharing the pool with him exchanged puzzled glances.

Perhaps his merriment was reaction to a narrow escape. It could just be excitement at his new powers. It was certainly not very manly. Rap forced himself back to sobriety, and shook Darad's hand again, in civilized fashion, and the deal was made.

So Andor and Jalon and Darad would help. Sagorn was effectively dead. Thinal they must not call, not here in dragon country. Rap had no illusions of holding off a dragon if there was real gold in the neighborhood. He relaxed for a moment, still enjoying the warm soak, and also relishing his new adept-hood.

He could listen to the distant murmur of dragons. His farsight was sharper and had a greater range. His ability to outbrawl Gathmor suggested that he would find he was expert at any skill he had ever practiced. He was as persuasive as Andor now, and he could read expressions in a way he had never dreamed was possible. His face was less blistered than Gathmor's, although he had been closer to the dragon; the scrapes on his toes had stopped hurting. He seemed to be healing very quickly, and he wondered what other abilities he might uncover in himself during the next few days.

He turned to meet Gathmor's scowl.

"You want to get even with Kalkor?"

The jotunn nodded warily.

"Then I suggest you stick around, too. There's another prophecy: I meet Kalkor again."

Gathmor's pale eyes showed interest. "You'll let me have him?

"You couldn't handle him. Darad might—"

The warrior growled. "Not a hope, sir! We tried a friendly bout once, and he mashed me. Half my ribs and a broken jaw, and he wasn't much more'n a kid then. Fists, swords, axes—he's the best."

That was an ominous report, because Darad also had a word of power. Either Kalkor had more native ability, or his word was much stronger.

Or else, like Rap now, he knew more than one word.

But that worry was far in the future.

"I want to hear the whole story," Gathmor said, "before I commit myself to anything."

It was his own fault he hadn't heard it all long since; Rap had tried to tell him often enough. "We can talk as we go. It's long enough to last till Zark."

"What next?" Gathmor heaved himself up stiffly. 'We going to get on our way?"

Rap's farsight nudged him, and he turned to stare at the watcher on the bank. Where had he come from?

He did not seem worrisome. He was standing on a fallen log and smiling shyly, although the smile was partly hidden by his hand—he had a finger up his nose. A gnome's nose was not much more than two holes in his face.

The scrap of rag around his loins was filthy beyond belief, and too tattered to serve its purpose; the natural mud color of his skin was visible only where sweat streaks had loosened flakes of dirt. Rap was sorry to discover that his sharp new farsight could detect the teeming multitudes within the odious tangle of the boy's hair. His head would have reached to Rap's navel; he was about thirteen, maybe, depending on how fast gnomes aged. The only clean places on him were two very gorgeous, bronze-tinted eyes.

Seeing he had the men's attention, he grinned more broadly and beckoned with his free hand. Then he jumped off his log and ran in among the trees.

Darad lurched to his feet, with Gathmor right behind him. They plowed across the pond in twin tidal waves, heedless of Rap's shouts.

It took a great effort of will and was only possible because his farsight still kept the boy in sight, but Rap managed to go the other way first and grab up five of the six wooden sandals. He wanted the sixth and the gowns, too, but the urgency of the summons became unbearable and tore him away. He ran around the pond on bare feet and followed the others.

In that overgrown riot of jungle, the tiny gnome boy had all the advantages. He could squeeze through bamboo thickets. He could roll or crawl under walls of thorns that three naked men dare not approach, or scurry like a beetle over marsh that would swallow them to the shoulders. He was fast and nimble and occultly inexhaustible. His powers included some means of telling direction, for he held to a straight course, and he never drew so far ahead that the chase seemed impossible. Always, his pursuers must believe that another two minutes would do it, and when they nagged from total exhaustion he laughed, and his laugh had some occult power also, for it drove the men on again like red-hot whips.

Rap easily caught up with his companions and handed over the sandals. He himself went barefoot, and soon they were all doing so, trying to gain speed.

His greatest problem was staying in contact with the others. He could easily have left them far behind, and the craving to do so gnawed at him like a starved rat. Darad had an occult warrior's strength, of course, and could keep up the pace and stand the punishment much better than poor Gathmor, who was only human and very soon exhausted. Rap took his hand and hauled him along, and their compromise pace was about what Darad could manage.

Eventually, as the hours passed and the young gnome led them up into the hills, jungle faded into parkland, and parkland into moor, giving welcome relief from the whipping and slashing of undergrowth. By nightfall, though, the chase was over rocky ground that chopped at feet like knives. Unable to rest for a moment, still staggering along after the gaily skipping gnome with his bewitching laugh and his beautiful eyes, Rap and his friends climbed ever higher between the barren peaks, and the muttering of dragons was very close.

Man's worth something:
No, when the fight begins within himself,
A man's worth something.
                          Browning, *Bishop Blougram's Apology*

6

Life and death

1

The Thume side of the mountains was a moister, kinder land than the desert to the east, with rich grass swaying underfoot and foliage-filled sky overhead. The air was friendly, heavy with woodsy scents. Inos could not identify the forest giants themselves, but among them she recognized some of the smaller, cultivated varieties she had seen in Arakkaran—citrus trees and olives, running wild. So whatever had destroyed the ancient folk of Thume had spared their orchards. She approved of fruit trees; unlike most others, they did something useful.

But she soon began to appreciate that even the others could be helpful. They cast shade, and shade discouraged undergrowth. The mules' little hooves swished through tall ferns, thumped softly on loam or moss. There was no obvious road, but the green tunnels of the woods were mostly quite passable, leading from time to time out into grassy clearings that reminded her oddly of the tiny sunlit courtyards of Krasnegar. In the meadows, of course, the sun was fierce, but on the far side there was always shade again, more gloom-filled hallways pillared with massive trunks that fanned out overhead into rafters, cross-braced with thin shafts of light. She knew the spruce of the taiga and she had seen hardwood forest near Kinvale, but nothing so magical as this.

For a long while the three invaders rode in silence. Kade was still uncharacteristically downcast, and Inos could only conclude that the uncanny encounter with the petrified army still weighed on her mind. She was old; any reminder of death must seem morbid to a woman of her years, but Kade would certainly spring back soon.

Azak was tense, vigilant, his eyes never still. Not wishing to distract him with conversation, Inos let herself become caught up in the birdsong. A steady flow of it filled the woods like musical rainbows. Once in a very long while she would see a tiny shape flash away; mostly the singers stayed out of sight and emptied their souls in chorus and counterpoint. *A thousand years we have practiced,* they said, *waiting for someone to return and hear our song. Welcome! Welcome! Welcome!*

Harness creaked and jingled, but the spongy ground muffled the mules' tread. At times the river made itself heard, chattering busily off to the left somewhere, telling the way, promising it would lead them to its bigger brother and that together they would venture to the sea.

The beauty of the morning was a balm to all fears, pure gold. Nowhere could seem less accursed than this.

The approach of noon lessened the birds' symphony, and Azak was the first to become talkative, as he began to relax. He pointed out some of what his tracker's eyes were seeing—ancient traces of buildings and trails, animal tracks and how old they were. Those scats were from a wild dog; domestic dogs' were less tapered. The bark of trees bore ravages of woodpeckers, the rubbing of antlers, old claw marks of bears.

"You didn't learn all this in the desert!" Inos said accusingly.

Blood-red eyes twinkled, "In the mountains, the Agonistes. When I was small."

If that was a hint of some personal history she did not know of, he failed to add to it. He went back to the wildlife. Deer and goats for certain, he said, and probably wild cattle.

But no people. When the time came to rest the mules and feed the riders, Azak was joyful. No cut trees, no tracks, no fences, no smoke. There were no people in Thume, he said. Anything else he could handle, of course, except demons.

Inos smiled, and assured him politely that she trusted both his eye and his arm.

Kade said nothing, frowning around and biting her lip.

"This is a splendid place to make camp!" Azak proclaimed royally, encompassing the glade with a sweeping gesture of approval.

Inos had been lost in a reverie of plans for Hub. Startled, she suppressed a snigger. At times that large young man assumed lofty airs that were not in keeping with his ragged robes and wildly bushy red beard—nor with his posture, for his legs were very nearly as long as his mule's. He had ridden all across the mountains with his feet almost trailing on the ground, and he could probably dismount by walking backward on tiptoe if he wished. Still, even if habit still made him pontificate sometimes, he had proved far more adaptable than she would ever have suspected back in Arakkaran. He had watched his dominion shrink from a kingdom to a single caravan and then to two women, and he had never complained or seemed to feel slighted. He had turned out to be a superb woodsman just as he had been a superb ruler of a kingdom. Whatever the game, whatever the stakes, Azak played with all his heart, and with all the native skill of a born winner.

He had his faults, Azak ak'Azakar, but he was a magnificent chunk of royalty.

Yet why this sudden change of heart? He had forced the pace ever since the hurried departure from Elkarath's caravan, so why a call to pitch camp now, with at least two hours' daylight left? They had no tent to erect and, while the clearing was a pleasant enough spot, it was no better than a dozen others they had seen.

Inos shot him a puzzled glance. "We hear and obey, Protector of the Poor, Beloved of the Gods!"

"Of course!" A smile flashed out of his red bush like an escaping bird, but Inos was certain that the ruby eyes had read every thought in her head. Who would ever have believed that Azak could handle her teasing so well? How had he ever learned?

Then his eyes flickered a signal. Inos twisted around to look at Kade, who was bringing up the rear.

Idiot! Furious that she had been so thoughtless—and that Azak should have noticed what she had not—Inos slid from her saddle, dropped her reins, and hurried back to Kade's mule.

"Aunt! Are you not feeling well?"

"Oh, I'm quite well, dear. Why are we stopping?" The pale-blue eyes made a great effort to find their old sparkle—and failed. No matter what she said, Kade was not better; she was worse. Whatever was wrong was taking a price. She was humped in her saddle, she seemed to have aged ten years, and for the first time in Inos's experience, her absurdly uncrushable cheerfulness had failed her.

"Azak thinks we should make camp now."

The news was not welcome. Kade twitched and looked around with evident alarm. "Oh, surely we can make a league or two before dark?"

"He thinks not. Here, let me help you down."

107

"Oh, I think we should continue!" Kade protested.

"Why?"

"The sheik? Queen Rasha?"

"The sheik is not going to catch us after all this time, Aunt. The mules need a rest." *And so do you!*

"Well . . . We might find a better campsite?"

"Azak insists that this one is perfect," Inos said firmly.

It was at least satisfactory, a grassy meadow in a wide loop of the busy river, with water on three sides and unusually bushy forest closing off the fourth. Even if the mules pulled up their pickets, they would not stray far unless the weather turned bad, and at me moment the weather was perfect: hot sunshine and cool breeze. Here and there the sward buckled in low mounds that hinted at ancient dwellings, perhaps a farm—given a little leisure time, those might be fun to explore for relics—and the only other landmark was a small copse in the middle, a dozen or so spindly trees. Inos knew enough of Azak's thinking now to guess his intent. He would embellish those saplings into an illusion of shelter, and it would have open ground all around. Practical man!

Still murmuring reluctance, Kade dismounted. Azak's mule, already stripped of its tack, was rolling in the thick grass with all four legs in me air, obviously agreeing with his opinion of this place.

In another half hour or so, the work was done. Azak had chopped saplings and branches from the woods and dragged them over to the copse to fashion a windbreak. Kade was sitting in there, brewing a peaceful pan of tea on a small fire. The mules were contentedly chomping grass at the end of long tethers, and Inos was standing on the riverbank with Azak. A brief inspection of the mounds had turned up nothing more interesting than old hearthstones, the day was not over yet, and she wasn't sure what she wanted to do next.

Azak was shielding his eyes with his hand as he studied the westering sun. Estimating time, likely.

Inos wondered idly how it would feel to throw her arms around that oversized camel jockey and kiss him till his beard smoked, to be herself kissed as Andor had once kissed her. Actually Andor's kiss had not been all that spectacular, even if he had used occult power. The kiss she really remembered, out of her very small collection, had been when Rap had been leaving for the spring drive and . . . but Rap was dead, and while she had a certain natural curiosity about how an overgrown, bush-bearded sultan might kiss, she could not detect any real excitement in herself in considering the prospect. Nor any real desire to try it, even were Rasha's curse to be revoked. So perhaps she was not making much progress in the falling-in-love department.

She could not imagine any man she would rather have here to guard her against the dangers of a savage land—as long as his curse was in place, of course—and very few men she could less easily imagine wanting to share the rest of her life with. *Trust in love?* Fun to have around, perhaps, but . . . every day? Every *night?*

Gods, but he had noticed her stare! She turned quickly to face the wind. "Is that the sea I can smell?"

There was a heart-stopping pause, then he said, "I think so. It can't be very far off—two days, maybe."

"Then we head west, to Qoble?"

"Maybe. We shall come to that large river, and we are on the wrong side of it."

She should have thought of that, of course! "I feel very grubby. This water will be warm, I expect."

He frowned at the arc of white sand fringing the meadow. "The current is swift, little kitten."

"Oh, I shan't go in deep. I can't swim. It's quiet this side."

Near the sand, the water was barely bothering to move the leaves drifting on its surface, but the far bank had been undercut into a small cliff and there the river was bundled in glistening, motionless waves below the overhanging forest boughs. Even as she watched, a floating stick went leaping through those waves at an astonishing speed.

Azak grunted, peering upstream and downstream, and also across at the jungle, which was thick and dark, casting shadows on the river. "Crocodiles?"

"No!"

"Well, I can't see any," he admitted. "But don't trust floating logs, especially if they smile at you."

Inos shivered. "I shall certainly keep that in mind. But I will wash the clothes—and me."

"I'll stay within earshot." He spoke seriously, his face expressionless.

Inos realized that she had been expecting a wisecrack, perhaps a joke about keeping careful watch—the sort of racy retort she would have received from her friends among the stablehands and servants of Krasnegar. Even the young dandies at Kinvale would likely have tried to mask embarrassment with wit. Not Azak. Of course the female body held no secrets for him, and to spy on her would be self-inflicted torment. His sense of fun was an intermittent, unpredictable thing anyway.

"You are going hunting!" she said firmly.

"Oh! I am?" He pursed his ups in astonishment.

"Yes, you are. You know we're short of supplies. Fresh meat will be a welcome change after all those pancakes and dates and things. You have time."

He nodded, amused. "And who will defend you?"

She began walking back to the shelter. "What is there to defend from? Mosquitoes?"

"Lions," he said, following.

"No!"

"I saw some spoor, a long way back."

Tramping through knee-high grass, she said, "Don't lions hunt at night?"

"That depends on how hungry they are, and how appetizing the prey. Some people look very appetizing. Sunset is a favorite time. Besides, they might be tigers, and I trust those even less."

"I would enjoy a nice slice of venison, or a plump bird." She was not a witless city girl who panicked at a mention of lions.

He shrugged. "As you wish. It won't take me long to find something."

Obviously he did not rank the lions and tigers very high as a danger if he was willing to leave two women alone for even a short while. They had all been together too much for too long; a break would do them all good.

"Don't mention lions to Kade."

"I won't, but you keep the other bow to hand while I am gone."

Clearly Inos was still one of the boys, and his faith in her competence was both flattering and reassuring.

She sat and sipped a pan of scalding tea with Kade. By the time it was finished, Azak had saddled up the largest mule and ridden it off into the trees. The others snickered to it a few times and then lost interest. Kade was still strangely twitchy and nervous and obviously trying not to show it.

"He won't be gone long, will he?"

"Azak? No." How odd! Inos thought that Kade ought to be finding Azak's absence restful—usually he made her jumpy. "Tell me what's wrong, Aunt."

Normally Kade's rosy cheeks were lighted by internal sunshine. Today strange shadows seemed to dull them. "Nothing! Nothing at all! Just superstition, the Accursed Land."

"Well, I have never met a name less suited. It's idyllic. Azak's quite sure there are no people here."

Kade nodded, uncertain. Then the old blue eyes steadied on Inos. "You're not changing your mind, dear, are you?"

"About what?" Inos had not seen Kade wear quite that expression since their first weeks together in Kinvale.

"Well, Azak. I know he's being very persistent." Kade blushed. "He's a very handsome man, in his way, and—"

"We're planning the announcement as soon as we arrive at . . ." Inos laughed and shook her head. "No, I have not changed my mind! I feel easier in his company than I did, maybe, and I do find him fun at times. But you needn't start polishing the state plate yet."

"Well, I just wondered. I hope you don't mind my asking?"

"Of course not! Now, do you want to sit here, or come and do laundry with me?"

Kade considered, and seemed to make an effort to overcome some daytime nightmare. "I'll stay here and watch the fire. I'll come and have a wash later."

Odd! But the mountains had been very hard going. A good night's rest was the least of what Kade needed, and had earned. Even an hour's solitude might be good for her.

And she might credit her niece with just a little more self-control. Handsome man indeed! There were lots of handsome men. And nice outside didn't necessarily mean nice inside. Things like honesty and reliability didn't always show in faces. Andor had been handsome, and who could have been plainer-looking than Rap?

Leaving her aunt sitting in her shift, Inos bundled up their two robes and all the spare linen, and stalked off toward the sand and the river. About a third of the way there she remembered Azak's warning to keep weapons handy. She stopped and considered. The idea of her bringing down a charging lion or a brace of tigers was not a very convincing one. On the other hand, he had been serious and he had trusted her. Azak had a very harsh tongue for those who disobeyed his orders. How would she feel if something dangerous did come and she had ignored so obvious a precaution? Feeling rather foolish, she marched determinedly back to the shelter, added a bow and three arrows to her load, and set off again for the water.

She untied her robe, and was amused to find herself pausing and glancing around before continuing to undress, even though she knew there had been no snoopers in these parts for a thousand years. She left her shift on. Adding her outer clothes to the others, she knelt down in cool water and set to work as well as she could with only a scrap of crude goat-tallow soap and with no rocks to beat them. Then she spread them on the long, warm grass to dry.

By that time, the air was chill on her skin, for the sun had ducked below the high treetops. As the air had cooled, so the water had seemed to become warmer. If she did not take her dip soon, the crocodiles might sneak up on her in the dark.

She took a careful look at the river and could see no floating logs, with or without smiles. A mule brayed in the distance, so Azak must be returning already, and she was surprised to discover how comforting that knowledge was—solitude had become an unfamiliar sensation.

Trying to remember when she had last been completely alone, she stripped to the skin and waded out into the river. Soon the current was unpleasantly strong, tugging at her legs and prizing the sand out from under

111

her toes. By the time she was knee deep, she dared go no farther. She knelt and soaped, splashed and rubbed.

Two mules whinnied.

She ducked her head for one last rinse, then started back to the shore, squeezing water from her hair. She rubbed wetness off her skin with her hands, wishing she had some of those seductively soft towels from the palace in Arakkaran. She reluctantly concluded that she would have to dress in damp clothes . . .

Mules did not whinny!

Then she heard Kade scream.

2

In the muddle of memories that Inos retained of the ensuing events, it always seemed as if the sun went down at that exact same instant—as if she left the water in daylight, leaped across the sand and up the bank with one jump, and landed on the turf in dusk. Deep shadows of the high forest crown filled the meadow as she raced across it, her bow in one hand, three arrows and a wet shift in the other, pursued by every terror her mind could conjure. Twigs and small pebbles dug at her bare feet, and thorny flower stems under the long grass scraped her shins. She stumbled over tussocks and hidden ridges. Her damp skin was cool, to match the icy horror inside her, and her hair was a wet rag flopping on her back.

Kade! Oh, Kade!

The mules had not screamed as they would have done for lions. The mules were still there, eating contentedly. Inos could see them, vague shapes in the gathering dusk. The whinny-noises had been ponies, or horses.

Why would Kade have screamed just once?

And a sudden flash of clarity—what did Inos think she was doing racing across the meadow in the nude? Why, oh, why, did she never stop to think? She should have taken the three seconds necessary to pull on a robe, instead of just grabbing up a sodden scrap of underwear that wasn't going to do very much good if the danger was human. Specifically, man-type human. That insight struck her about halfway from the river to the little windbreak; she stumbled, recovered, decided she could not desert Kade, and kept on running, heart pounding now from fear and exertion both.

Smoke still drifted from the tangled screen of branches Azak had woven between the saplings. Nothing looked disturbed. Kade was in there, or behind there. With what? With whom?

A mule brayed, and they all raised their heads—

Eight of them! Four mules and four horses. Saddled horses. Full-size horses, dim in the twilight. Well-trained horses, with their reins left dangling, cropping grass. Maybe a minute had passed since Kade screamed, and then a man stepped out of the shelter.

Inos dug in her toes, windmilled her arms once, and stopped dead, gasping for breath and simultaneously tucking the arrows under her arm and trying to arrange her skimpy covering like a curtain in front of herself with her free hand. It wasn't very satisfactory.

He had seen her. He held out his hands in welcome and called something. She made out not a single word, but his meaning was clear enough: *Here she comes.* Three other men emerged at his side, indistinct in the gloom. She could see few details, but they were men, young men, and she had no clothes on.

For a moment Inos just gaped in horror and disbelief—Azak had been so certain there were no traces of people. And the four strangers likewise stood and gazed at her. These were no primitive savages; they were decked out in long pants and some sort of neat shirts or tunics, all of the same dark-green shade. Each man wore a jaunty forester's cap with a feather in it and they carried longbows, the longest bows she had ever seen.

Then the first one made a beckoning motion and shouted to her, inviting. *Come all the way.*

Inos's feet began backing up of their own accord. To meet four strange men in a forest was bad enough, but to do so with no clothes on was the stuff of nightmares. There was no way she could even pull on her stupid slip without laying down her weapons.

The strangers conferred briefly. One gestured at the horses, and the others jeered at him. The leader said something and they laughed. They laid down their bows, slid the quivers from their shoulders, and dropped those also.

Again the leader called to her, and she made out enough to know he was telling her to disarm, also. She had three arrows, only three. Plus one bow and a white flag.

"Who are you?" she shouted. "What do you want?" She eased back a few more steps—nearer the river and the forest beyond, nearer her heap of clothes. *Kade!* What had they done to Kade?

What? the leader shouted. Or so she assumed—he cupped an ear.

"What do you want?" she cried again, ashamed other shrillness.

One of the others said something, and they all laughed again. The leader shouted, pointing: *You!*

Then one of the others made a joke, and they all laughed, and quickly spread out in a straight line. The leader glanced along the line, then called out two or three words. Then two more . . .

On your marks . . .

Get set . . .

They were going to run her down on foot. She would be first prize in the men's cross-country sprint.

And perhaps all the other prizes, too.

If she tried to escape from the loop of the river, the men would run her down easily. She could not swim. Crocodiles were a trivial evil now—she whirled around and took to her heels.

Another obvious shout: *Go!*

And a glance over her shoulder confirmed that word. The race was on.

Three arrows, four men, fading light . . . she would not dare shoot until they were at point-blank range, and if they charged her together, she would not have time to draw her bow a second time. Could she bring herself to shoot an arrow into a human being? Even to try might be a stupidity, for if she felled some or wounded some, then how would the others retaliate?

She ran as she had never run, and the river was horribly far off. Beyond it lay deep forest where she could hide if she could ever reach it alive. Harsh breathing and pounding heart and tangles of grass grabbing at her legs to trip her . . . Somewhere on the run her useless slip caught on a bush and was lost.

She would never make it. She had provoked enough chases in her life to know that female legs were no match for men's when it came to running. Even when she had been taller than Rap and Lin she had never been able to outrun them.

Then a chorus of mule noise in the distance, and a thump of hooves—Azak! With a cry of relief, Inos stopped and spun around. The men were dangerously near already, closing in on her like talons, but they had stopped and turned also, to see who came. *And they had left their bows at the shelter!* Had she had any breath left, Inos would have cheered—Azak would ride them down and fill them fall of arrows and chop their heads off in the first half minute.

The mule came into view, coming from the upstream side, the way Azak had gone.

A largish mule, riderless.

Skittering and jumpy, it raced around in tenor and indecision, and then headed for the others. It was Azak's mule. No Azak. The implications of that were not thinkable.

The four men laughed and jabbered and lost interest in the new arrival. They turned to face their quarry again. They were so spread out that it was hard to keep all four in view.

The leader called out to her and she thought she picked out some of the words: *lady . . . friends . . . be friends . . .* He repeated the beckoning gesture he had used before. Inos shook her head and stepped back, speechless with terror and lack of breath.

Blood roared in her head. Terror . . .

The man laughed. He pointed an aim at the mules then raised a hand high to indicate height. He pulled an imaginary bow, swung his arm around, jabbing a thumb in his chest. He made falling gestures. The other three gasped out fits of laughter at this dumbshow.

Azak bushwacked? Shot down from cover? So his panic-driven mount would have fled and then eventually circled back to join its companions.

Azak shot . . . What had they done to Kade?

Azak . . . Kade . . .

Now Inos.

She dropped two arrows and heaved on her bow to string it—faster than she had ever done that—and she had the third arrow notched at once, pointing at the leader. In this twilight, with her heart bouncing all around her chest, she was probably not capable of hitting a rain barrel from the inside.

The men on the ends were edging around, moving to encircle her. Again the leader called out in his singsong dialect, unfamiliar and yet teasingly close to being intelligible: *hurt? . . .* no, he meant *not hurt . . . promise, promise, promise . . .* She would trust his promise like a viper's kiss. The meanings came more in gesture and inflection than words, but the mockery and gloating came more clearly still.

"Go back!" she shouted, drawing the bow. "Call off your men. I'm not bluffing!"

The leader cowered in pretended fear and backed a couple of steps. But the others . . . Evil take it! She couldn't watch all three and aim an arrow at the same time.

Three? She whirled, and the fourth was not a dozen paces off, between her and the river. As her bow turned on him, he stopped and threw up his hands in mock surrender. He was taller than the others, fresh-faced, not very old. He spoke, and again the main words came through: . . . *mercy . . . have mercy . . . lady . . . mercy . . .*

"Stand aside!" Inos shouted, and moved to edge past him. He stepped to block her. She glanced around at the others. They were closer. The tall one shouted to attract her attention; then the others did. Now they were openly playing a child's game—whenever she was looking, they stood still; when she wasn't, they moved.

That river was horribly wide and swift, but it could contain no monsters worse than these. She dashed for the widest gap. The tall youngster dived for her. She struck with her bow, and he grabbed it. She let go, staggered, and was taken from behind by two arms like barrel hoops. She kicked screamed, twisted, butted . . .

Her captor cursed in her ear and squeezed until her ribs creaked. She cried out with her last puff of breath, going limp, as dark spots danced before her eyes. He eased the strain a little. The three other men were clustered around, inspecting the spoils, all winded, panting and grinning.

They were not tall, but then Inos had become accustomed to djinns. Imp height, then—middle size for a man, but still taller than she. Their faces and arms were a middle shade of brown, too, but they were not imps. Their hair was paler, curly not straight; they had too much shoulder and not enough hip . . . and their eyes were set at a curious slant, like an elf's. Pointed ears. Pixies. Living pixies! Young men out for devilment, two of them little more than boys.

But old enough. Four of them.

God of Mercy!

They were panting too much for so short a run. They kept smiling, chuckling, breathless with excitement. They spoke words that meant nice girl and much happiness. That meant horrible things.

They wore sleeveless shirts and long pants and boots—all of them well-made garments, embroidered, fitted. All the same olive green. Clothes and wearers smelled of woodsmoke, and horse, and male sweat.

The leader reached out to stroke her cheek and she tried to bite his hand. He laughed and fondled her breast instead.

"Brute!" she shouted with all the wind she could find. "Animal! Evil!" She kicked, and he caught her leg and hung on to it, so she reeled on the other foot, held up only by the man behind her, who chuckled in her ear.

The leader said something and stroked her thigh. Her skin came up in gooseflesh and he laughed at that.

"Don't understand! Don't know what you say. Monster! Four against one? You're brutes! Cowards! Spawn of Evil!"

Still holding her ankle in one hand and fondling with the other, the leader spoke, tried again, and finally found a word she knew and reacted to: "Outsider!"

He glanced at the others, then at her again, and he discarded his smile. "Outsider?" he repeated in his strange accent. He turned his head and spat on the grass. "Outsider!"

It made sense. Outsiders—intruders. Nonpixies were fair game. Shoot down the men, take the women. Then what? And what had they done to Kade? Whole legions could vanish in Thume.

"No!" She shook her head wildly and tried to struggle again. The same thing happened as before—her captor crushed her into helplessness. She whimpered, trying to wrestle her leg free, trying to butt, but she had slid down until her head was against her chest and butting did no good. Again she slumped into quiescence, but her heart was going mad inside her.

One of the others spoke sharply, impatiently.

The leader snapped, telling him to be quiet, but he dropped her ankle and began unlacing his shirt. She was half sitting now, unable to straighten her legs, and gradually sliding lower in her captor's arms.

The leader threw down his shirt, grinning at her. By some trick of the light, she could see the sweat glint on his chest with every harsh breath. He hooked his right heel under his left boot and tugged out his right foot.

"You bunch of animals!" she sneered, not shouting now. "Beasts! Filth! What sort of man treats—"

Again a sound of hooves, many hooves, shrills of alarm from the horses.

The men looked around, and Inos twisted her head to see. The shirtless man rammed his foot back in his boot and took to his heels, bellowing orders. The other two followed at once, leaving only the one holding Inos. He turned to watch, giving her a better view also.

The three men were running as if chased by lions, running for their horses. Horses and mules were in wild panic and uproar. In their midst, one horse plunged and leaped as its rider scrolled the dark with lines of fire, waving a flaming branch.

Nothing like fire to spook horses! Two were off into the trees already. The third had caught in one of the mules' tethers and was down. The mules were breaking loose but two of them had gone over also, and all were screaming in terror. Still the mysteriously glimmering figure on the horse flailed the torch around, and now the mules were up. Pounding hooves seemed to shake the clearing, gradually dwindling as the stampede faded into the forest, until all the animals had gone into the night and only two horses remained: one rolling helplessly, obviously injured, the other still bearing the maniac with the torch. Three young men ran impotently, uselessly, over the meadow, howling in wordless rage.

Then the rider hurled down the dying brand and wheeled the horse, and came across the clearing like an avenging hurricane, hooves hardly seeming to touch the ground. It was Kade! Incredible Kade, riding a mad horse as if she were Azak himself, wearing nothing but her flimsy cotton slip, white hair fluttering in the night.

Had she been armed with a lance, she might have skewered one of the marauders in her charge. As it was, he leaped to catch the reins, stumbled aside at the last minute, and fell heavily.

The jailer's grip had slackened. Inos straightened her legs, slamming her head up into his face with a satisfying impact, throwing all her weight back against him, then letting it all drop again. The two of them sat down simultaneously, hard. She lashed out backward with an elbow, hoping to hit him in the belly, but he grabbed her hair and pulled her over at just the same moment, so she tilted and missed and caught him between the legs instead. He seemed to have a sensitive spot there, for he spasmed and cried out. She pounded again, harder, and he lost interest in her altogether. She scrambled free.

She was on her feet and running as the horse came thundering by, and she made a wild grab for the harness as if she were an acrobat, but all she caught was a glimpse of Kade's terrified face above her. Brutal impact threw her aside and into the ground hard enough to explode the world into fragments.

For a moment she was stunned . . . in pain and breathless and too battered to care what happened. She tried to rise. A stab of white-hot agony in her ankle stopped her. Reality flooded back.

Grass was burning over by the shelter, a fountain of yellow light in the dusk. Kade was still somehow clinging to that berserk horse. It must have balked at the river, or she had wheeled it, for now it was pounding back toward the two men still on their feet. Again it seemed one must be ridden down. Again the man leaped aside in time, and this one did not fall.

And the other stepped between Inos and the spreading grass fire—and he had a bow! He was taking aim; the horse had turned again. The arrow flew, Inos yelled a warning, the horse reared, hooves flailing the sky. Then it sank back on its haunches and toppled over sideways. *Kade!* Inos could not see what had happened to Kade.

Silence.

No rider rose from the fallen horse.

Again Inos tried to stand, and again was stopped by that fearful pain. She must have broken her ankle.

One by one the men limped over and stood, glaring down at her.

The one who had fallen was clutching his arm in a way that reminded her of Kel breaking his collarbone years ago, going after birds' eggs on Windle Scarp. The man who had been her jailer was holding his groin, bent over and muttering horribly. His nose had bled badly all over his chin and his shirt. The other two were gasping for breath and looking just as mad.

She wanted to cringe, to make herself as tiny as possible before their fury. There was no amusement or mockery now in their slanted eyes, only *Hurt* and *Pain* and *Revenge*. Two of their mounts had run off, two been killed or crippled, two men injured, and all four had been made to look like idiots. They were not after fun now. They were going to make her pay. Long and hard.

Her fingers scrabbled on the ground, gathering sand and grit for throwing in eyes. She wasn't going to cringe and she wasn't going to cry out no matter what they did. She was a queen, for Gods' sakes!

"Animals!" she shouted. "Serves you right. Wait till my other friends arrive! You! Go and bring my robe from over there . . ."

One of the younger pair, one of the uninjured, said something emphatic and stripped off his shirt. She couldn't do much against those muscles, even if the other men did not help him. He kicked off his boots, glaring at her. Then he dropped his pants, and she instinctively averted her eyes. *Oh, Gods!* The drumming of her heart was making her feel giddy. This time there could be no escape, but whatever happened she wasn't going to give in. She would make them fight for every scrap of satisfaction, and if she could claw out an eye or two then Evil take the consequences because they would surely kill her afterward anyway.

Was all that noise just the beating of her heart? Hooves?

A third time Inos was saved by a distant sound of hooves.

A third time they all turned to look.

A horse came galloping out of the trees. It was huge and spectral, gleaming white as if wrapped in glory. Its rider was garbed all in white, and his cloak streamed like aurora in the night. Horse and rider glowed alike with unearthly silver radiance that brightened as they came thundering across the meadow, making the ground tremble. The pixies started to shout in alarm, the stripper hastily hauling up his pants. And they all fell silent, freezing in position. Inos felt a wave of calm and peace flood over her. She was saved. The occult had arrived.

3

The sense of serenity was as distinctive as a signature. That, and a flicker of red fire around his head, told Inos who her savior was even before he drew close and reined in his magnificent luminous stallion.

When she had first met him in the seclusion of his home, Sheik Elkarath had worn a sumptuous robe of many colors. On leaving Arakkaran he had set aside such unbusinesslike ostentation in favor of plain white garb. Of all his finery, he had retained only his gem-adorned agal, as if it were a small vice he could overlook in himself. Now a halo like blood flashed from its rubies. The trailing edges of his kaffiyeh shone brighter than moonlight alongside his snowy eyebrows and beard, making them seem to glow also, while the draperies of his kibr flowed to his boots in waves of white glory. He was almost too bright to look upon, and he lighted the glade as far as the trees.

"Greatness, you are a welcome sight," Inos said weakly. She could feel herself floating in strange surges of emotion, like long ocean swells, up and down and up . . . There was pain and terror and screaming-horrible-hair-tearing hysterics inside her somewhere, there was a broken ankle and worry about Kade and Azak, but all those were overlain by the silken web of calm that she had recognized as Elkarath's. It was an intensification of the spell he had used on her every day from their first meeting until she had fled from him at Tall Cranes. It was magnified now to soothe her after what she had endured. The slow ups and downs must be variations in the intensity of the magic as he sought to adjust it to her needs.

119

He nodded calmly from the eminence of horseback. "I regret that I did not arrive sooner, Majesty. However, it would seem that you have suffered no harm I cannot heal."

Her ankle had stopped throbbing already. She fingered the swelling absently. "My aunt?"

Elkarath glanced across the clearing to the body of the felled horse. "She has been stunned, but she is in no danger. I shall attend to her when we have meted justice here."

"And Azak?"

"He also will survive. I was just in time for him, also."

A wave of relief burst through the emotional blanket, and Inos muttered a swift prayer to the Gods. "This is good news indeed, Greatness!"

"Humph!" The white brows came down in a scowl, and Elkarath turned his regard on the four frozen youths. They twitched slightly and mumbled. Harmless as flies in amber, they drooled and rolled their eyes in their efforts to move lips and tongues.

"These vermin," the sheik said idly, "shot down a man from ambush and then did not have the grace to kill him. He might have lain there suffering for days so far as they knew, or cared. As it was, he had almost drowned in his own blood when I arrived. Else I had been here sooner."

He swung a leg and dropped as nimbly as an adolescent, although the stallion stood at least seventeen hands. Then it didn't. The great horse shrank and faded and in moments had become merely another shaggy mountain pony like many Inos had seen in the foothills on the far side of the Progistes. Its occult glow dimmed and vanished. Even through the euphoria spell, Inos felt prickles of shock, and she heard the four immobilized pixies mumble gutturally.

The least surprised seemed to be the pony itself. It flickered ears and swished tail in a sort of equine shrug, then lowered its head to crop the lush grass.

The sheik knelt to examine Inos's ankle. Inos had no clothes on. He chuckled softly. "Do not be shy. No woman has secrets from me." He laid a cool hand on the swelling and it subsided. Her other scrapes and bruises were healing also.

"There! That will do for now." The old man rose, with none of the stiffness he displayed when there were others around to tend him. He held down a courtly hand to help Inos rise also. Silver sandals appeared on her feet and, as she came erect, a silken robe enveloped her. A filmy shawl materialized over her filthy, tangled hair. He had either forgotten underwear or was too tactful to use magic so intimately.

She mumbled thanks and bobbed a shaky curtsy. He bowed in response and laughed softly, as if he were enjoying this rare opportunity to exert powers he normally concealed. He did not look straight at her, though. He never did. Being a sorcerer, he could see without looking, she supposed, and that had become a habit to him. But she always found it irritating.

The prisoners moaned and slobbered and twitched in their efforts to move. Lighted by Elkarath's awesome light, they all seemed younger and slighter than they had before—unusually broad, perhaps, and with a curl to their hair that she had rarely seen on men before, and only by artifice on women. Their eyes were large and angled like elves', stretched wide now in terror. The irises were pale hazel, almost gold. But they were no hideous monsters, merely youths little older or taller than herself. How could they have behaved so?

"Scum!" said the sheik.

"Who are they?" Inos asked.

He shrugged. "Not formal guards at their age. Just a hunting party, I fancy."

"They are well groomed, civilized-looking. Their clothes are well made."

"Ha! Their behavior was not civilized. They had been stalking you for some time. Their lives are forfeit, so it matters not who they are, nor whence they came."

The amber eyes rolled in their sockets. Curiously, Inos was discovering that she felt very little hatred toward her attackers. Perhaps it was because they looked so helpless and she could remember how it felt to be pinned down by sorcery, or perhaps because she had escaped without permanent hurt. Maybe it was only the sorcerer's spell working on her emotions, but they seemed very young to die.

The sheik was stroking his shining white beard in dignified consideration. "They did not actually consummate their violation of your person, Queen Inosolan, but the intent was manifest. Your escape was narrow enough to justify granting you the traditional satisfaction." He drew his dagger and offered it to her with a flourish, hilt first.

Inos stared at it in bewilderment. "What am I supposed to do with that?"

"Take what they were so eager to give." She recoiled a step and turned to meet the horrified gaze of the immobilized youths. "No!" she said. "I am not a public executioner! And I would not stoop to barbarity like that."

"Indeed?" Elkarath murmured, and snatched away the occult blanket he had laid upon her emotions.

A thunderbolt of rage and hate struck her, followed at once by a shivery wild joy at having the tables turned. Again her heart thundered in her ears. She tasted bile burning her throat as she recalled what these four moral cripples had done to her and what they had intended. The gloating, the mockery, the actual pain, and above all the planned degradation . . . four men against one woman . . . her hand trembled as she reached for the dagger. Revenge would feel very good.

And she heard her father's voice. "Do what *is* good," he had told her once, "not just what feels good." When? Why? She could not recall the occasion—perhaps something very trivial in her childhood. But the precept was not trivial. With a great effort she mastered her fury and turned to face the old man.

"No! They deserve punishment, I agree. But not by me."

The sheik raised his snowbank eyebrows in disbelief and for once looked at her squarely.

"Punishment and vengeance are not the same," Inos shouted. "You are judge here. Yours is the power. They are your captives. Judge then, and execute your judgment." She took a deep breath, steadied her voice, and added, "And if it please your Greatness—I prefer the world this way. I want to take life as it is and as I am, not a painted replica seen through the eyes of a drunkard."

He frowned. "You are trembling."

"I am not ashamed of that under the circumstances. I would rather tremble than be a puppet."

A faint smile rumpled the folds of his chubby red face. "Spoken like a queen! So be it." He replaced the dagger in his sash and turned to the four captives. "You are judged unfit to live. Die, then, and may the Gods find more good in you than I can."

They jerked into motion, turning on their heels and starting to walk. Inos stuffed knuckles into her mouth as she saw the nature of the sentence. Of course the old man would be watching her, but if he expected her to have a fit of hysterics, then she would not give him the satisfaction. So she held herself rigid and watched, and by some occult trick she was allowed to see through the darkness as the four boys advanced over the grass, stumbled down the little bank, and continued across the sand. They waded into the river until the water reached their waists, and the tall one lasted until it was halfway up his chest. Then the current took him, as well. None of them reappeared.

Inos released a long breath. She felt nauseated. She was still shaking. She would have nightmares for years . . . so be it!

If had been the sheik's justice, not hers.

"Now my aunt, your Greatness?"

"Of course. And First Lionslayer will be here shortly. Come, then."

He led the way across the meadow, walking within the moving circle of his own radiance. The grass fire that Kade had started had died away to a few red flickers and pale smoke drifting among the trees, so the forest was not going to burn down. The sky was full of stars already—night came more swiftly here than it did in Krasnegar.

Do what is right, not what feels right. No, it had not been her father who'd told her that. That had been one of Rap's little homilies. Rap had been full of such sayings. She'd often teased him about them. The whole gang had teased Rap about his proverbs; not that teasing Rap had ever been difficult or even very satisfying, because he'd never seemed to mind much. He'd never lost his temper like a jotunn or screamed like an imp; he'd just shrugged and gone his own way.

Why should she be thinking of Rap now? Because of the chase? Because of running from the men in terror, as she'd often run from Rap in play? She could well remember him catching her and pulling her down on the sand, and holding her there until she let him kiss her—when they'd been smaller, of course. Not in the last year or two. They'd only kissed once after kissing had become a serious activity.

Or was it because Rap had died for her, and now four more men had died because of her? Maybe that was it.

And the sheik had already reached the dead horse, and Kade was clambering to her feet, decently dressed already, like Inos herself, but looking very bewildered.

Inos ran to her, and they hugged.

4

Elkarath was throwing power around by the barrelful. The dead horse vanished, and in its place appeared a bonfire, a pyramid of logs crackling and sparking and casting a welcome light. Then he created a circle of rugs around it.

"We have a little time to kill," he said. "Let us enjoy this fine evening." He glanced around the clearing. "There is no danger . . . yet."

He sat down and crossed his legs, chuckling at the women's exclamations of wonder. "Be seated, ladies! Now, have you a preference in wine, Highness?" His occult glow had faded away, and he was only a plump old man in a white robe and white headcloth. Firelight twinkled in his rubied headband.

"Oh, I defer to your expertise, Greatness," Kade simpered, settling on one of the rugs and tucking her legs around in the usual Zarkian position, with no more than her usual stiffness. If she had sustained injuries in her fall, then obviously the sorcerer had cured them, and her previous uneasiness had gone completely.

How much her emotions were being suppressed Inos could not tell. It would not be out of character for Kade to survive even her recent ordeal without losing her poise. She had the barest trace of a tremor in her hands and her eyes were jumpy, but otherwise she was almost her old self. Indeed she was in much better spirits than she had been since entering Thume that morning. Whatever fears she had felt were apparently now dispelled by the guardian presence of the sheik.

Misted silver flasks of wine arrived beside each of them, and a first sip convinced Inos that the vintage was as fine as anything in Duke Angilki's cellar, or Azak's. It was cold, too, and even the Palace of Palms had trouble maintaining an adequate supply of snow for chilling the princes' wine, snow brought from the mountains by fast camels.

Kade glanced around at the looming night. The treetops were dark fingers waving against the stars. "Those . . . er, ruffians?" She had been told that they had been disposed of, and had asked no questions. "They were pixies? Live pixies?"

The sheik nodded, sipping his wine. Snow-bearded, cheeks rouged by desert life, he seemed like everyone's ideal grand-pappy. His voice was slow and placid as a glacier. His eyes would twinkle under the heavy white brows once in a while; but to catch a real look at those eyes was almost impossible. Inos wondered whether his benevolent air was genuine, or if he was again projecting an occult glamour to fog her mind. Perhaps he did so automatically, without thinking, as a shopkeeper used politeness, "It would appear that there are still pixies living in Thume," he agreed.

"Then there may be more of them around?" Again Kade eyed the darkness beyond the firelight.

"I strongly suspect that there must be women somewhere, as the race continues to thrive." He chuckled. "And other males. And yes, they may seek vengeance." He sipped his wine to heighten suspense. "There is a band approaching. They are coming upriver, but they are still a long way off. They may not know about us at all. If they bring a sorcerer against me, of course, then we are lost, but at the moment I detect no one within a league of us— other than a rather footsore young djinn making slow progress in the dark. I have kept him heading in the right direction," he assured Inos, "and he can see the fire now."

Inos shivered. Elkarath was human; he needed sleep and he could he deceived, as she had proved at Tall Cranes. How strong a defense could he maintain against the dangers of Thume? "But when these others arrive . . . how many?"

"I don't know. Many."

Why didn't he know? "But even if you . . . if you deal with those, a whole army of pixies may creep up on us before dawn?"

The old man shook his head, studying the condensation on his goblet. "We must be gone by dawn."

Apparently he was not about to explain, and Inos felt a twinge of uneasiness.

Elkarath beamed, though, smiling toward each of his companions in turn, but indirectly. "Shall we dine, ladies?" Three silver dishes appeared, sparkling in the firelight, heaped with fragrant curry, vegetables, and snowy rice.

Inos knew that she was hungry, but her insides were still very quivery. Nevertheless, she had rejected Elkarath's occult soothing, so she must keep up a pretense of calm. She reached for the food and promptly scalded her fingers. For a few minutes, silence . . .

"The . . . ruffians . . . did you no harm, Aunt?' she inquired between mouthfuls.

"No, dear. They shouted a lot of questions at me, but I could only understand about one word in four. So they gave up on me." Even in the flickering firelight, Kade's blush showed. "I'm afraid a fat old woman was of no interest to them. You were what they wanted." She looked anxiously at her niece. Inos had assured her that there had been no lasting harm done, but even so . . .

"You were fortunate that they did not cut your throat at once, Highness," Elkarath remarked placidly. "But I congratulate you on your diversionary exploit with the horse. I was near enough to observe, but not yet close enough to exert any influence. That was a rare display of courage, and of horsemanship."

Kade blushed more deeply. "One does what one can," she murmured.

"And I congratulate you on your skill at *thali*, also!"

"Oh, dear!" Kade turned redder than Inos had ever seen her and avoided her niece's eye.

The sheik chuckled deeply. "Her Majesty the Sultana warned me to look out for you. I admit I had grown careless."

Curious! The sheik thought Kade had planned that little deception? For a moment Inos was tempted to claim the credit, and then decided to be discreet, for once. Odd, though! Why had Rasha been wary of Kade?

The conversation had strayed onto dangerous ground. For a while all three attended to their meal in a silence broken only by the busy crackling of the fire. Flame-tinged smoke drifted away in the wind, and sparks soared up to join the stars. Inos was still trembling from her experience with the pixies. The thought of a band of many others arriving was unnerving, but she was not going to start jumping at shadows, and if the old man was hoping to rattle her, then she would disappoint him. She told herself sternly that an encounter with the mythical pixies was a once-in-a-lifetime experience, and this firelit picnic in a haunted forest was at least a memorable one. She did not need occult swaddling to let her enjoy herself, even if her mouth did seem drier than usual and swallowing harder.

"This curry is superb, Greatness," she said.

"Thank you. My dear mother made it like this, you see."

"And you have taught me that the protection of a sorcerer should not be discarded so lightly."

"Ah!" He sighed. "I am no sorcerer, ma'am. I dearly wish I was, at the moment. You would not have escaped from a sorcerer so readily."

"Then . . . Not a sorcerer?" Inos looked at Kade and saw a reflection of her own astonishment.

"I am but a mage," Elkarath said. "Like my grandfather before me, and his, also."

"A votary of Sultana Rasha's, though?"

He nodded—sadly, she thought. "That is so. She detected me before I knew of her existence. But I am content to serve her."

Given that lead and the old man's benevolent mood, Inos sensed a chance to satisfy her longstanding curiosity about magic. Was he seeking to distract her, though? "We are ignorant in such matters, Greatness. Will you explain the distinction?"

He chuckled as if he had expected the question. "A mage, knowing but three words, can perform only magic, not full sorcery."

"What is the difference?"

"Sorcery is permanent, magic only temporary. It varies—people are more easily influenced than inanimate objects. Healing the lionslayer and your aunt was relatively simple. I put a sleep spell on you every evening. That happens to be one of the easier magics, and it lasted until morning without reinforcement. But the euphoria spell I used on you by day tended to weaken unless I remembered to restore it at frequent intervals." He sipped his wine thoughtfully. "A sorcerer would have called you back out of the hills easily. And of course, I had to delay my pursuit until I had sorted out the tangle you had created. I tell yon true, Tall Cranes was in considerable uproar."

Inos gulped.

Kade glanced at her warningly. "You are gracious not to bear us ill will, Greatness," she murmured.

"I was a trifle irked, that first morning," the mage said, "but at my age, one sees the humor in such situations. It was well done."

Relieved, Inos began to frame more questions in her mind, but then Azak came stalking in from the dark.

The front of his kibr was black with dried blood, and the expression on his face was blacker yet. About to leap up and welcome him, Inos abruptly changed her mind.

Oh, poor Azak! To be defeated by sorcery was a permissible defeat for a mundane—hard as that admission would be for him—but to be bushwacked by a band of ragtag youths was abysmal incompetence.

Perhaps never in his life before had he known real humiliation. His reputation for infallibility was shattered. He had failed his chosen. He had been rescued from his own folly by hateful magic, and that might be hurting worst of all. His mood was obviously murderous as he folded his arms and glared across the fire at the sheik.

Never in Arakkaran had Inos thought she could ever feel sorry for Azak ak'Azakar, but she felt sorry for him now. And to offer sympathy would be to rub salt in the wound with a stonemason's brush.

"Welcome, Lionslayer," Elkarath said mildly. A very large dish of food appeared on the rug at Azak's feet.

The big man ignored it. "I am no lionslayer!"

The old man frowned warningly. "Be seated, ak'Azakar."

Azak ground his teeth. "You are a votary of that unspeakable slut, Rasha!"

Inos felt her heart sink lower still. Azak did not know how to be humble, how to handle humiliation. He was not familiar with failure as ordinary mortals were—how he must be suffering! She kept her eyes on her dish, but the food had turned to sawdust in her mouth. Poor Azak!

"I offer you hospitality," Elkarath said quietly

"I refuse it."

Azak's legs seemed to collapse beneath him, and he tumbled to the ground. Inos choked back a protest, and Kade gestured warningly to her. This was not fair! He struggled to sit up, supporting himself with his arms, and livid with fury.

"Yes," the sheik remarked, to no one in particular, "I do serve her Majesty. Why she did not bind you all to her service likewise, I do not know." He glanced a brief smile in the direction of Inos. "I suspect that in your case it may be something to do with the warlocks and your destiny as queen of Krasnegar—great sorcerers may be able to tell what spells have been cast on a person in the past. I don't know that, but such may be the case. Anyway, my instructions were to use deceit as long as possible. It was an amusing sport."

He chuckled, and a sound of grinding teeth came from Azak's direction.

But he had mentioned Inos's homeland. "Then Krasnegar is still . . . The matter has not been settled?"

"I have had no recent news," Elkarath said calmly, popping a wad of rice into his mouth.

"And the sultana truly intends to put me on the throne of my fathers?"

He shrugged. "So she says. I do not question her purposes, you understand."

Kade was beaming.

"She also intends to marry me off to a goblin?" Inos demanded.

Elkarath shot her a brief, elusive glance from under his shaggy white brows. "And if she does? To defy a sorceress is incredible folly, young lady. You told me tonight that you dislike having your emotions dictated to you. Queen Rasha may now decide to make you *want* to marry a goblin."

Inos flinched and felt suddenly ill. She rubbed her fingers on the grass, lacking the stomach even to lick them clean in approved Zarkian style. Fall in love with a goblin? She looked across at Azak's insensately furious face.

127

His hatred of sorcery suddenly seemed more understandable. It was indeed a great evil.

The prospect appalled her. The sorceress could make her fall in love with anyone—Azak, or some eligible imp, or even a detestable goblin. And she would accept her fate with joy! Horror!

"So her Majesty was aware of our intention to leave Arakkaran?" Kade inquired politely.

"She instigated it, I am sure."

"To conceal my niece from the wardens?"

"Correct. Warlocks are accustomed to getting their own way. Inosolan is a valuable property, as I understand the politics. They would certainly have penetrated the palace quickly."

Kade's extractions of information were usually subtle, but now she was clearly exploiting the old man's willingness to talk. "The wraith my niece saw, that first night," she queried. "That was your doing?"

The old man frowned. "No. That was nothing of mine."

"Then it was Rasha's?" Inos demanded.

He shook his head, and fires flashed from the rubies. "I think not. She was expecting to be under surveillance. She told me she would not even observe our departure, lest she reveal our whereabouts."

"But . . ." Inos shivered. "You mean it really was a wraith?"

Rap? Oh, poor Rap!

Elkarath shrugged his bulky shoulders. "Or else it was a sending fiom someone else. I did not awake in time to observe whether there was sorcery at work."

"Sending?" Inos repeated. "What sort of sending?"

"From another sorcerer. A warlock, perchance."

Inos's heart thumped hard with shock. "You can't mean that Rap may still be alive?"

The old man shrugged again. "Who knows? I expected trouble . . . but nothing further has transpired. Strange! I cannot explain that either, ma'am."

Rap alive? For some reason that information was stunning. Inos took a long draft of wine while she mulled over the news. She had never wanted to believe that Rap had been so wicked that he would have remained after death as an evil wraith. How could he ever have escaped the imps? How could he have arranged a sending? How . . .

No. Sadly she decided that it was impossible. Rap could never have survived the legionaries' wrath.

Kade was still interrogating the old man. "And what happens when we reach Ullacarn?"

He chewed and swallowed. "There we shall await further instructions. It is a pleasant city."

Inos glanced miserably at Azak, whose scowl could not nave been deeper. *All things include both the Evil and the Good.* Her joy at being rescued from the pixies had blinded her to the evil in that deliverance. Would even four pixies have been worse than one goblin, a lifetime with a goblin?

Once Ullacarn had been the first stop on the way to appeal to the wardens. Now it might be the first stop on the way to permanent slavery. She would be turned over to the warlock of the east, while Rasha reclaimed her favorite plaything, Azak.

Kade glanced uneasily at the encircling night. "But first we must reach Ullacarn. You say we shall be gone by dawn . . . Must we return through that dreadful pass in the dark?"

Elkarath shook his head in a vigorous torrent of red fire. "No! That pass would not be wise at any time, I fear."

"I am glad to hear it!" Kade said sharply. "Nothing has ever so depressed me as the sight of all those . . . statues."

"Why unwise?" Inos asked.

He sipped his wine, studying the fire over the lip of the goblet. "I am only a mage, ma'am. I cannot normally detect the occult at work. That ability is beyond my powers except in a few special cases, such as knowing when my farsight is blocked. I assume that others of my standing are similarly limited. But I think I felt something when I came through that pass. Even if I was mistaken, it may well be that some of the spell still lingers."

Inos frowned, not comprehending.

"The spell would have been directional," he explained with a trace of impatience, "It was cast against the fleeing refugees. We all came safely into Thume. We might not go out so easily."

"Turned to stone?"

"Maybe not. It may be too weak for that now, but it might still cripple us, or kill us. No, I would not try to go that way for all the gems in Kerith."

Inos shot another glance at Azak, and now he was looking marginally more interested and less murderous.

"I have other means," Elkarath explained, deflecting the next question before it was asked. Again Inos wondered if he was less confident than he wished them to think. "You have led me a merry dance these last few days, but I enjoyed it." He raised his goblet in salute to Kade.

"And how did you catch us, Greatness?"

"Oh, it wasn't hard to follow your trail. Compared to a mage, a lionslayer is a blind kitten."

Azak bared his teeth in fury and the old man smiled softly at the fire.

"Did you truly expect to escape me, ak'Azakar?"

"I was hoping that you would not dare exert your foul ability so close to Ullacarn."

"Ah! Well, that was a consideration, I admit, but of course I must accomplish my mission, and I had to take the risk. First, though, I had to make arrangements for the rest of my goods and people. I did not set out until yesterday at dawn."

"Then you made excellent time," Kade said approvingly.

Elkarath nodded to his hands in smug agreement. "This is a very pleasant evening, is it not? I hope you have noticed that magic is efficacious in deflecting mosquitoes?" He glanced benignly across at Azak. "You are quite sure you will not dine with us, Lionslayer?"

Again Azak angrily refused hospitality. Angry or not, he must be starving, so he was letting his sense of failure make him act very childishly. Why must some men be stubborn, so pigheaded? Inos felt herself oppressed by a strange nostalgia that she could not place.

"It was not difficult to follow you," the mage said mildly. "Although it became a little harder this side of the mountains."

"When the trail was warmer?" Azak growled skeptically. Using his arms, he levered himself back, moving his feet farther from the fire.

"When sorcery was interfering with it."

"I saw no signs of people."

"But obviously there are people." The old man glanced out at the darkness, and Inos instinctively did the same. Shapes moved in the gloom and she thought her heart had stopped forever, until she saw that they were the horses and mules, all returned, silent as ghosts, a cordon of mute spectators. She shivered.

"I also saw places with occult shielding," Elkarath said, "or rather I did not see them. My farsight was blocked, and I suspected that my eyesight was being deceived also and that what seemed to be woods were otherwise. Sometimes your tracks vanished altogether, and sometimes they made no sense. Thume is inhabited!"

"Then how did you find us, Greatness?" Kade inquired, licking her fingers with panache, although she had probably never done so in her life before she came to Zark.

"I had some assistance." The old man stretched out a hand, letting firelight flicker on his jewels.

"The ring?" Azak said. "That was not all pigswill you threw at us?"

"No." The old man's voice dropped half an octave. "But I lied when I said it was a family heirloom. Her Majesty created it specially for me." He peered thoughtfully at his fingers. "It isn't showing anything very much at the moment . . . Normally it lets me detect sorcery as a full sorcerer can, but Thume does not seem to influence it. There is nothing indicated from along the valley there, where the people are. And yet they are approaching very swiftly."

"Could Thume magic be different?" Inos was definitely uneasy now.

The mage shrugged. "Possibly. Earlier today, though, it was flickering green all the time; jumpy as fleas on a dead dog."

"And how did that help?" Azak asked sharply.

"I followed you with it."

For a moment the other three stared blankly at one another. The mage sipped his wine in silent amusement. Then he peered obliquely at Inos, his gaze guarded below his brows. "You inherited a word of power, child. Her Majesty was quite puzzled that it had not yet manifested itself in some special talent. She told me to watch out for it, and she gave me this device to detect it. Today, for the first time, I saw the gadget react."

"I . . . I was using magic?" Inos hoped that this was some complicated Zarkian joke. She had never told Azak about Inisso's word of power, and she dared not look to see how he was reacting to the news. Azak detested magic in any form.

"One of you was," the mage said. "Green light means one word, a genius. The areas I thought might be occult enclaves did not register. If I was right, then they are very well shielded. No, the power came from you. One of you, and if not you, who else?"

"I couldn't have been! Aunt—did you see me doing anything unusual? Azak?"

Kade shot a worried glance at Azak, then told Inos, "No, dear."

The old man stroked his beard. "I am puzzled, I admit. It was merely an occult talent at work; no moving of mountains. You weren't . . . well, taking tracking lessons from First Lionslayer, perhaps? Pathfinding? Singing? Sensing magic, maybe?"

Inos shook her head. "I don't think I've done anything today that I haven't done a thousand times before. Except nearly being raped, of course."

"No—earlier than that. On your way here."

Kade would always seek to break an awkward silence. She coughed softly to gain attention. "In the Impire, Greatness, they have a saying about frying pans and fires. You know it?"

"In Zark we talk about 'dodging the lion and rousing the lioness.' The same idea?"

"Exactly. I am beginning to think that my niece has an occult talent along those very lines."

He chuckled. "I do believe you have solved the mystery!"

Kade smiled thinly. "But even if this magic finder pointed in our direction, sir," she said, "is it not conceivable that it was seeing someone else? Might there have been someone following us closely, and that person was the source of the magic?"

"I suppose . . ." The mage nodded thoughtfully. "Invisibility, for example? If you had an invisible companion . . . but no. That would require a higher grade of power than I detected. Magic, at least."

Azak made an angry growling sound. "I had not been informed of this word of power. It explains many things." He glared at Inos with a red intensity that shocked her.

"You have another explanation?" inquired the sheik.

"The four who ambushed me?"

Elkarath shook his head. "They came from the north. They found your trail and tracked you. Quite separate from what I had been seeing."

Azak grunted. "But have you considered *why* they might have trailed us?"

Elkarath just shook his head. "Only that possibly all visitors to Thume are hunted down as fair game."

"I thought their purpose was quite evident," Inos snapped.

Azak snapped back: "Exactly!"

She began to feel her own anger rising to deflect whatever accusation he was about to make. "They called me an *outsider*. I think that was what they said. As if it were a dirty word, like . . . like *vermin*."

Hastily Kade interjected, "This would explain the mystery, the disappearances—"

But Inos was glaring back at the smolder in Azak's eye. "You have another idea?"

"I mean that the four might have been reacting to magic, also."

"I don't think I quite grasp your Majesty's meaning," Kade said sharply.

"It is clear enough. Your niece is very attractive, like a lodestone! That might explain why the four curs were drawn here."

"Azak!" Inos cried. "What are you saying?"

"I am saying that mayhap you bewitched me, woman, and mayhap you bewitched those others today."

"No! No! I—"

"Oh, maybe you don't know you're doing it," Azak roared. "But why should four young men out on a hunt suddenly turn into ravening rapist monsters?"

And why should a djinn sultan fall in love?—but he did not go so far as to say that.

Had he slapped her, he could not have shocked her more. She cowered back. The idea was unthinkable—that she might have used occult mastery on Azak, as Andor had once used it on her? Yes, of course she had tried to impress him, but not that way. Horrible! Odious! That she might be a sort of occult mermaid, luring innocent youths and inciting them to attack her, and thus provoke their deaths at the sheik's hands . . . No! Inconceivable!

Horrorstruck, she turned to appeal to Elkarath.

He was frowning and stroking his beard. "You are a very beautiful woman, Queen Inosolan, and I am not surprised that Sultan Azak is smitten by your charms, occult or not. But that you could summon four strangers, sight unseen, and enrage them into a mating frenzy . . . I suppose anything is possible to the occult. But you do not provoke riots wherever you go! Why should it only have happened today?"

Azak curled his bushy red mustache in a sneer. "Perhaps pixies are especially susceptible."

Again Inos recoiled from the thought. Four young men bewitched unknowingly by her and then executed by the sheik because of it? And now there was an even larger band of men hastening up the valley to find her? No, no! Madness! Filthy madness! "You mean I'm a sort of bitch in heat, summoning all the dogs in town?"

The two men avoided her eye. Kade bit her lip and colored.

The sheik sighed. "Well, I shall report the event to my mistress and let her draw conclusions. Meanwhile—" He peered up at the stars, "—it would be about the second hour of the night, I think?"

"About," Azak agreed.

"Then we can be on our way. Lionslayer, I have summoned the mounts. Go and strip off their harnesses; we shall give them their freedom. And bring me the saddlebags from my pony."

Azak's jaw snapped closed. "To hear my lord is to obey!" He accompanied the words with a glare of hatred. Scrambling to his feet, evidently now cured of his paralysis, he marched off into the dark. As he went, he adjusted the hang of his scimitar, perhaps dreaming of what he would like to do to a merchant who treated him as a flunky.

"Your Highness," Elkarath said, "is there anything in your baggage that you wish to retain? We can take little with us, but any special things?"

"Oh!" Kade glanced in the direction of the little windbreak that Azak had built. "Well, my breviary . . ."

"Then perhaps you would fetch that now, ma'am? Here Elkarath gestured, and then held out to Kade a large ball of bluish light.

Kade said, "Oh!" again.

"Take it. It is not hot."

Kade rose stiffly. She took the globe uncertainly in both hands. Holding it well away from her, she plodded off through the long grass.

Inos poured a small amount of wine into her goblet, and sipped it while she waited to see whether she was to be given secrets or a scolding.

For several minutes, though, the old man merely toyed with his bejeweled fingers, seeming to study the sparkles as he moved them in the firelight.

133

At length he said, "I do not speak as a mage now. Nor as a votary of the sultana, although I could not speak at all if I thought my words would hurt her interests. I speak only as a very old man to a very young woman. I seek no good but yours, Queen Inosolan. Can you accept, just for a few minutes, that sometimes the elderly do indeed possess wisdom?"

"I shall try, sir," Inos said with Kinvale sweetness. It was to be a scolding, obviously.

"That is all I ask. Listen carefully, then. I am very old. Much older than you perhaps suspect. If I tallied up my years . . . well, just say that I have spent as many of them, in total, in desert lands as you have been upon this earth. At least. And there is something in the desert that breaks away the husks from people. Desert light is very strong, very revealing."

Inos said nothing and he did not look up to appreciate her carefully crafted smile of interest.

"And I have spent many more years—in total—in Ullacarn, and Angot, and other outposts of the Impire. I probably understand the imps and their ways better than any other man in Arakkaran; or any woman either. I realize that you are not one of his Imperial Majesty's subjects, but your background and the ways in which you were raised are closer to those of an imp than they are to anyone else's. Is this not so, my dear?"

"Of course, Greatness."

He sighed. "And I say that he is not for you. Oh, he is besotted with you, and you may think you are in love with him. No, hear me out, child! He is a fine man, in his way. He is a perfect sultan for Arakkaran, unless he survives long enough to become bored with accomplishment. Then he will wade the red path of war. They always do, his kind. Fortunately for us humbler folk, sultans rarely live that long. Physically, of course, he is unmatched . . .

"And what he is to my mistress I do not even begin to understand. The purposes of sorcerers are cryptic and obscure. She has come by strange ways to her power. She seeks to punish men long dead, I fear." He sighed again and reached for his goblet.

Inos waited politely. There was more lecture to come.

"If he would only compromise . . ." Elkarath droned. "Bow the knee just once! Say the words she wants to hear! I think she then would gladly be to him whatever he wanted: lover, mother helper . . ."

"She would see through his lies at once," Inos muttered, disgusted.

"Perhaps," the old man said softly. "But he would have said them! And I think she might then be content. I expect a sorceress can deliberately deceive herself, just as any of us can. We all believe what we want to believe, not questioning, lest we lift scabs from unhealed wounds. We all seek happiness. Who knows what she seeks—now, after such a lifetime? Might not one kind word won be counted a triumph?"

He drank and the goblet faded from his hand. Then he raised his face to peer at the stars, or perhaps the restless treetops, and she had a clear view of his blood-red eyes and the haggard folds of his neck

"But even without the dangers from Sultana Rasha, child, I tell you that you are making a grievous error. Even if the two of you flee to your kingdom at the far end of the world, you shall not find happiness with Azak ak'Azakar. Yes, he has promised. I am sure he has promised. He lusts after you and cannot have you, so he will persuade himself of anything. Yet many a good marriage has sprung from that seed! No, it is his background that is wrong. He loves you? Meaning he wishes to possess you and breed sons with you, and, yes, I suppose he wishes to make you happy. But he is not capable of making you happy, no matter how sincere he is."

"I entirely agree."

"I am serious, child."

"So am I, Greatness. Perhaps my Imperial ways have deceived you, and I do fear they may have misled His Majesty. It is not unknown within the Impire for men and women to be merely friends."

"When I told you that he had not been killed by the pixies—"

"I was delighted, yes. Naturally! Azak and I have much in common, from our royal birth to our problems with sorcery. It is natural that we should find grounds for friendship. I admire him, enjoy his company, appreciate his invaluable help. On my side, at least, there is nothing more." So there!

The mage studied her sadly, in the longest straight gaze he had ever given her, firelight chasing odd shadows over the desert landscape of his face. Then he sighed deeply and looked away.

"There may be more than you think already," he said. "And how long can you resist his wooing? To be sought after by a man of his power and presence—it is very flattering."

"Very!" Inos said through clenched teeth. First Kade, now him! Could the old never learn to trust the young? "But Sultan Azak is my friend and political ally. Nothing more."

The mage sighed again, and looked away.

An elderly djinn . . .

Silly old man.

Azak emerged from the darkness holding a bulky leather bag.

"Ah!" The old man sprang to his feet with youthful agility. "The newcomers are advancing very rapidly. We must depart before they draw any closer. Now, let me see . . ."

He fumbled with the bag's fastenings and then pulled out a bundle that glittered like cloth of gold. He turned to study the ground nearby and wandered off with his head bent as if in search of something. Azak tossed away the bag and folded his arms. He scowled after the sheik, ignoring Inos.

Kade came stumping wearily back across the meadow, still holding the blue light. Inos walked over to meet her, and they exchanged worried smiles. Kade put the light down on the grass as carefully as if it were fine crystal. She straightened and took her niece's hand. Her fingers trembled slightly. Or maybe that was Inos herself.

"This seems flat enough here," Elkarath announced from the far limits of the firelight. "And that way is north."

He shook out a cloth, which flashed and gleamed, and spread surprisingly large. It floated to the ground, then seemed to wriggle and squirm of its own accord, until it was lying flat—completely fiat, although it was obviously extremely thin.

Almost dragging her aunt, Inos hurried over.

"I've seen this before! Rasha called it a welcome mat." Inos also recalled that the mat had been dangerously hypnotic in the palace. Here in the starlit dark of the forest it lay like black water, displaying faint shimmers of light that seemed to come from deep within it, as from goldfish moving in a shadowed pond. She tried not to look at it.

"Indeed?" The old man beamed briefly. He seemed to be reveling in some secret anticipation, like a child expecting a treat. "It is a magic carpet. Her Majesty gave it to me for just such an emergency as this. It may be the very one you saw."

Avoiding Inos, Azak paced over to the edge of the mat and glared down at it.

Elkarath studied the sky again for a moment. "Yes, that is north . . . To make return journeys, of course, one needs three of them. We have only two; but then we do not plan to return to Thume, do we?" He chuckled and rubbed his hands.

Then he glanced thoughtfully downriver.

"Where is the other, then?" Inos asked, feeling prickles of apprehension. She tried to catch Azak's eye, but he was watching the sheik.

"If Skarash did as he was told, it is now laid out in my house in Ullacarn. If he didn't . . . then we may shortly be in some difficulty. Ready?"

"What do we have to do?" she asked, feeling Kade's grip tighten.

"Just stand together on the carpet. I shall come on last, as it is prespelled to my person."

"And then?" Azak growled, fingering the hilt of his scimitar.

"Then it will position itself upon the one in Ullacarn. That is how they work."

Azak was suspicious. "You told me you dared not use much power near Ullacarn, yet now you work a major sorcery like this?"

"Be silent!" the mage said sharply. "Silence beseems the ignorant. The whole point of magical devices is that they are much harder to detect than brute power. Now—must I coerce you?"

Azak shrugged and took two long strides, which put him in the center of the mat, but it did not flex or dimple under his weight. Inos glanced at her aunt, and they advanced gingerly together, holding hands. The surface felt rigid, and rather slippery.

"There!" Elkarath said. "I suggest you stoop a little, Lionslayer—the ceiling may be a trifle low. Right! Now me."

He took two fast steps onto the mat, causing it to twist, and lurch. Kade cried out, and Inos steadied her. Then they found their balance again, blinking in the sudden brightness of lamps hung on crumbling plaster walls.

Azak cautiously raised his head and scowled at the sloping rafters just above him. Street noises of hooves and voices and wheels drifted in from the dark beyond the open window. The scent of grass and trees was replaced by smells of candles and spices and old cooking.

"Welcome to Ullacarn," said Elkarath.

Life and death:
  O to dream, O to awake and wander
  There, and with delight to take and render,
  Through the trance of silence,
      Quiet breath;
  Lo! for there, among the flowers and grasses,
  Only the mightier movement sounds and passes;
  Only winds and river,
      Life and death.

                              Stevenson, *In the Highlands*

7

The splendour falls

1

B
efuddled with exhaustion, Rap stared blankly at a hole in a cliff. The night was bright with stars, and the air pleasantly cool on his skin, but for a while he did not understand what he was doing. Then he remembered the last part: darkness and picking his way through the tangled and shattered rocks with his farsight. His feet were slashed bloody, his ankles and knees swollen like dropsy, even his arms all gashed and bruised. In the foggy nightmare that was what he recalled of the journey, he could vaguely remember carrying Gathmor for an hour or two, but now he was alone, and at the end of his powers. His companions were long lost behind him, their mundane strength broken by efforts to obey a sorcerous command.

The gnome boy had vanished, last seen still skipping as freshly as ever. So this cave must be Rap's destination. It was perfectly circular, bored by sorcery through draperies of black rock where a cliff had been melted. Dragons had been at work here, obviously, and his farsight was blocked; which likely meant that he was close to a sorcerer's lair. But it could be anything's lair—leopards or bears might lurk inside.

For a moment he leaned wearily against the rock. He ought to be terrified. He ought to be fighting the compulsion that he could feel growing in him again. Perhaps he was merely too exhausted to think straight, and yet some strange inner hunch was telling him that the summoning had been a good thing, an opportunity—that fortune was favoring him by bringing him here.

That crazy illusion must be part of the summoning itself! Unable to resist longer, he dropped to hands and knees and crawled into the pipe. The wind blowing through it was cool with the chill of ancient stone and long-forgotten caverns.

The barrier was thicker than any mundane castle wall, but he emerged eventually into a deep crevice, open to the stars. Rugged rocky walls towered up on either hand, close enough that he could touch them. The floor was smooth and level, but speckled with unpleasantly sharp pebbles. Here and there giant blocks had fallen from the peaks and jammed in the gorge to make archways; any smaller debris must have been removed. He hobbled along, following its turns and twists into the mountain for ten or fifteen minutes, recognizing that this cryptic entrance had been designed to be dragonproof; he could guess at its immense antiquity. Finally the burrow was blocked by a wall of rough masonry. Faint, spectral light spilled out through a kennel-size door.

He crouched down and recoiled before the familiar stench of gnome. Gnomes were scavengers and carrion eaters, tolerated in many places because they removed every scrap of garbage. They were certainly better than alternative vermin such as rats, but never pleasant companions. No one but a gnome would ever enter a gnome burrow—except that Rap now seemed to have no choice. Even a moment of hesitation was bringing back his compulsion to chase after the little boy.

Very reluctantly, and holding his nose, he ducked through and straightened up at once, gagging and retching. His eyes watered.

This was no burrow. He was inside a huge hall, whose walls soared up like great cliffs of masonry to an indistinct luminous fog that hid the ceiling and shed a dim bluish light over the rest of the vast space. There were many deep shadows, though, not all of which seemed readily explainable.

The floor was carved from the living rock, buried now below an oozing carpet of corruption—gnomes did unpleasant things at their front doors to discourage visitors. Here and there his farsight was blocked, or at least blurred, as if by ancient, forgotten barriers. He could see shapes that didn't feel quite solid, including gigantic rings of stone set in the walls; other shapes he could sense and not see in the dimness. The whole place had a sinister, sorcerous feel to it. And it stank worse than any pig farm he could imagine.

On a low stone wall at the far side of this enormous chamber sat his elusive quarry, the little boy. He, at least, was real. He was watching Rap with an understandably satisfied grin, while again stirring the inside of his nose with a finger.

Water! That parapet enclosed a circular pool of water! Holding a hand just below his nostrils in the hope that the smell of his own skin would overcome the other smells—it didn't—Rap limped carefully across the vast room. There was no way he could avoid treading in filth, but he hoped not to slip and sit down in it. The water, when he reached it, proved to be coated with green slime, but he brushed that aside with his hand and knelt to drink. Although it tasted about the way he had always suspected stable washings would taste, he was dried out like a raisin, and he sucked up bucketfuls of the odious brew. At least he could be sure that gnomes would not have been using it for bathwater.

Then he sank down on his buttocks and wiped his face with his hand, and realized that he was sitting in the mire after all. What the Evil did it matter?

His second word of power seemed to have granted him some occult ability to ignore pain, and he suspected that without it he would be screaming. He knew it was there, though—his butchered feet, his joints, his muscles—but at last the compulsion had gone, the spell was lifted, and the mere act of sitting down at last brought a wave of fatigue that threatened to push him over into instant sleep. And the pain came rushing in as soon as his attention faltered. He sat up straighter, suppressed the pain, and glared blearily up at the boy who had led him here.

"I'm Rap."

The boy sniggered.

"Don't you have a name, sonny?"

The boy removed his finger long enough to say, "Ugish," and giggle. He had more teeth than a pike. And sharper.

"You're a sorcerer, Ugish?"

A bigger grin and a head shake. Gnomes were by preference nocturnal, but Rap had met them in Durthing. He had seen them in Finrain and on his trips to Milflor. Their eyes were very large, and round, showing almost no white. In daylight they showed almost no pupil either, only a shiny black iris. Ugish's eyes were large, but different—the whites bright amid the dirt, and the irises bronze, with an intense luster. So perhaps there was more than one type of gnome.

Not all the inhabitants of Krasnegar had been notable for their personal cleanliness and some were notoriously unpopular companions indoors, but no other race seemed to enjoy filth as gnomes did.

Rap tried a smile. "Then who—*ulp!*"

A woman had emerged from a doorway and was striding around the end of the trough, coming toward them. Rap quickly pulled up his knees and clasped his arms around his shins.

She was no gnome—tall as he, and of a striking build. At first he could not even guess at her race. She wore a loose dress, dirty, sleeveless and short, and so tattered that it was indecent, but she moved with grace and poise. She was every bit as filthy as the boy, her skin color indeterminate and her long hair a disgusting slimy tangle halfway down her back. Then he saw the sweat-washed tufts in her armpits, and they were bright gold.

And her eyes! They were very large, and oddly slanted, their irises gleaming with a wonder of rainbow fires, like opal or mother-of-pearl. So her skin would be golden also; she was an elf. He had glimpsed a few elves in Milflor and Finrain, but never close to. He could not tell her age, but he thought she might be very beautiful if she were clean.

And now Rap understood Ugish's eyes, although he had never heard of a gnome halfbreed before.

Rap hugged his knees tighter as she stopped and bobbed a hint of a curtsy to him.

"I am Athal'rian, of course." She smiled rather vacantly, making faint cracks appear in the coating on her face. She scratched her scalp absent-mindedly.

"I'm Rap, ma'am. I . . . I haven't any clothes."

She frowned. "Oh, but . . . Well, Ugish, give him yours for now."

Grinning, the boy untied the rag that was all he wore and held it out to Rap, who recoiled in disgust. It was not something he would willing touch with a long stick, but he did not want to offend his hosts. Gnomes were normally shy and inoffensive, but they must have feelings like anyone else, and elves certainly would.

So he accepted the tattered relic and its passengers, and rose to his feet with all the dignity he could feign. Fortunately the cloth was not long enough to tie around his hips, so he just held it in front of him like a towel, not letting it touch him. It was even less adequate for him than it had been for Ugish.

He could not stand without swaying.

Athal'rian smiled again and offered a black-nailed hand. "You are welcome to Warth Redoubt, Sorcerer. It is long since we had company for dinner."

Rap gulped and ignored the hand, as both of his were occupied. "I am no sorcerer, ma'am. I am merely an adept—and a very new one, at that."

She looked puzzled. "But I thought Ishist said you were using mastery on a . . . Oh, dear!" She was staring down—at his feet, Rap was relieved to see. "Don't those hurt? Ugish, run and tell your father to come."

The boy shrugged and sauntered away, taking his time and idly kicking at fungoid growths sprouting amid the ordure on the floor.

"You must forgive us, Adept! My husband must have thought . . . Tut! Do, please sit down." She waved at the edge of the trough.

Rap perched himself on the crumbling stone and reluctantly spread the slimy rag over his lap. Then she again offered a hand to shake, and he had no choice but to accept. He hoped she hadn't expected him to kiss it.

Still standing, Athal'rian began to talk in a tuneless singsong. "It is wonderful to have visitors! I haven't cooked a proper meal in ages. I mean, one gets used to gnomes' tastes, but . . . well, it was nice to dig up some of Mother's old recipes. Ishist made some really fresh things for me to use. Eating at table will be a good experience for the children. I thought he said three of you?"

Even sitting, Rap was swaying with fatigue. He wondered whether he was mad or she was. Or both. "My friends have less power even than me, ma'am. They are out there somewhere."

"Tsk! Well, we must have them brought in at once. There are leopards and other bad things out there. This is wild country, I'm told." She peered vaguely around the great empty chamber. "Do you dance, Adept Rap?"

"Er, not very well, ma'am."

"Oh."

Rap's eyelids began to droop, and at once a fire of agony consumed his feet. He jerked awake again. Keep talking . . .

"Ma'am, what is this place?"

"Place?" His hostess smiled, and for a moment said nothing more. Then her wits lurched into action again. "We call it the Mews, but of course we just use it for—" Rap had already seen what it was used for. "— but it was a mews, long ago." She gestured apologetically at one of the walls, and Rap saw that there was an archway there, blocked up. But originally it would have been big enough for . . .

"*Dragon* mews, ma'am?"

Another pause. "Dragon stables? We don't bring dragons in here."

"The castle is very old, though?"

"Older than the Protocol, Ishist says." She laughed.

"And now?" Was it just a refuge taken over by gnome squatters, or was there some reason for Rap to have been dragged here?

"Now?"

"This castle, ma'am? Who owns it?"

"Owns?" She smiled at his left ear for a moment. "Well, my husband—he's the great sorcerer Ishist, you know—he's dragonward. Has been for many years. So we live in Warth Redoubt. It's a very important job, but somebody has to do it."

Rap tried to work that out and felt himself slide away down the slope to sleep again. Again a jolt of agony focused his attention and jerked him awake.

He was surprised to note that three small children had appeared and were clustered around Athal'rian, clinging to her and regarding the stranger with deep suspicion. They were all naked, filthy, and stinking, all smaller than Ugish.

And they all had the big, gorgeous eyes. Each set was different—blue, magenta, rose pink—but all had the same intense brilliance. Most crosses resembled one parent more than another, just as he himself looked mostly faunish, and the only features these little gnomes had inherited from their elvish mother were those lustrous bright eyes.

"What exactly does a dragonward do, my lady?"

"*The* dragonward. There's only one! He keeps the dragons from straying beyond the Neck, of course. They keep nibbling away at the fence, and he has to keep putting it back. And he counts the hatchings and doles out metal and spells the fire chicks never to fly over water. It's very important!" She stooped to hear what one of the children needed to whisper to her so urgently.

What sort of a woman would marry a gnome? Live like a gnome? Let her children live like gnomes?

And obviously the dragonward was a warden's deputy, like the proconsul of Faerie. "So your husband works for me warlock of the south, ma'am?"

Athal'rian glanced up, beaming, her opalescent eyes flashing amber and viridian. "That's right, Warlock Lith'rian! Have you met Daddy?"

2

Ishist was me first tubby gnome Rap had ever seen. His bald scalp did not reach to Athal'rian's breasts, but she stooped to hug and kiss him as if they had been apart for some days or weeks, and he rose on tiptoe to return the embrace with what seemed to be equal affection. He had arrived with an escort of six fire chicks, and they now swooped and soared around the lovers, shining wisps of yellow and orange light in the murky dimness. Five of the six were the sort of incorporeal flame-being that Rap had seen before, brilliant wisps of no settled shape or substance, and some were no bigger than hummingbirds. The sixth, though, was the size of a seagull and visibly solid, a sinuous silvery dragon body writhing within a nimbus of fire. Flying with much more purpose and confidence, this one came swooping over to inspect him.

He froze nervously while it circled. He was sure he had not summoned it, and he hoped that the sorcerer would know that. Before he could decide whether he ought to send it away, it glided in and landed on his shoulder, heavier than he had expected, uncomfortably warm against his ear and neck, like a freshly baked loaf. Its claws were both sharp and very hot. He had to divert some of his pain-suppression efforts to the points where they were digging in, and his farsight saw beads of blood fizz and darken. It also kept shifting its grip. He did not care! The chick's corona turned bright blue, and when it rubbed its warm, scaly neck against his, he felt a wash of pleasure that was astonishingly enjoyable. It was a romp with a puppy. It was a dog's tongue and tail telling him he was the nicest guy in the world. It was almost as good as kissing a pretty girl. Now he understood Bright Water's pleasure at having a baby dragon as a pet.

He raised a hand to stroke the smooth, hot scales, and the fire chick purred in his mind, radiating love, blazing up in washes of blue flame brighter than all the five others together, even casting shadows where there had been none before. It felt so good Rap wanted to weep.

There were now six young gnomes gathered around Athal'rian, ranging from Ugish down to a pocket-size baby. The baby was crawling off on business of its own, but the others all burst into shrill laughter at Rap's conquest of the dragon.

And Ishist had turned to stare, with his bulbous gnome eyes as round as black buttons. He was no cleaner than his wife, and much older. The fringe of hair around his scalp was probably gray—even Rap's farsight could not be certain—but his face was certainly entrenched with wrinkles like ditches. His beard was the most nauseating thing Rap had ever seen near to a human face. He wore some sort of uniform, anonymous in a stiff coating of dirt, and the front of its tunic gaped over a pot belly. Barefoot, he squelched forward through the muck to peer at Rap more closely.

The wall on which Rap was so uncomfortably sitting was no higher than a normal chair, and yet his head was higher than the gnome's. Rap decided to remain seated, and tried not to show nervousness as he was scrutinized by the hard black eyes.

Small though he was, the man's stink was powerful enough to register over all the others. Could this disgusting little scavenger truly be a powerful sorcerer?

"Lily seems to think she has met you before, Adept."

So that was it! "She may have . . . my lord—"

"Just call me Ishist. I always detect overtones of irony when day men offer me titles. Your name is Rap. You say you are only an adept?"

"Yes . . . Ishist."

There was shrewdness in those inkwell eyes, and sudden surprise. "You have indeed met Lily before!"

"She was called Precious then."

The fire chick reacted to the name with a flash of blue-green flame that made Rap wonder when his hair would start smoking. His ear and neck were turning painfully red.

"Bright Water?" the gnome muttered. "Well! I did not know that. My master did not take me into his confidence." He grinned, showing innumerable

144

little teeth, still white and needle sharp despite his age. "You wander around bearing strange secrets, Adept!"

He chuckled at Rap's horror. "Yes, I am poking around in your memories. Don't worry—you have no more bizarre obscenities in there than most men do. Remarkably few, in fact." He showed even more of the tiny teeth. "Some minds can disgust even a gnome, Master Rap, but I congratulate you. Now I must attend to your injuries; but I'm not going to try it with a fire chick on your shoulder. Come away, Lily."

The dragon turned a sulky green, and crouched low, while trickles of Rap's blood oozed out around its tightening claws. The other fire chicks, meanwhile, were circling him in flickers of curious pink, gradually daring to approach more closely. He thought he would be scorched or shredded if they all tried to land on him.

"I'm not doing this, sir! Ishist, I mean."

The sorcerer scratched thoughtfully at the old carrion caked around his mouth. "I know you're not. It's very unusual, and probably a very real compliment. But we can't stay here all night. Be off with you all!"

Lily shot up from Rap's shoulder in a stream of purple fire, and the whole juvenile blaze of baby dragons went swirling high into the ghostly upper reaches of the chamber, to race around like six violet comets, while their squeaks of anger and fright echoed as discordant bell strokes inside Rap's head.

Ishist ignored them, frowning at Rap. "Now, Master Adept, it is safe to use a little power around you! Never entered my head that you might not be a full sorcerer. You terrified poor Primrose. Fools rush in where mages fear to tread . . ." While he was muttering, Rap's wounds were closing and healing, from his mangled feet to the dragon scratches on his shoulder. ". . . so I overdid the summoning spell . . . at least we know you're not holding back anything if you had to endure this . . . there. How does that feel?"

The black-button eyes twinkled shrewdly, and Rap suddenly realized that even his fatigue had been lifted, or most of it, and he had lost his sense of smell also. That was the greatest blessing of all. He took a deep breath of relief.

"That's much better, Master Ishist. Thank you."

The gnome nodded with ironic amusement. "I was planning to throw you in a dungeon, but my wife is very anxious that you dine with us."

Athal'rian had been staying back, as if not wishing to interfere with business. Now she said, "Oh, yes!" breathlessly. and came over to cuddle against her husband and place a hand on his shoulder. Ishist took it and kissed it; she stooped to place a kiss on his bald pate, although it was plastered with what seemed to be old bird droppings. The elderly gnome and the much-younger elf woman were behaving like two lovesick adolescents, yet she had apparently already borne him seven . . . no, there were eight children present now. What *was* that baby eating?

"It will have to wait awhile, my love," Ishist said. "I must go and find Master Rap's two companions before the wildlife does."

Athal'rian wailed. "You won't be long, though, darling?"

"No, no! And it is still dark. I shall be as quick as I can, dearest." He patted her lovingly on the rump, as if she were a horse.

"But the food will spoil. And I did so want the children to see what a proper dinner party is like."

As a mother she seemed to have strange priorities. Ugish and the oldest girl were now fighting furiously, rolling around in the mire and biting each other, but Athal'rian was paying them no heed at all.

"It won't hurt them to stay up past dawn for once," Ishist said firmly. "Now, magic is magic, but sleep has its own magic. I'm sure that our guest would appreciate a little rest. Where are you planning to put the visitors?"

She hesitated, shuffling her toes in the dirt. "I thought . . . the northwest tower?" She waited anxiously for his opinion.

"Very good choice, my dear. So you show Master Rap to his chamber. I promised Ugish he could come with me. Stop that, you two!" He separated the combatants with a couple of well-placed kicks. Then he accepted a very long, tight embrace from his tearful wife, before plodding off toward the door. Young Ugish trailed after him, angrily licking a bleeding arm with a very long black tongue.

Still holding his wisp of dirty rag, Rap followed his hostess along innumerable corridors and up narrow, winding staircases. The walls were rough stonework, the floors soft with dirt as if they had not been cleaned since the founding of the Impire. Mummified carcasses and gnawed bones lay in drier corners, while wetter parts were ankle-deep in sewage and the doors had rotted away to rusty relics of hinges. In other places the ceilings had collapsed, requiring painful climbs over heaps of rubble.

He could not assess the full extent of the huge ruin, but he could easily believe that it was old enough to have known the Dragon Wars. Everywhere he detected ancient occult barriers, although once in a while he caught shadowy vistas running off for incredible distances between them. Sometimes then he glimpsed far-off groups of gnomes going about their business.

Many parts were more or less illuminated by the sort of sorcerous mist he had seen in the Mews; others were pitch black. Athal'rian seemed to find her way through those mostly by memory and touch, but he followed her with farsight, trying to ignore the details: the rashes under the dirt, the close-packed insect bites, the elven grace of her slender hips. She glided like a moonbeam, confirming all the tales he had heard about elves and dancing.

She sickened him—how could any human being exist in such condition? But in a gruesome fashion he found her fascinating. He kept trying to imagine her cleaned up and properly clad.

If Ugish was thirteen or so, then his mother must be over thirty, surely, but she had a figure any adolescent could envy. Perhaps sorcery had helped there, and bearing tiny gnome babies might not be very taxing to a woman of a tall race. Also, he had a vague idea that elves were long-lived.

Although he kept reproaching himself, he still felt very uncomfortable at the idea of an elf marrying a gnome. He was convinced that her obvious infatuation must be a product of sorcery, and yet Ishist himself seemed equally besotted. Could a sorcerer bespell himself? Would he ever want to? And who was Rap to question the follies of love when he had been crazy enough to fall in love with a queen?

Finally, at the top of a breathlessly winding spiral staircase, Athal'rian brought him to a place that was uncomfortably reminiscent of Inisso's chamber in Krasnegar and almost as large, the uppermost room of a circular tower. The floor creaked alarmingly under his feet. Starlight seeped in through gaps in the corbeled roof, but the four tiny casements were tightly sealed, opaque with grime. The only furniture was a giant four-poster bed whose draperies were mostly cobwebs.

She waited by the door, peering doubtfully at him.

"It's magnificent, my lady," he said gamely. "I shall feel like a king in such royal quarters."

Relief showed through the dirt, but her laugh had an awkward ring. "I know how difficult it can be to adjust to gnomish ways, Adept. No one has been here for a long time, I'm sure."

He saw no need to mention that he had been relieved of his sense of smell. "It is a beautiful room," he insisted. "And it must have a wonderful view."

He walked over to one of the casements and rubbed the glass. His farsight was blocked and he could see nothing in the starlight except that the walls were enormously thick, doubtless dragonproof.

His approval had filled the simple Athal'rian with delight, although she was smiling in the wrong direction, not having heard him move. "Well, you will want to rest. I'll send Ugish or Oshat to call you when dinner is ready." She floated into a curtsy.

He bowed, clumsy as a drunken troll. He thanked her and watched for a moment as she padded down off down the stairs on her bare feet. Then he took another look around the room. The holes in the ceiling had admitted bats, and some were already flitting around over his head, returning from their nocturnal outings. He could certainly use some sleep—but where? The bed would collapse if he laid as much as a hand on it. Beetles had fretted the woodwork; the thick feather mattress had been tunneled out by centuries of mice. There were hundreds of them still in there.

The floor might be as soft as the bed, though; both of them were inches deep in bat dung. He tried to pull the top cover from the bed and his hand came away holding a fragment of rag no larger than a kerchief. He sighed, chose the floor, and lay down.

3

Endlessly rolling from side to back and then back to her side, Inos had never spent a more miserable night, wondering a million times if she had somehow lost the ability to go to sleep without the aid of Elkarath's sorcery. Whenever she did begin to slide below the surface of drowsiness, the four pixies were there at once, all around her, gloating and hurting, repeating their cruelties of the day and going on to achieve worse and worse things, until she awoke in spasms of terror, soaked and shaking and choking back screams. She despised herself then for such cowardice, but that did not help her escape the nightmares.

The little room was so packed with its four small beds that to move around without climbing over them was almost impossible. Two had remained empty, as a gesture of respect to royalty. Kade snored peacefully on the fourth, not stopping once all night. After months in a tent, the stuffy garret seemed confining as a coffin, and although its little dormer window looked out only on a sagging tile roof, it had an inexplicable ability to gather up the racket of the street below: sounds of carousing sailors until an hour before dawn, and then the wheels of wagons rattling over cobblestones. Where now were the peace and serenity of the desert?

Demons haunted the night, spinning giddy circles of mockery in her mind. She had not escaped from Rasha, nor from Rasha's plans. Rasha would proceed to trade her to Warlock Olybino, and he in turn would marry her off to a goblin. Rasha might reasonably resent Inos's attempted flight, and be in future even less considerate than before.

What spiteful punishment would she inflict now on Azak?

Perhaps Inos should have married the sultan while she had the chance. For both their sakes.

Inos and Kade were royal guests, but also prisoners, for the door was locked. Only a cat could depart through that window. Having refused to give his parole, Azak had been led off to a dungeon somewhere.

Escape would not be so easy at Ullacarn as it had been at Three Cranes, with Elkarath now alert and watching for it. To slip away in a strange town with no friends or plan would be madness. No, the next escape must be prepared much more carefully than the madcap flight from the oasis, and Inos had no idea how much time she might have to plan. Perhaps none—Olybino might appear in the morning to take delivery.

Azak might no longer be a willing ally. Since Elkarath had suggested that Inos could use magic, the sultan had spoken not a s ngle word to her. Had there been any truth in the accusation, then Inos could have understood. She knew how she herself had felt about the late Sir Andor and his foul sorcery, but in her case the suggestion was ludicrous. Kade had not helped by hinting that Azak was just angry at himself for his own shortcomings. Azak now regarded Inos as one of those shortcomings. And that hurt.

The House of Elkarath in Ullacarn was a great rambling old building, yet it seemed to be crammed with people from cellar to gable. The cramped little attic room was not exactly the Palace of Palms in Arakkaran, nor yet even Kinvale, but it was comfortable enough for just two. An attic was certainly preferable to a dungeon, a dungeon with fleas and chains and rats, Elkarath had said.

Azak had chosen the dungeon.

Pigheaded idiot!

A mage could probably detect lies. Would Azak have given his parole to a mundane, meaning to break it as soon as he could find the opportunity? Were all men so stubborn?

And here was Inos, dancing naked on the grass and shouting unthinkable promises to dozens of young men, as they came running toward her to accept. But they kept turning to stone and sinking into the meadow as they drew near. Hundreds and thousands of them drowning in the ground, and every one of them was Azak. Then she awoke again, gasping and shaking.

Would she ever again be able to stand close to a man without expecting rape, without breaking out in a sweat of terror?

She had remote relatives in Hub, some of them very influential people. Senator Somebody, for example. Kade had innumerable friends there also. Ullacarn was allied with the Impire, and so the post must call here. If Kade could write a letter, enclosing a petition to the imperor or the other wardens, then they might be able to deliver it for her. That was one possibility. Ullacarn was a busy port. That was another.

But how could one ever deceive a mage and a sorceress?

Again Inos was back in the forest meadow, and this time Rasha was there also, laughing uproariously. She had rooted Inos's feet to the ground, as she had once done in Krasnegar. She was watching and gloating as the pixies . . . but they were not pixies, now they were goblins.

A faint glimmer of dawn smiled in through the window. The entire Imperial army seemed to be shoeing its mounts down in the street, but the yearlong night was ending at last.

And again Inos was back in the forest, and this time the men tormenting her were djinns, and the glowing figure riding up to rescue her on a shining white horse was Rap.

Rap, who had remained loyal when the imps and jotnar of Krasnegar had turned against their queen.

Rap, the only man who had ever accepted a kiss from her without expecting more.

Rap, who had died for her.

Rap, whose wraith had haunted her the night she left Arakkaran.

Crazy dreams!

4

"Why aren't you sleeping in the bed?" Ugish demanded, nudging Rap with a toe.

Rap groaned, rubbed his smarting eyes, and sat up. Then he sneezed six times in rapid succession. Faint traces of dawn showed through the eastern window. He was stiff and chilled, and filthy as a gnome.

"Is that for me?"

"Uh-huh." Ugish had brought a robe, a fine-looking linen garment whose obvious newness suggested that it had been specially made by his father. Unfortunately Ugish had been dragging it, and that showed also.

There would be no chance for shaving or washing here. Rap heaved himself to his feet and took the robe. "You can have your loincloth back, thank you very much."

Ugish shrugged. "Don't want it. Why do I have to get all dressed up just because we have visitors?"

"Mothers are funny about things like that."

"Uh-huh. Why didn't you sleep in the bed?"

Rap ran fingers through his hair and regretted the action. "Because it's full of mice."

The little gnome's glorious bronze eyes widened. "Babies, too?"

"Yes," said Rap. "But you'd better save them for later. If you spoil your appetite now, your mother will scold."

Ugish nodded reluctantly. "Awright—if you promise not to tell the others!"

As Rap walked out onto the great terrace, the first pinks and peaches of the rising sun were just starting to blossom on a forest of crumbling towers and turrets behind him. Warth Redoubt was ten times vaster than he had even guessed, a sprawling landscape in its own right. Once it must have clasped a whole city within its throbbing heart, but it had long since fallen into ruin. Shattered pillars and broken statuary lay thrown around in weed-strewn rubble.

Warth perched like an eyrie on the lip of a huge natural arena. On all sides jagged peaks stood dark against the brightening sky.

Ishist was waiting, with Darad and Gathmor. The two jotnar had been healed and restored, as Rap had been, and they wore white robes like his. Their faces showed great relief when they saw him.

"I thought you might like to watch the dawn rising," the sorcerer remarked. "We are sheltered here."

Rap had already registered the occult barrier enclosing the terrace, and he supposed that there would be other spells that he could not sense, for it was not the sun they would be watching rise.

Far below, the blasted, barren valley was still dark except where awakening dragons were glowing and breathing jets of many-colored fire. Their rumbling anger echoed from the rocky walls. He wondered if the worms themselves could have excavated so enormous a pit, even if they had started before the coming of the Gods.

"This is Warth Nest, of course," Ishist said, "home of the largest surviving blaze. In its prime it nurtured several times as many as it does now. It was from here that Olis'laine drew the sky army that he used to waste the Cities of the Ambly Pact. From here too came the Legions of Death in the Second Dragon War." He droned on for a while, obviously enjoying having an audience, however unappreciative. Rap did not know much history, and soon concluded that he did not want to.

Then a dragon spiraled up and up, until it was a dark shape against brightness; and yet the sun flashed brightest on its scales and wings. It was followed rapidly by others, and the sorcerer fell silent. Deadly the monsters undoubtedly were, but their beauty was undeniable, too. Soon the sky was filled with them, a hundred or more, and they danced for the dawn. They soared too high for sight, they swooped like falcons girt in thunder, they spun and rolled in pairs or groups, in wild confusion like schooling fish or in the rigid ranks of geese. Some were as small as ponies, others longer than longships and older than storied cities. Their voices roared and rang like every instrument ever known, reverberating in chorus from the peaks, and Rap thought he also heard some hint of mental song, the secret melody of dragon serenading dragon.

They shone in the hues of pearls and dew and the wings of butterflies; they blazed like a Winterfest ball. They were at once the most awesome thing he had ever witnessed and the most glorious. He felt tears run down into his stubble and he did not care. He wished Jalon had been here to see this, or Inos to share it with. And when the blaze had scattered and noise had faded and the last few were vanishing into the distance, he felt both crushed into insignificance and yet strangely uplifted.

He wiped his cheeks as he looked at the tiny old sorcerer. "Thank you, my lord. Thank you!"

"You are welcome, lad," the gnome said wryly. "You enjoyed it."

"It was so beautiful! How many men have seen that?"

"Very few in these times." Ishist glanced at the stunned horrified expressions on the faces of the two jotnar, and he chuckled. "Not many deserve it. Let us go and have this meal my wife is so excited about."

Oftentimes the banquet hall had rung to the laughter of famed heroes, Ishist said, and mighty kings. From here Alshth'aer had marched to meet his doom foretold. Olis'laine had feasted here, and the grim Jiel, and their noble companies had cheered them, clashing silver goblets in toast and making sterner metals ring in pledge of honor. Here the brave and the beautiful had trod and sung and sworn historic oaths. Trumpets had brayed to the banners on the hammerbeams, viols had lamented, and many a nimble dancer had been showered with gold. Warlock Thraine of high renown had visited Warth more than once, 'twas said, and had wrought many marvels in this very chamber for Allena the Fair.

But now the fine-arched windows held no glass and the subtle panels had all fallen from the walls. Now it belonged to the rodents, the birds, and the gnomes. In places the planks had rotted away, and a careless step might drop a man four stories to the cellars.

But in the center of the dusty, windswept desolation stood a long and shining table. Gold plate glinted on damask, and crystal sparkled. The sorcerer had been at work, Rap saw, and he wondered whether the gold was shielded from the dragons or was merely an illusion that would not deceive them. As the men approached, Athal'rian was adjusting eight children around her, while clutching a baby. Her family seemed to increase each time Rap turned his back. The smaller ones kept pulling off their wraps, and she kept telling Ugish and the older girls to dress them again. Ugish himself was setting a poor example.

She handed the baby to one of the older children so she could embrace her husband. By the time the long kiss was ended, more than half the children had stripped again and one of me toddlers was heading for a chasm. Rap himself went after it and brought it back. It bit him.

"Now, are we ready?" Ishist inquired.

"Chairs, dearest?" Athal'rian said.

"Chairs of course. Describe them."

Athal'rian became flustered and made vague gestures. "Blue velvet. Oak. About so high. Backs carved, tall . . ."

Three chairs appeared at one end of the table, and about a dozen at the other.

Her greasy face lighted up. "Thank you, my love. Master Adept, perhaps you and your friends would like to sit at that end, where the children will not disturb you?" Such tact was oddly touching in a woman so obviously addled.

Rap seated himself at one end of the long table, with Darad and Gathmor flanking him. Both seemed too overcome by emotion to speak, and from the greenish tinge of their cheeks, Rap suspected that their noses were working at normal efficiency. There was a fair breeze blowing through the ruin, but even so tile idea of dining with gnomes was enough to stun anyone.

For the first time he now saw inhabitants of Warth Redoubt other than the dragonward and his family. He had already sensed them with farsight, and the Mews floor had certainly suggested a large population. A troop of servant gnomes brought in dishes and laid them before the diners, and then mercifully departed.

The first course was a thin soup. It was cold and greasy, but Rap gulped it down manfully, choking on me gristly lumps and ignoring floating feathers. The others copied him with grim dedication. The wine had a sour flavor but it was drinkable, and probably occult.

Then the gruesome company of ragged footman returned with the second course. And departed.

"This was . . . is . . . fish," Rap remarked cheerfully. "Her ladyship tells me that she uses freshly ensorceled supplies, prepared according to famed elvish recipes." He gave each companion in turn a steely look, and each groaned softly and grudgingly addressed his high-piled plate. The fish was a sort of pike, mostly bones, and smothered in sickly caramel sauce.

At the other end of the table the children were having great difficulty adjusting to the idea of chairs, and reasonably so, for the small ones could not see the fare even if they stood on the seats. Ignoring their mother's ineffectual protests, some of them settled on the floor as usual, but most crawled up to sit on the table itself, eating out of the serving dishes. The food at that end was traditional gnomish cuisine, and Rap wished his farsight was not so efficient. Sweat prickled on his forehead as he tried to force sticky, bony pike down his throat.

Ishist himself had magicked his own chair to a suitable height and was eating in rather moody silence, using both hands, seeming to be balanced somewhere between annoyance at this folly and tolerant affection for his wife's odd notions.

"This fish is most delicious, ma'am," Rap said.

Athal'rian flashed him a smile of relief and thanked him for the compliment.

He nagged his mind to give him something else to say. He knew how formal affairs should go, because he had watched Holindarn entertain guests at the high table in Krasnegar. Gentlefolk chatted while they ate. They made jokes, and laughed.

Jokes about what, though?

Darad must have the right sort of experience in his multiple memory, but his wits were too dim to use it or even see the need. Gathmor's idea of dinner conversation was planning the brawl to follow.

Inspiration came to Rap like a pardon to a felon. "I have never seen so magnificent a chamber, my lady! The king's hall in Krasnegar would fit in here a dozen times."

"Oh, do tell me about it, Master Adept!"

So Rap described the palace in Krasnegar, and if the dragonward's lady somehow assumed that the raised dais was where he had sat and the servants' end was not, well, that was what she expected, not what he said. Then he asked about dining halls in Hub, and she became quite animated in describing them, ignoring her ironically smiling husband and the chaos of children squabbling amid the gold plate. As daughter of the warden of the south, she had moved in the highest levels of society. At fifteen, she had been presented to the imperor. She knew the Opal Palace itself.

"I hardly think of Hub anymore," she asserted, smiling at her husband, "and I would never dream of going back." They kissed on that.

She could not have been very old when she left, Rap decided, unless her age had been occultly altered. Mentally she was a small child. Was that the reason she now lived as a gnome, or had she been sane when she came here?

Something was licking his toes . . .

Rap slid his plate unobtrusively from me table and laid it on his lap. Soon he could hear satisfying sounds of pike bones crunching. When he brought it up again, it had been polished. The two jotnar at his side were chewing grimly, their faces running sweat.

The servants came trooping in again with another course, and Rap found himself facing a stag's head with antlers gilded and a potato in its mouth. He was expected to carve from this, apparently, but the cooks had neglected to skin it before boiling it, and it looked rather too rare, anyway. There was still a reproachful look in its eyes.

In an attempt to seem busy, he ladled out generous heaps of vegetables, comprising unwashed tubers and soft-boiled lemons. The other two nibbled listlessly at them while he prepared to do battle with the stag. He must also continue the insane conversation with the girl-woman at the far end of the table.

Yelling over the rioting children between them, she asked about his travels. Rap told a vague tale of being kidnapped by jotunnish raiders, and of shipwreck. Eventually he mentioned that he had visited Faerie and had been a guest of the proconsul. That convenient euphemism caused Ishist's globular eyes to twinkle like cabochons of jet. He must have ransacked all of Rap's memories by now, and probably the others' also.

"I have always wanted to visit Faerie," Athal'rian remarked wistfully, "but of course my husband's duties make it so difficult for us to get away."

Rap thrust his fork into the stag's head, and one of its soggy eyes winked at him. He recoiled and then glared reproachfully at the sorcerer, who seemed to be totally engrossed in biting lumps out of a shapeless mass that might have been a bird's nest. Ishist, Rap suspected, had a dangerous sense of humor.

Athal'rian had noticed his hesitation. "Is that knife not sharp enough, Master Adept?"

"Quite sharp enough, ma'am! I am letting the pleasures of your conversation distract me from my duties."

"Oo, flattery! But Daddy always says that wit is the finest sauce, and a meal without discourse has no flavor. Let me see . . . Who is proconsul of Faerie at present?"

"Lady Oothiana, ma'am."

"Oh!" Athal'rian seemed taken aback. She glanced uneasily at Ishist, then her eyes wandered briefly over the children. "Don't do that on the table, Shuth. Go to the Mews. Dear Oothie and I took viol lessons together. How is she?"

Rap cursed under his breath, feeling he had chosen to ride at a dangerous fence. "She is very well, ma'am."

"I forget if . . . Did she finally many that musclebound soldier? What was his name? Yodello?"

Tricky takeoff, landing unseen . . ."Yes, she did, ma'am."

Athal'rian bit her lip and seemed to slip away into a memory. "He was very pretty. Too pretty for a man, you know."

"Yes, ma'am."

The glorious opal eyes came up to stare along the table at him, and their fires nickered through a mist of tears. "He wanted me to marry him, but Daddy had promised me to Consul Uppinoli's youngest."

Ishist frowned. "My dear—"

"How furious he was when I told him I would rather wed a gnome." She looked hesitantly down at Ishist, and seemed suddenly aghast at what she had said. Then she smiled. "And I was right!" She bent for another lass.

The conversation ended when two of the smaller boys began to fight over the last rat and than pulled it apart in a tug of war. Darad leaned sideways in his chair and threw up everything, triggering Gathmor's reflexes also. That was bad. Even worse was the way the children all rushed over to clean it up.

5

The visitors stood while Athal'rian departed with her brood, sent away by an angry-looking Ishist. The table vanished abruptly, and so did all the chairs except the sorcerer's.

Obviously the time had come to talk business. Rap walked forward, aware that his two companions were following closely and leaving everything to him. He was an adept, and they were relying on him to save them. But he was also the cause of their danger, for he had used power against a dragon. He had violated the Protocol that had ruled Pandemia for three thousand years.

He stopped before the foul little sorcerer, who was lounging back in his high chair and picking his teeth with a slender bone. The seat was so much too big for him that his muck-laden bare feet stuck straight out. His bulging black eyes were unreadable.

Gruffly the gnome said, "Thank you. Master Rap. I'm grateful."

That made no sense at all! Rap had done nothing to earn the sorcerer's gratitude—it must be a trick. Yet why should a sorcerer need to use tricks?

"For what, my lord?" Then Rap remembered that he was not supposed to give the gnome titles. But apparently it did not matter, for Ishist just shrugged inscrutably and switched his gaze to the two sullen jotnar.

Rap knew how hard this must be for them. They had grown up around gnomes. All the towns and cities in the Impire had gnomes to keep down the vermin and deal with the garbage, and all large ships carried one or two, but there had been none in Krasnegar. He had not met gnomes until he was an adult, and then he had merely filed them away in his mind as another race of people new to him, like fairies or trolls. Gathmor and Darad, humbly waiting to hear their fate from this squat and squalid old ragamuffin, must be feeling as if a mongrel dog had suddenly ascended the Opal Throne and started barking orders. Come to think of it, Ishist did rather resemble a pug dog, with his pop eyes and upturned nose, with the bloodstained cake of hair around his mouth and all those teeth he was picking.

With a shiver of fear, Rap realized that the sorcerer might still be reading his thoughts.

The ugly old man flipped his toothpick away and scratched reflectively at the hairy bulge protruding above his belt. "Sailor, you are an innocent mundane caught up in occult matters that do not concern you. You are free to go."

Gathmor scowled, shot a glance at Rap, and said, "I'll wait for my shipmate."

"As you wish."

"No!" Rap said. "For the Gods' sake, Cap'n—"

156

"I'm staying." Gathmor folded his arms and set his jotunn jaw looking every bit as stubborn as man could be. He stepped back a pace and scowled. Rap saw that argument would be useless, and was again miserably aware that he had led the man into this danger.

The gnome's jet eyes had moved to Darad. "We'll handle the gold problem next. Call Thinal."

Darad grunted in shock and looked reproachfully at Rap.

"He didn't tell me," Ishist said. "If I have to force the change, I may hurt you."

The threat worked. Darad's gown crumpled toward the floor, uncovering Thinal within it. He bent his arms to stop it falling off him completely. Then he just stood there, staring at the gnome in terror. He was bare from the elbows up, hugging himself, and gradually turning pale all over. As usual, he was unshaven and ratty-haired. His teeth chattered with a curiously metallic clink.

Somewhere a dragon roared, and then another.

Thinal choked, worked one hand free of the overlong sleeve, and spat something into it.

"Pass it over."

Another roar, closer. The little thief shuffled forward with the folds of his robe tangling around his feet. He thrust the gold into the sorcerer's hand, then backed away quickly. Ishist flipped the coin; it rose in a gilded flicker and never came down. The dragon roars died away.

The sorcerer glared very sourly at Thinal for a minute or two. "You have unpleasant ideas about gnomes, guttersnipe. I'm tempted to . . . but then I don't like scroungers skulking around my castle, so it's mutual. Call Andor."

Thinal had just time for a quick nod before he vanished, not having spoken a word. From his point of view he had made a fast escape, which was all he would care about.

Andor raised the gown and adjusted it properly on his shoulders, somehow transforming plain homespun into elegant menswear in the process. He was clean, freshly shaved, washed, combed. He bowed.

"The honor of meeting me famous dragonward—"

"Quiet!" The gnome wrinkled his pug nose, causing me entrenched dirt around it to writhe and flake. He glanced at Rap. "They get worse all the time. Do you want them around, or shall I not bother?"

Rap was befaddled again. "My lord?"

Ishist shrugged and told Andor, "Call Sagorn, then."

Andor stiffened. "Your Omn—"

"One more word of flattery and I turn you into a troll."

"But the old man is—"

"I know. Call him."

Andor's mourn opened, then he nodded in understanding. He vanished.

Sagorn's face was me color of wood ash, a shade only a jotunn could ever be, and then only when close to death. He swayed as if about to fall. Before Rap could move to catch him, the sorcerer did so, with magic. The old man steadied. Color flowed back into his cheeks, his eyes flipped open. In a moment he took a deep breath and straightened. His face took on a healthy glow and even seemed to swell, becoming less gaunt and haggard than before. Suddenly Sagorn looked about ten years younger, and fitter than Rap had ever seen him.

He stared at me gnome for a long moment, as if waiting for the transformation to reach completion, or perhaps to see if there was more to come. Then he bowed.

"I am truly grateful, Sorcerer. It feels as if you found every ache and hangnail." His voice sounded stronger, too.

Ishist scratched at his beard, digging stuff out of it. "I found a few problems you didn't even know about. Tumors, for example."

Sagorn bowed again, and there was an ironic amusement twinkling in his pale-blue eyes. "I thought the prophecy of the dragon signified my death, but it seems to have brought me a new lease on life. I admit I have been prejudiced against gnomes, Dragonward, but I shall regard them differently after this."

The gnome grunted skeptically. He turned his gaze on Rap.

"Sorcerer," Sagorn said hastily. "There is another—"

"No." Ishist scowled horribly at him. "First of all, I just tried, and I made no impact at all. Your Orarinsagu must have been enormously powerful— it's much too strong for me. You'll need a warlock or a witch, likely. And second, that would make five of you around underfoot, and your word of power would be shared six ways. So, no." He switched his attention back to Rap again.

"You have demonstrated power within South's sector, boy. By ancient custom, your words belong to him." He waved a black thumb at Sagorn. "His, also, of course."

"I used mine first in the north," Rap said cautiously.

Ishist nodded. "Yes, and in West's sector later. It's very odd that neither of them imprinted you with a loyalty spell. If they did, I can't find it. But you're an odd case all round, lad. Neither of them could foresee you, could they?"

"I don't think Zinixo tried, but Bright Water said she couldn't, my lord."

"Ishist," Ishist said softly, showing his myriad teeth in a smile.

"Ishist."

"That's better! You're an adept, and we sorcerers must stick together! But if Bright Water tried and failed, then I certainly won't succeed. You're the first person I ever met that I can't foresee, though. All I get is a sort of white blur. It hurts! Did she explain?"

"No."

"I wish I had a preflecting pool handy . . ." The gnome sighed and leaned back to stare up at the ruins of what had once been a magnificent roof. For a moment nothing moved except wraiths of dust, swirled across the floor by eddies of wind. A dragon rumbled in the distance.

Ishist straightened, as if reaching a decision. "Take a seat."

One of the vanished dining chairs magically reappeared at Rap's back. He sat down obediently, aware the Sagorn and Gathmor had been left standing, wondering why the old gnome was favoring him so much over them.

"I'm imprinted. Rap," Ishist said. "You understand that? A votary. Most sorcerers get trapped by their warden sooner or later—it's why so many of them try to become wardens themselves, instead. Whenever a warlock detects magic at work in his sector, he'll try to track it down and lock it up with a loyalty spell. He may not do anything more about it than that . . . depends how many words and votaries he has already and what his needs are. I'm dragonward for Warlock Lith'rian, and very happy in my work. Perhaps he spelled me to enjoy it. I don't know, but it feels like worthwhile employment, and the quarters are ideal for gnomes." He leered.

Rap smiled, also, thinking of the ancient heroes who had built this enormous redoubt and how appalled they would be to see it now.

The bottomless black eyes fixed on him. "And I'm happily married."

Was that happiness also a spell? "I can see that, Ishist." Rap spoke as matter-of-factly as he could manage. "And Athal'rian seems to be very happy, also. I'm sure you love each other and you're proud of your family. They wouldn't be my choice of children, and I would not be happy living here, but my tastes are different—not better, just different . . . That's the best I can do," he added uneasily. Who was he to pass such judgment?

The gnome chuckled, glancing briefly at Sagorn and Gathmor. "Its a lot better than most can. Yes, she's happy. Misses her family sometimes. Her father hadn't been around for five years or more, but he turned up a few months ago, in a hurry, one evening. Needed a fire chick. None of my business why—he's the boss. He brought it back me next day. That's the only baby dragon that's left here in years. It was Lily you met."

He waited, giving Rap time to think. The fire chick could hardly have been a gift or a bribe if it had been returned the next day.

So despite what Bright Water had told Zinixo, she must be in league with Lith'rian.

"What exactly does a fire chick do to magic?"

Ishist smiled nastily. "All magic gets unpredictable around all dragons, young or old. You're only an adept, so Primrose ought to have charred you to ash yesterday, yet you almost drove her out of her wits. Poor thing was gibbering when she got back here! On the other hand, the occult fence across the Neck has been there for thousands of years, and all the greatest sorcerers in history have worked on it, yet the worms just seem to eat it. They throw off their bindings sometimes and fly over water. I don't know why Bright Water wanted a fire chick, or why Lith'rian loaned her one—but I expect they had their reasons." His button eyes twinkled.

Bright Water had been around for centuries, and must know all the tricks there were to be known. Zinixo, of course, was new to me warlocking business and . . . Rap saw that his reverie was causing me gnome to smirk approvingly. They were on me same track.

"Why can't you foresee me?"

"That I don't know either." For the first time the gnome seemed to hesitate. He turned to look at the jotnar, and they both spun around without a word and walked away. When they reached the nearest window, they stood and stared out at the unworldly scenery, sage and sailor chatting cozily side by side, while the wind ruffled their hair and tumbled the flow of their gowns. Ishist's somber eyes came back to Rap.

"Tell me about this God who appeared to Inosolan."

Rap frowned. He had almost forgotten that. He could remember sitting on the floor with Inos, holding her hand, in among the old gang and all the dogs, and listening to Jalon singing. In retrospect, that had been the last evening of his childhood.

But that moment had come later, after she'd told him about the meeting with the God. "I just know what Inos said. They didn't say which God They were. They told her to try harder. I think that's all."

The gnome shook his head. "There's more. Try harder!" His eyes seemed to grow even larger, and blacker, and deeper, and shinier.

"They said the king would give her many gowns. She was excited about that, but upset because—"

"They said more."

Rap leaned back in his chair and stared up at the warped rafters and fretted roof. "That she must . . . trust . . . remember . . . remember love! Trust in love!"

He started, as if he had been dozing and had heard a loud noise. "What did I just say?"

"Nothing much." Ishist showed his pike teeth. "But be sure to mention the God to my master when you meet him. He may know already, of course."

"How?"

The gnome sat up straight and scratched vigorously. "Even warlocks are very careful around the Gods, friend Rap. Gods rarely manifest so close an interest in human affairs, but when They do, then sorcery is nothing! The power of the Gods is unlimited. That could be why you . . . but I'm just guessing. I have to send you to my master, you understand? I have no choice in the matter."

"I understand." Oothiana had said much the same.

Ishist eased forward on the seat so his legs dangled over the edge. "But I do have discretion in how I do it. I'm his agent, not just a trained dog. If I had a magic portal, or even a magic carpet, then I could transport you at once to Hub, or to his home on Valdorian—he spends more time in Drane than he does in the Blue Palace. But sorcerous paraphernalia like that is tricky stuff around dragons. They might wreck the rest of the redoubt trying to get at it. So we haven't got any." He blinked solemnly.

"Then how . . ." But that was none of Rap's business.

Apparently it was, though. "How does he come visiting? Just by sorcery. A magic device like that casement of Inisso's . . . such things are handy, but they can never be stronger than the sorcerer who made them. They're quicker, often, and easier. And another of their advantages is that normally they don't make so many ripples. Sheer brute power is as subtle as a thunderstorm. It attracts attention, and all sorcerers are cagey, secretive people. When Lith'rian came here twice in two days, he rattled the ambience something awful. Took me weeks to get the livestock calmed down."

Rap began to feel more hopeful. Perhaps he was not going to be enslaved right away.

Ishist regarded him with quiet amusement. "And he's a lot better than me. I might magic you partway to Hub, at least, but I might well start a stampede in the process, and that could lead to a major disaster, if they got over the fence. So you're going to have to walk. Your two friends will go with you, of course." He glanced at the two jotnar by the window, lost in admiration of the bleakly alien scenery. Rap's future was concealed from the sorcerer, but he had not said that theirs was. Rap decided not to ask.

"Now," Ishist said softly, "I must decide how to send you. I could use a compulsion, like the one I used to bring you here. Less urgent, of course, but I can give you an irresistible command to go to Lith'rian." He smiled gruesomely. "Or I could put the loyalty spell on you myself; not as strong as he could, but strong enough. I can make you *want* to go to Lith'rian, to serve him."

Cold fingers of horror touched Rap's heart, and he shook his head vigorously.

"You would be happier," the gnome said mockingly. "You'd be doing what you wanted to do."

Just like the once-lovely Athal'rian, besotted with a gnome? Such power was obscene, perverting its user as much as his victim. Yesterday Rap had become an adept and in minutes had found himself using mastery on Andor.

"I . . . I should prefer just to obey an order, my lord."

He knew that the sorcerer knew what he was thinking, but the little man did not seem to take offense. He cocked his head at Rap. "You want to help Inosolan, don't you? That's your aim: to put her on her throne?"

"To serve her as a loyal subject. That's all." Rap's farsight told him he was blushing like a child.

Ishist chuckled gently. "Mmm? All? You can't do it alone, you know. Fauns like to go their own way, but even an adept can't find one mackerel in all the oceans, Rap."

Zark . . . but he did not know that Inos was still in Zark, even. She might have heeded his warning and fled. Or not. Or one of the wardens might have abducted her, or the sorceress recovered her. He had a terrifying vision of all Pandemia stretched out endlessly before him, and himself spending his whole life wandering from place to place, searching for Inos.

Put like that, his dream seemed hopeless. "I suppose not."

"You can't fight the Four! No one and nothing can fight the Four. Except the Gods."

"No," Rap said. He was a fool.

"So my advice would be to go and ask Lith'rian to help you."

For a moment Rap was speechless. Ask help from a *warlock?* Common sense had hysterics at me idea. Yet he also felt an odd shivery prickle of excitement. Was that some sort of occult ability of his own, or was the sorcerer playing tricks on him? Or imagination? Baffled, Rap said, "Would he?"

Ishist shrugged. "I honestly don't know. It would be dangerous for you, of course. The sorcerous normally stay well away from warlocks, and you're an adept. He may just give your words to someone else and kill you out of hand. I don't know where Krasnegar fits in his current political strategy, but elves . . . They're funny folk. They put style before substance. They admire *qualities—beauty,* wit, grace, elegance. Lith'rian might just be amused enough by your presumption. That would be like him. He can be generous beyond all reason, and he's ruthless when he's balked."

The shadow of Athal'rian fell across the conversation. Ishist frowned, then continued. "But he enjoys a good joke. He admires courage, too. I'd say he's about your only hope, being realistic."

"Well, you're going to send me to him. I'll ask then."

The old man shook his head gently. "If I send you, you won't ever get to see him. Not in person. You'll be thrown in the vau ts like a rent payment, until needed."

"But . . ." Rap stared incredulously. "Oh—you mean I just promise to go and ask the warden for help? You'd trust me?"

"That's it. No spells. No sorcery."

Could Rap even trust himself to obey such an order? Warily he said, "An oath made under duress isn't worth much. Do I have any choice?"

"That's the whole point, lad—I'm giving you a cho ce."

He wouldn't have much of a choice if he'd made a promise, would he? Not unless he reneged, of course.

Ruthless when balked. "You're steering pretty close to the rocks yourself, aren't you . . . Ishist?"

The gnome smiled into his nauseating beard and waited. He wasn't telling the whole truth, though, or else he was testing, somehow. Or wanting Rap to think those things. Or just lying, and planning to spell Rap anyway.

But Rap would much rather be his own man than a puppet, or at least think he was—and that spooky internal nudging was registering approval again. "Then I promise to go and find your master and ask him to help Inos—if you'll tell me how, and you promise not to . . . to mess about with my mind."

Ishist chuckled. "Typical faun! Always convinced his own ways are best." Abruptly he slid down off his chair.

Rap rose from his, and clasped the tiny hand being offered, having to bend slightly to do so. "I promise," he repeated.

"And I." For a moment a veil seemed to lift from the little gnome—a small, ugly, filthy old man, girt with enormous occult power, but just a man doing his best in a hard job, living in the style of his people, caring for his children, deeply in love with his wife. It was not his fault that his race ate carrion. Then the odd moment had passed, and he was a sorcerer again, even if his head was barely higher than Rap's elbow.

He examined his own hand, which Rap had just released.

"That's two," he remarked softly. "You and Athal'rian."

"Two?"

"Touched me." He looked up with a cryptic gleam in his black button eyes. "Few day men will shake hands with a gnome Rap. Even fewer would think a promise made to a gnome had any value at all. But you . . . I think you're a man of your word."

The splendour falls:
> The splendour falls on castle walls,
> And snowy summits old in story . . .
>> O sweet and far from cliff and scar
> The horns of Elfland faintly blowing!
>>>>> Tennyson, *The Princess*

8

To the seas again

1

"*T*he here is something very aesthetic about bacon and eggs," Kade said. "The meld of shapes and colors, perhaps? Or is it because I associate it with childhood? Or winter mornings in Kinvale?" She dabbed her lips with her napkin and sighed like one who could eat nothing more.

Kade was in ecstasy. She had slept in a bed with real linen sheets. She had been granted hot water for washing, and promised a hot tub later in the day. A maiden who was probably one of Elkarath's innumerable granddaughters or great-granddaughters had shampooed her hair and curled it for her afterward quite expertly. The matronly Nimosha, who was one of his daughters or granddaughters, had produced a gown of *almost* Kade's size, in *almost* the current fashion, and had asked if it would suffice until Kade herself could have the merchants bring around better, and of course that could be arranged to happen right after breakfast. Then Kade had eaten bacon and eggs, and with silver cutlery instead of fingers.

The two ladies had consumed their leisurely breakfast in the sheik's personal dining hall. The hour was late enough that everyone else was feverishly occupied elsewhere.

Like all the other chambers they had seen so far, the room was tiny, with only six chairs squeezed in around a table, and the rest of it taken up by a grotesquely awkward sideboard. The furniture was old and rather ugly; being the property of a merchant, even a wealthy merchant, it lacked the ducal opulence of Kinvale. But it was *Imperial* furniture. Bacon and eggs were an *Imperial* dish, and Kade's rather overlong dress was an *Imperial* garment. The casement was closed, but the voices that drifted up from the street were *Imperial* voices. And she was going to summon *Imperial* dressmakers.

Kade was floating on pink clouds.

Inos was gritty-eyed and slack-shouldered from lack of sleep. Flocks of impractical ideas for escape thundered around inside her head like a riot of startled seagulls, but none of them would come to her hand. Realizing that she was being poor company, she now laid her plotting aside for a moment to find some tactful way of dealing with the bacon-and-eggs question—for the real reason Kade liked bacon and eggs had nothing to do with esthetics and was merely that she enjoyed anything soaked in fat and grease.

At that moment the door was, firstly, tapped briskly and, secondly, thrown open to reveal a young man already swooping a low bow. He straightened up, adjusted a snowy lace cuff very slightly, and flashed a dazzling smile. "Mistresses, I am at your service! Guide and fearless protector! Poet, troubadour, humble slave!" Then he stepped into the room and bowed again.

Inos blinked hard and exchanged a bewildered glance with Kade. This was either Skarash or a twin brother.

Skarash was one of the sheik's many grandsons and one of his favorites. But Skarash had been a solemn, surly youth in his late teens, and Inos had never thought of him as dashing before. In all the weeks since leaving Arakkaran, he had neither smiled nor spoken ten words to her, although that was admittedly correct Zarkian behavior toward a woman.

Now he was decked out like an imp, in silver-buckled half boots and hose of sea green, in puffy silken breeches and a white shirt with innumerable ruffles—a very tall, slim-waisted young man with a mop of copper curls flopping cutely over his forehead. Without his straggly ginger beard he seemed somehow older and certainly better-looking. His cheeky, toothy grin was pure imp.

So was the way he lifted Inos's hand to kiss. Kade was right—it was nice to be back in the Impire.

"Good morning. Master Skarash."

"A magnificent morning! Beautiful weather outdoors, beautiful ladies indoors. The Gods are generous." He bowed again.

Skarash could not match Kinvale standards in polish and finesse, but he was certainly coming much closer than any other djinn Inos had yet met. He babbled like an imp.

"What is your pleasure for this magnificent day? Grandsire thought you might care to visit the shopping district—there is no real bazaar here. Or just go sightseeing? Ullacarn is famous for its flowers." His garnet-red eyes twinkled at Inos.

Kade and Inos exchanged more glances of surprise.

"I would enjoy seeing the stores," Kade said wistfully. "Mistress Nimosha mentioned a couturier's establishment on this very street, I think?"

Skarash laughed loudly. "She also mentioned it to Grandsire, and he bit her ears off! He said that for apparel I must take you to Ambly Square, where the rich ladies go." He produced a washleather bag and jingled it suggestively. "I have never known him eager to spend money before, but he threatens I shall eat every groat I bring back. So you will have to help me, and see it all gets spent."

Inos felt cold fingers of suspicion stroke the nape of her neck. What was the mage up to now? "His hospitality brings honor on his house. Are there by chance some conditions attached to such bounty?"

The impudent smile on Skarash's face did not fade or flicker by one eyelash. "He did mention that he would enjoy a word with your gracious self before we set out. Possibly you might put that question to him in person?"

So there were to be strings. Unbreakable strings, most likely. Would Inos feel bound if she gave her parole? A promise made under duress might not be as binding as one freely made, but then she would likely be given the option of staying in a cell . . . and that thought reminded her of Azak.

"First Lionslayer is still in the dungeons?"

"One dungeon. Actually, it's only a subcellar, but it's too damp to store anything of value."

"May I visit him?"

"Certainly! Mistress, I assure you again that your slightest whim is my life's desire." Skarash opened the door and held it.

Inos rose. Kade cast an indecisive look at the puffy rolls and the peach preserve. "I don't much care for dungeons. I think I'll wait here for you, dear."

"Shall I have more tea sent in?"

"No, that's not necessary," Kade said, "I've certainly finished eating.' She sat well back in her chair and tried to look innocent.

The corridor outside was narrow and twisting and uneven. The whole edifice was like that, a maze of low ceilings, peeling plaster walls, and uneven floors—a conglomeration of umpteen buildings, altered and connected and rearranged. "To the left, Inos," Skarash said softly.

Inos stopped and met his eye. "You know who I am? Why I'm here?"

He smirked, stepping close to avoid a woman passing with a load of laundry. He stayed close, looking down at Inos with a twinkle and a scent of rosewater.

"Of course! I'll call you Hathark if you wish, but it's almost as bad as Phattas." His voice had lost the djinn harshness, and his gestures were impish. Could this be sorcery?

"You are strangely changed from the surly young man I knew in the desert."

"Here we are in the Impire. *When in Hub . . .*"

" *. . . do as the Hubbans tell you?*"

"Correct." He took her arm, holding it tight. "This way. And remember also, I am a merchant. I always try to please, especially beautiful ladies. I give whatever you want to receive."

Was a flirtation what she wanted? Skarash seemed to be heading that way like a stampede of camels. But it would be fun to try a little banter again.

"The alteration is an improvement, I think. Which do you prefer being— imp or djinn?"

He grinned, and slid his arm around her. "With you, an imp." Again they had to make way for passing baggage, and this time he contrived to crush Inos into a corner. "Djinns can't peek down a girls cleavage very often," he added, doing so and licking his lips.

Inos placed a heel threateningly on his instep. Her borrowed dress was admittedly tight across the bosom, the neckline strained. She recalled that not so very long ago she had worried about putting padding in her clothes.

And then—but only then—she remembered the pixies. Her heart leaped into her throat. Sudden tremor. Man, too close. Hands. Eyes.

"Something wrong?" Skarash said.

"No!" Mouth dry, skin damp. She struggled to control her breathing. Flirt was not rape! She must not give in to this now or it would haunt her all her days. Could she remember how to flutter an eyelash? "Not at all. I expect I am merely overcome by me sight of a shapely male calf, after being deprived so long."

He gulped, and was djinn enough to need a moment on that one. Inos raced ahead, sternly not thinking of pixies. "I could almost believe that the change in you was due to sorcery."

"Sorcery? I know nothing about sorcery," Skarash said solemnly. But the rosy eyes seemed to change color slightly, and what they said was. *Nobody else knows anything about that, and if the mage chose me to be your guide it was to make sure that there is no loose talk about sorcery.*

Elkarath had mentioned that Skarash was the one entrusted with laying out the first magic carpet. He had been standing guard outside the door when the second arrived with its passengers. He was very likely the Chosen One, the heir who would receive the words of power when the sheik died.

"Just a joke," Inos said.

He nodded as if satisfied, and they continued along the bustling corridor, then down yet another winding staircase, the sixth cr seventh Inos had met already. The noises that infected the whole house were growing louder. "We have to go through here anyway, and Grandsire wants that word with you." Skarash opened a door and ushered Inos into me largest open space she had yet seen in Ullacarn.

Obviously it was the business area of the House of Elkarath, and with the annual caravan having arrived only the previous day, disorder and tumult were rampant. Light poured in through three open doorways, each large enough to admit a six-horse wagon, but the air was so thick with dust that Inos began to sneeze at once, and her eyes to water—so Skarash considerately put his arm around her again, guiding her between the high-piled clutter of barrels and bales and boxes. The odor of cloves and cinnamon and caraway was intoxicating, but the whiff of camel and horse was undeniable also. Porters and wagoneers and customers milled to and fro, arguing and shouting over the din, loading and unloading, taking and bringing.

The legionaries standing by the doors were a surprise. Outside in the fiery sunshine the busy street was thronged with people, all of them apparently imps: ladies in bright gowns, with unveiled faces; many men, and even woman, with their heads uncovered—although persons of quality wore fancy hats, of course. Sudden nostalgia snatched Inos's breath away.

With eyes streaming and nose tingling, she found herself arriving at a short flight of steps, leading up to a platform. There, in a large chair behind a long table, sat Elkarath, writing with one hand, finger ng his beard with the other, an oasis of calm amid the hubbub, quietness within the racket. No sheik now, within the Impire, he was merely Master Elkarath the merchant, yet imposing enough in a bulky scarlet robe and a gold skullcap. Great ledgers stood stacked beside him; clerks rushed in and out through other doors, or merely hovered, waiting for his attention. Here the master could oversee the loading and unloading, the trading and tabulating.

Grateful that she need not raise skirts, for her hem was well above her ankles, Inos climbed the worn wooden treads, assisted of course by the willing hand of Skarash.

"You may have to wait a moment Mistress," he muttered in her ear. "That one looks important."

Elkarath was rising stiffly to greet a visitor, a legionary. The white horsehair crest on his helmet denoted a centurion.

"Why soldiers?" Inos murmured, stepping back to where she would not impede the swarming clerks. "What has the army to do with merchants?" There were at least a dozen helmets in sight, all with black or brown crests.

"Guards," Skarash said, moving close. "This stuff is worth a fortune."

"And who would steal it?"

"The army might." He chuckled at her glance of surprise. "Watch Grandsire closely. There!"

A leather bag passed unobtrusively from merchant to centurion.

"Graft?"

"Of course."

Hands were being shaken across the table now, and the centurion saluted.

Inos let her attention wander over the bustling throng on the lower level. "Red hair? Obviously most of these men are djinns?"

"At least half of them are relatives."

"Then why dress like imps?"

Skarash showed his teeth in a snarl. "Believe me, having red hair is bad enough. Dressing like a *barbarian* is asking for trouble."

"Is Ullacarn part of the Impire, then? I thought it was an independent city-state."

"Only on paper. An Imperial protectorate, allied by treaty. But there are legionaries here. Lots of them."

Oh! Like that, was it? There were legionaries in Krasnegar now, or there had been the last time Inos had heard.

Skarash said, "You've been noticed."

Elkarath had resumed his seat and was beckoning. Inos picked her way across the platform, between the dodging, hovering flunkies. The centurion was still standing there, but as she approached he removed his helmet to show that his visit was now social. He was inspecting her with brazen approval, but she had been away from imps long enough to notice the swarthy, pocky complexion, the thick waist and narrow shoulders. Short by djinn standards . . . but handsome enough in his shiny bronze. More muscle than fat, dark wavy hair. Not bad.

"Mistress Hathark!" Elkarath boomed. His voice and manner had changed dramatically also, although not as much as his grandson's. "You slept well, lady?"

Had he been spying on her insomnia? Inos donned one of Kade's witless social smiles. "Never better, thank you, sir! I was weary from the journey." She wondered if a curtsy was appropriate, and compromised with a dainty bob. The centurion's eyes were still peeling her, and she wished her dress were just a little more Zarkian, or not quite so stretched in places.

Elkarath nodded to her bob, without rising. "Skarash will see you have everything you need, Mistress. May I present Centurion Imopopi?"

She bobbed agan, the imp saluted.

"Your first visit to beautiful Ullacarn, ma'am?"

Inos felt an odd twinge of indecision. She was not sure what she was supposed to say. Elkarath would hardly have explained that she was a refugee queen from a kingdom at the other end of the wor d. On the other hand, his deceits were his own problem, and she needed information as a fish needs water.

"Yes, it is. Indeed I am a newcomer to this part of the world."

That should have led the conversation toward Krasnegar, but Elkarath moved to block it. "Mistress Hathark and her party will not be staying long. They are merely passing through, on their way back to Hub."

They were? Why would Rasha . . . had Inos then been sold already? Was she to be delivered to Olybino in Hub? What use trying to escape if she was bound for Hub anyway, or was this a trick?

Before she could question. Centurion Imopopi laughed harshly, and Inos felt her skin prickle as if in premonition of something wrong, but she had no time to analyze, for he was speaking to her.

"I shall not venture to praise Ullacarn if you are familiar with the city of the Gods, ma'am. You had best not linger long, though. The season is late. The passes will be closing soon."

"Passes?" Inos fished frantically for geography that had momentarily slid down behind the back of her mind.

"The Qoble Range, of course." Why did his voice bother her? "You are not from Hub originally, though?"

He himself was, or from somewhere close to it. Perhaps it was merely his accent jangling her alarms, and yet she had heard tones like that often enough at Kinvale.

"Not by a long way."

"You have traveled far, then?" A small frown showed that the soldier's carnal inspection had become tinged with more intellectual interest. He was wondering what she was, as she did not quite fit any of the standard races. Golden hair meant either elf or jotunn in the family tree—plus what? What she was would be defined by her homeland.

"Oh, very far?" Inos said. "So far that—much as I regret to say so—we had never heard of Ullacarn where I come from."

A gentleman dandy might have prolonged the verbal sparring; a soldier went straight to the point. "And where is that?" Again his voice rasped a nerve. It was not the voice of a common swordbanger, she decided. He spoke like an upper-class Hubban. But rich families' sons were not thrown in with the common herd to work their way up through the ranks.

"I'm sure you won't ever have heard of it," Inos said, with her best two-sugar-lump simper. "A faraway kingdom called *Krasnegar?* It—"

Centurion Imopopi dropped his smile. Color flooded his face, giving it a hard, dangerous look. He paced forward menacingly, ostentatiously replacing his helmet. "Whatever rumors you may have heard, miss, were malicious falsehoods. When we apprehend persons spreading such slanders, we deal with them in appropriate fashion."

Despite herself, Inos backed up a step. The centurion followed her, dark eyes blazing. "The men are flogged for acting against the public good. Women are punished as common scolds. Is that not fair?"

She was off balance. She was taken by surprise. It was too soon after the pixies, and this man was potentially just as dangerous, albeit in other ways. He could tie her behind his horse and drag her to the jail if he chose. Skarash had warned her, and obviously an Imperial legionary on street duty was not the same thing as a tribune or a proconsul sipping tea in a Kinvale parlor. Suddenly she thought of pixies again, and began to shake again, and could find absolutely nothing to say. Her mouth was too dry to say anything, anyway.

"On the second offense we tear out their tongues."

Inos tried to say, "But, Centurion," and produced a croak. She backed another step.

The collapse of her conversational efforts had been amusing Elkarath, but now he came to her rescue. "Centurion, I think there must be a misunderstanding. I'm sure that Mistress Hathark intended no harm to the public good. She meant no slight to the imperor or his army. Indeed, I think that you may have misheard her. She hails from a small island state named Har Nogar, located near Uthle."

Centurion Imopopi kept his glittering gaze on Inos. "Did you say 'Har Nogar,' mistress?"

Inos nodded vigorously. Elkarath's hand moved to a row of leather bags, and closed on one of them with a faint clink that caught the centurion's attention at once.

"Mistress Hathark and her aunt will likely wish to see something of the town today," the mage remarked innocently. "Possibly visit the markets. I wonder, as she is a stranger here, whether an escort ought be advisable?" The bag moved a handsbreadth closer to the legionary.

His anger faded as reluctantly as a summer sunset. "We brook no trouble on the streets in Ullacarn, but I can understand how well-born ladies feel happier with personal protection. I shall gladly assign some men to escort them."

The bag moved the rest of the way and clinked again as it was removed by a strong military hand. Imopopi turned back to Inos. "Enjoy your visit, ma'am. Don't believe everything you hear. And certainly don't repeat it." With a final glare of warning, he saluted, spun around, and stamped away as if he were patrolling a siege line.

Inos was left quivering, wishing she had a chair. Aghast at her own timidity—and appalled at the thought that her experience with the pixies might have broken her nerve forever—she leaned both hands on the table. "What provoked that?" she shrilled.

Elkarath shrugged. "Ullacarn is a snakepit of rumors. Obviously you stepped on one of them."

"Krasnegar? An Imperial defeat at Krasnegar?"

"That would seem to be likely. Did you hear anything, Skarash?"

Skarash stroked imaginary lint from an immaculate lace cuff. "Not much, Grandsire, only that a legion was jumped by goblins while returning from a courtesy visit to a flyspeck place no one had ever heard of before. *Courtesy* visit? I like that a lot! Half the men were cut to pieces, or worse. There is talk of prisoners enjoying traditional goblin hospitality. Nothing more than that."

His uncle nodded and looked in the general direction of Inos. "Avoid the subject when talking to soldiers, I suggest." He reached for a massive ledger, ancient and tattered.

"Obviously. It wasn't a full legion, though."

"Almost half of one. Rumors always exaggerate. Certainly bad enough. And defeat by goblins . . ." He opened the book, but Inos thought he was chuckling silently. "No wonder the bronze bullies don't like to discuss it."

Her head was spinning. Four cohorts savaged by goblins? The forestfolk had always been treacherous, but never warlike. Now the warlock of the east had suffered a shattering blow. Where did that leave her? Would he seek revenge on the goblins? Had the legionaries been driven out of Krasnegar by Kalkor and his jotnar, or had they fled voluntarily?

And there was another matter—

"I am truly going on to Hub?"

The old man nodded, dipping his quill in a silver inkwell. "Her Majesty has so decreed."

"So! So I've been sold? She's made her deal with Olybino, and now all that remains is to deliver the goods?"

"Not at all. You are still her Majesty's guest. Enjoy your stay in Ullacarn, it will be brief."

His eyes! She wanted to see his eyes!

"I can't imagine why she would be sending me to Hub, then!"

"I didn't question. But if you can't, then perhaps others may be less likely to?" The old man's voice had sharpened half a tone, but he placidly ran a finger up a page as if counting.

"You mean I was hidden in the desert, and now I'm going to be hidden on the road to Hub . . . least likely place to look? And when the contract is finally signed, I'll be—"

"Draw your own conclusions. Meanwhile I have work to do."

"And Azak? Is he going back to Arakkaran, or coining with me, or will you leave him rotting—"

"He goes with you." The plump finger stopped on the numbers, but the old man did not look up. "Your cabins are reserved on *Dawn Pearl,* which sails in three days. It was to Hub you were headed, was it not? Well, to Hub you are going."

"I wish to see him!"

"Of course. By all means. Just one *friend* calling on another, I assume? Skarash will take you." Elkarath reached into the folds of his scarlet robe, then dropped a rusty key on the table. "You may give him this."

"No parole?"

He sighed crossly. "None at all. You will find no better ship than *Dawn Pearl,* and certainty none leaving sooner. Begone!"

Confused and suspicious, Inos watched Skarash take up the key, and then allowed him to usher her back to the steps. A horde of clerks and menials took this as their chance to rush forward and consult the merchant. Inos was left to ponder her fate. Why should Rasha send her to Hub? Stranger yet, why should she send Azak? It might be all a deception.

She, at least, was going to have a military escort, which would not make escape any easier. Had Elkarath deliberately arranged the little scene with the angry centurion?

There had been something odd—something very odd—about Imopopi. Just thinking of him gave Inos crawly feelings. She needed to talk with Azak. Him, at least, she could trust.

2

"Odd people, elves," Ishist said, and his voice echoed away into the black hollow ahead.

There was a sinister note in that remark, somehow. Or perhaps it was just that Rap was feeling jumpy, marching through, the bowels of the earth with a sorcerer.

"They live a long time?" he said hastily, unable to think of any comment more intelligent.

"They don't, actually. They just don't show their age like other people."

The oppressive silence returned, broken only by the gentle pad of footsteps and the whispered swish of long robes.

Nothing but sorcery could have carved a tunnel so smooth and regular, and so astonishingly long. "Thraine's Wormhole," the gnome had called it, with a private chuckle at some obscure historical joke. It sloped downward, never steeply and sometimes almost imperceptibly; but it held a steady bearing just west of north as if bored by a homing bee. It was dry and empty and musty-smelling; he had mentioned earlier that decades might pass without it being used. It was understandably dark and quiet.

"Odd people," he repeated. He walked boldly into the blackness with Rap at his side. A spectral glow at their heels provided light for Gathmor and Darad, who were following closely, and the dark closed in behind. The light was faintly pink, had no detectable source, cast no shadows.

Ishist had sent Sagorn away. Apparently he preferred Darad to any of the others, perhaps because he did not put on airs. Darad was just a brutal killer, and proud of it.

"Odd in what way?" Rap asked then.

"All sorts of ways, lad. What they'll tell you is that every elf belongs to a clan, and owes all his loyalty to his clan. Each clan owns a tree, or the tree owns them, maybe. And each clan has a chief. Sound simple?"

"No. Sky trees?" Rap's deeper voice echoed even more than the gnome's. He could not detect the surface now. A whole mountain seemed to lie above, pressing down relentlessly.

"Of course." Ishist was barefoot; the others were shod in elven boots of leather soft as gossamer. Their tread was spookily soft.

"And it's more complicated?" Rap asked, sending rumbles down the long tube.

"Nothing is ever simple around elves. It doesn't help that they never tell nonelves anything. Clans have alliances and feuds, which they don't talk about, which seem to come and go like the tide. There are subclans and over-clans. A clan may have more than one tree, and more than one clan may have rights in one tree. Any clan may have more than one chief—a chief for justice, a chief for wisdom, a chief for war, a chief for law . . . Gods know how they're chosen or how it all works, if it does." He fell silent for a few paces, then added, "But historically the elves have held off the imps better than almost anyone, except the dwarves, so I suppose it must work after a fashion."

"Anthropophagi?"

"Ah, yes. I'd forgotten the anthropophagi—I wonder how many imps they manage to eat in an average year? The merfolk have their little ways, too. Anyway, that's elves. If there's a complicated way to do something, an elf will find it; especially if it looks pretty or sounds good. The clan's the important thing. Even if an elf's family's lived within the Impire for generations, he'll still regard himself as belonging to one particular clan, one especial tree, although most clans control several trees. He may well have other, personal loyalties and allegiances within his clan."

Rap wondered why he was being given the lecture, but he supposed he would find out soon enough—either the little gnome would come to the point, or events would. He blinked a few times, before realizing that the speck in his eye was actually a gleam of light a long way ahead. His farsight told him that the hillside above was back within his range, and dropping steeply.

"This comes out not far from the fence," Ishist said, changing the subject. "About a league. And about another league beyond that is the imperial highway from Puldarn to Noom. Straight as an arrow. Imps have no sense of artistry at all. So the elves say."

"It must be a very busy highway." Rap was not experienced with crowds on the scale of the Impire. The thought of big cities made him nervous.

"Lords, yes! All the traffic between the Dragon Sea and Home Water goes along it. It ought to be farther from the fence. My pets sense the metal going by and howl like dogs. They go mad when the annual tax train passes. You taking your two friends with you?"

"Er . . . their decision."

"I think you should."

"But one of them has a word of power, and Warlock Lith—"

"True, but he can get that one out of you anyway," Ishist said callously. "If he has to damage someone, I suspect his sense of artistry would be more impressed by a well-matched sequential set than an oversize faun with goblin tattoos."

That sounded like a threat. Despite the gnome's apparent friendliness, he was dangerous; very dangerous and very unpredictable. His comically disgusting appearance concealed not only great occult power, but also a mind of deadly sharpness. His ways of thinking were as alien as the dragons'. Rap could not imagine what many years of tending those monsters might do to a man, and he did not know how a gnome would have thought in the first place. Who ever talked with gnomes to find out?

The speck was a visible circle of light now. The air felt damper, and cooler.

"They can come with me if they wish—or not, if they wish," Rap said stubbornly. Then he realized that Ishist could just change his friends' minds if he thought it a good idea. With sorcerers, as with elves, nothing was ever simple.

The tunnel ended abruptly in a small natural cave. Weeping gray sky and wet greenery were framed in the entrance arch, its ragged edges blurred by moss and fern. A steady vertical rain was soaking the hills as if willing to do so for weeks, hissing on rocks and mud, drumming on leaves. The four men stood under the lip of the cavern and peered out. Water dribbled and splashed everywhere, even dripping from the roof.

Gathmor uttered a long sigh of satisfaction. "Glad to see daylight," he muttered. "Don't like caves."

Darad grunted agreement, and Rap wondered if dislike of caves was a jotunn characteristic. He did not care for them either.

Ishist looked up at Gathmor. "West on the highway'll take you to Puldarn. If you're heading home, that is."

The sailor gnawed his silver mustache for a moment, then spoke to Rap over the gnome's head. "You meet Kalkor again?"

"That's the prophecy."

His pale eyes narrowed icily. "I'll stay aboard, then."

"Thanks, Cap'n."

"East to Noom," the sorcerer said. "First Tithro, then Noom. There you choose—overland to Hub, or sail to Ilrane. Valdorians in the west, near the coast, which is handy for you."

Ilrane!

Eastward? Closer to Zark? No, that wasn't it . . .

Rap realized that the sorcerer was eyeing him with a very curious expression. "Sir?"

"You having a premonition?" asked the gnome, scratching busily.

"I'm not sure." The idea of going to Ilrane had certainly stirred something in Rap, something encouraging. He remembered he'd felt a twinge when Ishist had first suggested a visit to Lith'rian. He'd even felt traces of . . . whatever it was . . . when he arrived at Warth Redoubt. And whatever it was, it seemed to be getting stronger every time. Was that practice?

Ishist still wore a puzzled pout. "Adepts don't usually . . . O' course, geniuses don't usually have farsight . . . New, is it?"

Rap nodded uneasily. "My mother was said to be a seer."

The gnome shrugged. "Possible, then. Fauns have a reputation for trusting their own feelings, don't they?" He chuckled to himself. "And I'm not doing it to you. You'll find it rarely comes to order, but when it does you can trust it. Now, which is it to be? Hub or Ilrane?"

"How far?" Rap ashed.

The gnome closed his eyes for a moment, as if consulting a mental map; perhaps he was farseeing a real chart. "A bit over four hundred leagues in either case."

"Water's faster!" Gathmor said quickly, and even Darac nodded as he struggled to keep up with the conversation.

"Not if you catch a ride on a stage," Ishist said.

Ilrane still felt right. Rap could walk ten leagues a day, maybe more on an Imperial highway. That was still more than a month to Hub, even if nothing went wrong. Water was faster and safer. "How do I get on a ship, though?"

"Steal a boat," Gathmor said impatiently.

"Then its owner may starve, and his children, too."

The jotunn grimaced at such sissy sentimentality.

"Thinal?" Darad said triumphantly.

177

I suppose so," Rap said sadly. If Thinal was willing to help, then he could steal the price of a ticket in Noom as easily as he had done the same thing for Andor in Milflor. Come to think of it, Rap probably could do those sorts of things himself now. He would just have to hope that whoever was chosen to support the cause could afford the honor.

The gnome was watching, scratching things out of his beard, and leering. "What do you advise, Ishist?" Rap asked, trying to feel trusting.

"Oh, sea! Your biggest problem isn't getting there, wherever you go. You need to worry more about getting in to meet Lith'rian. An audience with the Imperor might be easier to arrange than a private chat with a warlock."

"If I used my powers right outside his gates? He'd sense me just like you did when I sent the dragon away."

"The guards will be votaries. They'll turn you to stone before you can blink."

Rap gulped.

"Besides," Ishist added, "Hub's dangerous. Other wardens, and would-be wardens. You'll be safest to stay in South's sector."

"Advise me, please," Rap said, as he was expected to.

"There's one sure way. Would only work for an elf, though."

"Yes?" Rap said cautiously. He distrusted a sorcerer's sense of humor on principle, and Ishist's in particular.

"I'd have to make you look elvish. It would be a low-power sorcery. It won't fool Lith'rian, of course, if you get to him; or any other full sorcerer. But otherwise you should pass."

"And?"

"And you can get taken right to Lith'rian." The old man chuckled. "Express."

Rap watched his own cheeks redden under the challenge—his new reversible farsight could be a disconcerting ability. "That's the fastest way?"

"Yes."

"Then go ahead! Make me look elvish."

The stubble that had collected on Rap's face since he left Durthing fell off like cottontree fluff. His skin began to turn yellow—and not just on his face. His eyes . . . he watched in astonishment as they grew larger and somehow tilted, as the gray of his irises developed the opalescent sparkle of the pure-bred elf. The skin change had almost reached his toes. His hair was curling and taking on the metallic golden luster—even his body hair, he noticed uneasily. His legs were shedding as his chin had. And were Little Chicken here, he could no longer call him "Flat Nose." His tattoos were gone.

Then it was done. In a vague way, Rap was still Rap, but he was an elvish Rap—about the same height as before, but slimmer, slighter. Better looking than before, of course, but an ugly elf.

His robe shimmered and faded away, revealing snug-fitting jerkin and long trousers, of the same delicate leather as his boots, and colored bright green and blue. He did not remember putting those on. A matching forester's cap fell from nowhere and settled lightly on his shiny golden curls. He fingered an elvish ear thoughtfully.

He sniffed, and realized his sense of smell had returned—woodsy scents of wet loam and leaves, plus the powerful stink of the gnome beside him.

"Gods!" Gathmor said, horrified. "You look just like an elf! Even your eyes."

"Yes, I know." Rap's voice was higher pitched, and somehow *sweeter.* "It may take some getting used to."

Ishist chuckled, greatly pleased with himself. "You needn't be so worried! Everything's still there, it just looks different. The hair will grow back afterward. Don't be tempted to try anything, sailor. He looks elf and feels elf, but he's still got his strength. And he's still an adept."

Gathmor pouted. He must have felt tempted.

"I've put a year's limit on it, lad," the sorcerer said. "You're going to L th'rian of your own free will, understand? That's still the case. But if no one takes the spell off, it'll fade in a year. And you others—I think you'd better be dressed the same, at least." Robes vanished, foresters' leathers appeared on Gathmor in red and yellow, green and white on Darad. Caps and all.

The sight of the mighty-thewed Darad in such clothing was not one to be taken lightly, Rap thought, and realized how much he had already adapted to the ways of sorcery. Gathmor hadn't—he swore under his breath, and squirmed.

Rap said, "Explain how this gets me to the warlock, Ishist."

The gnome's black eyes twinkled. "There'll be lots of elves in Noom. In the Impire they're usually artists of one sort or another. They can't compete in business with imps, and they profess to despise fighting. They sculpt and sing and so on. Pick a big one."

"Big one?" Rap repeated warily.

"Important. A chief elf in a group of elves."

With a strange sensation that this conversation was somehow familiar, Rap said, "Then what do I do?"

The little old man cackled. "Then you punch him on the nose."

3

Like the rest of the House of Elkarath, the cellars were a jumble of mismatched levels and shapes—innumerable separate constructions that had grown together over the ages like some gigantic family whose members could never agree on anything. Most of the vaults were stacked high with merchandise, and much of it could be identified by smell alone: brandy and vinegar and turpentine in kegs; hides and cedar planks in stacks. But the dimness also held mysterious bales and barrels and baskets; ingots, crates, and flagons; urns and ewers and hampers. And shadows! With one hand comfortingly gripped by Skarash, and the other holding her lantern high to watch for uneven footing and low beams, Inos told herself very sternly that queens were not frightened of shadows. Or dust. Or rats, if rats there be.

Or Skarash.

But she hoped he could not feel the tremor in her hand.

Once in a while she saw other lights flickering beyond arches or down tunnels; rarely she heard distant voices and footsteps. It was all very creepy.

She soon began to suspect that the curiously brash Skarash was leading her around in a circle, up and down, in and out, in a tour of the whole bewildering catacomb, but she was *not* going to allow yesterday's experience with the pixies to turn her into a nerveless ninny frightened of anything that grew hair on its chin. Her behavior when the centurion blustered had been shameful, but she ought to be able to handle Master Starash no matter how friendly he became. If all he was trying to do was frighten her, then he could tunnel his way back to Arakkaran first. But their two lanterns did make the odd-shaped shadows shimmy in a sinister silent dance.

Something rustled . . . she jumped. Evil take it!

"Just rats, I think," Skarash said, stooping low under a tangle of beams that seemed to have been added as an afterthought to hold up part of the roof. "Or gnomes, which are worse. Every year or two gnomes get in here, and they're the Gods' own pests to get rid of. Mind the cobwebs. This next door is especially tuneful, as I recall."

He was right—it opened with a long, ear-rending scream of agony.

"I first came to Ullacarn when I was ten," he said, leading the way down more stairs. "I thought the desert was the most wonderful place in the world—until I discovered these cellars." High-vaulted and quite empty, the chamber gave his voice an eerie echo. The air was dank, the wall streaked with niter.

"And every year since, Grandsire has brought me along. We kids used to make up . . . Sh!" He stopped on the last tread and turned, staring up at the door they had just come through. "Hear anything?" he whispered.

"No."

He stepped down to the floor, then turned again, looking up at her intently. "Sure?"

He was playing a game, she thought, but she cocked her head and harked. "No."

Skarash frowned and laid down his lantern.

Above her, the door shrieked like a trampled cat, then slammed shut in a reverberating roll of thunder. She leaped, he reached up and caught her. She slammed her lantern against his knee, clawed at his eyes, instinctively banged a knee at his groin, and broke free.

Then she was cowering back against the wall, fighting down a crazy spinning panic, panting madly, with her heart beating inside her head and a vile taste in her throat, hefting the lantern to strike him if he came closer. *Enrage them into a mating frenzy,* Elkarath had said.

Her knee had missed the tender spot that had worked on the pixie, but Skarash had retreated several paces. He raised a hand to his cheek and then inspected the blood on his fingers.

"Gods, lady! I didn't mean . . ." Even in the uncertain light of the lanterns, his shock was obviously genuine.

She had not screamed, though. She struggled to calm her frantic breathing. She glanced back up at the door. "Kids?"

"Always. The place swarms with them. But—"

He dabbed at his face again, staring at her. Worried.

No mating frenzy, just a cruel practical joke.

Kids! "What exactly did you have in mind?" Inos asked, furious now.

He was blushing, dark in the dim light. "I thought . . . It was only a joke, my lady. I meant no harm."

She shouted. "Explain!"

He squirmed. "We used to do it to the girls. Make them jump into our arms. No harm, really. Just . . . I've never kissed a queen."

A queen. She was *not* going to let yesterday's escape scar her. She was *not* going to shy at shadows all her life. Pixies, centurions . . . now she had fallen for a stupid, juvenile, childish prank. Men!

She laid down her lantern with a clatter. "Then let's try that again!"

"*What?*"

Inos stamped up the stairs to where she had been standing before. "I said let's try that again!"

Wide-eyed, Skarash walked back to his former place also, and then just stared up at her.

"Well?" she demanded, ignoring the pounding of her heart and the wetness of her palms, wishing he would get on with it.

Skarash whispered, "Bang?"

Unencumbered by a lantern, she jumped; he caught her and set her down. Then he took a deep breath and kissed her lips.

Apparently Skarash had not been planning much of a kiss, or else was now frightened to, but she clung tight, closed her eyes, and kept it going, turning it into a long, intimate thing. He wasn't as experienced as Andor had been. He probably had no more experience than Rap had had, but he caught on quickly. And in the end it was she who broke it off.

"Gods!" he muttered. "Majesty! Gods!"

Skarash, she suddenly realized, might possibly be a valuable ally, if she could ever trust him at all. Centurions, pixies . . . she had not panicked. In fact she had withstood that better than he had—he looked much more scared than she felt. Nor had she roused him to a mating frenzy. Apart from a curious shaky feeling, she had come out of that quite well.

"I definitely do like you better as an imp."

Skarash just murmured, "Gods!" again, as if bewildered by impish ways.

"Well, then, let's go."

He nodded dumbly, and picked up the lanterns. Inos accepted hers, and followed him across the cellar floor with her heart still thumping.

She had exorcised the pixies! She had not used some unconscious magic to drive the man mad, but neither had she panicked when he touched her. She had almost enjoyed the kiss. Not quite, though.

And in spite of what Elkarath had said—and what Aunt Kade so obviously feared—she had not been thinking of Azak.

She had been thinking of Rap.

4

Another door groaning open, and another few steps down, and yet another door. Skarash paused. "This one's never used for storage," he said softly. "Except for people. We used to frighten the small fry to death in this one!"

Inos ducked through the doorway after him and then recoiled in disgust. Walls and floor gleamed wet in the lantern's flicker, and drips fell steadily from the low roof. Azak was sitting on the bare stones, an arm raised to shield his eyes from the light. She was horrified—no bedding, no light; damp, foul air. The only furniture was a bucket; the kennel was barely big enough for him to stretch out, and a rusty metal chain connected his ankle to a staple set in the middle of the floor.

"Good morning, my love. Or is it evening?"

"Haven't they fed you? No water? What kind of brutality is this?"

"Standard persuasion." He uncovered his eyes cautiously and peered up at the other visitor, blinking.

"Skarash ak'Arthark ak'Elkarath, Sire." Heedless of his expensive hose, Skarash knelt on the wet stone and bowed his head.

"Sire?" Azak filled a little word with infinite scorn.

Skarash looked up. "A true Arakkaranian, your Majesty! One of your loyal subjects!"

Where had he come from, this serious young man? The prankster had vanished, and the face in the lanterns' glow was hard and intense. Even his voice was harsher, pure southern Zarkian.

Azak shrugged. He moved his feet and the chain rattled. "Then I suggest you demonstrate your devotion by getting me out of here."

"I am honored, Sire!" Skarasb produced the rusty key and reached for the padlock.

"Stop!" Azak barked. "I am not giving my parole to any flea-ridden camel trader!"

"Sire—"

"No! If you came to tell me to behave and promise to be a good boy, then you're wasting your—" Azak broke off in a fit of coughing. "And the same with you," he told Inos hoarsely.

Stubborn ox! Mule! He wouldn't last a week in this tomb. She could feel the damp burrowing into her bones already, and he had been down here all night. Pigheaded idiot!

"Please, Sire?" Skarash begged. "One word?"

"I can spare you a few minutes, I suppose."

"Sire, there are Imperial legions in Ullacarn—"

"There are always . . . Go on!"

Words spurted from Skarash: "Far more troops than I have ever seen, Sire! This is the tenth time I have visited Ullacarn, and I have not seen this before. I arrived not long before you did, Sire, and I haven't had time to investigate properly, but the entire XXth Legion came in last month, and now the van of the XXXIInd is arriving. It's said the emir is under house arrest, and there is talk of rebellion in Garpoon and the Impire is behind it."

"God of Torment!"

"And the IVth Fleet is in port."

Azak looked to Inos, and then changed his mind and addressed the worried-looking Skarash. "You swear this?"

"Aye, Sire! May the Good spurn my soul!"

"Your grandfather put you up to it?"

"No, Sire. I doubt if he even knows. He hasn't been out yet. I mean, I rode into town with the caravan. He . . . well, you know."

Azak grunted and pulled his knees up, clattering rust flakes off his fetters. He leaned his arms on them, and then put his chin on his arms, saying nothing, staring at the lanterns.

"They'll strike Garpoon first, won't they?" Skarash whispered. "Then round the coast . . . one at a time . . . city by city?"

Azak shot a glance at him. "Merchants deal in strategy now?" But there was amusement in his voice.

"Ji-Gon's last campaign—I learned it in school. And the Widow War began that way, didn't it?"

"Yes, it did, Master Skarash. You can't move an army across the desert, so they always come by the coast, one way or the other. Usually from the north, but they have tried the south, too, at times."

"And we djinns never unite until it's too late! Why wait for them to chew us up? Get back to Arakkaran, Sire, and raise the black banner yourself, while there is still time!"

"God of Slaughter!" Azak shook his head in wonder, staring at the lanterns. "It doesn't make sense! They can't move supplies over the Qoble Range in winter. They might come across Thume again . . . the elves'll never let them through Ilrane. Maybe the Keriths? They may be going to try the Keriths again!"

"I don't know, Sire! I'm only a trader."

Azak grunted. "They might take Garpoon now, and make their big move in the spring . . ." He groaned. "What are his terms?"

"None, your Majesty!" Skarash began twisting the key, but the lock proved stubborn. "You are released. No parole."

"What!" Azak looked up at Inos.

Her neck was growing stiff under the low ceiling. "It's true. He says we're going to Hub! He has bought passage for us. We sail in three days."

Azak grunted with astonishment and stared at her, not heeding as the lock squealed and opened. Skarash unwrapped the chain from the sultan's ankle.

Then Azak looked down, and rubbed it. "I am grateful, Master Skarash! Mayhap we can talk later? Meanwhile, I could surely use a bath."

"At once, Sire!" Skarash was on his feet and out the door already with a lantern. His footsteps died away, then loud hinges wailed in the distance. Azak snorted. "Didn't wait for formal dismissal, did he? Weak on etiquette!"

"What else is he weak on? I've never heard him speak like that, and he was playing imp dandy all the way here." Imp lover.

"Skarash? Bah! He's a mimic, the man of a thousand masks. I've watched him trading. He'll make a great merchant. He shows what you want to see, says what you want to hear."

Kisses you when you want to be kissed.

So Skarash could never be trusted. Did Inos have any allies at all? She took the lantern and backed out of the tiny cell. Azak followed, then straightened to his full height with a groan of relief. He rubbed his back.

Reconciliation! She said, "Azak, I did not use occult power on you! I swear it."

He peered down at her for a moment, then shook his head sadly. "No. If you had, it would have faded, wouldn't it? Unless you're a full sorceress it would have gone away in the night?"

"Yes."

"It didn't! I am still quite hopelessly in love with you."

That, to her surprise, was a huge relief. Perhaps she also had wondered. Perhaps she was starting to return his love.

Perhaps that was why he had chosen to spend the night in the cellar. She turned away quickly and headed for the stair, hoping she could find a route out of the labyrinth.

"I shall be glad to see daylight again," Azak growled behind her. "I don't like caves . . . but what is this tale of sailing to the Impire?"

"I don't know. It's what Elkarath says. It may be just a lie, to keep us from trying to escape."

"Or Rasha may have sold us both to Olybino. You to be puppet queen of Krasnegar, me to be returned to Zark as traitor."

"Traitor?" She stopped and looked up at him. "You?"

His expression was bleak. "You heard Skarash. It is coming, as we suspected. Always when the Impire invades, we djinns unite and throw them out again. If we did it sooner we could keep them out, but we always do it eventually. Eventually a supreme leader raises the black banner. I am the obvious candidate."

"Er . . . of course."

"And if the warlock of the east has laid a loyalty spell on me?"

She nodded, horrified once again at the dark workings of sorcery. Azak might be in greater danger than she was.

She started up the stairs, with her shadow dancing on the wall beside her. "You should take Skarash's advice. Find a ship bound for Arakkaran as soon as you can."

They were through the door at the top before Azak said, "No. I shall stay with you. I care more for you than I do for Zark, or Arakkaran, or anything."

Again she halted and spun around to look at him in wonder. "This is madness!"

"Yes. But love always is, isn't it?"

"Your kingdom? Your sons?"

"I would give away my kingdom forever if I could just kiss you just once."

She could find no answer to that.

To the seas again:

I must go down to the seas again, to the lonely sea and the sky,
And all I ask is a tall ship and a star to steer her by.
                                        Masefield, *Sea-Fever*

9

They also serve

1

With rain dribbling down his neck and only two hours of daylight left to reach Puldarn, Ulynago thumped the reins and bellowed at his team. Ahead of him the ancient highway ran like a beam of gray light through the black woods, straight for the notch in the trees on the ridge ahead. Had he been able to see back over the load, the view behind would have been just about identical; traffic was almost nonexistent in this weather. He'd met none since Thin Bridge, just outside Tithro.

On the bench at his side, Iggo slumped and nodded, two-thirds asleep. No man ought to be able to sleep in such a downpour, but Iggo wasn't very much awake at the best of times.

In Puldarn there was hot food and beer and a certain well-padded waitress. Ulynago was a man of simple tastes.

Until four years ago, he'd been a legionary. He'd seen no real fighting, but he'd cut up a few rebellious gnomes in his time. Revolting gnomes, the legions called them—gnomes were always revolting. Joke! Good sport, though, gnomes. He'd struggled his way up to centurion near the end of his term. Then there had been better opportunities. He'd retired with a lot more than his official requital, enough to buy his wheels and hooves, back home in South Pithmot where he'd been raised. And he'd hired as swamper, Iggo who was big and stupid—stupid enough once to tackle a drunken troll and a lot stupider afterward. An ideal helper, who couldn't always remember when he'd been paid.

So everything was just as the Gods ordered, except for this Evil-take-it rain. Ulynago hoped the wet wouldn't get into his wheat, good northern wheat that had come all the way from Shimlundok, destined for rich folks' fine bread. The damp would do it no good, and him no good, therefore. The merchants would try to chew him down on the price.

With no warning, he forgot the wheat. He had a different problem—the horses breaking step, trying to slow to a walk. What the Evil? The wagon rocked. He yelled and pulled out his whip. He cracked it. It made no difference. Something had spooked them, they were fighting the weight, all on the wrong feet. The rig twisted. Hastily he grabbed the brake. Iggo lurched forward and awoke with a bellow of oaths.

"Shut up and get the blades!" Ulynago yelled.

"Wha's'matter?"

With a few lurid additions, Ulynago explained that he didn't know. The rig clattered to a halt. The horses stood and steamed in the wet, but all calm as jelly pudding. Silence. What the Evil?

Ulynago thumped reins again. Ears twitched . . . nothing more. God of Madness! The horses were all staring at the trees just ahead. He felt the hairs on his spine rise. Who would hijack a load of wheat? Of course he did have eighteen gold crowns in his moneybelt. If men were behind this, what had they done to his team?

He rose and peered back over the load at the highway behind—bare rock, shining in the wet, running straight and empty as far as he could see in the rain mist. He didn't like these parts. Too close to dragon country, but one whiff of dragon would have put the team in Puldarn by now. Not dragons.

A man stalked out of the trees ahead and headed for the rig.

With a roar, Ulynago tried to rouse the team again, and again nothing happened. Grinding out a mixture of army oaths and teamster technicalities, he shook water off his hat, took up his sword, and jumped down. Then he saw that the newcomer was only an elf. The tightness in his gut eased a lot—he could handle elves. Only one? Iggo's boots thumped down on the other side of the wagon.

Ulynago headed for the elf. He certainly was no threat—unarmed, just a kid in fancy blue and green, all soaked and smeared with grass stains. Hard to tell with elves, so he might be older. He was striding . . . elves usually pranced. Odd sort of elf.

They met beside the lead pair, with the point of Ulynago's sword at the brat's midriff.

"Who the Evil are you? What you do to my team?"

"I'm truly sorry about this," the kid said, looking at him with eyes that sparkled green and blue like his clothes. He was ignoring the blade.

"Sorry about what?"

"This."

Lying flat on his back, Ulynago could feel the rain falling straight into his eyes. The sky was fall of wildly gyrating trees. He thought back to when something like a ballista had impacted the point of his chin, all of five or six seconds ago. He was still holding his sword. No one had ever gotten by his guard like that before. No helmet. His head had hit the stones . . . God of Torment!

Somewhere Iggo yelled, just once. Then a clatter of metal struck the roadway, and a muffled thump.

An elf? A skinny, good-for nothing, yellow-bellied, pantywaist elf? Then other voices . . . There were more of them. Sounded like jotnar. Ulynago tried to rise, and everything went very black.

Some time later be discovered he was lying under the wagon, out of the rain, with the bench cushion under his head. Iggo was beside him, snoring. The highwaymen were long gone.

He wondered why jotnar would have sent an elf.

And to the end of his days Ulynago never understood why they'd taken only three of his horses and only one of the eighteen gold crowns in his moneybelt.

2

'Twas the fourth hour of the night, and things were heating up in the Mainbrace Saloon. Bithbal could hear the threat notes under the mind-wrenching roar of conversation. He could smell anger through the fog of oil fumes and yeast. Even the dim flicker of lamplight was enough to show the shiny red faces starting to change color, and some deep primitive sense of battle was crawling over his skin like ants, telling him the time was near for action. He fingered the sap in his belt. All those blond jotunn heads shining in the gloom—how many would he bloody tonight?

Bithbal was twenty-two, tow-haired and big, even for a jotunn. He'd skipped ship here in Noom when he'd discovered what a bouncer could earn. The chance to fight every bleeding night and even get paid for it had been irresistible, sheer jotunn rapture. After six months, he was a veteran. He'd swallowed his pride enough to take up using a blackjack when the odds got impossible otherwise, and he'd had the front of his pants armored. He'd been hurt and healed and been hurt again almost daily, but he'd never bounced less than eight in a single night's work, even when his arm was broken, and his record was thirty-seven. He loved his work.

Now he thought he might just have time to sell one more round of beer. He headed for the cage and thrust in the money he'd collected for the last lot, watching to make certain it went in his tally pot so he'd get his share of the take. Then he hung a dozen horseshoes of sausage over his elbow, hefted a full tray of steins, and went weaving off into the roar and the dark and the crowd. With hard-earned skill he held the tray high on his sore left hand, whipping off the beer and taking money with his right. There was no wasted conversation in that din, and no one had smiled seriously for some time.

Checking faces as he went, he felt a tightness growing in him, a thrill of pure joy somewhere down around his bladder. Yes, it would be a bone grinder tonight. There was a good sprinkling of imps for tinder, and the jotnar were well up to standard. He'd learned to spot difficult ones, and tonight they were all over the room. He'd never seen so many obvious hard cases. Oddly, it usually wasn't the real toughs that raised the anchor, but once they got going they soon became the survivors, so they were the ones he had to remove afterward, before they started on the furniture. The furniture was solid bronze, all bound to the flagstones, but sailors enjoyed a challenge.

He emptied his tray and headed for the door. Krat and Birg were there already, for it was the safest place to watch the early stages, and the most strategic. You worked inward from the door, usually. God of Battle, but there were some big ones around tonight! And yet . . . and yet somehow the tingle in his gut was not throbbing like it used to, couple of months ago, even. Was it possible that a guy could get *tired* of fighting? Not scared, just *bored*? Or just need a night off once in a while? Missing the sea, maybe?

Leaning back against the wall, Bithbal folded his arms and thus managed to jostle his broken fingers. He winced. That had been done two nights ago, and the buzzing in his right ear . . . four nights ago, or was it five? It wasn't showing any signs of quieting down.

There was a whaler in town looking for hands.

He smirked at Birg and Krat on the other side of the doorway, and they winked back to show they were ready and eager. The room was rocking like a lugger in a nor'wester—not long now. He wondered where it would start. The big part-djinn over in the far corner was sure to be irresistible to someone.

Then the doors flapped open, and closed. Three men.

Holy Balance!

One of them was bigger than anything else on two feet, a middle-aged jotunn, big as a troll—weird tattoos all over a punchbag face. A jotunn wearing forester garb? In garish colors like a namby elf? *God of Blood!* Bithbal revised his opinion of where the action was going to start. His scalp prickled, and he wished he was a little farther from that very spot—for the newcomers were just standing there, in a patch of good light. The noise level was falling rapidly as they gained attention.

And the one on the far side, near Birg and Krat . . . another jotunn, with a sailor mustache, and dressed up in the same sort of frippery! What was this— mass suicide? That one had the twitchy-shoulder look they did when they first hit port and were ready to fight anything.

The shouting had almost stopped. Men at the far side of the room were reeling to their feet to get a better view, rubbing their eyes and looking again. Some who had been almost at each other's throats were exchanging grins of incredulity and anticipation. Any moment now . . . Bithbal began planning his retreat. Tough was good, but being trampled to death could seriously hurt a man.

Then the third newcomer turned to him and smiled.

In six months' hard service, Bithbal thought he'd seen everything possible in the Mainbrace, but an elf was new. A three-way suicide pact? He wondered if elf blood would dry in the same brown-black color as the rest of the floor.

"Excuse me," trilled the elf. "There wouldn't be any tailors' shops open at this time of night, I suppose?"

So his many-colored finery was dirty and Little Precious wanted something prettier to wear? There was a strong smell of wet horse about him, detectable even over the odors of beer and sweat.

"Not a chance!" Curious . . . elves and their shiny curls usually made Bithbal's knuckles itch like crazy, but this kid had a winning sort of wry grin.

"It's just that my friends feel a little conspicuous."

"Sonny, if you want my advice—"

"Yes, I do. I don't suppose a tailor would have the big one's size in stock anyway." The elf frowned. "Should have thought of that! Well, what I really need is an *elf* saloon."

"Elf saloon?" The ringing in Bithbal's ears must be getting worse. "You didn't say 'elf saloon'?"

"Don't elves—I mean, aren't there any drinking establishments for elves?"

"Not here," Bithbal muttered, aware that the whole room was silent as a crypt now. Even to be seen talking to an elf hereabouts was plain stupid. You could hear blood pounding. You could hear fists clenching. "Never see elves near the docks."

"Near where, then?"

"Dunno. Theaters, maybe?"

"Direct me . . . quickly!" The elf's eyes twinkled in sea green and sky blue. Lamplight flashed where the metallic gold of his hair peeked out from under his cutesy cap.

"Dunno," Bithbal repeated dumbly. He was streaming sweat. The Mainbrace was going to explode into full riot from a standing start. He could smell it coming. This poor elf kid would be stamped flat for starters, and Bithbal for associating with him. He wondered why he didn't just turn the brat around and boot him straight out the door. Krat and Birg would handle the two jotnar. But he just said, "Sonny . . . for your own good, please go away. Quickly."

"First tell me where I might find an elf saloon."

Bithbal could not even imagine an elf saloon. 'Go west to the square, then nor'west and veer starboard at the fork and up the companionway, then bear west again to the temple and tack northerly about three cables' length there's theaters around there. Best I can do, sir."

Since when had he ever called an elf *sir?*

"Thank you. Come, guys."

The elf turned on his heel.

His companions started to turn, also, very obediently.

Someone whistled at the back of the room.

The two jotnar spun around to see who had whistled at the back of the room.

A chorus of whistles, then . . .

. . . but Bithbal did not *really* see what happened then. The door closed behind the strangers and the room erupted in deafening booms of mirth. Bithbal stared across at Krat, who was laughing, and Birg, who had turned as pale as pack ice.

So maybe Birg had suffered the same delusion he had.

Sensing the customers' change of mood, the waiters all hurried over to the cage to get more beer, and Bithbal never did ask Krat to tell him exactly what had really happened.

What he *thought* he'd seen was the two jotnar leap forward to start the rumble. And then . . . then it had seemed as if the weedy elf boy moved even faster and took both of them from behind, by the scruffs of their necks . . .

And stopped them in their tracks?

. . . turned them around?

. . . and pushed them out the door ahead of him?

God of Madness!

When he eased his bruises into bed around dawn, Bithbal discovered that he was strangely unable to sleep. He soon decided that his buzzing ear must be worse than he'd thought, and might even need a little peace and quiet to heal.

He pulled on his boots, slung his bindle on his shoulder, and departed—by way of the window, as he was slightly behind in the rent. He swaggered along the harborfront till he found the whaler that was hiring. The bosun offered a hand to shake and Bithbal won, so they took him on. He made his mark in the log and sailed with the tide.

Sailor Bithbal lived to a fair age, but he never again dropped anchor in Noom. And he never again had anything to do with elves.

3

The two legionaries still gleamed in the torchlight like bronze statues, flanking the entrance to the Enchanted Glade. With a sigh of relief, Arth'quith tiptoed back around the corner to the inner vestibule, silent on opulent carpet.

He had been afraid that the boors might have slipped away while he was busy with the guests, not watching. And they *were* boors, too! They had come an hour early in the *filthiest* armor he had ever seen, and they had eaten four meals apiece while his already overworked staff polished it up for them. Parasites! But of course they expected to be stroked like everyone else, and at least he had not had to shell out money for them. The senator had thrown in guards as part of his contribution. Big, impressive types, too, if your taste ran to imps, or *beef.* Arth'quith's did not, but the apes were a sensible and necessary precaution.

He winced at a twinge of dyspepsia. The doctors had warned him to avoid excitement, but an *artist* must pursue his *art.*

Arth'quith gazed lovingly into the main dining room—only his third night in business, and every table filled! Gold plate reflecting blazing chandeliers . . . the finest elvish orchestra in Noom serenading discreetly in the corner . . . sumptuously dressed women dancing with rich, fat men. Mostly imps, alas. It was a *tragedy* that so few elves would ever be able to afford his prices. Odors of the best food in all South Pithmot Province mingling with heady flower scents. Fine fabrics, shiny wood, damask like fresh snow on the tables . . .

All his life Arth' had dreamed of owning his own restaurant, an establishment of *class* and *taste.* How proud Mother would have been of what he had achieved! With the theater crowd here now, there was not a vacant seat in the house.

Of course he had been forced to take in an imp as business partner, and of course the inkstained little grub had turned out to have more needy relations than a queen termite, but an artist could not be expected to soil his mind with such *sordid* matters as *money.* And enlisting the senator as silent partner had been a shrewd move, too, however much it offended one's sensibilities. All the *best* people in Noom were showing up because the senator had come on the first night.

The future looked very secure. The senator would dine here every few days when he was in town. That was the arrangement, and it would cost him nothing, no matter how large his party. The quality would always be *unsurpassed*—Arth'quith himself would see to that, implacably. He had studied impish customs in Hub itself. He had trained in Valdolyn and Valdopol and even Valdofen, been instructed in high cuisine by Loth'fen herself. Father would have wept with pride to see the Enchanted Glade.

The decor was a *miracle* in pink and gold.

The orchestra ended a gavotte and struck up a minuet. It was time for the host to begin mingling discreetly with the diners.

Something went *clang* out in the street—a collision of carriages, perhaps.

The lictor's guests were returning to their seats. Arth'quith must make a good impression there, too—perhaps send over a couple of bottles of the Valdoquiff? Or even the Valdociel?

Another muffled clang . . .

Arth'quith felt more twinges from his despicable innards and a sudden trickle of iced water down his backbone. He wheeled round and headed for the entrance.

An elf came around the corner. God of Trees!

Arth'quith shied like a startled foal and stepped in front of him. "May I be of assistance, sir?"

The elf raised an eyebrow. "I don't think so." He was just a youth, and his clothes were *disgusting*. He stank of . . . of animal!

This time Arth'quith's ulcers clenched hard. "Have you a reservation. sir?"

"I have quite a few," the yokel remarked calmly, peering over Arth'quith's shoulder at the assembly, "but I also have instructions. This seems to be a likely place."

"Sir, I regret we are full this evening. If you do not have a reservation—"

Round the corner came—a jotunn!

And *another!* A giant! A *monster!*

Hot knives stabbed into Arth'quith's abdomen, twisting. He felt *defiled*. Those two metallic noises he had heard from the entrance . . .

"Is this some kind of shakedown?" he screamed. "Because I would have you know that the lictor *himself*—"

The youth smiled faintly at him, and he forgot what he had been about to say.

"Whom would you select as the most important elf present?"

"Imp-important?" Arth'quith stuttered.

"Elf. Important elf?" The lad was staring across the room. "Who's he?"
Reluctantly Arth'quith turned to see where the insolent finger pointed.
"That is Lord Phiel'. The others with him—"
"He is an important person?"
"Lord *Phiel'nilth*? He is Poet Laureate of the Impire!"
"Excellent. Excuse me."
With astonishing agility, the lad slipped past Arth'quith, and before he could move to follow, a fist like an alligator's jaws closed on his shoulder. The smaller jotunn stepped close and snarled, "Be silent!" through his *revolting* walrus mustache.
And the smelly young elf in the bedraggled workclothes went stalking across the floor toward the table where Lord Phiel'nilth was holding court among his admirers.
It was pure *disaster.*

4

Never before in her life had Inos known such a headache, a genuine eye-popping, suicide-provoking bone-splitter. It might be due to the bright sunlight, although she ought to be used to that and she was shaded by a fringed canopy. It might stem from the continuous tooth-jarring rattle of wheels on stone as Skarash played at being charioteer when he was only driving a one-horse chaise. The most likely cause was just simple frustration.

Kade was back at the couturier's again. Azak had gone spying. Feeling her head starting to ache, Inos had asked Skarash to take her for a drive in the fresh air and show her some of the sights. She had not expected chariot races.

This was her second day in Ullacarn, and she was being torn apart by too many questions chasing too little information. Should she try to escape from Elkarath? If she believed his story, he was going to send her on to Hub, and that was where she wanted to go, to appeal to the Four. But Elkarath was certainly capable of lying, and whether he served Rasha or Olybino, Inos was not likely to have much freedom of action in Hub if she was still controlled by any one of the three of them.

And how could she escape anyway? Even if she could avoid the mage's far-sight, there was still Skarash hovering everywhere, and Imperial guards. Worse still, in Ullacarn she had no friends, and she had no money. Azak's gold had been taken from him. Stealing mules in the desert had been easy compared to the problem of stealing horses in a big city and then evading pursuit. Moreover, the only possible way to travel from Ullacarn to the Impire was by ship, and Inos could not imagine Kade and herself as stowaways.

Money was the worst problem of all. The sheik was being incredibly generous. Skarash would offer to buy anything that caught her eye, price no consideration. But he would certainly demur if she asked for actual gold to use for bribes and disguises.

Had Rasha already sold Inos to Olybino? Had Elkarath actually been East's votary all along? The answer to those two questions seemed to be no. If she belonged to the warlock, then she would be magicked to Hub in no time. That much at least seemed clear—Rasha was still in control.

Ullacarn was admittedly a fair city. Most of its streets were straight and wide, typical of Imperial planning and completely unlike the chaotic alleys of Arakkaran. A few patches of ramshackle native construction still lingered here and there like unhealed wounds, including the ancient House of Elkarath itself, but all these old slums were scheduled for demolition in the near future, to be replaced by modern, more sanitary construction.

So Skarash had told her.

"How do you feel about that?" she had asked.

"Do you want my imp answer or any djinn answer?" Which was an answer. Even Skarash seemed out of sorts today. Around his grandfather he was submissive and self-effacing. For Azak he played stern patriot, for Kade dutiful escort, for Inos flippant playboy and now charioteer. The day before he had never missed a step, but that morning he had fumbled a few times, displaying the wrong face or having to change voice halfway through a speech. Either he was attempting too many roles at once, Inos thought, or something new was worrying Master Skarash.

The sightseeing had been a mistake; her headache had grown worse. Now, thank the Gods, she was on her way to pick up Kade and go home; if she lived that long. The wheels rat-tatted on the cobbles, shooting bolts of fire from her eyeballs, and the chaise lurched and rocked down the hill, scattering pedestrians and pack animals alike, swerving around on one wheel between wagons and carriages. Spectators roared in anger and shook fists. Dogs barked and horses shied. Dwarves with hammers beat on her brain like an anvil.

Skarash being charioteer . . . the two hussars sent along to guard Inos had objected to his fast driving. Mainly they'd just been throwing their weight around, hassling a rich djinn. So Skarash had challenged them to a race down the Way Imelada, the steepest, narrowest, nastiest alley in the city, so far as Inos could tell. He was going to win it, too, if it killed her.

Ullacarn was a flatter city than Arakkaran, or Krasnegar, but it did have the Way Imelada, and it did have a palace on a hilltop. The emir was rumored to be under house arrest, Skarash had said. There must be a strong anti-Impire faction in the city, so perhaps Azak could enlist some secret allies among the local djinns.

In three days? And why would the enemies of the Impire aid a sultan who wanted to go to Hub? More like they would see him as a traitor and push a scimitar through him; and the problems of a refugee queen from the far northwest would interest them not at all. Bury that idea.

Or bury Inos! The chaise skidded around a corner on one wheel, narrowly missing a cart laden with vegetables.

And now the way ahead was flatter, wider, and packed with people. Skarash was screaming warnings, cracking his whip in the air. Inos clung tight and tried closing her eyes, but that did not help much. Every jolt flashed flames inside her head, and they just seemed brighter when she had her eyes closed. Somewhere behind the bouncing chaise came the two horsemen, but Skarash had outwitted them right at the beginning by getting them to agree to give him a few paces' start, and ever since then they had been unable to find a place clear enough to overtake. Unless he killed someone, he was going to win the race.

Yesterday Azak had escorted Inos; today he had gone off on his own. He had reluctantly agreed to wear impish costume while in Ullacarn, for otherwise he would be conspicuous and might find himself harassed by the soldiers. As always, he had gone full measure. He had shaved off his beard and had his hair cut to impish shortness; it was coppery and lighter than his beard. In hose and breeches and ruffles, he was a sight to catch every female eye in town. Suddenly the idea of Azak in Kinvale or even Krasnegar was not quite so hard to imagine—but that was another problem altogether.

The chaise lurched extra hard and skidded and swung sideways. Inos muttered a prayer and clung tighter. Then she heard yells of triumph close by and opened her eyes just as the hussars went thundering past. Ambly Square was right ahead.

"You lost! "she said.

Skarash dared not turn to look at her yet, but he grinned. His face was bright scarlet and shiny with perspiration, his hair flew loose, and his plumed hat had vanished completely. He was obviously very pleased with himself. "Of course I lost! You think I'm crazy enough to win?" He was still hauling on the reins to slow the horse.

Two minutes later he brought Inos safely, if not soundly, back to the couturier's door. He began passing gold to the hussars, along with his congratulations. He was still being a trader, still giving what was wanted.

The couturier's establishment was a grand house on a grand square. Djinn servants came hurrying to lead the horse to the mews, and Skarash again flashed coin as he demanded that the hussars' mounts be taken, also, to be walked and rubbed down. Then he gave Inos his hand to help her descend, followed by his arm to mount the wide stairs to the door. He was puffing and still excited from the race. He could have won had he wished, so losing was a double victory for him.

Inos fought for concentration through the thumping surf in her head. "Master Skarash?" she murmured as big white doors swung open before them.

"Yes, my beloved?" he replied softly.

Inos ignored that. "I have relatives in Hub. My aunt knows many people there. I was wondering if we might write letters to forewarn them of our arrival?"

They stepped together into a hallway richly furnished, although possibly at secondhand, for the rugs and draperies seemed mismatched. Inos started toward the room where she had left Kade, but the footman was leading the way across to the stairs, so Kade must have moved.

"Letters?" Skarash mused. "There would be no point at the moment, would there? No ship is due to sail before *Dawn Pearl*, so you would merely be paying to send mail on the same vessel as yourself. When we reach Qoble, of course, then the case may be different. You may not wish to travel at the posts' pace then."

"You will be accompanying us?" For a moment that surprise even cut through the headache.

Skarash smiled innocently. "Only as far as Angot, to deliver some messages for Grandsire."

So Elkarath was not going! Yet how could he risk sending his prisoners off unaccompanied? Winds were fitful. Even if *Dawn Pearl* had no preliminary landfalls scheduled before Qoble, the Gods might arrange one. Rasha would not dare withdraw all occult restraint—what did that hint about Skarash?

Then Inos was being ushered into a room where Kade was preening before a pier glass. She spun around and beamed. "Ah! Did you have a pleasant journey, my dear? Do sit down and advise me. These pearls are such a problem."

Inos set her face in a rictus of smile and sank onto a chintz-covered chair. The draperies were rich purple velvet, the rugs soft and thick, in a discordant mauve. The furniture was an odd assemblage.

Kade, of course, was exultant at the thought of journeying to Hub. All her life she had wanted to visit the capital. She had almost attained her ambition twice, and each time something had come up to prevent her leaving Kinvale.

Kade, in a sense, was being as deceitful as Skarash. Having played the role of desert nomad for months, enduring hardship and discomfort without complaint, she had now reverted to being a brainless Kinvale lady, totally engrossed in gowns and frippery. Well, if she enjoyed the procedure, she had certainly earned it, even if it was only a comfortable sham.

"What do you think of this string?" she inquired. "Or this one?"

The impish assistants fussed and exclaimed around her, delighted to have a customer with such exquisite taste and such impressive wealth. Of course pearls were plentiful in Ullacarn, on the shores of the Sea of Sorrows. Despite her worries and her pounding temples, Inos was impressed by the glowing heaps being displayed.

"Why not take both, your Highness?" Skarash suggested. "And the stomacher, also?"

"You really think so?" Kade said, seeming tempted. "And what about earrings and brooches? Look at these, Inos!"

Inos murmured appreciation and offered opinions, and then reluctantly moved to a chair before a mirror so that she also might try on clasps and brooches encrusted with fine pearls. Skarash encouraged and applauded, flaunting wealth and pressing the noble ladies to buy whatever they fancied. The clerks murmured and enthused.

Inos's head continued to throb, but even while she babbled about settings and matches and sizes, her mind went on wrestling with the main problem, rejecting this whole charade as being unbelievable. There just was no reason why Rasha should be sending her prisoners off to Hub. The promised voyage to Qoble must be a feint to keep them happy while something else was planned.

But what could three penniless, friendless fugitives do in an unknown city? They could not pay their fares on a ship, they could not bribe guards, or sailors. They seemed to have no option except to play along with the pretense until such time as Elkarath revealed the sorceress's true plans.

"And you should see the lacework!" Kade exclaimed. "Do you remember those lace cuffs—no, they were before your time, my dear. I had a pair of lace cuffs that moved from gown to gown for ten years at least, until they were dishrags. Lace was so expensive in Kinford! And here they have lace like I have never seen. Collars and cuffs—"

"The best lace comes from Guwush," said Skarash, the trader in him emerging briefly. He began describing how the gnomes harvested silk from forest spiders, and then went into technicalities of quality and grading.

Half an hour or so later, Inos could rise thankfully to her feet, prepared to leave. The sun was near to setting, and the thought of lying down on her lumpy little bed in the House of Elkarath was heavenly. Kade had shamelessly frittered away a fortune, but seemed content at last—dear Kade! She had earned it. The assistants were hastily wrapping all those riches, and Skarash was counting out gold as carelessly as if it were millet.

Kade caught Inos's eye briefly.

Inos blinked and looked again, but the odd expression had vanished and her aunt had turned to ask about alterations to the turquoise tea gown.

By then Inos understood. Right under her eyes, Kade had solved one of the problems. The fugitives might not have gold, but they now had an enormous supply of valuable earrings and brooches and pins. For bribery, at least, those might do as well.

Three in a one-horse chaise were cramped, and although Skarash did not indulge in any more chariot races, he seemed to have picked up an inexplicable sense of urgency. The streets were crowded with homebound workers, and he fretted impatiently, muttering under his breath.

Inos considered him out of the corner of a bleary, pain-filled eye. Jumpy or not, he had been flirting all afternoon, at every chance. Dare she attempt to seduce Elkarath's grandson from his loyalty? Would she ever trust anything this devious young man promised? If he were indeed the Chosen One, he would be crazy to risk losing his chance of inheriting such powers just for a mild flirtation, for Inos had no intention of going any further than that. If he was indeed going to be her guardian on the ship, then he might already have been granted occult powers, and thus he might already know what she was thinking—and a flirtation would get out of hand very quickly. She decided not to pursue the matter . . . pursue Skarash. The way her head was thumping, she was not capable of producing even one winsome smile, anyway.

At last the rattling vehicle turned into a narrow alley and came bouncing to a halt outside the merchant's house. Skarash growled something inaudible. There were too many legionaries milling around there too many horses, too many citizens excited about something.

Suddenly apprehensive, Inos followed him down and ran ahead, awkward in her city shoes, not waiting for Kade. Then she heard a familiar voice and stopped abruptly.

In a moment she located him. Centurion Imopopi. He was barking out orders, and again she felt an uncanny unease. She had not seen him since the previous morning, but she had thought about him several times without deciding why he had so disconcerted her. His voice was arousing the same mysterious alarms as it had before. The soldiers were gathered in a group, with the djinn workers emerging from the big loading room to cluster around them. What were they all looking at?

She began to push her way through the crowd, even shoving at the leather and bronze of legionaries, and suffering a few pinches and fondlings in the process. She saw Elkarath himself appearing, large and hot-looking in his scarlet gown, his skull-cap perched awry on his white hair, his ruddy face ruddier than ever. Everyone was staring at something on the ground.

She reached the center before the sheik did. Azak lay flat on the cobbles, obviously unconscious. His face was battered, his clothes tattered. He was red with blood. As she dropped to her knees at his side, a hand closed crushingly on her wrist and hauled her back upright.

"You know the man, ma'am?" The centurion's black eyes were fearsome with suspicion.

"I . . . Yes." Shocked by the pain of his grip, Inos tried to pull free, but she might as well have tried to uproot an oak. "Sheik—I mean, Master—Elkarath employed . . . employs him. *You 're hurting me!*"

Imopopi ignored her complaint, directing his attention to the far side of the circle, where the legionaries now moved apart to admit the portly Elkarath, glowering like a thunderstorm.

"He was one of my guards, Centurion."

Imopopi released his painful hold on Inos, leaving white bracelets that slowly flamed red.

"Was, Master?"

Elkarath shrugged. "He may not be any longer. May I inquire?"

The centurion folded his thick arms. "He ventured where he was not supposed to."

"He appears to have suffered for it."

"He is lucky to be alive. You want him, or shall I dispose of him elsewhere?"

Still scowling, Elkarath glanced around the ring of armored men. Then he shrugged again. "I suppose I can take him in until he recovers. Is the matter closed?"

"There will be a fine."

Elkarath sighed. "Five imperials, I expect?"

"And damages of ten more."

The sheik pouted, then nodded resignedly.

"Plus a bond for future good behavior . . . say, another twenty?"

Now the old man glared, ready to rebel. "He still has some wages due, but he is not heir to an emir's ransom! I may summon a litter and have the fool taken within?"

Imopopi nodded, satisfied. Most of his men were openly smirking as they calculated their share of that neat extortion. Elkarath turned to growl instructions. In the center of the gathering, the cause of it all twitched and groaned, and then became still again.

Idiot! Had he thought the imps would allow a djinn to go spying around their barracks, or naval base? Served him right!

Of course Elkarath could cure his injuries, if he dared exert his powers within Ullacarn itself.

"A friend of yours, Mistress Hathark?"

Inos jumped, and turned to the sinister centurion at her side. Why sinister? Familiar? Not the face, the face was totally strange.

The voice?

The eyes! Recognition struck her like a fist.

She reeled back, and cannoned into a nearby legionary, who felt as solid as a stone pillar. He chuckled and steadied her and continued to hold her as she stared at Imopopi.

"Something wrong?" Mockery danced in the centurion's hard face.

"I think we have met before," Inos said, and her voice was a croak. Olybino! The warlock himself. He had grabbed her wrist earlier because she had been about to lay a hand on Azak and would have been burned by the curse. He knew! She squirmed, and the man behind her tightened his grip. But her eyes stayed locked on the centurion.

"Yesterday?" He knew! He knew she knew! He meant her to know.

"Before that, sir!" Inos pushed away offending hands and the young man at her back sighed loudly. Soldiers chuckled.

Imopopi looked around his men and then leered. "I don't recall. How could I forget such a lovely face? Were we in the dark, perchance? Or were there other things visible to distract me?"

The legionaries barked with laughter. Inos felt her cheeks flame red as a djinn's.

"Perhaps it is I who am mistaken, Centurion."

Imopopi considered her, his head on one side. 'Perhaps. But we could discuss the matter elsewhere. At length."

"No . . . er . . . no!" She tried to back away and was again gripped firmly by the man behind her. She squirmed, and he squeezed warningly, tethering her to bear his leader's baiting.

The warlock licked his lips and stepped closer. "You are enjoying your stay in beautiful Ullacarn, mistress? Or are you too impatient to be on your way to Hub?"

Oh, Gods! It was so obvious now why she was going to Hub! Why he would send her by ship instead of by sorcery was a mystery, but she knew now why she was going.

She shook her head and managed to say "I am enjoying my stay, sir."

"We could make it more enjoyable for you, I'm sure." Imopopi glanced around the group, and his men laughed obediently. He was playing to two audiences at once, and enjoying it.

Two husky warehousemen had arrived with a stretcher, and Elkarath close behind them. Inos caught a glimpse of Skarash peering at her over shoulders, and his face had paled to a sickly salmon shade. So Skarash knew! He had not known the previous day. That must be why he had been so jumpy—because he had discovered that there was a warlock involved.

She glanced back to meet the terrible mockery in Olybino's eyes.

"You should have gone to Hub sooner, ma'am." *The first time we met.*

Inos swallowed a few times and then found her voice. "My aunt was unable to accompany me sooner, sir."

"Unfortunate!" The warlock shrugged. "Well, I bid you a safe journey, Mistress Hathark." Reverting to his pretense of being Centurion Imopopi, be nodded to the man holding Inos to release her and turned to accept a heavy bag from Elkarath. Hugging herself, Inos backed away into the crowd, her knees still knocking with terror.

And just in case she had any doubts, the warlock had cured her headache. It had gone completely.

Male hands were lifting Azak onto the litter. Azak had been given a lesson, and a warning. Escape would be impossible now.

All Inos could do in Ullacarn was to wait for a ship to take her away.

5

Chains rattled and Gathmor opened his eyes, or tried to. He groaned and licked his lips. "Rap?"

"I'm here," Rap said calmly, jingling fetters in his ear. The two of them were jammed into a very small box. "You have a broken finger bone and you've lost a tooth. Your nose looks as if it will straighten all right. The rest is bruises, and cuts—you got those when the chandelier came down."

"You?"

"Broke a few bones in my hand and cracked a couple of ribs." No need to mention that they seemed to be mending very quickly.

Gathmor tried to move, and groaned louder. After a moment he said softly, "That was a very fine little fracas."

Remembering the devastation. Rap shuddered. "Then I wouldn't like to experience a big one."

"Who would have thought that imps could be so much sport?"

"Numbers and motivation, I suppose."

"Darad?"

"Not present." Probably Darad had called Thinal at the end, or possibly Andor, and he had then escaped in the confusion caused by the fire.

Again Gathmor groaned. He tried to sit up and thought better of it. "I can't see."

"There's not much light, and you wouldn't see too well, with those shiners you've got. We're in a cell. About gnome size, so it's a little snug. Three sides stone, one side timber."

"Smells like gnome, too." Gathmor smiled, or tried to. "Better than *Blood Wave*, anyway. This is becoming a habit, me waking up like this. But that was a very satisfactory bumping. Do you happen to know the final score?"

"No!" Rap bit back some angry remarks.

202

The cell was two floors belowground, and one of a hundred or so similar cells, all overcrowded with men and chains. The air was a foul, dead brew that had not been changed in centuries.

Gathmor gritted his teeth and sat up noisily. He leaned back against the wall, wincing as he tried to straighten his legs.

"I think we've got a visitor coming," Rap said. Jailers went by outside all the time, but now an elf was being escorted down the stairs at the end of the corridor, and Rap was the only elf in the cells. In a moment light flickered in the judas hole, and bolts grated.

Rap moved his knees aside to make room as the newcomer ducked into the cell and stopped, blind. The door boomed shut behind him and he flinched. He was slight, yet he could not straighten under the roof, and overall he seemed so like an adolescent that he might even be one. His clothes had a very homemade look to them, his golden curls needed trimming, but his fingernails were neat and clean.

"Rap'rian?" he said warily, peering straight ahead.

"That's me," said Rap at his feet.

The visitor jumped and banged his head. "I'm Quip'rian." He choked and slapped a hand over his mouth. "I think I'm going to throw up."

"I shall certainly kill you if you do," said Gathmor.

Another shock. "Who? There's more of you in here?"

"My associate, Captain Gathmor."

"A jotunn? They locked you up with a jotunn? How can you stand this place?"

"I don't have much alternative," Rap said, beginning to feel better already. "Your name—Quip'rian?—we're related?"

"I doubt . . . I'm an Aliel, cadet branch of the penultimate Offiniol sept. You?"

"No." Rap was even further out of his depth than he'd thought.

For a moment the conversation failed. The youth reached out and felt for the walls. His face twisted in horror when he realized how small the kennel was.

"Master Rap'rian?" he whispered. "Are you crazy? Will you plead insanity?"

"No. Would I be any better off if I did?"

"They might just cut your head off."

That classed as better off? "I did it right, didn't I?"

Quip'rian shut his eyes and shuddered. "You can't believe that!"

"Well, it came unstuck later," Rap admitted. "But I said the formula— 'I spit on Valdonilth!' That was right, wasn't it? And then I slapped his face. I didn't hit very hard. And the old boy said whatever it was he was supposed to say: 'Foul varlet' and so on. He did it rather well, I thought,

203

as he couldn't have been expecting anything like that. And then I said, 'I kneel in the shadow of Lith'rian.' That was all that was supposed to happen, I thought."

The real elf wiped his streaming forehead. "How should I know? Nobody does things like that nowadays! If you'd picked anyone but Lord Phiel', he probably wouldn't have had a clue what you were raving about. I know I wouldn't."

Rap grunted noncommittally. When the silence became oppressive, he said, "Who're you? How do you get involved?"

"I was the nearest male kin when you challenged."

"How old are you?"

"Fifteen. I'm a trainee waiter! I was clearing plates off the next table." He seemed ready to weep.

"And what does the nearest male kinsman have to do?"

"You mean you don't know all this? You utter the Sublime Defiance and you don't know how it works?"

Rap thought a few unkind thoughts about Sorcerer Ishist and his sense of humor. "Tell me."

Quip'rian's lip trembled. "You're really asking me? I only know what they've been babbling upstairs. I have to be your escort. I have to accompany you to Valdorian, if you get to go."

Rap's insides lurched. "You mean there's some doubt?"

"Doubt?" the elf yelled. "The lictor himself has a broken arm! The hall was wrecked, utterly wrecked! No one's died yet, but eight legionaries were injured, and two or three *dozen* civilians. Poor Master Arth'quith had a fit. It was awful, just awful! There's an almighty argument going on upstairs. It's going to cost *millions!*"

Gathmor sighed happily.

Rap scanned and eventually discovered a meeting in progress on the third floor. He could not hear the words, but the ten or so men up there were doing a lot of arm-waving.

"Well, I admit the fight wasn't part of the plan," he said sadly. "I was told— I mean, I intended—to find an important elf with other elf witnesses. I didn't realize that imp witnesses might not understand what was going on. I should have chosen a time when there were only elves present. I'm truly sorry, because of course no elf would have spoiled a solemn ceremony like that by trying to hit me with a bottle." It had been a sorry blow, and Rap had dodged easily, but . . . "My friends thought I was in danger, you see."

Gathmor and Darad had come to his rescue like twin avalanches.

Quip'rian sniffled. "Well, the lictor himself was there. He was hurt, and his wife went into labor, and half his guests are still hospitalized."

Now Rap began to grasp the enormity of the problem. "And he doesn't recognize ancient elvish customs?"

"They don't apply within the Impire."

"No. I see."

"He says he'll bypass normal procedure with a summary edict—to save time, because you're so obviously guilty."

"And then?"

The boy moaned. "You're going to be flogged to death in Emshandar Plaza at noon. The notices are being posted."

Rap recalled Kalkor's odious cat-o'-nine-tails and his throat felt as if it were being squeezed. "And my friend here?"

"Him first, you second."

"Then what's the argument about?"

"Lord Phiel'nilth says his clan honor is involved. He's delighted! No one's uttered the Sublime Defiance in three hundred years, he says. He wants to go through with the whole ritual."

Nothing was ever simple where elves were concerned, Rap remembered. "Can he swing that?" he asked hopefully.

For a moment the kid just wrung his hands. Then he whispered, "If they can find the actor's price." He was looking sicker by the minute. What sort of a fifteen-year-old was he?

"I'd have thought," Rap said, "that the chance of a free trip to Ilrane would appeal to you. Better than dirty dishes, surely?"

Quip'rian shuddered convulsively. "Go *on a ship?*"

"No? Well, cheer up! They may flay me yet, and then you can polish all the glasses in Noom in celebration."

"Don't mock me!" the elf snapped, showing a little spark at last. "I didn't ask for this."

"True! I'm sorry," Rap said, and meant it. "I suppose I'm just trying to whistle up some courage. Will the lictor blink?"

"How should I know? I'm a nothing . . . But that way the damage would be paid for. I think some important people like that idea."

In Milflor Rap had cost Gathmor forty-six imperials. He was going to be considerably more expensive this time. "Who pays for all this?"

"Lith'rian, of course. You knelt in his shadow."

Well, a warlock could create gold to order. If he wanted to.

"I get taken to Lith'rian for judgment?"

The elf nodded, looking sorely puzzled again.

"Then what?"

"Then he judges, of course. If he decides you were wrong to spit on the Nilths, then he sends your head to Valdonilth."

"Literally?"

"In a gold bucket is the tradition."

"And if he doesn't? If he thinks I was right?"

Quip'rian sniffled loudly. "Then you've started a war."

6

Either the execution scheduled for noon was postponed or there was a last-minute change of cast, because arguments over the elvish affair continued all day in the lictor's office. Rap watched the crowd there grow, but for information on what was being said he had to rely on Quip'rian.

The young elf was a loose ball in the game. The ancient rituals gave Nearest Kinsman a major role in all proceedings, but senior Imperial officials preferred not to discuss confidential financial matters in the presence of a trainee waiter, so they sent him off to attend Rap.

A short time in the cell was enough to make him nauseated, palsied, and likely to faint. At that point Rap would suggest he go and gatecrash the meetings again, and after some shouting for the jailers, he would be released. In an hour or so, someone would notice him in the lictor's office and toss him out again. Then he would force himself back down to the dungeon to report to Rap, for he had an elf's compulsion to perform duties conscientiously.

He told all he could, but young Quip', while he was sensitive and willing, was clearly neither well educated nor especially intelligent, and he had no inklings of finance or politics. He did report that the entire elf community of Noom was involved now, rallied around Lord Phiel'nilth. If the distinguished visitor chose to regard the insult paid him as an honor, then he must be given every assistance. Arcane rites had an undeniable appeal for elves.

The imps were seemingly divided between those who saw the practical advantages of accepting compensation, and those who insisted that the law must be upheld—meaning that the two culprits should be disassembled as soon as possible, in public. Rap began to suspect that the contest was unfair, that the elves were outmatched in the bargaining, caught between two grindstones that opposed each other to a common purpose. As the day wore on, Quip' was gasping out numbers even Gathmor could not comprehend.

And certainty the negotiations were only possible at all because the patron lord whose name Rap had invoked was a sorcerer. Lith'rian's credit was infinite.

Of course Lith'rian himself must be still unaware of all the good things being done on his behalf. The imps proposed leaving the felons to marinate in jail for a few weeks while a message went to Hub. The elves insisted that the rituals must be followed exactly, and Rap should be sent immediately to Lith'rian's enclave, the sky trees of Valdorian.

And the warlock was not available to sign and seal. Bankers could advance the necessary funds upon suitable security, but all bankers were imps, more or less by definition. Few elves were wealthy, and Quip' reported that every elf in the city was having to mortgage all he owned to provide the necessary bond. Rap glumly concluded that an agreement might be attainable when the last groat was pledged, and that did seem to be what happened.

Just after sunset, Quip'rian and a jurist came down to the cells and joyfully informed Rap that he was to be sent to Ilrane, to be judged by the ancient ceremony he had invoked.

Rap stayed on the floor. "How about my friend?"

"Noon tomorrow, I'm afraid."

Rap used some nautical expressions that neither Quip' nor jurist would have met before. "Both of us or neither," he added, in case of misunderstanding.

The exhausted negotiators upstairs were just starting to leave when a horrified Quip'rian came rushing up to break the news. The bargaining started all over again.

It went all night and most of the next day. Rap would not leave his cell voluntarily, so he was hauled out bodily and dragged before the lictor. He was warned that this was his last chance to avoid a terrible death. He refused to accept better treatment than his fellow felon. As he had spent a whole day and night in the dungeons, his mere presence could contaminate even the largest of rooms. He was quickly returned whence he came and thereafter the visitors came to call on him, speaking through the judas hole.

Elves came, pleading both the impossibility of fitting a jotunn into the traditional ceremonies and their inability to raise any more money. The jurists came, muttering that the procedure was highly improper and if word got out then it would have to be stopped. The lictor himself, the families of the injured, representatives of the city . . . all came to argue and beg and be turned down. He was denied food and water. Two stalwart jailers came with boots and other hard things. Still Rap refused. He wasn't certain just what leverage he had, but apparently he must travel voluntarily, and both ancient ritual and underhand dealing had now gone so far that they had taken on a life of their own and could not be reversed. So he did have leverage, somehow. The graft seeped steadily upward until it reached the praetor himself, and then the cost rose enormously. By now, of course, the imps knew that they had stumbled into a gold mine, and the elves were hopelessly trapped.

When the first round of appeals failed, they all came back and tried again, including the two jailers.

Rap stopped talking altogether.

He knew he was being crazy. He was tormented by the thought that he was breaking his word to Ishist, but he could not bring himself to desert Gathmor.

He could have used mastery to convert the visitors to his cause, but that use of power might alert any sorcerer in town and the goodwill would evaporate soon after they left his presence; so he tried not to, although he did ease the beatings a bit.

Even Gathmor started telling him he was crazy.

Rap told him to shut up, he wasn't helping much.

One elvish worthy called him a stupid troll, and another a brutish jotunn. The imps said he was being as stubborn as a faun. Quip'rian broke down and wept, then explained apologetically that he always reacted to the smell of blood like that. And he had not slept the last two nights. None of them had.

When the second round of visits failed, everyone came round a third time.

In the end they all just succumbed to exhaustion, and Rap had won.

They also serve:
     . . . Thousands at his bidding speed,
And post o'er land and ocean without rest;
They also serve who only stand and wait.
                              Milton, *On His Blindness*

10

Moaning of the bar

1

L
ate afternoon, and the fine harbor of Ullacarn was teeming with ships, a magnificent sight. Kade loved ships—sailing on them or even just looking at them. That was the jotunn in her, of course.

In her brief stay she had seen only a tiny part of the city, but she had certainly approved of that much. Bouncing along in an open carriage with Inos and Frainish, she had almost wished that she were staying longer, to see more. The streets were wide and clean, the many parks overflowed with flowers. The natives were djinns, and yet they all dressed in impish style in public, and with their height and slender build they mostly looked very good in it, better than the heavyset imps themselves ever could. Kade had long since noticed the same thing about the jotnar in Krasnegar, for while she herself had inherited jotunn coloring from her so-entangled family tree, her figure was as impish as imp could be. Still, she must not let the Gods think she was ungrateful or unmindful of Their many blessings. After all, she had viewed Ullacarn tinted with magic gold and filtered through draperies of silks and laces, velvets and poplins, to linger

might let realities dispel the illusion. No, it was time to go. Time to board
Dawn Pearl and sail away.

Time to head for Hub! Kadolan said another small silent prayer of thanks.
Her instincts still insisted that Inosolan would have been wiser to have
remained in Arakkaran, under the sultana's protection, but ancient knots could
never be untangled, and a chance to visit the Imperial capital was a most
uplifting prospect.

Inosolan was hunched in the corner of the carriage, morosely ignoring
even the exciting dock sights and the harbor view. A pity she had not yet
learned to let the future wait. That was a lesson that only age could teach.

Frainish was almost falling out in her excitement. Frainish was very young,
a descendant of Sheik Elkarath, and had been sent along as lady's maid. The
personable and deferential Master Skarash would also accompany them, as far
as Qoble. The sheik had been very kind, no matter who his ultimate master.
Inosolan really should have been more gracious when saying farewell.

And now the ships were very close, as the carriage jingled along the quay.
Frainish was twittering questions, making Kadolan rack her old brains to try
to answer. Caravels and dhows were easy, but she could not remember the difference among a galley, a galleon, and a galleas. What splendid vessels,
though! Vastly larger and more beautiful than the little cogs that had carried
her so many times between Krasnegar and Shaldokan.

As Kadolan was still trying to parry the child's questions, the carriage clattered to a halt alongside a ship that was very large indeed. It must be their
destination, for here was Skarash, pulling down the step, offering a helping
hand. So this beauty was their vessel, *Dawn Pearl*, and the noisy mill of people
around the gangways was clear evidence that departure was imminent.

She let Skarash guide her through the throng, as he could see over heads
much better than she could, while she kept an eye on Frainish, who was short
enough to disappear completely in such a crowd. Inosolan could look after
herself.

Kadolan caught a glimpse of Azak's head above the surging sea of shoulders. His face was surly and enraged. Then Skarash made room for her to step
forward, and she was already at the gangplank. She paused halfway up and
peered back, regardless of the line of persons following her, locating Azak's
red head again. He was the only djinn who towered over the crowd like a
jotunn sailor or a troll porter. The imps present seemed squat by comparison.
Inosolan was beside him, within a squad of legionaries. Azak was probably
being awkward. He had been in a bad mood ever since the day the soldiers
had beaten him, and although Elkarath had cured his broken bones and bruises on that occasion, he had probably incurred no thanks. Azak was one of
those people who enjoyed making things difficult for themselves, and thus for

210

everybody else, as well. That sort of behavior Kadolan could never comprehend.

Realizing suddenly that the vulgar shouting was being directed at her, she resumed her progress up the plank with suitable dignity. She stepped through a doorway into Dawn Pearl. Galleon or galleas, it was easily the largest ship she had ever boarded.

She was astonished by her stateroom, large and luxurious beyond anything she could have imagined on a ship, with a proper bed instead of bunks, with real windows along the aft wall. Plump, elderly ladies would only get in people's way, so she decided to wait there, knowing that Inosolan would find her. She sent the excited Frainish off in Skarash's care to explore, and to watch departure from the deck. Unpacking could wait.

Meanwhile, she could indulge herself in an inspection of the fittings admiring the shiny woodwork, the ingenious catches on cupboard doors, and the drawers that would not open if the ship rolled. Porters knocked and entered with baggage and departed. The room was still not crowded, even then.

Eventually she pulled a deliciously comfortable chair around to face the great windows and settled into it with a sigh. She kicked off her shoes and prepared to enjoy just watching the harbor.

A few minutes later the door opened and then thumped closed. Inosolan stalked across to the window in silence. Feet were running overhead, voices calling out, blocks squealing. Already the ship was drifting away from the quay. Dawn Pearl leaned slightly as the wind began to catch her sails. Inosolan had not said a word yet.

"Where is his Majesty?" Kadolan inquired.

Good guess—Inosolan turned around and scowled. She wore a full dress of cool emerald-green silk with half sleeves and a low neckline. She had let her hair grow during the past few months, and now it was coiled high on her head below a pearl tiara. She was as beautiful as a poet's dream of maidenhood. Her expression of suicidal sulks would have shamed a six-year-old being sent to bed without supper.

"Down in what they call Gnome Quarters. In irons."

"That doesn't seem like a very wise choice."

Inosolan turned her back and told the window, "He refused to board and demanded leave to appeal to the emir. The imps ran him up the plank at swordpoint, of course."

The noises outside continued; a thoughtful silence settled into Kadolan's stateroom. It would be interesting to see what happened to Azak when Dawn Pearl reached Angot. The journey on to Hub would mean a long trip by stage, over the Qoble Mountains and then across much of Shimlundok Province. Skarash swore he was going no farther than Angot.

Would there be magic waiting for them in Angot? Or was there magic on board already? Would Azak be shipped in irons all the way to the capital? It hardly mattered at the moment. Kadolan bent to find her shoes.

"Stubborn idiot!" Inosolan muttered.

"His own fault."

Inosolan had done very well, really. For months in the desert she had kept the sultan at arm's length without ever seeming to hurt his feelings or rouse false hopes. That was no mean feat of balance. Now Kadolan was a little worried that the relationship was starting to change in some way she had not defined. The terrible events in Thume had shaken everybody. Azak had nearly died, Inosolan had almost been ravished. Things had been different since then, attitudes altered, values reassessed. Perhaps Ullacarn, as a return to civilization, had helped the change. Azak in imp clothing had been a shock—certainly to Kadolan, and probably to Inosolan. He had not been a barbarian any more.

It might be better for everyone concerned if he did complete the rest of the journey in chains, all the way to Hub. Inosolan could sit inside the carriage and that dangerous young man could be strapped on the roof with the baggage.

Kadolan rebuked herself for unworthy thoughts.

"Well, this is true luxury," she said. "Is your stateroom as magnificent as this?"

"I haven't looked."

Respectably shod again, Kadolan pushed herself to her feet. "Then let's go and have a look now, and then go up and—"

Inosolan swung around and glared at her. "And have a nice time, I suppose?"

"Why not?"

"Well, it's easy for you! I'm on my way to marry a goblin. I've been captured by a warlock, and from the way he looked at me, the goblin may very well be going to get me as secondhand goods. Azak's down in the bilge, and I hate ships, and I'm a lousy sailor—"

"And you sound like a spoiled child."

"And I—What? You don't get seasick!"

"Are you seasick now? Is seasickness what is bothering you?"

Inosolan made a snorting noise and stalked toward the door.

And Kadolan felt a rush of anger. "Answer the question!"

Inosolan stopped and spun around, her mouth open in shock.

"You are still behaving like a spoiled child," Kadolan said—having gone so far, she would have to continue. "You are not married to a goblin at the moment. You are not being importuned by any warlocks that I can see. You are, in fact, about to enjoy a voyage in royal luxury on the finest ship I have ever seen, across the Sea of Sorrows, an expanse of water renowned for its fair weather and good sailing. You are likewise going to continue on the journey of a lifetime, through some of the world's finest scenery and across half the Impire to Hub itself, where you will very likely be granted royal honors and all the hospitality of the Imperial court. If you do believe that you are going to be married to a goblin—and I personally find the idea so absurd that I cannot take it seriously—then I suggest that you attempt to appreciate the good things that are happening at the moment, instead of making yourself miserable all the time brooding over a future that may never happen."

"Absurd, you said?" Inosolan was pale with fury. "Absurd?"

"Absurd." Kadolan sighed, wishing she had kept her annoyance safely bottled up. "I've told you before. The principle of compromise is to find something, or someone in this case, which . . . who . . . is equally acceptable to both sides. A goblin, I think, would be equally unacceptable to both sides. All four sides, really: you, and the citizens, and the Impire, and—"

"You didn't see that warlock—"

"No, I didn't, and I'm not certain you did."

Inosolan drew a deep breath, but before the angry torrent could flow, Kadolan added, "He might have been Rasha."

"Rasha? That's crazy!"

"I don't see why it's any crazier than what you say, though. A warlock can change his appearance, but so can a sorceress. You met someone who upset you. You claim you knew the voice, but I am sure his Omnipotence of the East is not so stupid as to disguise his face and forget his voice. You say he cured your headache, but that could have been a result of shock. In fact, the whole episode may even have been a delusion promoted by Elkarath. You agree?"

Inosolan shook her head, wide-eyed. "You'll go mad if you start thinking like that."

"Exactly," Kadolan agreed. "That's why I try not to. I'm sorry I was rude, dear. Do let's go and get some wind in our hair. You're going to die, you know."

"I am?" Inosolan gaped—and then suddenly smiled, still pale. "We all are, you mean?"

"Exactly, dear. Eventually. We just mustn't brood about it. Now, let's go. After you . . ."

2

Whether he looked like an elf or a faun, Rap was still much the same divided boy who had hung around the harbor in Krasnegar whenever he hadn't been hanging around the stables. Almost nothing could ever thrill him more than actually boarding a ship, and the *Allena* was a very splendid ship, a luxury four-master—square-rigged on the two foremasts and lateen on the aft—and she was the grandest, cleanest, most breathtakingly beautiful thing Rap had ever seen. When possible, elves traveled as they did everything else, in style.

He spared a few admiring glances for the bustling harbor of Noom, which had been dark and deserted when he first arrived in town. He admired the variety and the volume of the shipping, the cutters and dhows and junks and caravels and a dozen other types, and he marveled at the hubbub and bustle of one of the great ports of the Impire, gateway to the Dragon Sea and half of Pithmot. He was impressed, almost embarrassed, by the comfort of the little stateroom assigned to him on *Allena*. But mostly he just stood on deck and gazed longingly in every direction at once.

He wondered if passengers were allowed aloft. Unless someone chained him down, he was going to explore *Allena* from stem to stern and keel to royals as soon as she sailed. Of course he could talk anyone into anything now, and the temptation to use mastery was going to be irresistible in this case, however much his conscience might grumble. Yet the expression on Gathmor's still-mangled face showed that he was not going to sit in his cabin and knit, either. Likely all Rap need do was stay close to the sailor, and he'd find a way.

Playful white clouds scudded across a wondrous blue afternoon. The tide was running, the wind rising as evening approached. Seabirds shrieked among the masts and rigging, tangs of tar and fish mingling with the heartrending smell of the eternal sea itself. Jotnar and imps and trolls and even a few elves jostled along the dockside; porters trotted up and down the gangplank, loading the last few stores from the bakeries and markets of Noom. The crew was almost ready to cast off. Rap was on his way to Ilrane, Lith'rian, and—please Gods!—to Inos. Yet even that thrill could barely compete with the sheer joy and excitement of just boarding a great ship.

"Ten knots in this wind or I'm an elf," Gathmor muttered.

"Then you'll have to dress like one," Rap said.

He himself was dressed like an elf and trying not to notice. Krasnegarians expected protection from cold in winter and gnats in summer; they despised short pants and sleeveless shirts. Rap scowled down at the multihued arms on the rail before him. Whoever heard of an elf with scrapes and bruises? The conical absurdity on his head was even sillier than the forester cap Ishist had given him—and a lace collar! Even if he was standard gold all over, he still would not suit magenta and peach. With his arms and face and legs bearing bright rainbow reminders of the brawl in the Enchanted Glade and even more of the jailers' persuasions, he was not a likely elf at all, and certainly not a beautiful one.

Quip' was. He was much more interested in his new outfit than he was in the view from the deck. The first *real* clothes he had ever owned, he said, and he was overcome by their glory. He'd chosen them himself: turquoise buskins cross-laced in silver, shorts and blouse in chrome red and sulfur yellow, with floral overlay in seed pearls and cornflower blue stitchery. He had lace everywhere, even on his pants, and his cap kept blowing off because of its oversize ostrich plume, which was green. And yet, amazingly, it all very nearly worked. Without the green feather, it might have passed. At least five minutes had gone by since he'd asked Rap if he liked the effect—*really* liked it—so the question was about due again. Quip' was the most glorious thing in port at the moment, and yet still the most insecure.

A little way aft stood a group of another six brightly clad passengers. Whatever the traditions said, the elvish community of Noom was not going to gamble its entire wealth on Apprentice Quip'rian. He was Nearest Kinsman and therefore official escort, but someone reliable must keep an eye on him. The leaders seemed to be Mistress Fern'soon, director of the city art gallery— who looked about twenty and was a grandmother—and Sir Thoalin'fen, who was chief choreographer for the South Pithmot Ballet and had danced for the imperor's grandmother in his youth. His face sagged slightly over missing teeth and a milky sheen dulled the opal fires of his eyes, but elvish skin never wrinkled, elvish hair never turned from spun gold to silver. A stooped or pot-bellied elf was unthinkable. Not fair, Rap thought. One day Thoalin' would drop dead of sheer old age, and he would still look no older than Rap, the real Rap.

Lord Phiel' had sent his warmest wishes, but etiquette did not allow him to be present, and he must return to Hub anyway, to prepare for the celebrations of the imperor's birthday.

The legionaries pacing the quay would be making sure that the agreement was being honored. Likely the lictor had a man or two on board as well.

A grand landau drew up alongside, bearing a strikingly beautiful and obviously wealthy lady, so engrossed in a passionate farewell to her gentleman companion that she had not realized she could be seen from the deck. When the tearful embrace ended, Rap saw to his astonishment that the man in question was Andor.

What could possibly have brought *him?*

Yet Andor it was, and he strolled gracefully up the gangplank, following his sea chest. Andor's hose would never wrinkle, no breeze ever dare ruffle his hair. Without a glance at Rap, he headed for the group of elvish worthies.

Ten minutes later, though, the lovely but slightly bewildered Fern'soon found herself presenting Sir Andor to Master Rap'rian and his . . . er, friends. Formal courtesies were exchanged, Andor trying to conceal his distaste at the welts, puffy eyes, and swollen lips.

And as he allowed Fern'soon to draw him away to better company, he muttered out of the corner of his mouth, "Later, in my cabin. Sagorn has news for you."

Even that intriguing word could not distract Rap from the excitement of the imminent departure. He went back to watching the preparations.

"She's a beauty," Gathmor muttered, and he was not studying women.

"Yes, Cap'n, she's all that."

"No disrespect to a fine ship, lad, but she even outclasses *Stormdancer*." He was comparing a racehorse and a donkey, but then his own admission upset him. He turned his face away, as if to hide tears from a seer.

"Infernal feather!" Quip'rian grumbled as the wind snatched his cap yet again. "Should I have chosen a smaller plume, do you think, sir?"

"No. That one suits you," Rap said. "It adds *dash*!"

"Oh, do you think so? Really think so?" The gold of Quip's cheeks turned coppery.

"This beats clearing plates, does it not? It doesn't?"

Quip' swallowed hard. "I had to go on the harbor ferry once."

"And?"

He shuddered. "You've never been on a boat before?"

"Oh, yes. And ships."

Quip' gave him a tortured, puzzled glance. "You don't get sick, sir?"

"Quip'!" Rap protested. "I keep telling you—stop calling me 'sir'! I'm not much older than you are."

"But you're so much more . . . *worldly*! Experienced. Manly."

"You'll get there soon enough. And no, I never get seasick."

"Really? I thought elves always did. I did. Horribly."

In the harbor? "It's all inside your head," Rap said airily. Then he began to wonder how deeply his own head had been penetrated by Ishist's magic. A sorcerer who enjoyed practical jokes might find seasickness a real belly laugh.

The gangplanks were being hauled in. The other elves were heading for their cabins. Quip's edginess was increasing rapidly.

"I may not be able to carry out my escort duties if I get seasick, sir-I-mean-Rap'."

Rap tried his encouraging smile. Could even occult mastery overcome seasickness? "Don't worry about it. It's only a formality. I'm not going to jump overboard."

The idea of jumping overboard made Quip' shudder and alloyed his golden face with silver. "You're frightfully brave!"

"No, I'm not."

"But you're going to Lith'rian! A warlock! He may cut off your head."

216

"I don't think he will," Rap said with all the confidence he could display, wishing he could use occult mastery to convince himself as well as he could others.

"Then you really want a war? The Clan'rians against the Clan'nilths? And of course all the allied clans will come in, or most of—"

"I hope not that, either! I'm sure a warlock can find a way around the problem, Quip'. I've nothing against Phiel'nilth. I chose him by pure chance, or maybe by good luck. I've nothing against his clan. I just need to see Warlock Lith'rian very urgently, that's all. I was told that this was the easiest, quickest way to do so."

The elf's big opal eyes seemed to grow even larger, flickering amethyst and pearl. "But why?" he whispered.

Rap wanted to watch the cables being cast off, but he decided he was going to have to talk at the same time, to give his Nearest Kinsman some sort of explanation. He deserved it, for Rap's actions had grossly disrupted his humdrum, insignificant existence. Some people were not made to hear the trumpets. Quip'rian would always be a lapdog, never a wolfhound.

And Rap himself was another. This mad pilgrimage had never been his choice. All he had ever wanted was to aid Inos by warning her of her father's illness. Now where had it got him? Had Andor and his gang not interfered, Rap would be driving a wagon now, bringing in the harvest at Krasnegar. Or he might be an assistant factor, charging to and fro on a pony and tallying supplies.

And who would be reigning in the castle?

Kalkor?

Rap pulled his mind back to *Allena* and the worried youth beside him. Gathmor had dashed off to haul on ropes with the sailors unable to stand idle any longer.

"Why? Because of a lady."

"Oooo!" Quip' sighed deeply. "Truly? All this for an affair of the heart? How wonderful!" His eyes misted.

"A little more than that . . ." Leaning his elbows on the rail, Rap started to explain. The elf pulled off his cap for safekeeping and then leaned at his side, listening in open-month fascination.

Rap began at the beginning, in Krasnegar. He did not mention that he had become an elf only recently—that was much too complicated. Indeed, he managed to keep almost all the magic out of it, especially his own, but he did have to include Rasha, Ishist, and Bright Water.

Even in that abbreviated form it was a very remarkable tale, yet the most remarkable thing about it was that young Quip' obviously believed every word. He sniffed, then sniveled, and finally openly wept, not even seeing the sails spreading out above him, pink in the sunset glow. Nor did he notice the gentle motion of the ship as *Allena* turned majestically toward the harbor bar. And when Rap at last straightened up and concluded with, "And that's where you came in," the elf blinked bronze-rimmed eyes at him and—being speechless with emotion—then tried to embrace him.

Rap used his occult agility to dodge the embrace, so Quip' draped himself on the rail again until he could control his tears.

"It's beautiful!" he sobbed. "The bards of Ilrane will sing of it for centuries! Oh, Rap'! That's the *loveliest* story I ever heard! Throwing your life away to help the lady you can never hope to marry!"

Rap took a hard look at that last statement.

"Huh? I'm not planning on throwing anything away."

"Well, I suppose Lith'rian . . ." The elf looked up, puzzled. "I mean, lots of clan wars have been fought for much less. The War of the Bad Apple, for instance. People sometimes forget that we elves can be ferocious when we choose, bloodthirsty as jotnar when necessary."

"I've heard that."

"And we can never resist suicidal last stands . . . but not in this case!" He had come to a decision. "No, it's much more satisfactory if the warlock puts you to death. Poignant! Heartrending!" He dabbed at his eyes with an apricot silk kerchief.

"Um. Do you suppose other elves would feel this way about the most appropriate choice?" Lith'rian, for one.

"Oh, yes! I can quote you all sorts of idylls. *Rap'!* You can't want to go back to being a stableboy, not after all this? You can't expect the princess to marry a . . . a *nobody!* It's so much more romantic you die, sending her your final word of—" He choked, and more tears flooded down his cheeks. "—final word of *love!*"

And two words of power to the warlock for his trouble? Ishist had never denied that Rap was going into danger; he'd made no guarantees.

"And what happens to Inos in this libretto?"

"She dies of a broken heart."

Rap felt a little better. Inos was much too practical to do any such thing, either to mourn a childhood friend or yet to satisfy all the bards in Ilrane. "Does she die on her throne, though?"

Quip' shook his head, so overcome again that he reached out his arms, and this time Rap let himself be hugged, self-consciously patting Quip's back as he buried his face on Rap's shoulder. He soaked it before he could sob out what he wanted to say. "That's the saddest part of all!"

"It is? Why?"

"Because . . . because it's all in vain, of course! Because Lith'rian can't . . . can't . . . can't help Inos!"

Rap grabbed his arms and straightened him up. "What do you mean *can't*? He's a warlock!"

Nods, gulps, sniffs . . . "Yes. But she's in Zark. That's east! Lith'rian's South. He can't interfere!"

"He can champion her cause among the Four!"

"Oh, Rap', Rap'! Even an elf won't start *that* sort of a war just for a girl. I mean, a civil war between clans . . . we have those on the boil all the time. But all of Pandemia . . . Warlocks and dragons and things . . . No, no, no!"

"How would you know?" Rap snarled, wanting to shake him.

"Oh, but I am sure! Ilrane's south. Lith'rian's been warlock for seventy years, and a good one for elves—he keeps the dragons away. Inos's kingdom's in North's sector. And jotnar are North's, also. The legions are East's, and Inos is in his sector. South isn't going to get himself involved, Rap'! Or West, either. I mean, that's obvious!"

"That wasn't what Ishist told the."

"But he's only a gnome, you said!" Quip' wailed. "You know how sneaky gnomes are!"

Perhaps Ishist's sense of humor was even more macabre than Rap had yet suspected.

"You *can't* trust a gnome, Rap'!" Quip' was staring at his friend in horror. "You mean you truly expected that Lith'rian would let you live? After all this? You're trying to *trap* a warlock! You can't expect a *warlock* to let you get *away* with it?"

South could be ruthless, Ishist had said. How many people even knew that he'd married his unruly daughter off to a gnome? If that one secret alone was jealously guarded, then what was Rap's life worth?

"No, Rap'," Quip' said resolutely, straightening his narrow shoulders. "It's wonderful and beautiful and people will weep for you for hundreds of—"

He gaped up in sudden horror at the clouds of canvas overhead.

Allena had reached the harbor mouth. She bobbed eagerly, rolling in a new motion, preparing to dance with the long swell beyond. Apparently Quip'rian only now realized that she had even left the quay. His eyes went to the shiny blue-green sea all around, the leaping white breakers on the bar, and the gathering dusk above the distant towers of Noom.

Before Rap's fascinated gaze, his face turned swiftly from gold to lead. and then to the exact shade of green found on old tarnished copper. He spun around, doubled himself over the rail, and lost everything he had eaten in the last five years.

Moaning of the bar:
   Sunset and evening star,
      And one clear call for me!
   And may there be no moaning of the bar,
      When I put out to sea.
                              Tennyson, *Crossing the Bar*

11

Rushing seas

1

R ap offered to help Quip' to his cabin, and ended by carrying him most
of the way. Having made him as comfortable as it was possible for a
man to be while convinced he was about to die and the sooner the
better, Rap then went off in search of Andor.

Allena was pitching seriously now, with a longer, slower motion than the
galley or the longship had ever shown, adding a sort of lurching, flying sensation on the crests of the waves. She had a pronounced roll, also, and the
wind must still be rising, for the crew was already shortening sail.

As he waited along the corridor, he noted that every elf on board lay as
prostrate as Quip', proving that the elvish compulsion to do things in style
included even seasickness. Impish passengers were now succumbing also.

Locating Sagorn stretched out on a bunk, reading, Rap knocked and called
his name, and was told to enter.

Allena had forty-two staterooms for first-class passengers on her upper
deck. Rap's cabin was far aft, and one of the best; Andor's was near the bow,
smaller and plainer. Although it would barely qualify ashore as a large closet,
it was still larger and more pleasant than *Stormdancer's* cubicles, or the cell Rap

221

had so recently shared with Gathmor. Floral drapes fringed the scuttle, the rug was thick, the woodwork and brass all gleamed. Two bunks were hinged to the forward bulkhead. The aft side held a mirror and a shelf with space below it for the occupant's baggage. With the upper bunk hooked back out of the way, the old man was lounging comfortably on the lower, his long, pale shanks protruding from a powder-blue gown. Andor's lady friend would have paid for that.

Rap folded his arms, leaned back against the door, and waited.

Sagorn had been holding his book close to his nose, catching the last dregs of daylight from the scuttle; now he closed it on a finger and regarded Rap with his normal sour disapproval.

"Why did you not consult me?"

"About what?"

Sagorn clenched his lips in exasperation. "About everything! My evaluation of the gnome sorcerer. The significance of uttering the Sublime Defiance. The choice of victim. You blundered into Noom like a herd of charging behemoths."

"I seem to have blundered out again much as planned."

"After being battered to a pulp several times."

Rap shrugged. He still had aches he hadn't catalogued yet, and that gesture had discovered more of them. "I'll survive."

"You are extremely fortunate not to have any broken bones."

"I have nine, mostly fingers, but they seem to be healing very quickly."

The old man's mouth shut with a click of teeth. After a moment he said, "So that is within the powers of an adept?" A spasm of envy and longing crossed his face.

For a few minutes the two stared at each other in mutual obstinacy. Sagorn's face was against the light, but of course Rap could make out every cleft and wrinkle. The old man certainly looked younger and healthier since Ishist had restored him—a pity the sorcerer had not done something about his disposition.

Again Sagorn was first to break the silence, and with a slash of nervy sarcasm. "You are practicing being inscrutable?"

"I'm trying not to use mastery on you."

Sagorn flinched. He marked his place in the book with a piece of ribbon, and then laid it on the bunk beside him. That gave him a moment to gather his wits, of course. He was pathetically readable now, and certainly plotting something. "Are you succeeding?"

"Apparently. You haven't been very helpful so far."

"I took a considerable risk on your behalf, in Noom."

"Your decision, not my request."

222

"Ha! Repartee is also within the powers of an adept?"

Ripple!

"What was that?" Rap cried, looking all around.

"What was what?"

"I felt something." Yet the ship continued to pitch and roll as before. The sailors on deck were showing no alarm.

"What sort of something?" Sagorn demanded irritably.

"I'm not sure." Rap wasn't even sure how he'd felt whatever it was. Neither noise nor motion, not in his ears or bones or skin. Nor could he tell from which direction it had come, but he was sure he'd felt something—it had been faint, but real. He shivered at the uncanny touch of premonition, but it said *important*, not notably *dangerous*. He disliked these strange new talents.

Sagorn dismissed the problem with a sneer. "Nerves"

"Perhaps. Tell me of this risk."

"I called upon an old friend, a scholar and something of an authority on Imperial politics. We have not met in thirty years."

"Why was this a risk?"

"Because I do not wish to be denounced as a sorcerer. I have not aged thirty years in those thirty years." His aquamarine eyes flickered with sudden amusement.

"And?"

"And neither had he!"

Rap chuckled. "Embarrassing for both of you."

"Quite! He is still much the same as ever he was. With the assistance of your gnomish friend, I may even look younger now than I did then. But my friend made me welcome, and we had a long gossip. He belongs to a very large and powerful family. He is its expert on political affairs and, I suspect, its strategist for meddling in them. He was exiled to Noom by Emthar and liked it so well that he never petitioned for leave to return. Yet he keeps a very steady finger on the pulse in Hub."

"Inos? Krasnegar?"

"He knew of Krasnegar." Sagorn thinned his lips in the callous smile that always reminded Rap of an animal trap. He waited, teasing. When he failed to win a reaction, he said, "The imps withdrew, as I predicted they would. There is much scandal over the cost. Many men were lost."

"I don't think I mourn." Rap cared little for goblins, but Imperial troops were worse, and they had started the hostilities. Their occupation would leave the little town with bitter scars—women violated and their menfolk killed or maimed in trying to defend them, property looted or destroyed. Those troops had been the dregs of the Imperial army. It was better not to know.

More interesting than the news itself was the implication of sorcery at work. Clearly whatever occult protection Warlock Olybino had tried to provide for his legionaries' retreat had been successfully blocked, either by Raspnex, the dwarf disguised as a goblin, or by Bright Water herself.

"The Marshal of the Armies has used the affair to justify some much-needed housecleaning." Sagorn sneered. "Long overdue! The high command is a swamp of toads. He is rushing the crack XIIth Legion north, because goblins have been raiding in Northwest Julgistro, coming over the mountains! He has other problems, too. Revolt has broken out in Farmer Shimlundok—the usual dispute with the dwarves and access to the Dark River, of course—and half of Guwush is in flames, also. Absolutely nothing will rouse the Senate more than any hint of mere *gnomes* defeating Imperial troops. That is anathema to—"

"So what happened in Krasnegar after the imps left?" Rap had heard Bright Water tell of the goblin raids, months ago, and the rest did not interest him.

The light was failing swiftly now. Sagorn was nearly invisible to Rap's eyes, but farsight said he shrugged. "Who knows?"

"The wardens, of course."

"Quite. But you are the only mundane I have ever heard of who goes around chatting with warlocks and witches as an everyday affair. Of course you're not a mundane, are you?" Again the hurt and envy showed for a moment. Sagorn considered that he, not Rap, deserved to be the adept.

"And what are the imperor's plans?"

The crabby old jotunn detested being questioned and would normally have turned stubborn then. Probably Rap was using mastery whether he liked it or not, because he got an answer.

"Warm soup and a soft bed, I imagine."

Rap studied the familiar cynical sneer and said, "Bad news?"

"Emshandar's health is failing rapidly, it seems. Pity! He was a good man . . . relatively speaking. He will be missed." Sagorn scowled, as if regretting this admission of sympathy. "But the Impire goes on regardless. His advisors have found a solution, of course."

"Tell!"

Reluctantly the old man came to the point. "Rumor—and it is only rumor—says that the Privy Secretariat has put out feelers to Nordland."

"Compromise?"

"Of course. Ironically, it seems that neither side has ever spared much thought for Krasnegar in the past. Might that be some lingering trace of Inisso's work, do you suppose? The Impire's bureaucrats have always just assumed it to be some sort of client state or protectorate; the thanes seemed to have looked on it as jotunn territory. It was never worth a raid by either side, anyway. It has some commercial value, because of the trading, but it is still not worth a war."

"If everyone agrees to behave logically."

Sagorn shrugged, as if unwilling to admit that Rap himself could be so logical. "The Impire's proposal is thought to be this: Duke Angilki shall be recognized as king, but stay where he is, measuring carpet and hanging drapes as usual. The actual authority will be in the hands of a viceroy, ruling in his name."

"Kalkor, I suppose?"

The old man waved a frail white hand. "Whoever is nominated—meaning chosen—by the thanes' moot. It could be Kalkor if he wants it, but why would he? Possibly even a local, like Foronod. In effect, the Impire is saying that Nordland can have Krasnegar in all but name. It may rule as long as it doesn't claim a victory. The chart makers will still color it Imperial . . . And please don't kill any more people man you have to, or you'll curtail our supply of fur collars."

So Inos would be dispossessed?

"The wardens must have approved this proposal?"

"Certainly. Only Olybino could have held back the legions from a full invasion of goblin territory. That is not on the table."

Inos bereft of her kingdom would no longer be a queen and . . . Rap recoiled in horror from the thoughts that lay along that road. Were she not a queen she would be free to marry a hostler, or a common sailor. What sort of selfish monster was he? He would not even consider the possibility.

Meanwhile, there was the problem of what Sagorn was hiding. He was gloating, so it had to be bad news.

Stewards were approaching, working their way along the corridor with a rack of lighted lanterns, knocking on doors to offer them, together with respectful warnings about the dangers of fire on a ship.

Overhead, the sailors were again shortening sail, while the timbers and cables groaned with the strain of the sudden storm. Certainly the captain would have never left port had he foreseen such roaring weather. Again Rap felt a crawly sense of premonition, as if he were overlooking something obvious.

Now the stewards had reached the cabin, two youngsters finely attired in white livery. As the taller of the two raised knuckles to tap, Rap turned and opened the door. He held out a hand for one of the little lanterns, and said a premature "Thanks!"

The fair-haired boy offering it just froze, his mouth hanging open as he gaped at Rap as if at something emerging from a graveyard by night. His already light-skinned face turned pale as parchment. His equally blond companion seemed equally dumbfounded.

Amused, Rap put a finger to his lips. "Sh!" he said. "I'm a jotunn in disguise. Don't tell anyone."

The boys blushed scarlet. The first quickly passed over the lamp, and the other found enough voice to say, "Will you be dining this evening, sir?"

Polite male jotnar? What was the world coming to?

But Rap had some prison hollows to fill yet. "I shall certainly be dining, and my friend here, also. What's on the menu?"

Exchanging renewed glances of amazement, the stewards rattled off a list of dishes that made his mouth water. *Stormdancer* had never been like this.

"Sounds good," he said. "If I asked for a double helping of the broiled pork, done rare and extra greasy, I imagine the chef could oblige?" Chuckling, he closed the door on them, still thunderstruck. He hung the lantern on a hook in the beams, where it swung crazily.

Sagorn was smiling sourly at the foolery. "The first-class dining room? What do you know of the gentry's table manners?"

"I think those should be within the powers of an adept." Rap had eyes; he could copy what he saw done.

Finding that life standing up was becoming too strenuous, he stepped across to Andor's sea chest and sat down. The sly old scholar was certainly hiding something. It was time to do some prying.

"Tell me about Lith'rian." He saw at once that his guess was wrong—the old man answered without hesitation.

"Phaw! He succeeded to the blue throne in the first year of Emthar's reign, sixty-eight years ago. Almost nothing is known of his background, but he is said to have been born on Valdojif, not on Valdorian itself. The Clan'jifs are a sept of the Clan'rians, the senior clan in the Eol Gens. He is naturally a hero to elves in general, and the Clan'rians in particular. He is High War Chief, a post of extreme honor, rarely granted, and equivalent to overlord of the whole gens—not that such honors are worth much to a warlock, I suppose. His age is unknown, and of course inestimable, as he is both a sorcerer and elvish, but it seems that he was chosen by Umthrum herself as her successor, and she told him her words on her deathbed, so I would guess he was around eighteen or twenty then—"

"Why would you guess that?"

Sagorn snorted. "Most sorcerers and sorceresses turn strange as they grow older, and Umthrum was at least two hundred. She was also a merwoman."

"Oh."

"She maintained an extensive entourage of handsome young—"

"I see."

" . . . selected from all races, and noted for their—"

"I understand!" Rap insisted, feeling distaste that had nothing to do with seasickness. "How do you remember so much?"

The old man sneered. "Training and practice, of course. I have an eidetic memory—I can recall a visual image of anything I have ever seen, or any page I have ever read. I should have thought that such an ability would lie within the powers of an adept."

"Would it, though?" Rap had not thought of that, and again felt a small tremor of premonition. No, a *thrill* of premonition. Somehow that scrap of information was important, and he was certainly overlooking something. An adept could master any human skill—why not memory? He had best go to his own cabin and do some thinking. And these uncanny premonitions . . . were they a sign of a developing foresight talent? Or only imagination?

His mother had been a seer.

He still had not discovered what ill tidings Sagorn was hoarding. "Do you think the warlock will aid me?"

"I have no idea." The old man's manner implied that he did not intend to find out, either.

"How long until I reach Valdorian?"

Sagorn shot a worried glance up at the window glass. Water was dribbling in around the edges. "If you can predict even where we shall be tomorrow, you are much more than an adept. You must know *Allena's* schedule. Malfin—"

"I know we are not expected in Vislawn for at least four weeks. I almost wish I'd not listened to Ishist's crazy ideas. I could have walked to Hub a lot sooner."

Sagorn bared his teeth in contempt. "So you may not have been quite the free agent you hoped? See why you should consult me before undertaking such rash actions?"

Once Rap would have felt anger at the old man's jibes. Now he was merely saddened by the petty spite that bred them.

"I understood that a serf could not walk up to the door of a warlock's palace and demand to see him."

"I have friends in Hub who could have arranged an audience."

"Quickly?"

"Maybe not right away," the scholar admitted.

"So this way may be quicker in the end?"

Sagorn nodded reluctantly. "Oh, once you reach Ilrane, you will be rushed to Valdorian. I have no doubt of that. The finest procrastinators in the world are Dwanishian customs officials, but elves run a close second, and they dislike strangers wandering around Ilrane. An elf who has uttered the Sublime Defiance, though—he's a matter of state! You'll be shipped like ice, posthaste."

"So how long?"

Sagorn shrugged. "Sixty leagues, maybe. A hard day's ride on good horses."

Sixty leagues in a day? While Rap was digesting that astonishing scrap of information, Sagorn rose stiffly to his feet. Balancing unsteadily, he closed the deadlight over the scupper. "The question may be moot, you know. We are hove to now, but we cannot have left Noom Bay yet. Our situation is perilous." He sat down again, probably more heavily than he had intended. Evidently he was enough of a jotunn to recognize the dangers of a lee shore.

A steward reeled along the passage, jangling a dinner bell.

"I do not think I shall essay the journey to the dining room," Sagorn muttered. "And Andor would nave no appetite. Jalon, perhaps, would appreciate a good meal, and the crew knows none of us by sight . . ."

"I still hanker after that roast pork," Rap said. Time to go, and therefore time for a direct offensive. "I am curious about your motives, Doctor. And your friends'. Andor and Jalon and Darad all shook my hand. Each of them agreed to help my quest in return for my promise of help afterward. You and Thinal I have not asked yet. But I was very surprised to see Andor embark on this ship. Fidelity is not Andor's favorite sport."

The old man flushed. "He harbors delusions of weaseling your word of power out of you somewhere on the journey."

Rap shook his head.

The sage scowled. "We may not accompany you all the way to Vislawn. The schedule calls for stops at Malfin and Dal Petr and—"

"No. Andor is not overendowed with courage, either. He would not risk any sea voyage without very good reason, and he would run a thousand leagues to stay away from a warlock. Must I conclude that Ishist bound all five of you with a compulsion to accompany me to Lith'rian?"

Sagorn paled. "Certainly not!"

"Then the obvious question is, what else did your friend in Noom tell you?"

Sagorn snarled, baring yellow teeth. "You are growing too smart for your own good, young man! Here it is, then. Inosolan is dead!"

No!

Cognizant of his own face, Rap was certain he had shown no reaction, and Sagorn's obvious disappointment confirmed that.

"Who says so?" Rap asked stonily. *No! No! No!*

"Emshandar. He so informed the Senate when he advised it of the Krasnegar matter."

"And who told the imperor?"

"I don't know."

Sagorn was not lying. His unnamed friend would have had no reason to lie. Months ago, on the night when Rap had seen Inos somewhere in the desert of Zark, at least three of the wardens had known where she was, and at least two of them had been planning to snatch her away. If Hub thought she was dead, then something had gone wrong . . . Rap fought against a screaming sense of despair, but he thought his premonition was helping him. Something in this tale rang false. "I don't believe it."

Sagorn's book began to move. He grabbed for it too late, and it slid swiftly to the end of the bunk. Losing interest, he leaned back and sneered at Rap.

"As you grow older and wiser, you will discover that one's first reaction to distressing events is often one of rejection. The mind just refuses to believe, at first, and the emotions rule. But this news is hardly unexpected. In a day or so, you will come to accept it."

"And then?"

"And then you will see that your quest has been terminated. It has become impossible. Under the agreement you made with the others, you are morally bound to help us now. I call on you to share the second word with us."

Rap said nothing, thinking furiously.

Sagorn frowned. "True, that was not spelled out exactly. My associates failed to establish reasonable terms with you. But you are certainly under an ethical obligation." He was not nearly so confident as he was trying to appear, but Andor's decision to board the ship was now explicable.

Ishist had told Rap to trust his premontions. "I don't believe it," he repeated stubbornly.

"Faugh! You are being childish! She may have died the very night the sorceress abducted—"

"She was alive when we were in Milflor."

"How do you know that?" roared Sagorn.

"Never mind! I want to know who told the imperor."

"Then go to Hub and ask him!"

"Who holds the power? Him or the Senate?"

Sagorn's eyes narrowed. "Ten years ago—even five years ago—Emshandar could make the senators dance jigs in their nightgowns These days . . . who knows?"

"So Krasnegar was an annoying problem for him. It was easier to find a solution without Inos, maybe, so he . . . simplified it?"

Sagorn laughed mockingly.

It sounded weak even to Rap, but he persisted. "A young queen in distress, and legionaries had already died to help her, and Emshandar wanted to give her kingdom away to the thane, but the senators might have—"

"Wishful thinking!"

And yet—

"The imperor may have been lying!"

Yes! said premonition. *Closer! Closer!*

229

Or was that only wishful thinking also? Oh, Inos!

"Your optimism is as far beyond belief as your claims of knowledge," Sagorn said. "Why would the wardens support such a falsehood? Tell me what you learned in Milflor." He was tortured by curiosity, and trying not to show it.

Taking pity on him. Rap began to tell him of the night he had met Bright Water and Warlock Zinixo, and the strange events in the Gazebo in Milflor. Talking was a welcome distraction. He told it all—how the two wardens had foreseen Little Chicken, how they had plotted against Olybino, how he had observed Inos in the occult mirror, and how he had tried to warn her.

By the time he had done, the officers and a handful of passengers were into their third course in the dining room, shadows were squirreling madly around the cabin, and he was shouting over the noise of the storm. Sagorn was a most unlikely jotunn, but he ignored the fearsome weather in true jotunn fashion, listening enraptly.

"You think she heeded your admonition and escaped?" he demanded doubtfully at the end.

"I don't know. I hope so."

"It seems unlikely she would have succeeded. And I find your touching beliefs even harder to swallow now. I should prefer to surmise that there was a struggle over her, and she was a casualty in the dispute. Or she tried to escape as you suggested and met with misfortune. The wardens told the imperor."

Rap's heart sank.

"We do not have enough information," Sagorn conceded. "Whatever we conclude must be a cobweb of speculation."

Rap sadly agreed with that. His hope sounded like a very thin whistling beside a very large graveyard. And yet his premonition was insisting that Inos was not dead.

"Lith'rian will certainly know."

"Let us hope you live to see him!" Sagorn was holding the side of his bunk now to avoid being tipped out as the ship pitched. "Does your farsight detect land anywhere?"

"None," Rap said soothingly. "Lots of sea out there."

The masts were almost bare of canvas, every rib and beam was creaking under the strain. Head to the wind, *Allena* was holding her station so far as he could tell, but the old man was right to be scared. Rap let him ramble, not listening to the nervous chitchat, idly nagging at himself to go and eat while there was still food to be had, yet letting his mind pursue its own researches . . .

Suddenly he had it. The picture he wanted flashed up from his memory, fresh-painted, clear in every detail as if he were again staring over an elf's shoulder.

230

He jumped up, and lurched across to the door.

"What's the matter?" Sagorn demanded.

Rap grabbed the handle with injured fingers, and a hot jab of pain distracted him. But his farsight was far out ahead of him, searching . . . He met resistance, insisted, was repulsed . . .

He stumbled back and slithered awkwardly to his knees. Nauseated, he put his face in his hands.

"Seasick, Master Rap? Not enough jotunn in you?"

It was a moment before Rap could reply. He licked his lips, swallowed twice. Then he lied, "Just a twinge."

"Eschew the pork, I suggest."

But Rap had recognized the familiar touch of an aversion spell. If he told the old man the truth about the storm, the news would only frighten him more. This weather had been summoned.

Inos was still alive!

Or else Little Chicken was.

2

When Rap awoke to a chill gray dawn, he found *Allena* still hove to in an unrelenting gale. As he set off in search of breakfast, his farsight was detecting sharp edges to the south, decorated with foam and spray. He concluded that he would have to do something about those.

An hour or two later, Gathmor went reeling aft in search of his companions. He had spent the entire night with the officers, joyfully swapping yarns and summing up potential partners for recreational mayhem at a later date. He threw open the door and lurched into Rap's cabin.

Jalon was stretched out on the bed, idly tuning a lute he'd borrowed from an unconscious elf. Since eating a hearty dinner the previous night, Jalon had shown no impatience to call back Sagorn, or Andor. Although he was unassertive toward people, he had treated wind and waves with total contempt. Either the fury of the storm left him unmoved, or he had not really noticed it.

Rap was sitting in one of the two well-padded chairs, with his feet up on the other. He removed those feet and waved for Gathmor to sit down.

"You know what that crazy skipper's doing?" Gathmor snarled.

"Hoisting more sail?"

"How'd you know?"

"Oh, I suggested it to him," Rap said, smirking. Not yet knowing how effective his mastery was, he had not been sure how long the compulsion would hold after he parted from the captain, but apparently it had held long enough. Andor's range was about an hour, he recalled.

231

Gathmor collapsed on the chair. "God of Storms! Why? We'll be dismasted or laid on our beam ends."

Rap waved a thumb. "Rocks thataway."

The sailor scowled. "I mean, why would he listen to you, a prissy landlubber elf?"

Rap shrugged. "We were having breakfast, and Captain Prakker happened to remark he'd never seen an elf on his feet in anything other than dead calm. One thing led to another."

"More canvas in this weather?"

"I persuaded him it was worth a try."

The sailor scowled blackly, recognizing that he was in the presence of the occult.

"She'll make good time in this, won't she?" Rap said. "If she stays afloat, that is. Skipper says Malfin's straight upwind, but we can tack. And if you'd care for a wager, Cap'n, I'll lay odds we won't see Malfin on this trip."

Gathmor scowled. "I don't bet against you, not ever. But Prakker'll just heave to again as soon as he's clear of Noom Bay."

"Sure you don't want to bet?" Rap said cheerfully.

He glanced over at the minstrel, who was quietly fingering out a tune and frowning.

"You've been to Ilrane, haven't you?"

Jalon shrugged without looking up. "Andor mostly. I was just there a few hours."

"Tell me about the sky trees."

"Andor told you once," Jalon said, still twanging quietly.

"But you've got the artist's eye and the poet's tongue."

Even Darad might have seen through such thick-buttered flattery, but Jalon didn't. He laid the lute beside him, put his hands under his flaxen head, and stared up at the beams. For a long minute he was silent, then he sighed. "They're glorious, utterly breathtaking. Like crystal artichokes."

Gathmor rolled his eyes at Rap and made a scornful noise.

Jalon had once admitted to Rap that he was part elf, and this seemed a logical time to mention the fact again, but he didn't. He might have forgotten having done so already, or he might be reluctant to inform Gathmor. "No, truly. They're not really trees, they're some sort of mineral growth."

"How big?" Rap asked.

"Huge. Lots are a league high, some of them more than that, with their tops all covered in snow. Valdobyt Prime was said to be so high there wasn't enough air at the top of it to breathe. It got knocked down by some sorcerer or other thousands of years ago. I'd give you a ballad or two about it if I could fix this E string."

"Artichokes?" Rap said. "A league high? Come on, be serious!"

"Should have been able to see 'em from Kith," Gathmor snorted, equally disbelieving. But Jalon was lost in remembered bliss.

"Oftentimes the clouds hide them. It can take days to climb up from the ground to where you want to be. That's how I got called—Andor was exhausted. I would never've left, I think, except that his hosts knew him and not me; never mind that tale . . . Each leaf is sort of like a hand. Think of hundreds of crystalline hands all sprouting from a common trunk, except you can't see much of the trunk itself. There's usually a little lake in the palm, and the fingers feather 'way out and up, into branches of crystals, and they branch more, and finally make petals like a mist of stained glass and butterfly wings in the distance. All day the sun strikes through them in all the colors you can imagine and a few you can't, and the clouds float by in pearly fires."

"Where do the people live?" Gathmor said, always practical.

"They build houses around the lakes, or higher on the slopes, in among the trees. There's real trees and grass, and flowers of course. Can't have elves without flowers around! Little fields. Each leaf is a separate village. You go from one to the other up long ladders or in tunnels winding up through the rock. The sky trees are the most beautiful thing in the world," Jalon said with unusual firmness. "No wonder elves love beauty so much."

Gathmor rubbed his eyes. "I think I'll catch some sleep."

Rap hid a smile. "Good idea. Any chance you could borrow a cape and a hat for me, Cap'n?" He would have to spend time up on deck to hold the skipper on course. Already he thought he could detect the wind being altered to react to the ship's new course.

If all else failed, he would just have to explain to the master that the warlock of the south wanted him, Rap, delivered to Ilrane as soon as possible; but he thought Lith'rain might regard that as cheating. Presumably he was not going to all this trouble just to steal Rap's word of power, so Rap must have some interest or value, and just maybe that meant he was a pawn in the Krasnegar struggle, and in that case the game was still on, and Inos was still alive.

This rationalization was a tapestry of moonbeams, but it was enough to keep him from brooding, except when he remembered he was trying to outguess a man who had married his daughter to a gnome.

Or when he wondered if the unseen hand belonged to Bright Water, needing Rap in order to fulfill Little Chicken's destiny. Lith'rian was the witch's ally.

Nevertheless, Rap would guide the ship to Vislawn as best he could. The rest of the time he would lounge in his wonderful cabin. He had eaten a very fine breakfast. Never before in his life had he lived in luxury like this.

And he had a whole new pastime to savor. With his new eidetic memory, he could call up detailed pictures of Inos from their childhood together—Inos riding, Inos running, dancing, laughing, playing, running. Next to actually having her there, it was the best thing he could imagine.

3

It was at some undefined time during the second day that Inos opened her eyes to find Kade standing over her, regarding her with concern, white hair tousled around wind-flushed face. Beyond the scuppers lay blue sky and sea and white birds—and waves. Inos closed her eyes again swiftly.

"I was hoping . . ." Kade said softly. "The wind has died almost completely."

"So have I."

Kade was not to be discouraged. "I did bring a little—"

"If you mention food or drink or . . . yecgh! . . . soup . . . I will start all over again," Inos said firmly. She heard a faint sigh and a fainter clink of china.

Then vague noises suggested a chair being pulled up. She opened her eyes just as Kade sat down beside the bed.

"Please, Aunt? Leave me. Maybe tomorrow?"

But Kade was descended from a long line of kings, and at times she could be implacably stubborn. Regrettably this looked like being one of those times.

"There is something you should know," she said firmly.

"Tell me then." Get it over with.

"I did try to tell Azak, but I was not allowed near him."

How would he be doing, down in the bilge? Azak swore that he loved the sea, and yet djinns were usually reluctant sailors. Inos wondered how Gnome Quarters smelled, and instantly wished she hadn't. She grunted noncommittally. She had too many worries of her own. He was a big boy and could look after himself.

"So I'm going to tell you," Kade said firmly. "This ship is not going to Angot."

Inos turned her head quickly on the pillow—too quickly. "It's not?"

"Not when it's heading south it isn't! I may be old but I'm not stupid." Princess Kadolan very rarely lost her temper. This must be one of those times, also.

"You're not old," Inos said automatically as she tried to comprehend the stunning news.

"Despite the calm sea and gentle breezes, this is not the Sea of Sorrows. We're in Kerith Passage."

"Then where are we going?"

"I have spent the last day and a half trying to find out! The crew and the officers are being extremely unhelpful. Frainish doesn't know—she was told she was going to Qoble—and I seem to be the only passenger capable of maintaining an upright posture."

"Arakkaran?" Inos whispered. It would have to be Arakkaran.

"Arakkaran, yes. I just visited the cabin of an elderly priest. He didn't want any fish chowder, either, but he did admit that he's on his way to Githarn, and expects the ship to call at Torkag, Brogog, and Arakkaran."

Seasickness did not promote clear thinking, any thinking. The planks in the ceiling had a very wavy grain pattern, and if Inos looked at them for very long, the waves started rippling.

Don't look, stupid!

"You are still convinced that your centurion was the warlock?" Kade demanded.

"Yes. Yes, even his eyes. Certainty his voice. And not even a mistake. He wanted me to know—he was laughing at me."

Her aunt tapped a shoe on the rug several times. "Well, I don't understand! If we were still Rasha's prisoners, I could see why we might be on our way back to Arakkaran, but I don't understand why the warlock of the east would send us there. I mean, either he wants you as queen of Krasnegar, or he doesn't want you at all, or I shouldn't think he would anyway."

That was not an unusually muddled speech for Kade, but in her insubstantial condition, Inos needed time to think it through. "I agree," she muttered at last.

"So, if you were right in thinking that the warlock stole us away from the sorceress, then it would seem that the sorceress has stolen us back again!"

At the moment it didn't matter all that much. "What does Skarash say?"

"Master Skarash," Kade said crossly, "is being a jotunn."

"Jotunn?"

"He's wearing sailor clothes, consorting with sailors. The one time I managed to get a word in with him, he was attempting sailor jargon in a broad Nordland dialect—a very bad imitation of Nordland dialect."

"And what did he say?"

"That was debatable. I couldn't understand him, and when I used a much more authentic Nordland accent on him, he obviously couldn't understand me and wouldn't admit it."

Inos made a mental note to find that story funny when she recovered her health and sense of humor. Trader Skarash must know the truth of the matter. If Azak were around, he could choke it out of the sleazy little twister.

"I don't know. How long?"

"We shall be in Torkag within the hour, unless the wind fails completely."

Inos roused herself enough to reach out and give her aunt's hand a sympathetic squeeze. "And you're not going to get your longed-for visit to Hub, are you?"

235

"Apparently not this time." Kade set her lips angrily.

And back in Arakkaran she would not get to wear all the fine clothes she had picked out. That would be hurting, too.

4

When *Allena* made landfall near the many mouths of the Vislawn River, the wind dropped as if cut down by an ax. The sailors were beyond being surprised by anything the weather did on this voyage. They hoisted more sail and began the cleanup chores that inevitably followed a storm. Spreading all the canvas she could carry, *Allena* came in nobly on the morning tide, nudged along by a faint breeze over mirrored waters. Real ship and reflected glory floated together between the wooded islets like dancers in embrace.

Rap and Jalon were leaning on the rail, admiring the scenery, the weather, the white-sailed fishing boats, the glimpses of picturesque buildings in the woods. After being called by Sagorn on the first night, Jalon had put off calling any of the others to replace him until it was too late, because he was known to the crew. Rap did not care, as he preferred Jalon's company anyway, but it was surprising—three days of anything were usually enough to bore the minstrel to frenzy. Fortunately he had discovered a sailor who knew a song cycle that he did not. He had spent his time in learning it and working out improvements.

Rap was feeling thick-eyed and draggy from lack of sleep. As an adept, he could talk almost anyone into almost anything, but not for long. For the first three days and nights on Home Water, he had barely slept at all. Later he had done better as he gained authority and as the sailors concluded that he must be a sorcerer, since he could either control the winds, or at least predict what they would do next. Tacking when he advised not to, for example, had been enough to put the ship in irons every time. Any attempt to head for Malfin had been frustrated; the road to Vislawn had been open. Had they realized the true limits of Rap's power, they would have thrown him overboard.

And now there was nothing to do except lean on the rail and admire the bobbing gulls and fine morning.

"God of Marvels," Jalon remarked softly. "Do my old eyes deceive me?"

Twitching out of his drowsy reverie, Rap twisted around and saw that an elf had just come out on deck. Right behind her came another. "We must be getting close to the city," he agreed.

"This *is* the city."

Ribbons of sunbright water snaking between green islands? Pole boats and a few barges? "Where?"

"Here." Jalon waved vaguely. "Elves would rather look at trees than buildings, although the buildings they hide would be flaunted by anyone else.
We've been sailing through uptown Vislawn for the last hour."

Rap hauled himself properly alert by the scruff of his mental neck and
scanned around. True enough, there were little timbered houses and quaint
shops hidden everywhere. Very few were more than one story high, and only
boathouses and a few storage sheds could be reached directly from the waterfront. *Allena* was easing slowly past a white-sand beach where a half-dozen
golden children were splashing and shrieking. Hidden in the trees behind it
was a pottery, of bright-enameled woodwork and glittering tiles. Its tall chimney curved in an impossible spiral.

"How many islands?" Rap asked.

He should have known better—Jalon looked totally blank at the question.
"Lots. Why?"

Sagorn would have quoted the exact number. "Never mind. If we don't
reach our berth soon we'll have to anchor. The tide's about to turn."

Jalon chuckled. "Then they'll ask you to whistle up some more wind." He
went back to his dreamy gazing at the scenery.

Ripple!

Gods!

Rap grabbed the rail tight and told his heart to calm down. He'd been half
expecting that ripple, but just because a guess proved right did not stop it
scaring a man out of his wits. It had felt just like the first one, the ripple that
had startled him when he was talking with Sagorn, but this time he'd made it
out more clearly. The whole world had shimmered—sea, islands, ships, buildings—in vision and farsight both, as if he'd been viewing a reflection in a bowl
of water and someone had tapped the side of the bowl. It had lasted only a
fraction of a second, but that was long enough to be scary Nor had he sensed
where the ripple had come from, although he could guess.

More elves were emerging. The imps had mostly gained their sea legs by
the third day of the voyage. Elves apparently never did, and Rap's unique ability to function was assumed to be merely one more proof of his sorcery On
this millpond channel, though, old Sir Thoalin'fen could strut around in silver and sea green. Fern'soon was displaying her gorgeous legs below an
extremely daring burgundy wrap. Grandmother or not, she was a lovely girl!
Jalon's golden jotunn hair was a faded washrag compared to elvish curls.

And finally came Quip', still pale, but resplendent in rose and peacock blue.

He paused in the companionway door rather unsteadily, glancing
around until he located Rap. Registering great relief, he walked over to join
him, adjusting a saffron cap topped with a scarlet plume. When he was still
a few paces off, Rap bowed. Jalon was lost in a trancelike contemplation of

a barge being poled past and did not notice, but Quip' stopped dead, suddenly worried.

"Why're you bowing to me, Rap'?"

"Because I don't think your name is Quip', your Omnipotence."

Ice! For a moment Rap felt more frightened than he could ever remember feeling before in his life. Then the opal eyes twinkled, and the elf stepped to his side, laying hands on the rail. His physical appearance did not change in the slightest—he stayed shorter than Rap and much slighter, and he still looked no older than fifteen. But he was a different person.

Had there been a hint of a ripple there, or was it just Rap's teeth trying to chatter? Or was he shying at moths now?

Still in Quip's husky treble, Lith'rian said, "Tell me?"

Rap found some saliva and said, "I've learned how to control my memory. There was no one clearing plates near Lord Phiel'nilth when I made my challenge."

The elf chuckled and shook his head sadly. "How the tiny flaw can spoil the great design! Well done, Master Rap! Anything else?"

"He denied it, but I think the dragonward must have some way of communicating with the warlock of the south."

"Yes, he does; a magic scroll. Whatever he writes on it can be read on its mate in Hub. It's a very small magic and the drakes don't seem to mind. That's all?"

"I got seasick a few times. I wasn't sure that you . . . I mean, I wanted to see if Quip' was all right."

Quip's cabin had not been on the ship, and the harder Rap had searched for it, in person or by farsight, the more violently his insides had protested.

The elf pursed his lips. "If you got close enough to feel nauseated, then you're a remarkably determined young man—you'd dug through three layers of . . . But we knew that about you, didn't we?" He chuckled. "And that reminds me, I must give Captain Prakker back his cabin!"

Ripple!

Lith'rian stiffened, staring hard at Rap. "You felt that!"

Rap nodded nervously. "Yes, your Omnipotence."

"You're only an adept! Reading the ambience? What else can you do?"

Rap listed the talents he had discovered, and they all seemed very insignificant compared to the powers of a warlock. But he had felt a ripple when the bogus Quip' departed and also when he returned a few minutes ago, and now he had felt Lith'rian remove the spell from the undiscoverable cabin. The elf looked impressed, but certainly not pleased.

238

With his eerily boyish appearance and voice, Lith'rian was somehow even more intimidating than Bright Water or Zinixo. "I jumped to Hub, and that used a lot of raw power. I came back the same way. And just now I was very close to you. Can you feel this? Or this?"

Rap shook his head.

The big opal eyes flickered from blues and greens to red and orange. "Your sensitivity isn't very high, then. But even so! Very few mages can feel disturbance in the ambience. Some sorcerers can't, or do it poorly. I recall no precedent for an adept being able to do it at all."

Rap forced himself to meet the warlock's glittering gaze and saw a nasty sort of appraisal in them. "What does that mean, your Omnipotence?"

"It means that you have some surprising abilities. That's all."

It mattered though, obviously. So did other things. "Inos, your Omnipotence?"

"She's well."

Rap sagged on the rail as if his heart really had taken flight and vanished into the sky. Logic and rationalization were fine, but they lacked conviction. *She's well!* How much those two words conveyed! How much they brightened the sunshine! Even the flowers were more vivid. Inos was alive and well. He really hadn't quite, *totally* disbelieved Sagorn. But now he knew. She's well! She's well!

After a while he realized that the warlock was regarding him with what looked for all the world like a juvenile smirk.

"Can you foresee me?" Rap demanded.

For a moment Lith'rian's smile did not change, and yet Rap thought of young boys dismembering insects or torturing kittens. He shivered, and reminded himself that this seeming kid was at least ninety.

"No, I can't," the warlock said softly.

His manner was a challenge to ask more impertinent questions, but Rap was not crazy, just too brash for his own good. He changed the subject quickly. "Ishist told me to mention to your Omnipotence that a God had appeared to Inos."

"Yes. I know about that. I think I know the whole story, Master Rap."

Blocks shrieked as sailors furled sails. On the far side of the deck, someone threw a line. *Allena* was about to tie up at a jetty, and most of the passengers were over on the far side. Jalon's dreamy inattention was excessive, even for him, so he was being occultly distracted.

The warlock was watching a passing pole boat. The boy in it was an elf who looked to be about Quip's age, wearing only a rag. He was shiny all over with the effort he was putting into his work, and his bony chest pumped. Lith'rian seemed to change mood again. He laughed and put both elbows on the rail.

"The dragonward may be in need of a vacation! He certainly is acting the clown. But he was right. This little escapade has amused me. Being Quip'rian was a gruesome experience!"

Rap decided not to ask, but the warlock told him anyway. "There really is a Quip'rian. He was in the kitchen when you uttered the Defiance. I merely borrowed his name and personality, just as I could have borrowed his appearance had I wanted to. He knows nothing about all this, and never will. No one knew what he looked like . . .

"Seeing the world through the eyes of a nobody—it's frightening! You know, I almost didn't *want* to go back to being my own self?"

Rap had not thought of the gentle Quip' as a nobody. He had felt much more at ease with him than he did with the sinister, deadly warlock, despite their identical appearance.

Lith'rian removed his cap. He pulled off the feather and dropped it into the river. As he replaced the cap itself, it changed color to match his shirt. The silence continued until Rap began to find it oppressive.

"You said . . . I mean, Quip' said that you must either cut off my head or go to war with Clan'nilth—your Omnipotence."

The warlock nodded. "That's what the rules say." He patted Rap's hand on the rail. "But there's a couple of ways out, very old precedents. Once a young man of the Clan'lyns uttered the Sublime Defiance against the Clan'ciels and knelt in his own father's shadow. His father was rich, and apparently stupid. Anyway, he sent the golden bucket, but the head in it was a replica."

Rap felt an invigorating surge of relief. "That was acceptable?"

"Perfectly. It was solid gold also."

"I can see how that would help."

Lith'rian nodded. "I think it will work in this case. We're in a civilized spell at the moment in Pandemia, when civil wars seem to be in poor taste."

Rap risked another step. "Then you don't share Quip's views on the most appropriate outcome of my quest, your Omnipotence?"

The warlock snorted. "His sense of the romantic is revolting. Gushy sentiment! What would you expect from a dishwasher?" He lifted his face skyward, staring at a circling seabird. He sighed. "No. I know a much more romantic ending."

"Tragic or happy?"

The elf sighed. "Too close to call. The balance trembles still."

No more answers, obviously.

"Still, Rap, you did very well in diverting *Allena* straight here."

No need to ask why it had all been necessary. Elves liked things done in style, never the easy, obvious way. "It was a wild trip, your Omnipotence."

"You're going to have a wilder one. I'd estimated eight days was the absolute minimum, twelve more likely, and you got here in nine. That will help."

"Help, my lord?"

"Time is very short. Very! I can't even take you to Valdorian to complete the Sublime Defiance ritual, appropriate though that would be. Regretfully, the Rap'rian who goes to Valdorian will be a facsimile, not the real you. Here comes your transportation now."

A small boat was gliding across the blue mirror of the channel, heading for the ship and pulling a lucent fan of ripples. *Allena* was t ed up now, and both crew and passengers were concentrating their attention on the far side of the deck. Nobody seemed to notice the mysteriously speedy boat, although its sail was flapping around chaotically as it came up against the slight breeze. It carried three young elves, skinny golden boys wearing almost nothing. Two of them were fighting for the tiller, but the boat was paying no attention to the rudder anyway.

On the other side of *Allena's* deck, shrill shouting had broken out as some of the passengers learned for the first time that they had been brought all the way to Vislawn and not to Malfin.

Filthy as a common sailor, wiping horny hands on his pants, Gathmor came striding over. He stopped and frowned, as if he had forgotten why he had come.

"Captain Gathmor," Lith'rian said pleasantly. "Bring a rope ladder quickly."

Gathmor opened his mouth and then took another, harder look at the adolescent elf. "Aye, sir!" he said, and ran.

Rap drew a deep breath, not sure whether he even dared ask the question. "My lord . . . Where is Inos?"

"In Arakkaran."

"Still?"

"Again."

"Bright Water said—" Rap began.

"If you mean that night in the Gazebo, I know exactly what happened, and what was said. Exactly."

Rap sensed a challenge. "You do? I mean . . . Oh! Fire chick?"

Lith'rian's eyes danced in rainbow colors and he nodded.

"You *were* the fire chick?"

"No, but I used it. They have odd properties, dragons. Useful, sometimes. Couldn't let Bright Water go into that nest of tunnel rats without support.

241

And you mustn't take anything she said then too literally. You do see why she betrayed Inos to the mole though?"

Of course elves liked dwarves no more than dwarves liked elves, and Rap sensed unsteady footing ahead. "No, my lord."

"It's perfectly simple," Lith'rian said snappily. "We're stuck with that dweller-under-rocks as a warlock, but we can't have him thrashing around on his own, threatening everyone, so we have to educate him into a few alliances. Allies can keep him under some sort of control, right? So Bright Water offered him Olybino's head on a plate, see? And the way that nervous meat-herder thinks, if you give him an opportunity, he at once suspects it's a trap and goes in the opposite direction. The same with Inos—Bright Water said I'd stolen her from the Rasha woman, but of course Rasha was merely hiding her from Olybino—the witch had predicted that, because only a woman can forecast how a woman will think, so she was waiting ready to track Inos—and that let her give the mole a chance to steal Inos away from me and from Olybino's sector and offer her to the imperor as a bribe for support or else to reveal the supposed plot to Olybino and try to bribe him and either way he'd think he had gained an ally, either East or Emshandar. Follow?"

"Er . . . What went wrong?"

"Olybino did, of course. Idiot! He cut the knot by telling Emshandar that Inos was dead, so the plan unraveled. Then Inos herself went and escaped from the Rasha woman's votary, and he had to use so much power to get her back that Olybino's locals tracked him down and he captured her, only she wasn't any value by then except a negative value as an embarrassment. He didn't kill her, so now she's back in Arakkaran. It's all perfectly simple."

Any less simple and Rap's head would fall off. "Yes, my lord."

"She's in danger though," Lith'rian said sternly, "in danger of making a terrible mistake. You must warn her."

"Me, sir? I mean, your—"

"You." The warlock sighed. "Quip' was right about some things, lad. Arakkaran's in East's sector. I daren't interfere."

"But—"

"But nothing. You've already met two of them—which would you say was crazier? And the fourth, Olybino, is a fool, a pompous, frightened fool. He is being stupid, but if I meddle in his affairs then he may get much stupider. Things are too dangerously poised. I mustn't give West a real ally!" He waved an expressive hand in an inscrutable gesture.

Rap said, "Oh!" His hopes spiraled down into endless dark. How could he help when a warlock daren't?

"You will have to do it," Lith'rian said firmly. "Or try, at least. I can give you help, but time is desperately short."

"Yes, my lord."

Gathmor came hurrying back with a bundle of dowel and hemp under his arm just as the little boat slid to a stop directly below the watchers, its sail hanging limp. The three youngsters gazed up with big expectant grins.

"Make it fast, sailor," the warlock said impatiently, and Gathmor began bending the lines to a convenient cleat.

"What exactly am I to do?" Rap asked, feeling both alarmed and suspicious. He had never liked being rushed into things.

"Do what the God told Inos to do—trust in love!"

"Yes?" Rap said nonconmuttally.

"And go and remind her of those instructions! Minstrel, you can play one of these?" Lith'rian held out a rack of silver tubes to Jalon, who had at some point begun to take an interest in the proceedings. Where the pipes had come from, Rap had no idea.

Jalon's dreamy blue eyes widened. "Of course. They're faunish, but I've used them."

"Do you know 'Swiftly Comes the Dawn'?"

Jalon pouted. "A Dwanishian melody on Sysassanoan panpipes?"

"Barbaric, I admit."

"But I expect I can come close enough."

"Good. And 'rest, My Beloved'?"

"That's worse—but, yes."

The ladder clattered down the side, and the boys began scrambling up.

"We're going in that?" Gathmor protested. "Square sail? The mast's set too far forward. It'll do nothing except run before the wind."

The warlock chuckled. "But this boat always has a following wind! Don't pull faces, sailor. Sometimes magic serves the Good. So you must steer and Master Jalon must whistle the wind. 'Comes the Dawn' for more wind, 'Rest, My Beloved' for less. Any questions?"

The three boys tumbled over the side in fast succession, panting, grinning, and clustering excitedly around Lith'rian. He flashed them a smile and tousled their curls.

Rap had been peering down at the bundles in the boat.

"That long package—swords?"

"Of course."

Rap looked distrustfully at the warlock, the man who had given his daughter to a gnome.

"I'm an adept. I can learn to play those two tunes. I can certainly steer a boat. The other two needn't—"

"No! No!" Lith'rian's juvenile face took on the soulful expression that Quip' had favored. His eyes misted. "Don't you see? The three of you, hastening to

Arakkaran . . . jotnar aiding a faun . . . that's beautiful! That's much more romantic than just one."

"Course it is." Jalon tucked the panpipes in his belt and clambered over the rail.

"Just try and stop me," said Gathmor with all his old menace. "Everything we need is there . . . er . . . my lord?" Perhaps he still did not know who the elf was, but he had recognized his authority.

"You'll find a chart in the big chest. There's an inkblot on it, somewhere. That's you."

The sailor tried not to pull faces again.

"And, Captain . . . a prophecy. Veer south of the Keriths. If you go to the north you wreak havoc on the shipping there, and if you try to go through The Gut, you certainty run aground. You know about merfolk! Remember that, whatever else they are, they are also madly jealous. The men have fast knives."

"Troublemakers!" Gathmor agreed. "Had 'em around Durthing a few times. Always brought bloodshed." He followed Jalon down the ladder.

"The Gods be with you, Master Rap," the warlock said. "Waste no time."

Still feeling that he should be arguing, Rap took hold of the rail and swung up a leg.

Gathmor had the tiller already and the sail was spread. The tiny craft rocked as Rap settled on the thwart amidship, next to Jalon, who grinned childishly and raised the pipes to his lips. At the first haunting notes, a shadow of ripples rushed over the waters, and the sail swelled.

"What's her name?" Gathmor demanded. He looked up to ask the elf, but already there was open water spreading between the large craft and the small.

"Call her the *Queen of Krasnegar*," Rap said between his teeth.

"So be it. May the Good go with her."

A stronger gust rocked the boat. Palms on the shore bent and thrashed. *Ripple?* The world steadied again at once.

That one had been faint, but Rap had felt it—either because he was learning to, or because the power had touched him personally. His arms and knees had turned from gold to brown in front of his eyes. He gasped in agony, and then his shirt burst open in a shower of buttons, his pants ripped across the seat. Jalon stopped trilling on the panpipes to join Gathmor in great bellows of stupid, raucous laughter. The boat rocked with their mirth. Idiots!

All the same, it was with real relief that Rap inspected his own familiar faunish face again, flat nose and goblin tattoos and all. It had never been much of a face, but he was glad to have it back.

He grinned at the very pink Jalon, and then at Gathmor. "Lay a course for Arakkaran, Cap'n!"

"Aye, sir!"

"Look!" Jalon pointed.

Quip'rian was waving from *Allena's* deck. Beside him stood the elvish Rap—
and Jalon, and Gathmor. All four waved. Rap raised his hand in farewell, and
then turned his face to the sea.

Rushing seas:

One port, methought, alike they sought—
　　One purpose hold wher'er they fare;
O bounding breeze, O rushing seas,
　　At last, at last, unite them there.
　　　　　　　　Clough, As *Ships Becalmed*

12

Female of the species

1

Morning sun sparkled on the great harbor as *Dawn Pearl* crept slow-ly toward her berth. Inos stood on deck with Azak on one side of her and Kade on the other, studying all the bustle and the astonishing variety of shipping—very much as she had wanted to study it that other morning, months ago, when she had been lumbered with the odious baby Charak. Now she was much less interested, for the bright hopes of that memorable day were tarnished. Spoiled! Crumbled to ruin. She dared not look at Azak, for his feelings must be as dark as her own. They had gambled and lost, and they still lacked even the tiny compensation of knowing for certain who had won.

Even the medley of scents was oddly familiar to Inos—the fish stinks of a harbor and the flower scents of the city. She felt far more like a return-ing resident than she would have expected, or wanted. The shining palace on the hill was a derision, a marble jail waiting to take her back, a sar-cophagus. She was draped again in the despicable chaddar of humiliation, a recaptured fugitive.

"Look!" Kade exclaimed. "On the dock. Isn't that a reception party?"

It was indeed, and Inos had detected it long before Kade had. Azak had probably seen it even earlier, for he had the falcon vision of his race. Neither of them had commented.

"Led by Kar," Azak murmured.

Inos could not see that yet, but it would be a welcome sight for Azak. If the devoted Kar still lived, then no other prince had seized the title of sultan. And that thought made Inos realize that Azak must have feared for his life since he learned *Dawn Pearl's* true destination.

Who had told him, or when, he had not said, but he had been released from the brig as soon as the ship cleared Brogog, the last port before Arakkaran. Gaunt and grim, he had spoken very little since. He was dressed again as a prince, all in green: trousers, tunic, cloak, and turban. Inos did not know where he obtained those. Likely they had been slipped aboard by Elkarath's women, as it must have been they who had smuggled the Zarkian costume for Inos and Kade into the baggage. The whole cruel buffoonery had been very well planned.

Azak had hardly spoken. She did not know how he felt about her now. Was he still in love with her? She could not read his thoughts.

But Azak was returning as sultan, and apparently his throne was still secure. His lack of jewels and scimitar would be soon rectified if the efficient Kar was in charge of the welcome.

Welcome? Public reception . . . they were not even to be granted the grace of an unobtrusive entry into the city. There would be bands and a parade. Rejoice!—the sultan returns!

Mockery.

Inos turned away from the sight of the band and the assemblage of princes. She glanced around her to confirm that the chests had been brought up and that all was ready for disembarkation. *Dawn Pearl* would leave on the same tide.

Well! Over there was the shrouded form of little Fra inish, who had been so chagrined to discover that she was coming home to Arakkaran instead of venturing forth to Angot. But at her side stood Skarash, inscrutable again in the flowing robes of a Zarkian merchant. Well, well!

Master Skarash had supposedly disembarked at Torkag. No one had seen him since, so no one had been able to question him. And here he was back? Either this was more sorcery, or he had been plying the sailors with gold to keep him hidden. There was one way to solve that question.

Inos strode across the deck and accosted him. "Master Skarash?"

He raised his chin and continued to stare at the harbor, arms folded, ignoring her. He was being a djinn again, and djinns did not speak to other men's wives, or pretended wives.

"I was hoping for a farewell kiss," Inos said.

He twitched. Garnet eyes flickered toward her, then away again. His Adam's apple lurched, but he did not speak.

"If I tell Azak about that episode," Inos said, "then he will kill you now, with his bare hands."

Again the hard swallow.

"I shall count to three, then I tell him how you forced your kisses on me in the cellars. One!"

"Go away!"

"Not until I have some answers. Two!"

Frainish was wide-eyed above her yashmak. Skarash did not look around, but gems of sweat gleamed amid the pink stubble on his lip. "What do you want to know?" he whispered.

Inos had already gained one answer—Skarash was not a sorcerer. "Whom do you serve?"

"My grandfather, of course."

"And whose votary is he?"

He licked his lips. The dock was very close now, Kar and the dozens of other princes clearly visible, all loyally smiling. The band lurched into the clamorous discords of the Arakkaranian national anthem.

"Warlock Olybino's."

Aha! "Since when?"

Skarash turned a furious, frightened gaze on Inos. "Since the night we reached Ullacarn. The centurion . . . You saw! That was the warlock himself!"

"Yes, I know. So your grandfather did serve Rasha when we left here?"

He snarled at her. "Yes, and now he doesn't, and it's all your fault!"

"Mine?"

"You escaped from Tall Cranes. He had to use so much power to find you and get you back that the warlock found him! You spoiled everything, Inosolan! Now go away!"

"I am not quite satisfied. So it is not Rasha's will that brings us back here. Does she know we are coming?"

"Yes. I think so. She must if they do." He waved at the quay.

"And why are we coming?"

Skarash's ruddy face was all shiny with fright. He glanced momentarily over at Azak, and then back to Inos. "He is watching! Please go away!"

"Not until you tell."

"The wardens do not need you! The Krasnegar problem has been solved. You are nothing, Inosolan! Nothing!"

She flinched. Yet somehow it was almost a comfort to have one's worst suspicions confirmed, the uncertainty laid to rest. Now the fairer hopes could

248

be discarded and put away. Now Krasnegar could be forgotten, for whoever
ruled there in future, an ex-queen would not be allowed to return. Other alternatives could be examined, and Inos could start to make some plans. The hurt
. . . The hurt could wait.

"So why bother to send us back?"

Skarash looked longingly at the dock, as if wondering if he might leap to
safety and disappear into the crowd. Then he sneaked another glance across
at Azak, and paled at what he saw.

"As a message to Rasha. She is nothing, also! Olybiro is the stronger—he
broke her loyalty spell. Grandsire was her votary and now is his. He can
enslave Rasha also!"

Aha! again.

"Please, Inos!" Skarash whispered. "Have mercy! You are killing me. He is
still sultan of this city and Grandsire is not here to shield me."

Inos hesitated, then nodded. "I shall not forget the kiss," she said sweetly.
Let him worry about what that meant! She spun around in a swirl of hems and
stalked back to the glaring Azak, picking her way between ropes and baggage
and hurrying sailors.

Things were a little clearer now.

"Well?" Azak demanded. There might be hint of twinkle in his scowl, making Inos wonder how much he had deliberately been aiding the interrogation
of Skarash.

"Rasha knows we are coming. Olybino has sent us back as a threat—his
sorcery is stronger than hers. She is in danger herself now."

"Gods of the Good!" The tall young man's face broke into a wide smile.

But Rasha was still a sorceress, and she would be waiting in the palace.

2

Nothing!

All during the bowings, the prostrations, the speeches of welcome, that
dread word kept echoing to and fro in her head.

You are nothing, Inosolan!

As the band played and the procession moved slowly up the long and hilly road
to the palace, she sat with Kade in a decently screened carriage, accompanied by two
anonymously shrouded women whose presence stifled conversation completely.

She thought about being nothing. If her kingdom had gone and she was
nothing, then surely she had been nothing before? Inosolan had always been
nothing. Krasnegar had been everything. Bitter taste.

The crowds were not cheering for her—they could have no idea who was
inside that opaque little oven bouncing by on its unsprung axle. They knelt

249

with their faces in the dust and they cheered their sultan on his big black horse. They were shouting *Azak! Azak! Azak!* but it sounded very much like *Nothing! Nothing! Nothing!* to Inos.

Now she need not worry about Krasnegar. Now she was free to consider the alternatives. There were not very many to consider.

She had no assets. She knew no trade. Her needlework was scandalous, her lute playing pained the ear. Who ever heard of a female hostler, or a cook who could catch the dish but not prepare it? With a royal title she had been useful timber for matchmakers like the dowager duchess of Kinvale. Without it, she might make a governess or a dancing instructor. Or she might marry a rich, fat merchant who hoped to rise in society and needed guidance in gentility.

Of course she had one asset. Doubtless she could soon acquire the skill required to use it to its best advantage; but that road led down to the pit that Rasha had known, the bog from which almost no one but Rasha had ever escaped.

Nothing!

If her father had told her a word of power as everyone believed, then she had mistaken it. So far she had displayed no signs of being an occult genius at anything.

Why had the warlock been so cruel as to send her back to Zark? Anywhere in the Impire would have been better for an unattached female with no skills, no title, no money, no friends.

She might have one friend, but one she was not certain she wanted. And she was not even sure of him any more. Since being released from the brig, Azak had not said he loved her. Was it she he had thought he loved, or only the romantic myth of a beautiful, dispossessed queen? What had he dreamed of—being her husband, or being king of Krasnegar? If he still wanted her, could she ever want him?

The Azak who had been good company in the desert had been Azak the lionslayer, a freelance swordsman with no kingdom to worry about. The Azak she had just glimpsed on the dock had been the ruthless sultan, grim and saturnine, terrifying everyone.

She might have learned to love the one; she doubted she could ever love the other.

If Rasha must now flee from Arakkaran to evade the warlock, then Azak would be free to be sultan as he wished to be. He would be free to marry, if he chose, although he could no longer marry a queen, because there was no queen available. He might prefer a woman of his own race, one who could do a better job of running the royal household. Who would not shock princely society by wanting to ride to hounds. Who would be properly respectful of her lord, not teasing and talking back.

He lusted after her, Elkarath had said. But Azak was never petty. He might withdraw his offer of marriage, from the needs of polit cal expediency, but . . . but surely there would always be a bed for her in the palace?

They had gambled together.

Inos had lost.

And Rasha had lost. So Azak had won.

And if Inos accepted the job of son-breeder, what happened when she was forty, with Azak long since assassinated and someone else on the throne? To whom would the chattel be reassigned?

She thought about all these things in the hot and stuffy carriage as it climbed the hill. She was still thinking about them as it rattled to a halt in the palace yard.

"After the rigors of the desert and the confines of a ship," Kade said brightly, "it will be nice to enjoy some really luxurious decadence again."

3

Their old quarters had been taken over by another prince and his household. Kade and Inos were ushered to a small suite of rooms that they had never seen before. Compared to the others they were dingy; compared to anywhere else they were still opulent. A half-dozen shrouded women waited to attend them, but they were surly and uncommunicative. There was no sign of Zana.

Inos demanded a bath, and enjoyed it. Then she defiantly scrabbled through her trunk until she found a slinky Imperial dress of cool green and white silk, and she braided up her hair herself. She smothered herself in pearls and admired her reflection in a mirror and wanted to weep.

Kade, when she appeared, had donned a Zarkian chaddar of white cotton, although her head was uncovered.

They hugged without words, and wandered out to a balcony overlooking a jeweled garden. Parrots screamed among the trees.

"Nice to be home?" Inos asked bitterly, sniffing the flower scents in the air.

"I enjoy the little comforts." Kade waited, and when she received no answer, added, "Don't believe everything that Master Skarash says, my dear. He's not a very reliable witness."

"But it makes sense. It all makes sense. And nothing else does."

Kade sighed and went to sit on a soft chair. "Well, you may have lost your kingdom. We can't be sure of that yet. And even if you have—it wasn't ever very much of a kingdom, you know."

Battling a lump in her throat, Inos said nothing.

"Kinvale was always more comfortable. And Kinvale is still there. We shall always be welcome."

"To accept charity from that sly old bitch who set Yggingi on us?"

"Inos!"

"It's true! And she will still believe I have a word of power. She will brew up some other foul scheme to rack it out of me for her precious moronic son."

Kade beamed, being motherly. "Well then, not Kinvale. We know hundreds of people in the Impire. We shall go and visit Hub."

"And just how do we get there? On camels? Will our earrings buy camels?"

"They would buy a lot of things." Kade smiled brightly. "You are young, and healthy, and wealthy, and well educated. You have beauty and grace. I am sure that Sultana Rasha will still be sympathetic, perhaps even more so now. You have been harshly treated—by men—and she disapproves of women being oppressed. She will see you on your way, back to the Impire where you belong. She may even magic you there. Now that the wardens know about her, she has no reason to conceal her existence or her powers."

Inos was not sure she believed all that. She did not trust Rasha, and certainly did not want to be beholden to her.

Kade tried again. "Remember the God's words? You were told to trust in love. Love is worth more than all the kingdoms of Pandemia."

"Whose love? Azak's?"

Her aunt hesitated and pursed her lips. "If you want my honest opinion . . . No, I don't think so. You do have a great attraction for men, Inos. He will not be the last man to fall in love with you."

"But none more truly," said Azak, coming out of the doorway.

Inos jumped and bit back a sharp comment about eavesdroppers. He was sultan again; she must watch her tongue.

He strode over to her and stopped, very close, and his jewels glittered in the sunlight. His fringe of beard was a two-week stubble, but it was enough to distinguish him from the dashing imp he had been in Ullacarn, or the bushy lionslayer of the desert. He stared down at her with his dark red eyes.

"I have not changed," he said.

She tried not to show how much that meant. Then she felt guilty. She wanted to use that love against him, to win favors, not to love him in return. Could she ever? Queens did not marry for love; they married for reasons of state.

Was that so very different from what Rasha had done in her younger days?

He smiled, but it was not a very warming smile. It looked too deliberate. "No answer?"

"Azak . . . I don't know what to say. Kade was just warning me that we still don't know for certain about Krasnegar. Skarash is not the most reliable of witnesses."

Azak snorted. "Of course not. Well, you shall remain here as—"

He twisted and went rigid. She saw beads of perspiration break out on his face. "Azak! What's wrong?"

He relaxed with a gasp and shivered. "I came to tell you that we are summoned. I must be taking too long. That was a nudge, that's all."

Rasha! The spider at the heart of the web.

"Then let us go right away!"

He was angry at having revealed weakness. "There is no hurry. Have you a shawl or something . . . for the walk?"

Inos nodded and ran ahead indoors to find a cloth to cover her hair and shoulders. Kade came close behind her.

4

Jeweled amber eyes rolled to inspect the visitors, and the carven demon face writhed into speech. "State your name and business!" On the other flap of the door, the matching demon merely curled its wooden lips in a sneer.

"Sultan Azak of Arakkaran and Queen Inosolan of Krasnegar!" No occult fakery could teach Azak anything about sneering.

"Who is the other one?"

"Her Royal Highness Princess Kadolan."

There was a pause then, as if the grotesque were reporting to its mistress. The corridor was dim; it felt as cold as a Krasnegarian midwinter. Inos was trying not to shiver, absurdly glad that Azak was there beside her. She doubted she would have had the courage to come and face the sorceress alone. Then she sensed him looking down at her. She glanced up.

"She has power," he said coldly, and there was no doubt to whom he referred, "but remember what she is. And what you are, Cousin."

I am nothing! "Of course, Cousin."

He nodded and went back to outsneering the demonic faces on the door. Inos's black mood darkened further.

He said he had not changed, but he had. He was sultan again, as he had been when she first met him. On the dock, back in the palace yard, he had spurned the fawning princess, made strong men leap to obedience with one cold glance. She had forgotten just how intimidating he was in his royal role.

And she had changed. She was a queen no longer. Royal status was much more important to Azak than it had ever been to her. Now she was an outcast, like one of the banished princes who sank to being family men in other palaces, or lionslayers serving tradesmen. Although he denied it, he despised them as failures. Rasha's nudge had come before they had finished their talk— had he been about to offer Inos marriage, or escape to Hub, or steady employment as a breeder of sons? Which did she want?

253

Rasha's curse still kept them apart.

"The two of you may enter, the third may not," the carving stated.

"No!" Kade looked ready to argue with the door.

Inos kissed her cheek. "You go back and wait in the suite, Aunt. Don't hang around here. We may be some time."

"I think it is my duty—"

"Go!" Azak boomed, and Kade capitulated.

Inos watched sadly as her aunt wandered back along the long gloomy corridor, and she felt loneliness settle over her like hoar frost.

Then a squeal from a hinge made her jump. The double doors had swung open.

She entered at Azak's side, and saw at once that the Kinvale influence had been discarded. Again the great circular bedchamber was overflowing with chests and tables in every possible style. The sumptuous floor was hidden again below a discordant mismatch of rugs, and the lewd wall hangings and erotic statuary that Kade had banished had now been replaced. Inos had been shocked by the first collection, and the replacements were even worse; she blushed to see them. The air reeked with syrupy scents.

Beyond the two big windows stood the white vertical blaze of noon. Light spilled also down the central well of the spiral staircase, and yet it was curiously muted . . . smoky? . . . less bright than Inos remembered or expected, so the big room seemed oddly dim, and cool.

The doors closed with a boom and a fading echo like a drum roll. The two visitors continued to advance, heading for the bottom step. Then Azak halted, and so did Inos. The enormous canopied bed still stood at the far side of the room, beyond the stair, and the sorceress was standing at one corner of it, leaning provocatively against the carved post as if embracing it.

Inos felt a shiver of apprehension and disgust as she saw that Rasha was in her seductress mode, more voluptuous than ever. Only a small space around her eyes was actually uncovered, but the mist of gauze and jewels that floated over the rest of her concealed nothing—not the long fall of russet hair, nor the hot glow of nipple and areola, nor the many ropes of pearls looped around her body and limbs, next the skin. Nor the skin either, the hot, ruddy skin of a nubile djinn maiden. Nothing above the bright enamel of her sandal straps was leaving any mysteries to tempt the imagination. She looked no older than Inos. Did men really appreciate such an obscenity? Did they not see the vulgarity, or the contempt?

"Come closer," said the moist red lips.

Azak and Inos advanced more slowly, stopped. Inos waited for his cue, until she realized that he would not bow to a dockside trollop. She had set her own precedents long since, and to change them now would be a defiance, so she curtsied. Rasha acknowledged the move with a flick of one shapely eyebrow.

Then Azak fell to his knees and steadied himself w th his hands. That fall had not been voluntary, and had probably hurt.

"You seem to have learned no lessons, Muscles," said Rasha.

"Oh, but I have!" Azak's ruddy-stubbled face parted in a joyful gleam of white teeth.

"Do tell."

"I have learned that you are no match for Warlock Olybino!"

Rasha leaned even more seductively against the carved post of the bed, stroking it with her breast. "So what do you expect to happen now?"

He shrugged. "I suppose, when he gets around to it, the warlock wi l come for you, to claim your words of power. But I hardly expect that an aged, malformed, mutilated whore will be of use to him. He will torture the words out of you and have your throat cut like a pig's!"

"You would like to be there to watch, of course."

"I would enjoy few things more."

"And volunteer to help?"

"Why not? You have caused me enough pain in the past."

Now it was Rasha who shrugged, and the gesture seemed to involve her whole body. She turned her gaze of languid contempt on Inos. It felt like impudence from a girl so young.

"I offered my help and you spurned it. Now you have been disinherited. You are a homeless refugee."

Woe! So it was true. Skarash might have been lying. but a sorceress had no need to lie.

"Your help seemed to involve marrying a goblin," Inos said, keeping her words slow and level.

The sorceress slid around, so the post was behind her. "If you just keep your eyes closed, honey baby, they're all much the same. Some are heavier than others, some hairier, some hurt more. That's all."

"I can hardly keep my eyes closed all the time."

"You have never had them open! You are a fool."

Inos felt no anger, only apprehension. "It would seem that my kingdom was disposed of without my presence being necessary. In that case, your help would have been no help. There never was any way you could put me on my throne—the Protocol forbade it."

The sorceress's eyes flashed in fury.

Inos did not wait for a comment. "I appreciate that you had good intentions, your Majesty. Now I humbly ask that you return my aunt and myself to Krasnegar, where you found us."

Rasha laughed hard scorn, like hail. "I may keep the dog as payment for services rendered, though? How about compensation for the votary I have lost because of your stupidity? No, Inosolan, you forfeited any claim on me when you fled from my city."

Her city? Azak growled wordlessly.

"You organized that whole affair!" Inos shouted, and at last she began to feel anger. "It was all your idea, and—"

"It was your idea, kitten. I did not put it in your head. And had my sorcery not prevented him, that slab of brawn on the floor there would have had you with child by now."

Fury! How dare this slut speak such lies? Inos took a very deep breath—

"Be silent, or I shall make you silent. He cannot look at you without half choking on his lust." Rasha chuckled softly, and shivers ran down Inos's spine. "No, we shall keep you here. We shall teach the royal parasites how to be useful. Your aunt we shall put in the sculleries, scrubbing floors. And you—you I shall assign to one of the guards. I have one picked out already. He has unusual tastes in recreation." She was watching Azak as she spoke.

Oh, Gods! She had found another way to torture him, by torturing the woman he loved. Inos felt her hands start to shake and clasped them behind her. She would suffer to make Azak suffer. Every humiliation inflicted upon her would be reported to him so that he would be humiliated also. He might even be forced to watch.

Silence. No one spoke.

Then the sorceress jeered at the man on his knees before her. "And you, Wonderstud? Let me give you some *disappointing* news."

Azak's eyes narrowed, but he still did not speak.

Rasha straightened up and laid hands on hips, thrusting her dainty chin forward in a curiously inappropriate gesture. "It is true that Elkarath's allegiance has been turned, so Olybino broke my spell. Possibly he does have more power at his disposal than I do, for he has votaries to aid him. But I did not put my full power into the spell—sorcerers almost never do, for this very reason. I still have power in reserve, and he can't know how much. More important, I am in my stronghold." She waved both hands high, triumphantly. "Why do you suppose sorcerers build towers? The whole palace is shielded, and it will take enormous power to defeat me here. If he sends in votaries, I may turn them. If they blast their way in, then the entire complex may be razed by the energies released. Think again, Pretty Man."

Azak studied her for a moment and then said quietly, "And did the warlock of the east spell me, also?"

Rasha hesitated, and Inos sensed that the tension had somehow changed. "Not that I can see," the sorceress remarked cautiously.

He sighed deeply. That news would be a great relief to him. "Let me up, please."

Please?

Rasha's smoldering eyes widened a fraction. "Rise, then."

Azak rose, rubbing a bruised knee. He drew himself up to his full height and crossed his arms. "On your promise to behave yourself, your Majesty . . . I invite you to my wedding, three days hence."

Inos gasped. Rasha's face blazed with fury at such defiance.

Before she could speak, Azak repeated softly, "Your Majesty."

It was the royal title she coveted. For a moment the silence seemed to grow unbearably, then Rasha said warily, "And what of the curse? She will char in your arms."

"I humbly request that you lift it, as your wedding present to us."

Humbly? Rasha made an effort to recover her disdain. "Lift it for all women, or just for her?"

There was unholy bargaining going on, and Inos groped to catch all the floating threads of it.

"All would be preferable, of course, but just for Inosclan would be acceptable."

Inos cried, "Azak!" and stopped, stunned. From him, this was an unbelievable declaration of . . . of love?

And surrender.

He could have offered nothing more, not even the whole of his realm.

Rasha's eyes glinted in a slow smile that chilled Inos's blood. "Only three days?"

Azak was as taut as a bowstring, his face unreadable.

"Seven days might be more seemly," he said hoarsely.

She stepped close and looked up at him in challenge. "And until then?"

"As you wish."

Horrors crawled on Inos's skin as she watched Rasha's slow smile of triumph. With delicate fingers, the sorceress unhooked her yashmak and let it fall, then raised her face to be kissed. Her appearance might be soft and youthful, but the open lips were too eager for any pretense of maidenly innocence.

But Azak knew all about that. He took her in his arms and kissed her.

She can inflame any man to madness he had said once. When the long embrace ended, he was breathless, and his always-ruddy djinn complexion burned red as a furnace. He kept his eyes on the seductress's, and did not look at Inos.

Then Rasha changed. The young beauty shrank and aged, reverting to the hideously battered, squat old woman whom Inos had glimpsed twice before.

The jewels and filmy gauzes became a dirty brown wrap, her hair a gray tangle, the silken skin shriveled and wrinkled.

Having to bend farther this time, Azak kissed her again.

Inos looked away, until she discovered she was staring at the contorted bodies of obscene sculptures.

Elkarath had known: "If he would only compromise! Bow the knee just once. Say the words she wants to hear."

And when the second kiss ended, Azak continued to clasp the sorceress in his arms. He lifted his lips from hers just far enough to speak—softly, but without hesitation. "Inosolan, you have seven days. Go and prepare our wedding."

"*Seek to find the Good,*" They had said, "*and above all . . . remember love! If you do not trust in love, then all will be lost.*"

Without a word, Inos turned and fled from the chamber.

Rasha had won.

Female of the species:

When the Himalayan peasant meets the he-bear in his pride,
He shouts to scare the monster, who will often turn aside.
But the she-bear thus accosted rends the peasant tooth and nail
For the female of the species is more deadly than the male.
Kipling, *The Female of the Species*

13

Out of the West

1

"**N**ice little place they've got on the hill there," Gathmor shouted. Holding tight to the gunwale, Rap leaned sideways and peered under the sail at the great white and green city—rich and beautiful, seeming strangely cool in the blazing sunlight. "Not bad," he yelled, knowing that the wind might steal away his words before they reached back to the tiller. "Be a brute to heat in winter."

The headlands slipped away on either hand as the *Queen of Krasnegar* raced into the harbor. There could be no doubt where this was, for the blot on the chart now lay directly on the name of Arakkaran. If Inos was living in that incredible palace, that shining wonder of domes and towers and spires, then she must be finding it very comfortable. Rap thought briefly of jungle and galley benches, of jotunn raiders and dragons and the nightmare journey now ending, and he felt an absurd twinge of envy.

Idiot! Where did stableboys live like queens? Nowhere. Never.

And he had seen her in a tent, anyway.

Now the voyage was over, the time for action was at hand. He turned to Jalon, who was spread limp on the gratings amidships, covered with a length

259

of salt-caked canvas. That was the only place aboard where anyone could even hope to sleep, where the boat's unending mad leapings would not shake a man's teeth out and bounce him until he was black and blue all over. A true storm raised a great swell, but the occult local squall that powered the Queen had lacked enough fetch to change the existing waves much, so the sea had remained relatively calm. Shrouded in flying spume, the boat had skipped and bounded over the crests in a strange unholy motion, all the way from Vislawn.

"Belay the wind, pilot!" Rap shouted.

Red-eyed and haggard, Jalon fumbled for the pipes. He had worn them on a thong around his neck ever since Gathmor had asked what would happen if they fell overboard.

"I hope I remember the tune!"

"If you don't, we're going to wreck a lot of shipping!"

Queen and her rigging were seemingly indestructible, but other craft were not. All over the bay, frightened men were hauling in sail as the freak storm roared in from the Spring Sea, turning silver water to lead and blowing a fog of spray. No one would notice one small unfamiliar boat in this sudden turmoil.

The minstrel began piping the gentle strains of "Rest, My Beloved," and the wind faltered, then began to subside. Jalon had played that song only once on the journey, after Rap's nagging had led him to summon a typhoon so hectic that both crew and cargo had been in danger of being hurled overboard.

Rap ducked under the sail and knelt on the baggage in the bow, being tossed up and down and soaked by spray. He had not been dry in two weeks. He peered anxiously at the huge city ahead. His plans were vague in the extreme—find Inos, yes, but how? The palace alone was bigger than all of Krasnegar, or Durthing. Arakkaran was twice the size of Noom or Finrain, the only real cities he knew. He saw much shipping tied up along the waterfront, but less activity than he would have expected in the streets. The hour was too late for siesta and too early for serious drinking.

And this was not the Impire. The laws and those who made them might frown on visitors with no credentials and no patron. There would be jotnar aplenty in a port of this size, but a faun would be a rarity, and an oversized faun with goblin tattoos round his eyes was a conspicuous freak.

The boat settled lower in the water as the wind continued to drop. For the first time in two weeks the haze lifted, and the Queen sailed in clear sunlight. Rap crawled back below the sail, to find Jalon stripping off his clothes.

"You'll not be wanting me, Rap?" he asked apologetically. "You can manage the pipes if you need them?"

"Of course."

"Darad?"

"Yes, I think so. And, Jalon—thanks worlds!" Rap thumped the slim minstrel on the shoulder and won a grin. Once again, as in Dragon Reach, Jalon had revealed surprising tenacity. He could have departed at any time just by wishing, yet he had stayed to endure two weeks of vicious battering and sleeplessness, cold and wet and salt sores, danger and boredom. He might not be a pureblood jotunn, but even Gathmor now conceded he was made of the right stuff.

"My pleasure!" The minstrel smiled through his stubble, wincing at the salt cracks in his lips. "I'm planning a romantic ballad about you, Rap, for the elves. And a saga for imps. Maybe a battle song for jotnar?"

"I hope not!"

"Don't be surprised! Go with the Good." Jalon shook Rap's hand, and the *Queen of Krasnegar* wallowed as Darad's great bulk replaced him. A whiff of spray blew over the naked giant and he roared like a sea lion in springtime. "Might have dressed me first!" he complained, and spread his wolflike leer.

"Welcome aboard! Your clothes are in there." Rap pointed at a bundle. He turned to the red-eyed, bristle-faced Gathmor. "See anything odd about this town, Cap'n?"

Gathmor narrowed his eyes and stared. "Like what?"

"Bunting? Streets quiet?"

"Public holiday?" Gathmor said, nodding. "Maybe. Celebration?"

Rap felt a twinge of premonition. He glanced at the bundle of swords.

"What we do now, sir?" Darad was busily hauling on pants vast enough to furnish the sails of a galleon. So far the boat's cargo had supplied everything her crew had needed, down to the last needle. Obviously Lith'rian must have perfect foresight, and Rap worried constantly over what else the warlock might have foreseen—some event too close to call.

"I think we dock." Rap pondered. Yes, he was learning to trust these twinges of his, this evidence of his adepthood. "And then . . . then I think you two stay and guard the boat. I'll go ashore and ask someone what all the flags are for."

2

Inos had been ready for hours, or so it seemed. Her gown was heavy and hot; she had wandered out on the balcony—to be alone, to enjoy the cool breezes, to stare down unseeing at the jeweled city and the blue enamel of the harbor. How brightly colors glowed under a tropic sun! How black the shadows. How very black.

Yet today the hard edges were softened by a curious and inexplicable mist, through which she saw another city—a smaller, drabber, shabby town under a grayer sky, by a harbor that most of the year was a white plain. She still had not quite adjusted to the certainty that she would never return there, although that possibility had been obvious ever since the sorceress stole her away. The good folk of Krasnegar might never know what had happened to their princess. And she might never learn what had happened to them.

May they find happiness.

May I.

A swirl of dust in her face brought her back to harsh reality. Palm fronds thrashed and danced; something tugged at her veils. As if to match her mood, a sudden squall had blown in from the Spring Sea, turning the lucent bay an umbral shade and shooing all the little boats before it like frightened duck-lings. Inos circled carefully and swept back into the room.

It must be almost time for her to go down. The Gut would be here any minute, Prince Gutturaz who was to escort the bride. He was Azak's oldest surviving brother, and a portly man.

Organizing a wedding in Zark had turned out to be quite easy. Inos had merely told Kar what she wanted, and Kar had done as he pleased. Then Azak had ordered it all changed. Finally Rasha had rearranged the whole plan. Not difficult at all.

Almost the only decisions Inos had been allowed to make for herself had concerned her gown, and those choices had been held to within extremely narrow limits, decreed by tradition. Now she was swathed in enough lace to drape every window in Krasnegar, enough pearls to ransom a warlock. Pearls were a Zarkian symbol of virginity. She wondered if the oysters believed that.

She paused to scowl at herself in one of the innumerable mirrors that had infested her apartment, crowding it like a bazaar—hanging mirrors, free-standing mirrors, square, round, and oval mirrors. There she was, scowling everywhere, the human iceberg. At the moment she still had her veils raised, but when they were down she could not be distinguished from an iceberg, not even by experts. The room was packed with icebergs. She could have left her hair in curlers and painted her face blue and no one would ever notice under all this.

"Ah, there you are, my dear," said a familiar voice. "You look charming."

Inos preferred not to turn around in case she tangled her train, so she located a Kade reflection and spoke to that.

"I do not look charming! I do not *look* at all! If we left this gown on the dressmaker's dummy, and wheeled that into the hall instead of me, then I think the iman could marry it to Azak without anyone noticing."

Kade fluttered, and for a moment Inos thought she was going to sug-gest that they do just that, but Kade would never be so unkind. Instead she said, "Well, every land has its own ways, dear. And weddings are always very traditional." With a satisfied nod at this insight, she turned away to consult a mirror, smiling politely to her reflection as if thinking it needed reassurance also.

Kade was almost invisible herself, bundled in rolls of a heavy gold cloth that did not suit her complexion; it must also be even hotter and heavier than Inos's wedding gown. Only the lower part of her face would be veiled for the ceremony, as mature male Arakkaranians could apparently be trusted not to riot at the sight of Kade's eyes.

She thought Inos was making a terrible mistake. She had said so when Inos had told her the news, a week ago.

Hot words then; cold words ever since.

Even now, Kade was visibly fretting, unhappy about the match, unwilling to upset Inos on her wedding day, aware that it was too late to stop the avalanche anyway—every word of that was written in her eyes and the set of her mouth.

Inos contrived to turn around without knotting herself. "Do you remember Agimoonoo?"

Kade blinked and then said, "Yes?" uncertainly.

"It was just after I arrived at Kinvale. She announced her engagement to that fat customs official. Remember?"

"Yes. I remember."

"I said some nasty things, as I recall. That he was odious and sneaky. That she didn't love him. That she was only marrying him for his money and because her mother was insisting." Inos smiled. "That was before you taught me to be more discreet, Aunt. But at least I just said them to you, not to anyone else."

Kade bit her lip. "What about her?"

"You told me that she would learn to love him. That unless a man was a real horror, a woman could learn to live with him and be happy, and often love had to come later."

A sickly little smile appeared on Kade's lips and vanished like a melting snowflake. "I may have said something like that. But—"

"And in this case, the God told me to trust in love. What Azak did for me—has been doing for me . . . he is doing for me. For love." She had seen Azak only twice, and briefly, in the past week. Both meetings had been very public and formal, and the two of them had hardly spoken to each other. His face had been unreadable, stern and wooden. The sacrifice he was making for her was a strange and cruel one, but no less a sacrifice for that. "No man enjoys losing, Aunt. Abject surrender is hard for anyone. From a proud man like Azak it almost ranks as a miracle! It proves his love, don't you see? We must trust in love."

263

Inos had been repeating that sentiment for a week now—to Kade by day and to herself by night—so she must really believe it. Mustn't she?

Kade nodded, slightly pink. "I wish you both all happiness, my dear." She meant it; she did not expect it.

At the height of their quarrel, Kade had said some very painful things, but Inos would forgive them and forget them. Today she could not hold a grievance against anyone, for today was her wedding day. Today she was to be happy. Wasn't she?

Every girl must feel nervous on her wedding day. Every bride must know this feeling of a lump of ice in her belly.

She had not told Kade about the sculleries. Rasha had been serious in her threats, and only Azak's surrender had stopped her from carrying them out. The sculleries alone made the marriage inevitable, to save Kade from being worked to a quick death scrubbing out acres of stone floors.

Unthinkable.

Ladylike banter? "A rather brief betrothal, Aunt."

"Yes, dear?"

"But longer than my last one, I believe."

"A great improvement. As I recall, we hadn't opened the wine to toast your engagement before you were lining up in front of the bishop."

"And then Rap—" Inos shrugged. The conversation wasn't going anywhere. But if Rap had not burst in and stopped the wedding, what would have happened then?

"I still feel that perhaps there has been too much haste in . . ." Kade trailed into silence, and in that hall of mirrors it was impossible to tell whether she had stopped because of Inos's expression, or because what she was about to say was much too late now, or because a dozen black-clad Zanas had suddenly appeared. Zana had mysteriously returned to the palace the day after Inos did, and had again taken charge of the royal guests' comforts. Without Zana, today would have collapsed into chaos long since.

"His Largeness is here?" Inos moved hands expansively.

Zana nodded, eyes atwinkle. With deft fingers she pulled down the veils to make Inos respectable. Inos peered out at the world through a mist of fine lace, seeing icebergs in all directions.

Suddenly the mirrors had a new reflection to play with as the massive green form of grizzled Prince Gutturaz filled the doorway, swaying stiffly forward in a bow. He advanced three paces and bowed again. Then two lines of excited young pages came sweeping into sight from behind his eclipsing bulk.

Chattering and giggling, the boys headed for Inos and their allotted places. Most of them were very small, but all twelve were princes, clad in green, come to bear the bride's train to their father's wedding.

3

God of Fools!
Running, running, he kept running. Hills were steep, and stairs were steeper. Not like home, where both were covered—open here, but steep and winding.
Lith'rian . . . The Evil take him. Must have known it!
"Let me by, please!"
Too close to call, that's how he'd put it. Maybe. Maybe. Just romantic? Just keep running. Sweat romantic, smell romantic? Dodge round corners . . . Push past donkeys, keep on running. Sword kept bouncing, people looking. Royal wedding, flags and banners. Inosolan getting married? Inosolan leave her homeland? Didn't sound like Inosolan!
God of Fools, he should have waited, just a moment. Should have stayed for just a moment, stayed to tell the other two.
Then they'd both have started running, running up the hill like him. He could run a great deal faster; the way he ran would surely kill them, they would burst their hearts for sure. Trouble was, he should have told them, told them he was going to Inos, not just dashed off like a crazy, leaving them to mind the boat. Sword kept bouncing, people looking. No one else was armed at all. If he didn't get to Inos, then he'd quickly be arrested, and the others wouldn't know. Gathmor, Darad couldn't help him, even so he should have told them; maybe now they'd come to find him—and that wouldn't help at all. He'd be dead by then for certain and that wouldn't help at all.
"Let me by, please!"
Worst of all was indecision—just what could he hope to do? Even if he got to Inos, what in heaven could he do? Tell her maybe that he loved her, put it into words just once? If that was all, he'd better hurry—get there while she still was single, even if she was engaged. Talk of love to married women likely made their men enraged.
Royal wedding in the palace, palace at the very crest. Palace didn't show on farsight! Sorceress was there for certain, hidden in that palace-blank. If a man climbed in a window, then the guards would surely kill him—all intruders in a palace were most surely put to death.
What a warren! It kept winding. Steeper, steeper grew the stairs. Heart was straining, breath was labored, and it didn't feel romantic. If he hadn't had his farsight, he'd have never found a way.

Now the palace loomed above him, but the gate was leagues ahead, and the scrimmage in the forecourt was the local population, being feasted by the sultan in a wedding celebration—there were thousands in the courtyard at the wedding jubilee. So the gates were being guarded, extra-guarded from the crowd. If a stranger with a saber tried to enter by the forecourt, then the guards would want to argue and provide some entertainment for the wedding jubilee.

The wall that ran beside him . . . it was high but it was old, and the mortar in the stonework had been weathered very deep. A criminal like Thinal could just scramble up the stonework, could just clamber like a fly; and an adept could do anything that anyone could do.

Stop!

Heart . . . lungs . . . legs shaking . . . head swimming . . .

Don't know . . . what's on other side . . . was that a whinny?

What have I got to lose?

4

The trumpets blared. Through the white mist of lace, Inos watched the great doors swing open before her. With one hand resting on the well-padded arm of Prince Gutturaz, she floated forward very slowly, mindful always of the stumpy legs of the tiny trainbearers behind her . . . mindful also of icebergs drifting through the pack, visible sometimes from the castle windows in Krasnegar. Never again.

She entered the Great Hall. She had not seen—had not even heard mention of—the Great Hall until the rehearsals began. She would believe anyone who told her it was the largest covered space in Pandemia.

Head up. No need to smile. No one could see.

On either hand stood the massed commonfolk worthies of Arakkaran in their finest finery; up ahead were the princes, from very young to very old, in green. The young outnumbered the old. All held their eyes forward, not turning around to gape at her. There was nothing to see but an iceberg.

The sun's sharp glare stabbed in through windows high overhead, to be diverted by filigree of marble and reflected from rib and pier and slab until it floated down upon the congregation like a mist of milk. All men. Kade would be on the platform, being official mother of the bride, and a side section had been reserved for Azak's sisters, few of whom Inos had ever met. Women played little part in even domestic affairs here, and the marriage of a sultan was not a domestic affair, it was state business. Kar had explained that. By rights this should be a political marriage—Azak should be wedding the daughter of some neighbor state, to cement an alliance. He was breaking a tradition and taking a risk by marrying an outsider, a homeless nobody. The official proclamation had named her as a queen, but who had been deceived?

Citherns and other instruments of torment twanged and whined faintly in an alien dirge . . . walk slowly . . .

Behind her, distant already, the great doors thumped shut with a reverberating impact like the end of the world, like the final reckoning of the Good and the Evil—*The End!* It rolled from arch to arch and pillar to pillar, raining echoes, fading away above the distant dais that was her destination.

Ahead of her white marble stretched, flat as a frozen canal, all the way to that dais where the rest of the wedding party waited. Back and center was the throne, and on the throne sat Rasha, victorious. She was even wearing royal green, although a very dark, lustrous green. Already Inos could see the hot red eyes above the filmy yashmak, the circlet of emeralds and pearls that was Rasha's only ornamentation, the crimson nails idly picking at the arms of the throne. She was girt in her illusions of youth and beauty. Inos had those, also, and by right.

Zarkian custom made one strange concession to womanhood, or motherhood—at weddings a woman presided from the throne. Had Azak's grandfather's wife been alive, she would have sat there until her replacement was installed. There being no true sultana at present, that throne should by rights stay empty until Azak led his bride to it at the end of the ceremony. But Rasha had insisted and Azak had consented without dispute. Her triumph complete, an ancient strumpet sat upon the throne of Arakkaran. What bitter satisfaction did it give her?

At least she had not tried to claim the royal sash, which still glittered green across the sultan's chest, and now he came in from one side, to stand and wait for his approaching bride. Tall and fierce and handsome, showing his eagle profile. Dear Azak?

Poor Azak! His long humiliation was over now, surely? He had served his seven days and nights of penance. Rasha would bait and harry him no more. Or would she? Inos had no guarantee of that; she had heard no promise. Must she share her husband with the twisted old harlot as well as with all the son-breeding women of his harem?

And tonight? What sort of replacement would Inos be? She had offered prayers that she would not disappoint him on his wedding night. She wanted to please him. She must trust him—he was certainly experienced.

He was handsome and virile and royal; and loved her. What more could a maiden's dreams require? This was a much richer land than Krasnegar. The God had promised her a happy ending.

She was almost at the steps. There was the iman, ancient and inclined to spray spittle. There was the ever-smiling, baby-face Kar, best man and vigilant bodyguard. There was young Prince Quarazak, proudly holding a green cushion, *tall for his age.* On the cushion lay the slender golden necklace that symbolized marriage in Zark. Inos had made a halfhearted effort to substitute a ring, Imperial style, but in Zark they preferred a necklace. Kade had been very upset when she heard of the necklace. Inos had tried to make a joke of it, claiming that a chain was merely less subtle than a ring, but they both meant much the same.

The whole Zarkian ceremony was less subtle. She mounted the two steps to the dais. She turned to face Azak, and Gutturaz steadied her as she knelt on the waiting cushion, awkward in her massive gown.

The music died and was buried in the sea-sound of the audience being seated.

The iman tottered forward, clutching a book. Azak advanced a few paces, flanked by Kar and shiny-eyed little Quarazak.

He couldn't see her face, but surely he could give her a smile? Kar was smiling.

It was amazing the sultan could move under all the jewels encrusting him. Even the fabulous emerald sash was dulled by their glory. He was absolute monarch of a rich kingdom.

And Inos was a nobody. She had explained that over and over to Kade.

Silence settled like the dust of the ages. Coughing and rustling faded. The last chair leg scraped harshly and alone.

The iman cleared his throat. He began.

Azak's responses rang out like the royal edicts they were. He promised many things: care, protection. Love.

Then it was her turn. Inos tried to make her voice carry, but she tried also not to shout.

She promised everything.

And Quarazak held out the cushion so the iman could bless the chain. He offered it then to his father and Azak reached for it, every link gleaming in the evening sunlight.

It slid out of reach again as the boy turned slightly to glance at the distant doors, puzzled. Then Azak heard what younger ears had heard first and looked that way, also. Kar . . . turbans in the audience were twisting around. A strange noise outside the hall?

Faint but coming closer? Shouting? Thuds?

Swords?

Azak turned his head to look at Rasha, and Rasha was frowning above the green gauze silk of her yashmak.

Rasha sprang to her feet.

Then the doors opened.

The ornate bar shattered in a cloud of flying splinters. The doors were hurled open, blasted open as if struck by a tidal wave or a thunderbolt. They flew back on their hinges and their impact with the walls battered every ear a second time. Echoes rolled unending.

The golden chain slid unnoticed from the cushion to the floor. Every eye was turned on the tumult in the entrance.

And in through the doorway came . . . the hindquarters of an enormous black horse.

Out of the West:

O, young Lochinvar is come out of the West,

Through all the wide Border his steed was the best;

And, save his good broadsword, he weapon had none,

   He rode all unarmed, and he rode all alone.

So faithful in love, and so dauntless in war,

There never was knight like the young Lochinvar.

Scott, Lochinvar

14

Tumult, and shouting

1

For a long, breathless moment the whole congregation was frozen in place, from Rasha and Azak down to the tiniest princeling, fascinated spectators of the battle raging in the doorway.

If that horse was not Evil himself, it was one of his brothers, yet the man on his back was handling him with the precision of an artist's brush— Azak himself could not control a mount like that. Whole cohorts of family men were striking and slashing at the intruder, but man and horse together held them off. The rider's sword danced like a silver mist, first on one side, then the other. Blades clamoring in unbroken carillon; the stallion whirled and clattered on slippery marble, but his hooves and teeth and bulk were part of the fight, and if he really was Evil, then the family men would be treating him with much greater care than they were trying to extend to the stranger.

The audience leaped to its feet in a crash of falling chairs, and those nearest the doors began to push away.

One guard stopped a full rear kick, and reacted much as the doors had. A *chakram* whined through the air like a deadly sunbeam, but the intended victim flicked it aside with his sword, parried a thrust on his right, slashed down an assailant on his left, deflected a lance. Bodies lay in disarray outside the

270

room and were starting to pile up inside, as well. Another man screamed and dropped his sword, then toppled over, even as the horse slammed into two more, spilling them aside. The rider ducked a second *chakram*, and airborne death flashed across the hall over the heads of hundreds of people. Horseshoes screeched on marble . . .

"*Hold!*" Rasha's voice rang out with the power of a bugle.

The battle stopped. The spectators froze again. So did the combatants.

Cautiously the rider backed his horse out from the petrified forest of his assailants. Satisfied that they were no longer dangerous, he turned the stallion and let him prance forward, high-stepping up the aisle. His passage dragged a ripple through the congregation, as heads turned to watch—Inos could see only faces beyond him, only turbans in front. More faces emerged from behind pillars.

The newcomer slid his sword back into its scabbard still bloody; he pulled an arm across his forehead.

The horse was indeed Evil, greatest of the midnight stallions that only Azak might ride, the pride of the royal stables. He was shivering and foaming, rolling eyes and baring teeth. His hooves clicked and skittered on the slippery stone, yet the shabby-looking rider had him in perfect control. He reached the space before the dais. Now all the audience was behind him, all faces.

Inos did not even dare look at Azak to see how he was reacting to this sacrilege, and she was staring in growing disbelief at the intruder. This was sorcery.

Then she saw that Evil bore no harness, no saddle.

Bareback! She had only ever known one man who—

Not again!

She surged to her feet, hindered and unbalanced by the weight of lace. She staggered, steadied, stared at the bashful little half smile, the ludicrous raccoon tattoos, the unkempt tangle of brown hair soaked with sweat. *No! Impossible! He was dead!* She swayed, the hall darkened. Again? The sun had not set yet; wraiths did not haunt in daylight. She had gone mad. She was hallucinating.

Then the intruder leaned forward, swung his leg, and dropped to the floor at Evil's side. He staggered, steadying himself against the steaming, heaving black flank. His clothes were filthy and soaked and blood-spattered. He was convulsed by his efforts to breathe, pumping air in and out in harsh gasps as loud as those of his horse. Sweat trickled down his face and every few seconds he would wipe it with a brawny bare forearm.

Nevertheless he squared his shoulders and straightened. He bowed unsteadily to Inos. His glance wandered between Azak and Rasha a couple of times. He stretched his tattoos slightly at the sight of Azak's finery, then chose Rasha and bowed to her. And finally to Azak.

The hall was filled with a silent, staring multitude, and still no one had spoken a word. The loudest noise in the room was the intruder's breathing.

"The faun!" said Rasha. "How interesting."

Again Rap smiled faintly, has usual diffident little smile that . . .

No! No! No!

"That faun is dead!" Inos shouted. "This is foul, cruel sorcery. Queen Rasha? Is this your doing?"

The green-shrouded sorceress shook her head, and Inos could not tell if that was anger or amusement glinting in those ruby eyes. And Azak . . . Inos quailed. Never had she seen such fury. Veins bulged on a scarlet face. He quivered, holding himself in by precarious power of will. The state wedding was a shambles, pomp had become farce, and no sultan of Arakkaran had ever been so shamed before his court.

"It is sorcery," Rasha said. "But not mine. Who are you?"

"I'm Rap, ma'am." He panted, then continued. "There are some wounded men out there. I may even have killed a couple. I hope I didn't—"

"Leave them!" Azak roared. "It will be a kindness."

Rasha shrugged. The petrified guards at the door thawed back to life. Seeing the orderly discussion in progress at the dais, they began shamedly sheathing their swords and stooped to tend their wounded.

The audience seemed to shimmer in doubt and uncertainty. Then chairs scraped and clattered as the guests resumed their seats.

"Rap is dead!" Inos shouted . . . screamed? "You can't be Rap!"

He smiled up at her wistfully, then patted the mighty foam-spattered shoulder beside him. "Master-of-horse and sergeant-at-arms both?"

Oh, Gods! Inos felt her knees start to buckle, and then Kade was at her side, holding her. Oh, blessed Kade! She clung tight. Rap? Not dead? Really Rap?

Idiot Rap! Maniac Rap! He'd fallen into the power of some sorcerer, and was being used to disrupt Azak's wedding, and, and . . . Except that this whole monstrous disaster had a horribly Rappian sort of feel to it. Just the sort of thing . . .

"Whose work is this?" Azak asked hoarsely, of Rasha.

She shrugged again. "Speak, boy."

Rap was gazing witlessly at Inos. "Are you married?" he asked in a very small voice.

"Yes," she said. "No. I mean—"

"Oh."

Was that all he could say? Returning from the dead? Disrupting a solemn occasion of state? Turning her whole world upside—Oh, that was nonsense! It couldn't be Rap. Not the same Rap. Not all the way from Krasnegar in less than half a year.

272

Azak reached for his scimitar, but Rasha held out a hand, warning him not to draw.

Rap licked his lips. "I bring a message to Queen Inosolan."

"From whom?" Azak roared.

"From . . . from . . . I don't seem able to be answer that, your Majesty."

A handsbreadth of blade emerged before Azak was again stopped by Rasha. "He's been blocked, but it's very shallow. There . . ."

"Thank you!" Rap said politely. "From Warlock Lith'rian, your Majesty. Majesties."

Azak hissed in surprise.

"Let us hear this message, then," Rasha said.

Why was she so poised? Her eyes were gleaming, but her fingers were relaxed, and there was no air of anger or alarm. Her calm was astonishing. She was behaving like . . . like Kade, or someone.

Inos hugged Kade a little tighter, and felt the hug returned. She could not take her eyes off Rap. Her cheeks felt wet and she had no idea what her face looked like, so it was fortunate that no one could see it anyway. Except Rasha, of course.

And Rap. Oh, damn!

He was deeper, broader than he had been. And more confident. Manly. Not big like Azak, or a jotunn, but bigger than an imp. Or a pixie. Why did she think of pixies? Ugly flat noses?

Rap on a white horse in her dream. When had she dreamed that? Several times, maybe.

"His Omnipotence said I should come and tell Queen Inos—"

"Silence!" Azak drew his sword all the way.

"Put that back," Rasha said brusquely, "If you go against the faun, he'll cut you to confetti. In fact . . ."

Azak's scimitar vanished, and Rap's sword, and Kar's, also. The whole hall was disarmed then, for the wedding guests bore no weapons. The horse shivered into motion, clattering around and heading for the door, where the platoon of the family men fidgeted in baffled rage—and likely in fear, knowing that Azak's vengeance would be bloody. They parted to let Evil leave. In a moment the doors closed as the last of the shamed and discredited guards followed the horse out.

By now the ceremony should have been long over, the guests on their way to the wedding feast. The light from the high windows was fading, and blushing, spreading blood on the vaults and pillars. Shadows drifted in like vultures coming to a massacre.

The departure of the horse left Rap looking small and lonely. He stood on the floor; the others were all on the dais, two steps up.

273

"Better," Rasha said.

"He wants a good rubdown," Rap agreed, folding his arms as if relieved of a worry.

"I meant . . . Well, speak up, Master Rap. The message?"

"That message will be delivered in private!" Azak snapped. "And messages to my wife come to me first."

Rap stretched his tattoos again at that and looked quizzically up at Inos. "Are you truly married, your Majesty, and did you do this of your own free will?"

Her mouth was full of sand. "Yes. And yes." Of course her choices had been limited, but she would not admit that now. A stableboy would not understand politics, of course. All Rap would see in Azak at the moment would be glittering riches. And big male animal.

What Rap thought did not matter at all.

Azak growled in fury. He took two strides back to the middle of the dais, snatched up the gold chain where it had fallen, and stamped over to Inos. She bowed her head in acceptance and he dropped the necklace over it. Then he marched back to the edge of the platform. "She is certainly married now, and if you address one more word to her, I will have you broken on the wheel."

Rap pursed his lips and shrugged. He had almost stopped panting and he seemed to be accepting the situation, accepting that he had arrived too late.

Too late for *what!*

"The warlock's message?" Rasha said calmly.

"He told me to tell Queen Inosolan to . . . to trust in love."

Inos recoiled as if she had been struck, and again Kade's arms steadied her. She pushed them away angrily. How dare he burst into her wedding like this! How dare he throw such vicious slurs! Yes, she had kissed him when they were children together; now he had turned her wedding into a circus and a bloodbath, and he wanted to lecture her about *love?*

Recklessly she threw up her veil and turned to face Azak, fearing she might be as pale as the lace enshrouding her. For her he had groveled before the hateful sorceress. Why else, if not for love?

"I have always trusted in love," she declared loudly. "And I still do."

He nodded in grudging satisfaction. "So the message was unnecessary, and we may now deal with the messenger."

Oh, Rap! Idiot Rap!

"Gutturaz!" Azak said loudly. "Lead our honored guests to the feast. And send in the guards."

The big prince rose and bowed. Chairs scraped again as the congregation rose.

"I am staying!" Inos said firmly.

Azak glared, but did not overrule her. Gutturaz hesitated, for the rehearsals had not covered these events. Improvising he gestured respectfully for the iman to precede him, then held out an arm for Kade. She shook her head, staying close to Inos. Pouting, the fat man beckoned the trainbearers to follow him and strutted off down the steps. Rap stepped aside and watched the dignitaries file past, heading along the aisle behind the tottering cleric. Front-row princes began streaming after. Only the soft-smiling Kar remained on the platform, and Azak, and the three women.

"Azak, my . . ." Inos stopped, and tried again. "My lord, this man is a very—"

Azak shot her a glare of disbelief and turned away.

"Wait, though," Rasha said. Her voice was soft. yet it came clearly over the noise of shuffling feet. "He may not have been entirely a free agent, your Majesty. I detected a trace of a compulsion there."

"I don't care if he doesn't know his ears—"

"Hold! I think there is another message, my dear."

My dear? How dare she! How dare she claim that throne, give orders to the sultan, set herself up as tyrant, and especially dare talk to Azak like that!

Azak frowned. "Lith'rian?"

Rasha nodded, studying Rap, who had flinched at the word "compulsion" and was now glancing uneasily from face to face as if he had only just realized his danger. Had he truly expected Azak to let him ive, after this?

The swift tropical sunset was over. People, faces, chairs, even the Great Hall itself, all were fading away into shadow. Yet there was no doubt that Rasha was pleased about something—exultant, even. Rubbing her hands, she advanced down the steps toward Rap, who backed away a pace and then stopped, staring at her apprehensively.

Apprehension became horror. "No!"

"Yes," said Rasha. She chuckled. "I think Warlock Lith'rian was sending me a message also. Or a gift!"

"This is not the time or the place!" Azak spoke as if he were leading his army in cavalry drill.

"It is the only time and place, my dear." Rasha did not look around. "I was told once that this faun knew a word of power. Obviously that was an understatement, or he has learned more words since. He is at least a mage, and possibly a sorcerer."

"Just 'n adept," Rap muttered. He was clearly worried now, the whites of his eyes shining like moons amid the dark blotches of tattoo.

"You would say that, of course." The sorceress floated nearer, her deepgreen robes now turned to black in the gloom. "But we saw you at work. An adept holding off the whole palace guard? Hardly! I have been an adept; I know what is possible!"

The hall was half empty now, the commoners starting to follow the prince's. The indistinct figures of the family men in their brown uniforms were slipping in through a side door, and forming up.

"What are you getting at?" Azak demanded sharply.

"Our alliance, darling, remember? Our pact against Olybino."

Inos gasped.

It was like shutting a finger in a door—blinding pain but also a deafening howl of injustice; an internal voice screaming that the Gods should never allow such things to happen. Was *that* what Azak had really wanted from the sorceress? Was that why he had whored for her all the last week? What coin had he accepted for his services—freedom from the curse so he could marry Inos, yes, but also an occult alliance for the coming war against the Impire? Suddenly Inos saw herself as part of a package, something thrown in by a merchant to make a sale of something else. A pretty ribboned basket hiding an unsavory purchase. *Azak, what did you promise? What were you really planning?*

Betrayed!

Rap was still protesting that he was only as adept.

"Perhaps sorcerer is unlikely," Rasha conceded."Even warlocks have limits on their generosity. But you are certainly too strong for a mere adept. A mage, I judge."

"He is meant as a replacement for Elkarath?" Azak asked, stepping down from the dais to join her. Imperceptibly Rap had been backing away, and Rasha stalking him. The last guests were filtering out the big doorway beyond a wasteland of empty chairs like the stumps of a ravaged forest.

"Perhaps. Obviously the elf has turned against East, as I predicted. Olybino is a failure, and elves despise incompetence. Also, I think this faun as been sent to me as protection."

"Protection?" said Rap and Azak together.

Inos took a step forward and Kade pulled her back. "No, dear!" she whispered.

She was right, of course—to plead with Rasha on Rap's behalf would be a disastrous error. Rasha did not approve of women having tender feelings toward men, any men.

"Protection! East has threatened to bespell me. Lith'rian is suggesting a defense, you see? This gift-faun is going to start making himself useful by telling me one of his words."

"No!" Rap cried.

"Most certainly."

"Four words is the limit!"

"Indeed? If your words give you that sort of lore, then you are certainly a full sorcerer. Else, who told you so?"

Rap stuttered and said nothing.

"I don't believe in that limit!" Rasha said. "At least it is worth a try, even if I gain nothing."

"Your sorcery can't get my words out of me!"

Rasha chuckled. "No?"

He screamed, doubled over, then toppled heavily. Inos felt her feet start to move, and Kade's hand tighten on her arm. The day they had arrived in Arakkaran, Rasha had tortured Azak just like this.

Rap curled up small, writhed, straightened, spasmed, thrashed as if every muscle was being convulsed by cramps. He did not scream again, but he gurgled, and somehow more noise would have made the spectacle less horrible. Nauseated, Inos tried to look away, and couldn't. She clenched her teeth in the effort not to cry out. To appeal to the sorceress would be as bad as appealing to Azak. *Rap! I can't help! Anything I do will make it worse.*

At last the whimpering thing on the floor fell silent, and was still. Inos wondered if he had fainted, or died.

"Had enough yet?" Rasha inquired sweetly. "Want a rest?"

After a moment Rap pushed himself up, leaning on his hands and one hip. His face was deathly pale and there was a crazy look in his eye as he stared up at the sorceress. He must have bitten his tongue, for his mouth was bloody; he said something so slurred that Inos missed it. It was also spoken in a very broad sailor dialect, but the sense was obvious.

Rasha laughed. "Very good! But how long can you stand it, faun?" Her voice flowed like poisoned syrup in the gloom. "An hour? A week? A lifetime?"

Again Rap's reply was an unintelligible obscenity.

"Ready then? You want to burn some more?" she asked.

And she must have cured his tongue, because the next reply was at least clearly phrased, if no more polite. Visibly shaken, Rap clambered to his feet. He swayed for a moment, then lunged forward as if to attack the sorceress and strangle her. He stopped after two steps, glaring, but Inos could not tell if he had changed his mind or if Rasha had blocked him. How could he know that courage and defiance were the worst possible responses to her torments?

Even through the gauze of her veil, her amusement showed. "Interesting! You present an interesting challenge. But we'll find your breaking point some other day. This is holding up the wedding celebrations. You'll talk soon enough when your sweetheart . . . Oh, I am so sorry! How careless of me to spill such dangerous little secrets! I mean the sultana, of course. This time she burns and you watch, faun."

Azak uttered a wordless roar of protest, and then reeled back as if kicked by an invisible horse.

Inos steadied herself, brushing away her helpers. She opened her mouth to shout a royal defiance, to tell the old harlot to do her worst, to order Rap to refuse—and she could not force the words between her teeth. Whether that was Rasha's sorcery or her own frailty she did not know, but silent she stayed. Silent, and already shaking. Never in her life had she experienced truly great pain. She had seen both Azak and Rap crushed by it, and she did not think she could be any braver or more stubborn than either of those two.

And what did it matter if Rasha's powers were increased? Already she ruled Arakkaran as she willed.

Glaring murder, Rap stepped closer to the sorceress, his fingers hooked. She shook her head mockingly at such folly.

"All right!" he shouted. "All right, you evil old hag!"

"You will rue ever uttering that remark. Meanwhile—talk!" She turned her head as Rap moved close, his face black with anger.

He went to whisper to her, and stuttered into silence with a gasp. Rasha glanced around and then frowned at Azak, who was closest.

"You have sharp ears, Muscles. Go back! Come here, faun." She marched over to the deserted front row of chairs. Rap trailed behind, looking broken and dejected. Azak turned away from the two of them and ran up on the dais. He came over to stand behind Inos, but he was glowering at the drama, and did not look at her. As an oven might radiate heat, so Azak still radiated fury. Oh, idiot Rap!

She hugged Kade tighter, aware that one of them was trembling. Or both of them.

The hall was growing so dim now that it was hard to make out the details, but again Rap had leaned close to the sorceress's ear. He choked, and again pulled away. "It still hurts!"

"Tell! Or I give Inosolan what I gave you! Last chance!"

Inos tensed again, mad with her own helplessness. Azak growled wordlessly. At the far end of the hall, torches flickered brightly where the guard was lining up.

Again Rap bent to Rasha. He began to whisper, and stopped with a heart-rending groan. There was certainly no one else within earshot now, but apparently to speak a word of power for even one listener hurt about as much as Rasha's occult tortures.

Someone shouted a command by the door, and the squad of family men began to move, starting down the aisle, at least fifty of them, bringing their flaming torches. Their boots thumped in steady cadence, and shadows began to shimmy behind the pillars.

278

Rap tried again, and this time seemed to finish what he was saying. Then he reeled back, doubled over and gagging.

"Ah!" Rasha stiffened in triumph and seemed to grow taller. "Yes, yes!" She spun around to face Azak. "Yes! Now I—"

Rap straightened, staring at her.

Inos gasped and moved closer to Kade—the sorceress's eyes were glowing red in the gloom. She tried to speak and produced only a gabble of gibberish. Azak took a step forward and stopped, grimacing. Now her face and hands were shining with a ghostly pink light.

Kade's fingers bit into Inos's arm. "Am I mistaken," she whispered, "or has her Majesty made a serious error?"

"Too much power?" Inos said. "Rap warned her!"

Rap clapped his hands to his head, as if hearing something inaudible to mundane ears.

Pale wisps of smoke trickled from the sorceress's garments, her head and arms glowed through the silk. Then she either realized the extent of her danger for the first time, or else the pain overcame her defenses. She screamed.

The leading rank of family men stopped abruptly, others ran into them, and the march fell into chaos. Men stumbled, knocking over chairs, or one another. The leader roared.

Rasha whirled around toward Rap and held out her arms. "Take it back!" she yelled. She staggered forward, and he lurched away in horror. Smoke poured from her wrists, lighted by the red glow of her hands. She tried to speak again and the words were lost in an animal howl as her sleeves exploded into flame, followed at once by her headdress.

The sorceress blazed then, a human bonfire illuminating the hall and the royal party on the dais and the terrified faces of the close-bunched guards, whose eyes reflected her brilliance like the eyes of a wolf pack peering from a forest. Sparks and smoke roared up to the arches of the roof. Inos saw the glare through her eyelids; she gagged at the vile stench of burning hair and cloth.

The fire dwindled, the light faded into darkness, but the screaming continued, and Inos opened her eyes again to see. Rasha was still there. Her clothes and hair had burned away, but she herself seemed to be fighting back, hanging on to her mortal existence by some supreme act of will or sorcery. There was no fakery or pretense now, no tall queenly stature or maidenly beauty, only a grotesque roly-poly figure of hairless flabby skin, staggering around and keening with a shrill thin note that froze the ears. And the whole of that hideous figure shone like a lantern with an internal pink light, brightening the gloom of the hall.

Inos wanted to run to Rap, and could not bring herself to release Kade. The two of them hugged and shivered together. The guards were backing away down the aisle.

Again Rasha tried to appeal to Rap, holding out her arms in supplication. Again he refused her. She tried to speak, and every word burst from her mouth as a spout of white fire. She wheeled around in search of someone else to aid her, and her eyes lit on Azak.

Except that she had no eyes now. Where they should have been were two dark shadows in the blaze that was the front of her head. The shape of her skull was visible, shining through her flesh, and when she spread her arms toward Azak, the bones were visible also, burning white-hot inside her.

She tottered forward, one unsteady step at a time, all the way to the dais. Azak advanced to meet her, holding out a chair as if she were a dangerous animal he must keep at bay. He halted at the top of the steps, barring her advance.

Again she tried to speak, whimpers mingled with vomits of flame like a smith's furnace. Inos could feel the heat; she thought she made out a few words—"Help," maybe, and "Sorcerer," and perhaps even "Lover," but that could have been imagination. The inside of Rasha's mouth was hotter than a potter's kiln.

She put a foot on the first step, and managed that, then swayed as she tried for the next. Azak was standing his ground against the heat, all his jeweled finery sparkling like a dew of blood, his face contorted in revulsion, but the chair he held extended before him was starting to smoke as Rasha neared it.

"No!" he shouted. "Go away! Monster!"

The Rasha thing raised its face to the sky and uttered one last, loud, ear-splitting howl of despair, and the word was clear: *"Love!"* It came out as a long jet of white fire squirting upward, and that cry of resignation seemed to burst the mortal bubble. The strangely resistant flesh exploded into flames, and for the second time the sorceress blazed as a bonfire—hotter and brighter than before, as her very substance burned away in a roar of sparks and fire. Azak dropped his shield, covered his face, and backed away.

For a moment the skeleton alone remained, standing on the first step, miraculously balanced, and every bone shone hot as the sun. Then it collapsed, even as it also was consumed in an upward rush of flame and ash.

The hall was plunged into silence and darkness. Inos could see nothing except a greenish afterimage of a skeleton and the stone glowing briefly red where its feet had rested, two faint footprints fading fast. The marble cracked like thunder.

"Bring those lights!" Azak roared, and the family men sprang to life. Two of the torchbearers hurried forward to brighten the scene.

Eyes recovered slowly, but soon Inos could make out the night sky framed in the high arches, their stone traceries speckled with stars, the faint curve of vaulting. Within the dancing yellow glow on the floor, nothing remained of

Sultana Rasha but a stain of lime on scorched marble and a cracked step. And a nasty, burned smell.

"She's dead," Rap said in a thin voice. "Quite dead. I felt her die. I felt my power come back!" He walked forward and peered at the step.

"Free!" Azak threw back his head and bellowed the word so the echoes boomed. He brandished fists in the air. "Free of the harlot! Free to be sultan at last!"

"I thought she was to be your aide-de-camp?" Kar muttered the question so softly that Azak likely did not hear him.

But Inos did, and it confirmed what she had suspected. Rasha would have been in charge of occult defense in the coming war. Azak had bought two sultanas. Gone, now, all gone . . .

Azak gestured, and the family men hastily advanced. then spread out in a cordon in front of the chairs. He pointed at Rap. "Bowmen! If that man speaks one word without my permission—shoot to kill."

With six arrows aimed on him at point-blank range Rap shut his mouth and kept it shut. He tucked his thumbs in his belt and rolled his eyes ironically at Inos. He looked much happier than he had a few moments ago. But of course—Rasha was dead and Elkarath had not returned, so far as Inos knew. Whether he was a mage or only an adept as he claimed Rap was senior sorcerer in Arakkaran. Her brain struggled to accept that idea. Rap?

"I have a couple of questions, prisoner!" Azak barked

"Azak!" Inos pulled away from Kade and hurried across the dais, her train rustling heavily after her.

Azak turned to face her, glaring. He put hands on hips. "You dare to plead for this felon?"

"I certainly do!" Inos snapped. "He is no felon. He rid you of the sorceress, didn't he?"

"No. She rid me of herself."

"Then you need a replacement advisor in occult matters. I will vouch for Master Rap's loyalty. He is honest and trustworthy."

"Loyal to whom? No, I shall have no hateful sorcery within my kingdom. He dies!"

Rap had killed guards, invaded the palace, disrupted the royal wedding, stolen Evil, made Azak look foolish. Any one of those would be a capital offense in Arakkaran.

"Azak!" She fell to her knees.

His face darkened in fury. "What is this man to you. Sultana?"

"Nothing! Merely a childhood friend and a loyal retainer of my late father's. May not I ask this small favor as a gift from you upon this, our wedding—"

"Silence! Do not begin your married life by incurring my displeasure, wife. In Zark it is unseemly for a married woman even to know another man by name, let alone take his part against her husband's wishes. Princess Kadolan, conduct your niece to the royal bedchamber."

Inos choked, speechless. She . . . she could not even find thoughts adequate, let alone words. The man she needed was the Azak of the desert, the lionslayer, but she did not know how to summon him in the place of this city tyrant.

"Majesty?" Kar strolled forward, his usual small smile just visible in the dancing flicker of the torches.

Azak grunted.

"Your Majesty, if this man truly was sent as a messenger by Warlock Lith'rian, then putting him to death might possibly be unwise. His arrival has rid you of the sorceress who was both a burden to you and who seemed destined to become an Olybino votary. His Omnipotence of the South may have foreseen these events."

Azak grunted again.

"At least take counsel on the matter, Sire. Be not hasty."

"Keep a mage prisoner?"

"No, impossible. But if he is a mage you cannot put him to death, either. The attempt might incur his enmity." Kar chuckled softly. "He claims to be only an adept. It should be possible to detain an adept, and I think these honest fellows here may be willing to attempt so dangerous and difficult a task as a token of their desire to be reinstated in your favor. A small recompense for their poor showing this afternoon?"

That was quite a speech, Inos thought gratefully.

Azak seemed to agree. "Very well. Captain, you will see that this prisoner is kept in close confinement, guarded at all times. He must not be allowed to speak, or he will subvert you, and you will use the thickest chains you—"

Rap moved like a streak. He spun on his heel, took two steps, and jumped. The archers were hopelessly late, and only one even released his shaft. It flashed across the semicircle and buried itself in a torchbearer, who toppled backward without a sound.

At first, few of the guards seemed to understand where their prisoner had gone. Then they heard the clatter of boots on marble behind them as Rap landed, already running, barely visible in the dark. He hurtled toward the door, a faint blur of motion like a cheetah.

But there were guards on the door, also, and he skidded to a halt before their line of swords. Inos heard him start to say something, and the swords seemed to waver. Then the rest of the family men arrived in a charge and engulfed him in a heaving mass of bodies. Even then, for a moment it seemed like a fair fight. Men screamed, others hurtled through the air. But the odds were too great. The struggle ended. The hitting and kicking did not.

Inos clapped her hands to her ears and screamed, "Stop them!" at Azak.

Azak merely shrugged, but the guards may have heard her, for they stopped. They brought Rap back facedown between eight men, two to a limb, and with a cap stuffed in his mouth so he could not speak; but he was probably unconscious anyway. His head dangled limply, dribbling blood on the floor, black in the wavering torchlight.

"Satisfactory!" Azak boomed. "Take whatever steps you deem necessary, Captain!"

Inos felt her heart twist. She did not know how to deal with this Sultan-Azak. Anything except abject humility infuriated him. If she could only call forth the solitary Azak of the desert, the one who had laughed and cracked jokes . . . him she might move, when they were alone together. So if she could keep Rap alive for a few days, perhaps she could do something.

"My lord! They will kill him!"

"Not quite!"

She was still on her knees; she raised clasped hands in supplication. "No bloodshed! At least promise me that!"

Azak scowled furiously. "Very well! Captain, you will shed no more blood!" He glanced over the whole troop, and his voice rose to include every man. "But none of you can imagine anything worse than what will happen if he escapes. Nothing at all! Do I make myself clear?"

The captain saluted, his face grim and hateful. He must be thinking of the sons by whom he was sworn, and what Azak was capable of doing to them. They all must.

"Princess Kadolan!" said Azak.

Kade stumbled forward, eyes wide and staring above her yashmak.

"We gathered here to seal a marriage. Escort the sultana to the royal quarters." He glanced down coldly at Inos. "Your women will be waiting to prepare you. You may expect me shortly."

2

Clunk!

Huh? The jotunn opened his eyes and shivered.

He was lying in the bottom of a boat, under a hard, damp cover, and a sky sickly pale with dawn. Stiff? Gods! He hadn't felt like this since the time he'd been sixteen and lipped Rathkrun and Rathkrun had told him he was ready for his first real lesson and given it to him, all over, inch by inch.

Rathkrun was dead. And the old man. And Wanmie and the kids.

Shiver.

Clunk! Plip!

Something bounced off the boat's side and hit the water.

Gathmor heaved himself up with a groan. He hadn't meant to go to sleep. Tyro trick! Fall asleep on watch? He deserved to have all his teeth kicked out. Other craft rocked gently all around, misty in the uncertain light. Shiny water, mist, sky bright . . .

A faint hail: "Krasnegar!"

That was the password. He peered shoreward, but the sea ended just before it got there. The boat must be visible, though—against the light?

Gathmor groaned again. Gods! Black and blue from two weeks of battering in this Evil-take-it elven magic tub. "Durthing!" he yelled, the countersign.

Feeling as if his joints had all frozen and that when he forced his aching, quivering limbs to bend he must be cracking ice, he reached for an oar, made it ready, rose. *Queen* rocked in protest, then lurched forward as he hauled on the cable. Up came the little anchor, dripping silver and breaking the stillness with an absurdly loud clatter when he threw it down. None of the other craft was showing signs of life yet. A dog howled somewhere northward, in the city.

One-oared he paddled the boat shoreward. Without her magic, she was a wallowing cow, a hulk, but a few strokes were enough to bring him within sight of the man waiting on the beach. Gray-on-gray, the shape wasn't big enough to be Darad. It was that sleazy, glib-spoken imp, Andor. Well, Darad had warned him that any of them was possible. Couldn't promise they'd call him back, he'd said. Crazy, Evil-begotten magic! Andor was too slippery.

Come to think of it, it had been that Andor who'd talked him into buying the faun in the first place. All his fault! Be a real pleasure to pound him a little, make something more manlike out of that pretty face. Due for a little exercise, and the imp would be a good warmup. Except he'd just call Darad— no satisfaction there.

Queen grounded with a scraping sound. Andor splashed out to her and tossed in a pair of boots and a string bag; then he pushed and simultaneously clambered over the side, all with an agility that produced grudging surprise in Gathmor. His mouth was watering at the sight of the bag.

"Hot loaves, Cap'n! Fresh from the oven. Not quite done yet, but they'll do. Too early for much else." Andor settled on a thwart and peered around for something to dry his feet with.

Gathmor wondered where the boots had come from—they weren't Darad's. He leaned on the oar, poling the boat until he was out of his depth. Then let her drift while he sat down and reached for the savory bag. "What news?"

Andor shook his head somberly. "It's all bad."

"Tell me anyway. I'm a big boy now."

"The faun went berserk. Whole city's twisted in knots."

"What sort of berserk?" Gathmor mumbled, tearing off hunks of warm dough.

"Apparently he broke into the palace, stole one of the royal horses, rode from one end of the grounds to the other, and then busted into the actual wedding with the entire guard in pursuit."

The sailor grunted admiringly. Great kid, the faun. Half jotunn, of course.

"Crazy!" Andor removed his cloak and distastefully wiped his feet on the lining.

"Did he stop the wedding?"

"No. But he blasted the sorceress somehow. Burned her up like a ball of tallow."

"How?"

"I've got no idea, and no one I talked with has, either."

"How'd you find all this out?"

"Just asked!" Andor flashed perfect white teeth in a perfect brown face. Gathmor grinned back—silly question! Who could resist that smile?

For a moment the imp chewed at a loaf. The sky was flaming in red and gold, and the mist lifting from the sea in patches. Other craft were coming into sight. Voices and bumping sounds drifted over from them, and a baby began to cry in one of the closer. Then Andor was ready to speak again.

"My associates helped. Thinal got us over the wall. I talked with a few of the witnesses. Most everyone was too shaky or drunk to question much, and Darad dealt with those that weren't. Wasn't dangerous with the sorceress gone."

"So the lady's happily married and the faun had his journey for nothing?"

"Married," Andor said. "Not happily, I suspect. Thinal broke into the royal apartments—"

"No!"

"Near as no-matter! He goes loony if there's jewels around, and that palace has sacks of them, enough to call him like a blowfly to a dead horse." Andor casually reached in a pocket and pulled out a glittering handful that had to be more wealth than Gathmor had ever seen in his life.

"Here, you can have 'em. These were just his warmup, sneaked on the roof. He located the sultan's window, and he was almost down to the balcony when out came the sultan himself." Andor was grinning again. "At least he was very big, and loaded with gems; don't know who else it could have been, not there. And he started pacing. He marched up and down for an hour, with Thinal hanging on a vine right over his head." The imp laughed. "The little scrounger hasn't been so scared in fifty years! He wet his pants three times and was waiting for the djinn to notice the smell."

Gathmor guffawed, then frowned. "What's a man doing walking around on his wedding night?"

"Not what's he supposed to be doing on his wedding night, there's a sure bet! And even more interesting was the sound from inside."

"What sound?"

"Weeping."

Gathmor grunted again. You'd never catch a jotunn letting his bride weep at a time like that. Keep 'em busy, that was the secret.

"So where's the faun?"

"In jail. Still alive, though. Surprisingly."

"How'd you know that?"

Andor wrinkled his nose and chewed for a minute, as if reluctant to continue. The vapors had all dissolved away. The sun burned as a golden blaze on the sea between the headlands, making the great palace shine as if lighted from the inside, bright against a distant backdrop of flushed mountains and a still-dark sky.

"The dogs," Andor said. "The horses. Remember he told us about the beatings he got in Noom? Said he could suppress the pain?"

"As long as he could stay awake."

"Right. Well, all night the dogs and horses have been raising the Evil, all over the palace. Not all the time, but in spurts. You don't want this last one, do you?"

"No, you have it." Gathmor was still hungry and had been eyeing that last roll. He wondered why he should suddenly have an attack of politeness now, at his age.

"Grooms and dogboys are going crazy," Andor said. "Everyone is. They're blaming it on the sorceress, or demons she summoned, or came to mourn her . . . I think it's Rap's doing."

"Why'd he do a thing like that?" The sun was warm already.

"I don't think he means to, but every time he loses control of the pain he sets off the livestock. You see?"

Gathmor felt a stab of horror. "What pain?"

Andor didn't answer for a moment, avoiding the sailor's eye. The boat rocked on a slow swell, gradually drifting away from the shore as the fisherman's wind awakened. The harbor was stirring. All over the great bay, sails were rising.

"He's in a Zarkian jail," he said at last. "Just leave it at that, mm?"

"No. Tell me."

"The wheel."

"What in Evil is the wheel?"

"Well, I gather they didn't use a real wheel, just the floor. They staked him out with chains. Then they smashed his bones with an ax handle."

The boat rocked in silence. Gathmor stared idiotically at his companion, unable to believe what he had heard.

"I even talked with one of the guards who'd helped," Andor said softly. "Then I handed the conversation over to Darad. That's one less, if it makes you feel any better."

The sailor's hands were sweaty, and there was a pain in his throat. He was surprised to realize that he hadn't even been swearing. How could men treat a man like that? *Chained down?* Unbelievable! Filthy djinns!

"I don't understand," he muttered. "He's an adept. He should have been able to talk them out of it. Gods! Talk them into letting him go, even."

"He can't talk. He'll never talk again."

"How?"

"Red-hot iron."

For a moment Gathmor seriously believed he was going to lose his breakfast. Then the fit passed. He wiped his forehead. "What do we do now?" His mouth was dry and cloacal.

"There isn't one thing we can do!" Andor shrugged sadly. "Not a thing. He'll certainly be dead in a couple of days. He was given to the guards he'd shamed, see. And he'd killed some of their . . . I can't believe even an adept can heal that kind of damage, and I expect they'll be watching for healing and work him over again if it starts."

He paused, as if inviting Gathmor to argue. Gathmor didn't.

"We go home, sailor. We provision the boat and head for the Impire. I've got gold . . . you can keep those baubles I gave you. I'd prefer we head north, to Ollion, but Qoble will do me if you want to go back west. Let me off somewhere civilized, you keep the boat. I'm sure Jalon will give you a lesson on the pipes if you ask him, and you'll be a rich sailor in no time, if the magic lasts." He sighed. "Ah, civilization! Fine wine in crystal, tasty food on gold plates, smooth women on silk sheets."

Gathmor felt a drowning sensation and tried to struggle. "Never! Leave a shipmate? There must be something we can do!"

Andor smiled sadly, holding the sailor's eye. "'Fraid not. I've got powers beyond most men's, and I've never met a man I'd rather have at my side in a tight spot more'n you, Skipper. But we're still just a couple of vagabonds really."

Gathmor shook his head fiercely. "Desert a shipmate? You think you can talk me into that? After what he risked for me in Noom? Think your damnable charm will convince me of that?"

"I wouldn't use charm on you, Gath," Andor said crossly. "Pretty girls, yes. All the time! But never my friends. And my eyelashes won't work on the palace guard. They're a tough bunch—I'd never try more than two at a time. I'm sure I couldn't bedazzle three. You think I can just walk into the jail and carry Rap out with me? Two of us couldn't carry him anyway, the state he must be in. Two of us can't fight a sultan and his army and his people. There's a war coming, so I hear . . . No shame in giving up when a job's impossible, Cap'n. That's just plain sanity."

Gathmor groaned.

"A sailor knows that," Andor said. "You furl your sails in a storm, right? And no one calls you a coward. This is the same thing. It's hopeless."

Trouble was, he was right.

"I like it no more than you do, Cap'n. Even Rap can't expect a witch to fly in the window every time he wants one—and you and I shan't be needed if one does. Even if we could get him out of the dungeon, he'd just die on us anyway. The wheel's not torture, it's a slow execution. He's as good as dead now. Two more deaths won't solve anything."

Very convincing, was Andor. Logical and clear thinking. A sound, honest man for an imp, and no shirker—he'd been around the palace in the night, and that had not been a mission for a coward.

"I suppose this was what Lith'rian foresaw when he said it was too close to call?"

"It isn't too close now," Andor insisted. "The girl's married and bedded, and in Zark she'll stay that way. Her kingdom's been divided between her enemies. The wardens have lost interest. The sorceress is dead and the faun as good as— the sooner the better for his sake. He tried and he failed! It's as simple as that."

"I guess so." Gathmor sighed. He glanced around and checked the wind. All the way around to Qoble was a fair voyage, but of course they could make landfalls on the way this time. They needn't take on stores for the whole trip. "I suppose so," he repeated.

"Ever been to a theater, sailor? *Tragedy in Three Acts?* That's it! The curtain fells and the play's over. The audience dries its eyes and goes home and gets on with real life."

"I suppose." Gathmor smiled to show his acceptance. "And I suppose I'm lucky to have you here to stop me doing something crazy. Just feels like there ought to be more, somehow."

Tumult, and shouting:
    The tumult and the shouting dies;
    The captains and the kings depart.

                                        Kipling, *Recessional*

"A Man of His Word" will conclude with Part Four, *Emperor and Clown*

About the Author

DAVE DUNCAN, born in Scotland in 1933, is a Canadian citizen. He received his diploma from Dundee High School and got his college education at the University of Saint Andrews. He moved to Canada in 1955, where he still lives with his wife. He has three grown children and spent twenty-five years as a petroleum geologist. He has had dozens of fantasy and science fiction novels published, among them A ROSE-RED CITY, MAGIC CASEMENT and THE REAVER ROAD, as well as a highly praised historical novel under a pseudonym.

Printed in the United States
25567LVS00006B/59